Transferring Credits

the With Honors series

Book 3

Addison Winters

Cover Design by Scarlett Ink Publishing, INC
Edited by Charlene Burgett & Eric Staeheli

This is a work of fiction. Names, characters, places, brands, media, and incidents are either the product of the author's imagination or are used fictitiously. Any resemblance to similarly named places or to persons living or deceased is unintentional.

Print ISBN: 978-1-948143-16-5
EPUB ISBN: 978-1-948143-17-2

Library of Congress Control Number: 2021922772

Acknowledgments

I appreciate everyone's patience while I struggled with how to conclude the With Honors series. I love these characters and have truly enjoyed spending time in their world.

To my husband, Eric

I am not saying you were right, but this book/series could not have been completed without you.

Chapter 1

MASON STOOD RED FACED AND fuming. I could see the glistening in his eyes as he fought hard to keep the tears welling up from spilling out into a world, he couldn't imagine ever being in. The music was still engulfing us, drinks were being consumed, and all around us people were laughing and preparing for the countdown to the New Year, but for the three of us the world had stopped.

"Mason?" Hayden took a small step in his son's direction, but Mason took a step back. He shook his head slightly, turned, and walked as quickly as he could to the front door.

"Oh my God," I whispered in astonishment as Hayden and I both followed closely behind Mason.

But I was in heels and Hayden, in his dress shoes, slipped on the residual ice on the steps on Debbie's porch, narrowly catching himself on the railing. The slight delay created an even greater distance between Mason and us. By the time we reached him, Mason was in his car and backing out of my driveway. Hayden hollered after him as we stood in the street watching as Mason's taillights faded around the corner and the street went silent.

I heard someone cough behind me. When I turned, I realized half of Debbie's guests were standing on her front porch staring at us, including Lisa, Erik, Mark, and Debbie herself. I was humiliated. I wasn't sure how many of them realized what had transpired but the uncanny resemblance between Hayden and Mason left little to the imagination.

I reached out and took Hayden's hand. I held my head up and walked as bravely as I could into my house with him and closed the door behind us.

"This is bad, Hayden." I stated the obvious out of sheer nervousness.

"I know, Alex." His voice was raised several octaves. I knew it was out of frustration of the situation and not me, but it still hit me.

"Don't yell at me," I said as calmly as I could manage.

"I'm not yelling at you," he said loudly. "Where's my phone?" Hayden began patting himself down before finally pulling it out of his back pocket.

He hit the button that would connect him with his son and then paced the family room. I leaned against the wall unsure as to what to do or say. It appeared Hayden's call went straight to voicemail, because every other minute he would hang up and try to connect again. I thought about trying to reach him myself, but I didn't think Mason would answer a call from me either.

Hayden's frustration continued to build as he wore a pathway across my floor. Finally, he flopped down on the couch, ran his fingers through his hair, and left Mason a voicemail.

"Mason, I really wish you'd talk to me. Son," he sighed heavily into the phone. "I'm sorry. I … I don't know what to say." Hayden pressed the button disconnecting his phone and then tossed it beside him on the couch. He looked up at me with big, sad, pleading eyes.

I felt horrible.

There were no words to say to him. I approached him slowly and sat down beside him. I gently rested my hand on his leg. Hayden sat there bent over with his elbows on his knees, his head in his hands. For the next thirty minutes the room was at a dead silence.

"I have no clue what to say to him, so I guess it's a good thing he didn't answer." Hayden tried to muster a smile but didn't pull it off very well. "This isn't exactly how I envisioned us starting the New Year."

"I know. Me neither."

"I thought we'd have this incredible romantic evening." Hayden reached over and put his arm around my shoulder, pulling me closer to him. "I really didn't want Mason to find out about us this way. I didn't want him to find out about us at all if that was even possible."

"I was hoping he'd never find out." I couldn't get the image of Mason's face when he saw the two of us standing there out of my mind. It was burned into my brain haunting me.

"It wasn't supposed to be like this. I knew there would be consequences for our actions. I was never naïve about that. But if Mason was ever going to find out about us, I wanted to be the one to tell him, a long time from now once he'd moved forward with his life and it wouldn't hurt him nearly as bad as what this is doing." Hayden scrambled for the right words.

"I know," I assured him despite his inability to say it properly.

"I do love you; you know that right?" His eyes were full of giant tears that finally breached the rim as he looked at me and spilled down his cheeks.

"Yes, I know. I love you, too." I rested my head against his shoulder.

"Looks like we're really in this together now, kid." He hastily brushed the tears off his cheeks.

"Yep, and I'm not going anywhere." I intertwined my fingers with his. "For better or for worse, right?"

"Are you sure that's something you want?" Hayden's eyes pleaded.

"I'm positive," I said without hesitation.

"It's going to be rough. You realize there are going to be some really bad days ahead of us and we're going to catch hell from a lot of people, especially my family," he cautioned me.

"I understand." I lifted our interlocked hands to my lips and kissed his hand softly. "I'm not going anywhere."

"Good, because I'm going to need you to be there if we're going to weather this storm."

"I promise," I whispered and kissed his lips softly. "Always."

Chapter 2

THE MORNING LIGHT SEEPED through the blinds in my bedroom. Hayden was sleeping soundly spooned up behind me with an arm and a leg draped over me. I sighed peacefully and snuggled back against him. His grip unconsciously tightened around me. Then I remembered the horrible events from the night before — the look on Mason's face.

It would haunt me for the rest of my life.

I climbed out of bed and went over to the window. I lifted the blinds just enough to gaze out over the vast lawn and the woods behind my house. It was barely dawn and the first rays of sunshine were cascading across the newly fallen snow. The world appeared so serene. I looked back at the beautiful man sleeping peacefully in my bed.

His hair was slightly tasseled, the scruff brazenly outlining his strong jaw. He was a breathtaking sight. I couldn't believe this handsome, charming man was in love with me. My heart was so far gone with love for him it was ridiculous. I wanted to be near him, touch him, feel his hand in mine every day. The way he brushed the side of my face with his fingers; the look in his eyes as they embraced mine told me how much he truly loved me.

He was too good to be true. I held my breath waiting for the other shoe to drop. Men like Hayden were a once in a lifetime and I was scared out of my mind that he would realize I wasn't worth the pain this would surely cause his family.

Yes, I made him happy. I knew that. But was his happiness worth everything else that was waiting on the horizon?

Of course, he reassured me it was. But when the chips finally hit the ground, scattered, and broken, would he still think so?

I wasn't so sure.

I knew what I had done, and I took full responsibility for falling in love with a man that was technically, morally, and ethically, forbidden.

But my heart …

I had allowed my heart to overrun my head and now here we were. I was about to be held accountable for what I had done.

Could I withstand the fallout?

Could he?

I gazed at the gorgeous dream man sleeping soundly in my bed and sighed heavily.

There was no backing out now.

Hayden's phone began ringing shortly before nine o'clock. I was coming out of the bathroom as I saw him reaching over to grab it off the nightstand.

"Hello?" He muttered still half asleep.

I could hear a loud female voice booming from his phone all the way from across the room. "Now wait just a minute. You don't talk to me that way! I am your father. You show me a little respect!" Hayden abruptly sat up in bed, his face red with anger.

Loud screaming came blasting from his phone once more. He looked up at me and shook his head. I slowly approached him, hesitating a moment and then sat down beside him. I could hear the voice on the phone now. And it was certainly not a happy one.

"How could you do this to your own son? What kind of woman would be sleeping with a father and his son? Seriously, Dad? There is something sick and twisted about this?" I could hear the female ranting.

"Would you calm down for just a minute and let me say something?"

"You cannot justify your behavior or hers!" The loud voice responded.

"Kennedy Rochelle, stop!" Hayden raised his voice for the first time.

"Fine," He took a deep breath and set the phone back on the nightstand. Clearly, she had hung up on him. He rubbed his eyes and climbed out of bed, walked into the bathroom and closed the door behind him.

I sat there looking at the closed door. I didn't know what to say. I was half tempted to call Mason, but he was obviously still upset and venting to his sister. Now was not the time.

I felt horrible.

I started the coffee and stood there with the refrigerator door open trying to decide if I wanted to cook breakfast or not. Hayden entered the kitchen and poured himself a mug before the pot was even finished. He sat down at the table without adding sugar or creamer; something he rarely did.

"Are you all right?" I knew how ridiculous the question was. Of course, he wasn't all right.

"No." He reached out and took my hand pulling me to him. He wrapped his arms around my waist and rested his head against my abdomen. I held him close and stroked his hair.

"I wish I knew what to say. Somehow, I'm sorry, just doesn't seem to even scratch the service." I said in a soft voice.

"This," he squeezed me tighter. "This is all I need."

My heart broke for him. Despite all their bickering, I knew how much Hayden loved his son. I also knew how much he adored his daughter, Kennedy. We were aware the fallout was going to be harsh, and we had tried to postpone it for as long as we could — me more so than him, but alas we were now going to be held accountable.

The word kept flashing through my mind more than once since I'd opened my eyes today.

"Would you like me to fix you something?" I offered.

"No, I'm not hungry. The coffee is fine." He finally let me go and took a sip of his coffee.

"You should put something on your stomach." I sat down in the chair beside him.

"Maybe in a while."

"I'm guessing Mason is at Kennedy's?"

"Yeah, and he gave her an earful as you can imagine." Hayden ran his index finger absentmindedly over the rim of his mug.

"I'm so sorry, darling." I placed my hand over his other hand.

"Well, there's no turning back now." He attempted a smile but didn't pull it off very well. "You're stuck with me."

"Always."

The hours passed by slowly. The winds howled around the house as the snow began to fall again. It was bitter cold, and the temperatures were dropping by the hour. Hayden and I curled up on the couch and started to binge on a *Game of Thrones* marathon. He was a fan of the show, and I was a fan of the books. It seemed like the perfect way to spend a snow day together. Not to mention a fabulous distraction to keep our minds off the outside world and the damnation that was surely headed our way.

Hayden was quiet for the next several days. We were pretty

much snowed in as the storm engulfed the Midwest and East Coast in a blanket of white and several inches of ice. It was risky to even attempt to make it to the mailbox.

Luckily, we hadn't lost power or heat like other areas. I had a difficult time bribing Billy to go outside because of the ice after she slid down the steps off the deck.

Hayden spent the first couple days glued to the television and saying little. By the third day he started rummaging through my books. He found the ones from my advanced sex class from the summer course I had taken 18 months ago. He found them intriguing, and I caught him becoming engrossed in them. I almost teased him about them, but then I decided against it. I was just happy he'd found something to take his mind off everything else.

By the end of the week, he'd began acting like his old self again. He was smiling again, being playful even. And suddenly, being snowed in wasn't so horrible.

Friday morning, I was awakened to the smell of bacon and hot coffee. After I brushed my teeth and hair, I found Hayden standing over the stove fixing bacon, eggs, and toast to go with our morning coffee. He was wearing dark gray flannel pajama bottoms and a thick, navy blue, terry cloth robe. His hair needed a trim and loose curls hung freely in soft waves. His bare muscular chest made his simple attire incredibly sexy. I walked up behind him and wrapped my arms around his waist.

"Good morning, darling. This looks wonderful." I leaned my head against his back and inhaled the lingering smell of his cologne on his robe.

"Good morning." He hugged my arms to his body briefly. "Did you sleep well?"

"Too well. I didn't want to get up." I let him go and helped myself to a hot mug of coffee.

"I figured as much so I thought I would entice you with my amazing cooking skills." Hayden looked over his shoulder and grinned.

"You spoil me," I sat down at the island absorbing the warmth of the mug through my hands and watched him. "Be careful or I could get used to this."

"I hope so." He came over and set down a plate with two soft eggs, three strips of bacon and a piece of toast smothered with strawberry jelly down in front of me.

"This looks great. Thank you, baby." I placed a paper napkin across my lap and waited for him to join me.

"Well, to be honest I was starving when I woke up and I didn't want to wait for you to get your lazy butt outta bed to cook me breakfast." He chuckled and joined me with his plate.

"Smart man," I smirked and dug into my breakfast. It was delicious.

The man can cook …

I loaded the dishwasher while Hayden filled me in on the busy upcoming week he was dreading. I found his work interesting and his office staff quite humorous. He figured that the roads would be clear enough by Sunday for him to attempt the drive. As much as I hated driving in it, I knew I'd be out there myself on Sunday afternoon to meet the boys at the airport. I couldn't wait to see them although I wasn't sure how I was going to explain Mason's absence to them.

I closed the dishwasher and dried my hands on a towel. Hayden was straddling one of the barstools leaning on the island finishing his third cup of coffee. I leaned back against the counter just watching him; listening to him ramble on about his work.

I loved how passionate he was about it. My eyes watched his face carefully, studying every chiseled line from his emerald eyes, strong jaw to his high cheekbones. He was so incredibly gorgeous.

Chapter 3

IT WAS ALMOST SIX O'CLOCK and our stomachs were grumbling. We had skipped lunch because were enjoying the spoils of being snowed in. I was curled up beside Hayden with my head resting on his chest, my arm draped over him and a leg lying across his. Our heartrates were beginning to slow, our breathing relaxed back to normal.

This was what I truly loved, lying in his arms listening to the strong rhythm of his heartbeat.

"I love you," he whispered in a low voice brushing my hair away from my face.

"I love you, too." I closed my eyes trying to ignore my rumbling stomach. I wanted to enjoy this moment before it escaped.

But reality found us.

Hayden's cell phone erupted from the nightstand. He sighed deeply and reached for his phone. "Hello?"

"Dad, can you talk?" I recognized Kennedy's voice from her screaming phone call earlier in the week. I was close enough to Hayden that I could hear her clearly.

"Yes."

"Mason's back at mom's. I did not call to start another fight with you. I'm just trying to understand how something like this happened." Her voice was much calmer than before.

"What did Mason tell you?" I knew he was fishing to see exactly how much she already knew.

"That you're sleeping with his girlfriend. He caught you with her, Dad — on New Year's Eve!" She squeaked.

"Yes, that's true to a certain extent. Alex was dating Mason. They met last year. They had a fling that lasted longer than it should have. Alex is a divorced mom who is 33 years old. I met her when your brother used the emergency credit card I gave him for a spring break in Cancun trip. He then lied about who Alex was — not once but repeatedly. I met her when Mason led me to believe she was his girlfriend's mom. Anyway, long story short, she told me the truth. We got to talking that evening and the next day I returned to Chicago." Hayden explained.

"How did that turn into you sleeping with her?" His daughter inquired.

"There was something about her. I couldn't stay away from her. I pursued her after they split at the end of the semester and your brother moved back to Chicago. It was not the other way around. I promise you that. I am responsible for this." I sat there silently listening to him take all the blame. He put his hand over my mouth when I slightly opened it and shook his head. "There was a connection between us neither of us could deny." Hayden breathed heavily. "Kennedy, I'm in love with her."

"You love her?" The sentiment clearly caught her off guard. "I thought this was another one of yours and Mason's pissing matches — granted, the worst of them, but you love her!" Her voice kicked up a couple notches.

"Yes, Kennedy. I truly love her."

"Oh, God," I could hear the sob fighting through in her voice and my heart broke a little.

"What? Why is that so hard to believe?" Hayden questioned.

"No, it's just I've never heard you say that about any woman before." Her words shook me more then I let on.

"I know." He confessed. "But it's true. And I'm not saying it to justify what I did."

"But dad, you do realize how sick and twisted this is?"

"Yes, I am aware. Do you honestly think I planned this? In an ideal world I would have met Alex first and in any other way and fallen deeply in love with her, but it didn't happen that way and here we are." Hayden's voice sounded so apologetic and sincere.

"You do know that Mason is still seeing that intern from last summer? Some girl named Megan." She told him.

"I know. We both know. Mason attempted to sneak around with her, but he isn't exactly Jason Bourne." For the first time in their conversation, Hayden chuckled a bit.

"True, but what I'm having a hard time with is that if they both knew it was over, why not just go their separate ways? From what Mason said he's been living with this woman for almost two years. It doesn't make sense." Kennedy pointed out the obvious.

"Alex's sons have grown attached to Mason and their dad moved to Arizona about seven years ago."

"So, they stayed in the relationship, so the boys wouldn't get hurt?" She questioned.

"Pretty much."

"And how's that working out for them?" Her voice was dripping with sarcasm.

"Kennedy, don't be a smartass." Hayden chastised his daughter.

"It seems a bit ridiculous to me and more of a flimsy excuse from both parties."

"You don't have children, nor have you ever been involved with someone who did. It does alter your perception of right and wrong." I sat there uncomfortably listening to Hayden repeat the same ol' excuses I'd given him.

"I'll have to take your word for it." She conceded. "So, what happens now?"

"What do you mean?" Hayden naively asked.

"Geez Dad, don't you think mom's going to have a coronary when she hears about this?" Kennedy chuckled despite her effort not to. I knew she didn't have the best relationship with her mother.

"Do you think I care?" Hayden finally smiled.

"Nope. But isn't Mason supposed to work for you after he graduates? When I asked him about it, he said he'd find another job."

"That's his prerogative if he wants to do that. But I have no problem hiring him after graduation. He's really talented." I knew he was being sincere, but I could also see the hurt in his eyes.

"You need to talk to him." She stated.

"I've tried — multiple times. He won't answer his phone."

"Then keep trying until he does; let him yell at you and get it off his chest. He's really upset and rightfully so. You've been sneaking around and sleeping with his sort of girlfriend for the nine months."

"Yes, Kennedy. I am aware of what I did." Hayden got a little red around the ears.

"I just hate to see something else come between you two." She lowered her voice. "I know he's always blamed you for everything and it's not fair but this — good Lord Dad, I think he has every right to be ticked all to hell at you and Alex for this one."

"I'm not arguing that fact."

"Do I get to meet her?" She asked after a moment of silence.

"I imagine you will at some point considering," My eyes darted up from watching him fiddling with the pen on my nightstand and met his. His green eyes sparkled and locked on mine, caressing them.

"Considering what? Is she pregnant?" Kennedy's voice raided a couple octaves.

"No. Of course not." Even Hayden laughed at the thought of that.

"Then what? She asked impatiently.

"Considering this isn't a fling. I love her." His gaze intensified sending shudders down my back. "I love her and want to marry her someday."

Monday morning hours after I had gotten the boys off to school, I was still in my pajamas curled up on the couch under a blanket watching reruns of Supernatural and on my second pot of coffee. The temperatures remained in the teens and although the roads weren't as treacherous as they were the week before, they still were not great. I was surprised the boys only had a two hour delay this morning for their return to school instead of a cancellation.

Hayden left before noon the day before to head back up to Chicago to face the wrath that surely awaited him. I had picked up the boys at three from the airport and was thrilled to finally have them back home. It felt like a lifetime had passed since they'd left, instead of just a short time ago. They hadn't inquired about Mason or rather his absence and for that I was grateful. I was certain they believed he would return before our classes resumed.

It was almost one and I had no desire or motivation to do anything. The blanket was toasty, and the fire was roaring in the hearth. I was dozing off when I felt Billy jump off the other end of the couch at the sound of the deadbolt turning in the lock. My stomach immediately knotted as I realized it was Mason.

The sight of him was like having a bucket of cold water dumped over me. He stood in the foyer fumbling to remove the key from the lock. "Hello." He said meekly when he noticed me on the couch. "I wasn't sure if you'd be here or not. Is it all right if I collect my things so I can move them back to my dorm?"

"Of course," I didn't know what to say to him. Sorry didn't seem to be enough for how badly his father and I had hurt him.

Then I saw it. A slight flash off the band sparkled in the twinkling lights off the Christmas tree — a gold band on Mason's left ring finger — a wedding band.

What the fuck has he done? He's married!

He closed the front door behind him and kicked the snow off his shoes on the front mat before slipping them off and putting them in 'their spot'. "I was hoping to avoid the boys."

"They are at school," I bit my tongue and kept my mouth shut.

"Good."

"How are the roads?" I couldn't think of anything else to say.

"Still slick, but passable." He took off his coat and put it on the coatrack. "Lots of black ice."

"That's what I figured."

He stood there for a long awkward moment before walking over and sitting down in the spot Billie had vacated only moments earlier. I pulled my feet beneath me and sat up a little straighter turning towards him.

"How did we get here? A year ago, we were so happy — so happy just the four of us. But even then, I knew it wouldn't last forever." He dropped his eyes to the floor. "Why didn't you tell me?" Mason's eyes looked as sad as they had the day he pleaded with me in my room after the start of the fall semester to give us a chance.

"I didn't want to hurt you." I told him honestly. "I didn't know how."

"It's easy; hey Mason, the man I spent the summer screwing behind your back is your dad." He gestured his hands widely, sarcasm dripping from his shapely lips.

"And what the hell is this?" I rose to my knees and grabbed his hand. "I can see exactly how heartbroken you are." I unintentionally snorted. "Let me guess; Megan?"

"Like you care." Mason huffed.

"Wow!" I got up from the couch and headed towards my room. "You truly are a child." I knew the words would sting him like nothing else I could possibly say.

"At least I know she hasn't fucked my dad!" He leapt off the couch and ran after me.

"I didn't just fuck your dad!" I spun around and screamed in his face. "I love him. I'm in love with him!"

"Yeah right! Kind of how you love me, too!" Mason spat at me.

"I do love you, you asshole. I'm in love with Hayden." I couldn't believe I was having this conversation. "There's a big difference."

"Apparently so!" I turned back around to my room and slammed the door behind me only to have Mason fling it back open a second later. "I'm not done talking to you."

"I believe everything has been said." I gestured towards his hand. "And done."

"I did this;" he held up his hand to show off his ring. "Because I wanted to. Nobody made me."

"I never said or implied otherwise." I lowered my voice and sat down on the corner of my bed. "When did you do it?"

"The day after Christmas. We eloped." He leaned against my dresser looking ashamed.

"So, you were married when you showed up here on New Year's Eve?" The disbelief settled fully on my chest.

"I was coming down to tell you. I hadn't expected to find you in the arms of my father when I arrived." He huffed again.

"I guess neither of us is any better than the other." I rolled my eyes. "We should have ended this a long time ago." I muttered.

"I thought we had."

Ouch!

"Obviously." I conceded.

"Lexie," Mason sighed heavily. "Look. It was clear when I came back last fall that this was over. I knew you were in love with someone else. I didn't know who, but I knew. Hell, you told me as much."

"And you begged me." I pointed out.

"I shouldn't have." He said in a low voice. "I was just so jealous. I know it's ridiculous and immature, "

"So," I suddenly became irritated. "You didn't want me, but you didn't want me to be with anyone else. Is that what you're saying?"

"Anyone? No. I didn't want anyone else to have you. And I sure as fuck didn't want you with my Dad!" He scoffed.

"We never meant for any of this to happen. It just did." I knew that didn't matter.

"How? How in the hell does it happen, Lexie?" He folded his arms and looked at me with such hostility. "How in the fuck did you go from being my girlfriend to fucking my Dad? Explain it to me because I really want to know."

"One. Lower your voice. Two. That day when Hayden showed up on my front porch looking for you; well, we sort of had dinner that night and he knew you were lying when you took Emma to breakfast as me. And thirdly, I didn't mean to fall in love with him, and I am sorry, but I did. I love him very much." I admitted.

"So, this started last spring?" Mason started getting red around the ears.

"No, I said he knew you were lying about who I was last spring. I started seeing him after you left for your internship." I conveniently left out exactly how soon after he left for his internship. "And for the record, no we weren't talking on the phone in-between."

"And that's supposed to make it better?"

"No." I sighed heavily. There was nothing left to say. "Mason," I reached my hand out to him. Thankfully, he took it and sat down beside me on the bed.

"I know." He whispered and then went silent.

We sat there on my bed, holding hands, not talking, each lost in our own thoughts for what felt like an eternity. I believe I was still in shock that this boy, this young man who had meant so much to me, who still meant so much to me, was married.

"What did your mom say?" I was positive Hayden didn't know because I hadn't gotten a call.

"She doesn't know yet. No one does." He confessed.

"Why is that?" I couldn't stop myself from asking.

"My parents don't like Megan." Mason admitted.

"I know you and your dad disagreed on her work performance, but that has nothing to do with her personally."

"No, he was pretty up front about his feelings for her after Thanksgiving." He chuckled sarcastically. "He really doesn't like her. I believe he referred to her as trash."

"Ouch," it was hard to fathom Haydon saying something like that without just cause.

"And my mom, well she's holding a grudge from last summer when Megan and I had a nasty argument." His eyes dropped to the floor as if he was embarrassed.

"What happened?"

"Megan's got a bit of a temper, and I was egging her on. So, really it was just as much my fault as it was hers." Mason quickly added. "But I called her a bitch, and she kicked me in the balls — hard. When I went down, she continued to kick me about the head, face, and chest." He shifted his weight uncomfortably.

"She was wearing hiking boots at the time. Our neighbors called the police and Megan was arrested for assault and battery." *Why hadn't I heard about any of this?* "But once my mom saw me and found out what happened, she was livid and has hated her ever since." Mason fidgeted with his new wedding band.

"I told her if I can forgive Megan, then she could but she claims that if it had been a man kicking one of her daughters, no one would ever expect her to forgive him. She claims it's no different with her sons.

"I hate to tell you this, but I agree with her whole-heartedly. I'd never forgive a woman for doing such a thing to my son." I told him.

"Well, my mom said Megan wasn't welcome in her home so this," He held up his ring finger momentarily. "Is not going to go over well."

"Does your dad know about what happened?"

"No. I never told him, and I've sworn Kennedy to secrecy. Although now I'm pretty sure my mom will tell him." Mason rolled his eyes.

"Probably, but why Mason? Why did you marry her?" I asked still holding his hand.

"I don't know. I was drunk; it seemed like a fun thing to do at the time when she suggested it." He shrugged.

"That doesn't seem like a very good reason." His maturity astounded me once again. I couldn't believe how much he had changed since I first met him, and not necessarily for the better.

"But it's done now. I guess I'll just have to deal with it." His eyes stared blankly forward.

"That's a pleasant way of looking at it." I reached over and took his face in my hand and turned him towards me. "Marriage is hard enough, Mason without going into it with such low expectations."

"Do you ever think of getting remarried?" His eyes looked sad once again. "Or do I even want to know?"

"Mason," My voice trailed off. I didn't want to answer him.

"Has my dad proposed?" He asked with a surprised tone.

"No. Of course not." Which was true.

"But you've discussed a future together?" He inquired.

"Some." Which was also true.

"Does he love you too?" Mason's voice dropped a bit.

"Yes, he does." I looked down at our still intertwined hands and nodded. "And you love him?"

"Yes."

"So, you could be my stepmom?" He laughed. "How cliché is that? Aren't you supposed to sleep with the stepson after the wedding?"

"I'm glad you're enjoying this." I smirked.

"Not really." But he continued grinning.

"It's strange, that's for sure." I rolled my eyes playfully at him.

"I'm going to miss you and the boys." Mason confessed. "Thank you for letting me a be a part of your family for a while."

"You will always be my family." I told him.

"Just perhaps in a more legal way." He teased and gently nudged me.

"We'll see," was all I was willing to admit.

"I supposed I'd better get packing." Mason half grinned before standing up. "Is it okay if I see the boys before I leave?"

"Of course. They've missed you."

"I've missed them." He walked over to the closet and turned back towards me. "And hey, if you do end up marrying my dad, I guess that would make them my little brothers." He snorted and shrugged. "At least I'd still get to see them." Mason smiled.

Mason spent the next hour tossing his things into bags and throwing them in his car. I did my best to go behind him and fold his clothes just so he wouldn't look like a wrinkled mess on campus, which only made him laugh and call me 'mom' — and then correct himself by calling me 'stepmom'. I playfully smacked his arm and continued my task.

I felt I got off easy for my part in this whole mess. I feared Hayden wasn't going to be nearly as lucky. I also feared what was to come once Hayden learned of his son's new wife. I was positive he was going to be livid. But I wasn't wanting to be the one to tell him either.

Mason had put me in a difficult position and one I certainly couldn't win. If I didn't tell Hayden and he found out I knew, he'd be ticked at me for not telling him. And if I do tell him and he tears into Mason then Mason would feel I betrayed his trust.

I zipped up the last of his duffle bags and handed them to him at the front door. We thought it best that everything be hidden in his car before the boys arrived home. The atmosphere between us had shifted dramatically and we both felt it. Strangely, it was oddly comfortable in a very weird way.

The boys showed up about twenty minutes later than normal because of the roads. They were so excited to see Mason. Henry ran up and gave Mason a hug and Max immediately challenged him to play his new Madden game he'd gotten for Christmas. Mason glanced over at me, and I nodded before he accepted. I hadn't planned on him staying that long, but I couldn't bring myself to say that in front of my boys.

I watched Mason follow my sons down the hall into Max's room. I also noticed Mason casually slip off his wedding band and stuff it in his front pocket along the way. For that, I was grateful. My boys were to observant for their own good and it would have only been a matter of time before one or both would have noticed it. And that would have incited a barrage of questions that neither I, nor Mason I'm sure, were ready to answer.

I started dinner taking comfort in the noise coming from the bedroom. It was so familiar, and I sighed heavily knowing it was about to end. I tried to push the thought out of my head and not think about all of that.

My phone went off and I glanced down to see who it was. Hayden. I muted the call. I didn't want to talk to him while Mason was still here. I figured it was more respectful to wait until I could give him my undivided attention. Plus, I wasn't sure what to tell him about his son's elopement. I was still angry with Mason myself for doing something so idiotic.

An hour later we were all seated around the kitchen table, just as we had done hundreds of times before. Yet now it was different. I could feel it. I knew Mason could by the uncomfortable look on his face. And I was pretty sure the boys could as well.

We made small talk and the boys rambled about their day; silly things that happened in class. Max and Henry had recently taken on a competitive stance even in their daily school events in trying to one up each other.

Mason and I listened attentively, grateful for the distraction. Neither of us sure as to how to tell the boys what we knew we must.

"So, this weekend, my team is playing against Jordie's team. He's the biggest bully in our class." Henry told Mason. "I mean, this kid is so tall he must have flunked at least two grades." Henry snickered.

"Henry, that's not nice." I gave him a cross look.

"But mom, I'm serious. It's not like I mentioned how stupid he is." He rolled his eyes at the ceiling.

"Henry!"

"But he is," he glanced at Mason with a sly grin.

"Be nice." I told him.

"Someone should remind him." My youngest muttered under his breath. "You'll see what I mean on Saturday." Henry looked directly at Mason.

"Well, Henry. I don't know if I'll be there on Saturday." Mason looked at me for help.

"Why not? Exam?" Max stopped eating and asked.

"Well, I'm moving back to campus guys." Mason said a little too bluntly.

"Why?" Four young eyes rested on me.

"Boys, Mason and I agree that it's time for him to transition back to campus. He's going to be graduating in a couple months and then moving back to Chicago." I said carefully.

"That's a lame excuse." Max looked between us.

"Max," I started, but Mason intervened.

"Your mom and I are great friends, and we love each other, but as friends." Mason added.

Ouch!

"Does this have anything to do with the necklace?" Max's eyes narrowed at me. Henry looked confused and Mason sighed audibly.

"Guys. I met someone when I went home last summer. We," Mason reached over and took my hand; "had agreed to remain friends when I left, but we weren't together. I guess we both sort of found someone closer to our own ages and fell in love. When I came back in the fall, I didn't want to leave you guys because I love you both so much. So, I asked your mom if I could still stay here. And she was nice enough to let me. but now, things have changed, and I need to move back to campus."

"I knew something was wrong." Max muttered.

"What's changed? Don't you love us anymore?" Henry asked innocently.

"Of course, I do. I will always love you guys. I've loved the time I spent here with you both and being a part of your family." Mason assured him.

"Then what's changed?" Henry looked on the verge of tears.

"I got married over Christmas." Mason stated abruptly.

"What?" Max stood up and glared at him. "You got married?" He shouted.

"Max," I reached for my son, but he pulled away.

"You married another woman?" Henry asked in a small voice.

"Yes. Her name is Megan and she," Mason attempted to smile and tell Henry, but Max cut him off.

"I could care less what her name is. How could you do that to my mom?" My eldest and fiercest protector shouted at Mason.

"Max. Calm down and sit down." I reached for him again, but he took a step back. "Mason didn't do anything to me."

"Did you know he was getting married?" His eyes narrowed on me.

"No. I had no idea." I answered honestly. "But as he said, we're just friends."

"But he was living with us." Max pointed out as if all of us were blindly unaware of that small fact.

"Max, I care about Mason. I love him very much. But over the last year or so it has become obvious to both of us that the difference in our ages made it difficult on our relationship. We have very little in common except for you boys. I want Mason to be happy and fall in love." I swallowed hard. "And if Megan does that for him, then I'm happy for him." I tried to explain.

"So, you're just going to leave us? We'll never see you again." Henry's eyes were filled with big fat tears.

"No. Of course, you will." Mason assured him, but Max grunted.

"Yeah, right." He muttered under his breath. It was obvious that Max was determined to make this as difficult as possible.

I cleared my throat and rose from my seat. I started clearing away the table and putting the dishes in the sink. I had my back towards the table and was rinsing the plates.

"I don't understand why you guys didn't just tell us this before school started this year." Max flopped back down in his chair. "Did you think we wouldn't understand?"

"No. We didn't want to hurt you. I know how much you both care about Mason." I told them.

"Did you think this would hurt less?" He countered.

"Well, obviously, Mason's unplanned marriage changed things a bit." I snickered unintentionally.

"I'll say." Max muttered.

I finished the dishes while the boys pulled themselves together and shifted the subject to Madden and the game they'd recently abandoned. I let out a sigh of relief and busied myself picking up the family room. Granted, it could have gone better but I also knew it could have gone a lot worse. I also knew that the forty questions with my boys was not over yet. This was merely halftime.

Mason stayed until the boys were down for the night. He had tucked Henry in and had a chat with Max before joining me in the family room. He sat down beside me on the couch looking none to worse for the wear. His sandy blond curls were askew giving him an even younger appearance than he already was.

I dearly loved those curls.

"I guess I'd best be going." He said but didn't move. "I'm trying to be happy for you, but it may take a while. I guess he does love you. I know that much." He offered me a tired smile. "I spoke with Kennedy."

"Oh," I didn't know what else to say.

"Hey," Mason nudged me gently and then took my hand in his; "it's okay. I'm over the shock of it now. I just want you and the boys to be happy."

"Thanks."

"When are you going to tell them who he is?" He inquired.

"I don't know. It's not going to be easy to explain."

"No. I would imagine not."

We sat in silence for several minutes; his hand still holding mine. I looked down at his strong familiar hand that felt so natural in mine. This hand I had held for almost two years; had kissed; had worked hard around my home to make it beautiful for my family. This hand that knew my body intimately; that had held my face tenderly; wiped my tears and whose fingers had run through my hair countless times. My heart ached at the thought of them belonging to anyone else.

But now they did.

"It's getting late. You should probably get going?" I reluctantly whispered.

"I know." But still, he didn't move. "I'll never regret our time together." Mason reached up and cupped my face in his hand. "I will miss you." He leaned over and kissed me very sweetly and gently. "And I will always love you."

"I'll always love you too." I said in a soft voice. With great hesitation, I stood up and took his hand leading him to the door. He put on his boots and coat before I wrapped my arms around his neck and held him tightly. "Please take care of yourself. And you make her take care of you." I whispered in his ear, fighting back the tears that stung my eyes.

"I will. I promise."

I let him go and watched him walk slowly to his car. As much as I dearly loved Hayden, it was still difficult to watch Mason walk out of my life in the capacity he'd been in it for almost two years. I knew we'd each made the right decisions for our future, but that didn't make the sting of it hurt any less.

I closed the door after his taillights faded off down the street. This chapter of my life was finally over. For something that had started out as a fling almost two years ago, it had grown into so much more. There was love, respect, and a deep friendship that I would treasure for the rest of my life.

I knew that the roads we had both chosen to travel were not going to be easy for either of us in the upcoming months. His parents were going to be hurt and enraged when they discover what he'd done. And I had no clue how to explain to my boys that the man I was in love with was Mason's father.

I turned off the television and the lights and slowly walked down the hall to my room.

Chapter 4

I CURLED UP IN BED CLUTCHING my cell phone in my hand. I felt torn between my loyalty to both men. It was so unfair for Mason to put me in this position. I quickly hit the button to connect me with Hayden and rested back against the pile of pillows.

"Hello darling, I've been waiting on you to call. Is everything all right?" Hayden's voice was light, but I could still hear the concern in it.

"I'm fine. I'm sorry I didn't answer earlier. Mason came by to pick up his things and moved back to campus." I told him.

"Oh, I hadn't realized. I'm sorry. Please tell me he was a gentleman."

"Of course, he was. He was a little irritable at first and rightfully so, but he came around and we had a good talk." I assured him.

"Did you sleep with him?" I could hear the hesitation in his voice.

"Hayden!" I was shocked. "No. Of course, not. Why would you even ask me such a thing?"

"Sweetheart, I know you care about him. I would be hurt if you did, but I would understand it." He stated flatly.

"No, I did not have sex with him. I helped him pack. I fixed dinner while he played video games with my boys, he tucked them in and said his goodbyes. Then he left and took his things back to campus." I sighed deeply and closed my eyes. "But I really think you should talk to him."

"I've tried to talk to him, numerous times. But he's not exactly been receptive." Hayden sounded irritated.

"You need to try again. He's going through some things right now and he could really use your support; even if you don't agree with some of the decisions he made." I danced carefully.

"Dear Lord, what has he done now?" He sighed audibly.

"Please don't put me in the middle." I begged. "I'm just asking you to please come down and talk with him. He's going to really need you."

"It sounds like Mason already put you there. Now you need to tell me exactly what's going on before I do get in my car and drive down there right now." The tone of his voice shifted to edgy.

"Hayden. Please call your son. I don't like being in this position. I told him the same. You know how much I love you, but I hate this." I sulked.

"Fine." I heard movement and then the distinct sound of the clinking of car keys. "I'll be there shortly."

"Hayden. No!" I sat up in bed. "Please, everything is fine. It's not necessary."

"I don't know what sort of stupid asinine stunt my son pulled this time, but I can guarantee by your reluctance to tell me, it's something to top all the others, isn't it?" Hayden huffed.

"Hayden, please. Just call him. Don't come down here." I begged, but I heard the unmistakable ding of his car door and then the engine of his car roar to life. "Hayden!"

"I'll see you shortly." He said roughly and then the line went dead.

"Jesus Christ!" I tossed my phone across the bed. "Shit!"

I reached over and grabbed my phone. I quickly clicked Mason's contact button and waited impatiently for him to answer the phone.

"Did I forget something?" His voice was lighthearted, and I could hear his buddies in the background.

"Mason, I just got off the phone with your father." I began but he cut me off.

"Did you tell him?" All the noise around him came to a sudden halt and I could picture the guys standing there staring at him in wonderment.

"No. I told him he needed to talk to you." I informed him.

"But you didn't tell him what about?" Mason questioned.

"No. But I hate that you put me in this position."

"I know. I'm sorry. I should have taken off my ring before I got there."

"You shouldn't have done it." I said before I could stop myself. "Thanks!"

"I'm sorry. I shouldn't have said that." I felt bad even though it was what I felt.

"Look, I can deal with my dad. I've gotten pretty good at it." He chuckled.

"I hope so. He's on his way down here because I wouldn't tell him what's going on." I told him.

"Damn it," he muttered.

"You've got a little less than three hours before he hits Indy."

"Do you think he'll stop by your place before heading here?" He asked.

"I don't know. I hope not. My boys are home. I'm not ready to explain all that to them yet." I confessed.

"Why do I get the feeling it's going to be a very long night, and no one is going to get any sleep." Mason moaned.

"I think you're right." I flopped back against the pillows already exhausted from an emotionally draining day.

"Why don't I just come back, and we handle this at your place. My dad won't blow a gasket in front of you." He reasoned.

"Mason, my boys are here. I cannot have this in my house in front of them. You know that." I explained.

"Even better. He'll definitely behave in front of them." Mason chuckled again.

"You are not using my boys to fix this crap with your father, Mason." I told him not finding the humor in this.

"I would never do that. You know I love those boys." He sighed heavily into the phone. "I'm just saying he's apt to be more reasonable and listen rather than shouting if they are present. Plus, he'd never behave like that in front of you."

"Mason, you don't know what you're asking of me." I told him.

"Please" I could hear the desperation in his voice. "Do this for me."

A million and one things ran through my mind, but the most loudly of them all was the word no. "Fine. But you will behave yourself. I will not have my children awoken in the middle of the night by you two screaming at each other. They have school in the morning." I closed my eyes and took a deep breath. "Come on over. I'll put on a pot of coffee and call your dad and tell him where you're at."

"You're the best, Lexie. You know that?" Mason exclaimed.

"Whatever. I'll see you soon." I hung up the phone and set it on the pillow beside me. I couldn't believe I had agreed to this. I knew I did it partially because I felt responsible for Mason doing something so stupid and partially because I was hoping to salvage the relationship between the man I was dearly in love with and the young man I loved.

I climbed back out of bed and wandered off into the kitchen. I started the coffee and leaned against the counter. I had no idea what to expect but I knew it was traveling towards my house at a good 75 mph with little regard for the black ice in his path.

I went back to my room and threw on a pair of sweats. I brushed my teeth again and pulled my hair up into a messy bun on top my head. I splashed some cold water on my face before I picked up my phone on my way back to the kitchen to get my first of many cups of coffee in preparation for the long night.

I settled down on the couch with a blanket pulled up around me, sipped my coffee and finally hit the button to connect me with Hayden. I was hoping that he had calmed down a bit after an hour on the road.

"What's going on?" Hayden answered the phone abruptly.

"Are you all right?" I didn't like the sound of his voice.

"Yeah, I'm fine. But the roads aren't great. They've managed to ice back over since rush hour." He complained.

"Please be careful." I hated him driving in this mess and making this unnecessary trip down here.

"I am. So, what's going on?" He asked again a bit impatiently.

"I told Mason you were coming down here so he's going to meet you at my house. He didn't want to get into a heated discussion with you at the dorms in the middle of the night." I told him.

"I thought your boys were there."

"They are, so no shouting." I warned him.

"So, basically you're telling me that my son is hiding behind your skirt instead of facing me?" I could picture Hayden rolling his eyes as he said it.

"No. He's just moved back today and doesn't want to cause any problems." I reasoned.

"Fine. I will come to your place."

"Thank you." I let out a small breath of relief.

"I'll be there shortly."

"Please be careful. I love you." I reminded him.

"I love you, too."

I barely got halfway through my first cup of coffee when I saw Mason's headlights come up the driveway. I patted Billy on the head and told her to be quiet. I was afraid she'd bark as late as it was, but thankfully she didn't. She only jumped on Mason when I opened the door to let me him. He rubbed her ears playfully before telling her to get down.

"You okay?" He asked removing his coat and hat.

"Tired." I walked over and curled back up on the couch. "There's fresh coffee in the kitchen."

"Thanks. I could use it just to warm up. It's freezing out there. My car said it's fourteen degrees." He rubbed his hands together and headed into the kitchen. He returned moments later still rambling and clinging to the oversized mug in his hands. "I'm so ready for spring. I hate this crap and the roads are shit." He nudged my feet, so he could slip down under them and share in part of the blanket. "Sorry love, but I'm frozen."

"I know." How many countless nights had we shared a blanket watching a movie together on the couch with my feet draped casually over his lap? More than I could fathom.

We settled comfortably on into a familiar bit. Mason turned on some reruns of Friends and started playing on his phone. I snuggled down into my pillow with the blanket wrapped up around my chin. Despite the coffee, I was so exhausted, all I wanted to do was sleep. It wasn't long before I drifted off.

"Well, isn't this sweet." The sound of Hayden's voice woke me up. Mason, apparently, had fallen asleep also. "You realize your front door was unlocked." He leaned over and kissed me quickly.

"That was my fault. I forgot to lock it when I got here." Mason pulled himself out of his slumped position and sat upright. "Sorry." He apologized rubbing his eyes.

"What time is it?" I asked sitting up myself.

"Almost two. It took me longer to get here than I anticipated. The roads are really slick." Hayden took off his coat and draped it over the arm of the chair by the front door.

"You really didn't need to make the trip down here. I would have been home in a few weeks for spring break." Mason told his dad as Hayden sat down on the loveseat.

"Would you like some coffee. I can heat it back up for you." I offered.

"I can get it." Hayden stood up. "I made the trip to see what shenanigans you've been up to, and I wanted to talk to you as well." He told Mason before entering the kitchen.

"Okay, is it me or is it weird that he knows where everything is?" Mason paused and looked at me. "I almost said *our* house, but I guess it's just your house now." He tried to smile but did not pull it off very well.

I ignored the comment simply because there wasn't anything to say in return. However, I did notice Mason quickly stuff his wedding ring back into his front pocket while Hayden was in the kitchen. He shrugged with a grin when I shook my head at him. There was no need for Hayden to see that right off the bat so I couldn't blame Mason for doing it.

"So, what's going on? Alex said you moved back to the dorms today. Why did I need to meet you here?" Hayden sat down on the loveseat and sipped his coffee.

"I did. I took my stuff there earlier." Mason shifted uncomfortably. "I just thought it would be easier if we talked here. I didn't want my friends to know that you've been seeing Alex behind my back."

Ouch!

"I appreciate that." I felt my face go red and Hayden cleared his throat.

"Alex and I did a lot of talking this afternoon before the boys got home. We both know our relationship ended long before I started my internship, and we know I shouldn't have moved back in here at the beginning of fall term." He took a deep breath before he continued. "Alex had told me she was involved with someone else. She told me she was in love with someone else, but I admit, I didn't want to lose her." Mason smiled over at me. "I do love her. And I love the boys. We've become a family."

His words hurt just as badly now as they had the first time he said them to me last fall.

"I understand. I really do. You two have spent a lot of time together." Hayden reintegrated.

"We lived together for almost two years." Mason emphasized. "Shared the same bed. I went to all the boys' activities, did their homework with them, played ball with them, video games, cooked for them. I learned what it takes to be the man of the family." He stated a little harshly.

"I know, I understand." Hayden nodded.

"You know, all those things you didn't do with me." Mason stated flatly.

"Mason, this is not about that. Stop it." I felt like a parent scolding a child and I hated it. Mason turned and glared at me.

"Son," Hayden began, but I cut him off too.

"Stop. I mean it. My boys are asleep and you two are not going to get into an intense argument and wake them up. If you two want to do that you can both just leave. Is that clear?" My patience was wearing thin already and exhaustion wasn't putting any of us in the best of moods. I couldn't help thinking again that this was a bad idea.

"Sorry," Mason mumbled, but Hayden just shot me a look.

"Mason, we never meant for any of this to happen. And I am sorry it did. But you should know by now you can't always control who you fall in love with." Hayden's face softened a bit, and I began to relax a little.

"I do understand that, and it is true." Mason looked over at me and I held my breath with every muscle in my body immediately tensed back up. I knew what was coming. I just prayed Hayden would hold it together. "You know dad, that I've been seeing Megan when I've been home." Hayden nodded. "Well, we've been talking every day and well," Mason looked at me with pleading eyes, but I wasn't about to open my mouth.

If he was man enough to get married, then he can be man enough to tell his father about it.

"Well, dad," Mason fumbled but couldn't find the words.

"Is she pregnant?" I could see Hayden's ears turning red from where I was seated. Mason nodded and tears immediately sprang to my eyes. "Oh, dear Lord." Hayden's head dropped in his hands. I went over to him and wrapped my arms around him. He looked up at me with big tears in his eyes and shook his head slowly. "How far long?" He looked back at Mason.

"Since Thanksgiving. She was late so we took a test over Christmas break." Mason said in a low voice. "I went with her to the doctors, and he confirmed it."

Of course, that was why he married her. What an idiot!

"I'm guessing your mother doesn't know because she'd still be screaming." Hayden took a deep breath and reached for my hand. Mason shook his head. "Kennedy knows."

"I figured as much." Hayden sat there for a couple of minutes staring at the floor before he looked back up at his son. "Well, let's not jump to anything irrational. If she decides to have the baby, then we'll do a paternity test. If it's yours, you're going to man up and pay child support. And we'll love it and spoil it." Hayden tried to grin, but it was heartbreaking. "Do you believe it's yours?"

"She says it is. She says she hasn't been with anyone but me since last spring." Mason picked at his fingernails and struggled to look at his dad.

"Do you believe her?" I couldn't stop myself from asking.

"Yeah, I guess so." Mason shrugged not sounding all too confident, but I couldn't help but think of what he'd told me about their sexual encounters.

"Son, you've been down here, and she's been in Chicago for the last four and a half months. Now, I'm not pointing fingers, but you haven't exactly been faithful to her. Are you sure she's not seeing anyone else?" Hayden asked.

"Not that I know of."

"Well, we, of all people, know how secrets can be kept and discovered." I mumbled.

"True." Hayden agreed. "What do you think, son?"

"I think I made a big mistake." Mason shook his head slowly with a flood of tears pouring down his face.

"Ah, Mason," I stood up and opened my arms. He practically jumped into them and wrapped his arms tightly around me. His tears poured down my neck with his face buried in my shoulder. "Darling, please tell me you lied to me earlier?" I whispered in his ear.

"I wish I was." He sniffled.

"Oh, God," I couldn't stop my own tears from falling.

Hayden stood up and wrapped his arms around both of us.

"I'm sorry. I'm so sorry." Mason continued to sob. "I just don't understand. I was always so careful. I always wore a condom, and I never even came with her."

"What?" I let go of them and took a step back. "Then it can't be yours." I exclaimed. "It's damn near impossible." I was completely stunned. "She's lying. You have to get this thing annulled." I slipped before I realized what I'd said.

"What?" Hayden almost shouted. "You didn't." His body went rigid, and he stared at his son. "Please, dear God, tell me you didn't" His eyes narrowed at Mason who slowly nodded.

"Hayden," I began but quickly shut up when I saw the look on his face.

"Tell me you didn't marry her." Hayden was barely holding it together.

"Dad," Mason brushed the tears off his cheeks. "I didn't know what else to do."

"Why didn't you come to me?" Hayden asked.

"Because when I went to your place, you weren't there. You were down here fucking my girlfriend." Mason said angrily.

"Don't give me that crap. You didn't know that then. Your actions are of your own making and have nothing to do with Alex nor me." Hayden spat back.

"Please guys, this isn't helping. We need to figure out what to do to fix this mess." I stepped in between them. "Let's sit down and talk." Both men sat back down in their seats, each with tears of frustration and aggravation. "I'm going to put on a fresh pot of coffee."

I picked up my mug and walked into the kitchen. I set it down on the counter and brushed the tears away from my face. I couldn't believe it hadn't entered my mind before. Mason was always so responsible when it came to sex — at least he always was with me. He said he was with Megan, but …

I took my time getting the coffee started. I wasn't sure exactly how Hayden planned to fix this situation, but I was certain Mason wasn't going to like it. And I was scared that somehow, I was going to be a part of it. Either way, I knew I was in for a long night.

"Are you okay?" Hayden asked when I walked back into the family room.

"I'm fine." I lied and joined him on the loveseat. I took his hand in mine and smiled as best I could. "Fresh coffee will be ready in a minute."

"Thanks, darling." Hayden squeezed my hand.

The three of us sat there in silence for several minutes. It was hard to think of something to say without sounding accusatory. We'd all made foolish mistakes in the last couple of months and none of us were sitting there with a clean slate.

I knew Mason was still talking to Megan, even suspected that he was seeing her when he went home, but I never imagined he'd gotten in this far over his head. I could still recall how Hayden had told me of his dislike and mistrust of her. He said she was a manipulator. And now that was all I could think of.

"So, what is the game plan?" I asked stupidly.

"We're going to get this farce annulled first thing in the morning." Hayden stated as a matter of fact. "If it wasn't three in the morning, I'd already have called my attorney."

"Is that even possible?" I knew very little about the stipulations for an annulment.

"Have you consummated the marriage?" Hayden asked.

"This is embarrassing," Mason dropped his head. "But no. We haven't."

"Why not?" He asked his son. "When do your classes start?" Hayden turned towards me.

Damn, I had a feeling this was coming.

"Next Wednesday, but what does this have to do with me?"

"Can Lisa watch the boys? Or maybe your parents or Debbie?" Hayden asked.

"You know Lisa and Debbie?" Mason looked a little surprised. "Huh...well, I guess you do, you were at the New Year's party. Have you met her delightful mother yet?" Mason smirked.

"Mason. Stop." I warned him.

"No, and from what I understand, I can wait." Hayden smiled over at his son. As thrilled as I was that the two were calming down and starting to talk, I didn't want my mother to be their mutual ground for hatred.

"She's a doll." Mason obviously couldn't help himself.

"Seriously — Mason." I sighed heavily.

"Sorry," he smirked again.

"Would you mind accompanying us to Chicago? I will bring you home on Sunday." Hayden looked at me with the sincerest expression. His eyes looked desperate. I knew he didn't need me there, but I knew he wanted me there.

"I will have to get a hold of my parents. They should be up by seven." I glanced up at the clock on the mantle. "We should probably try to get a couple hours of sleep before we head out." It was almost four and the boys were going to be up by six thirty.

The men got to their feet, and I didn't move. They both paused and looked strangely at me.

"Sorry. Habit." Mason sat back down. "I'll sleep on the couch." He smiled awkwardly at his dad.

"My boys are home. You can't sleep in my room." I turned to Hayden and placed my hand on his chest. "I'm sorry, but they don't know who you are, and I can't have them find out this way."

"I understand." He leaned down and kissed me sweetly. "I'll be right here."

"Okay," I kissed him again and hugged him tightly. "It's so good to see you. I love you." I whispered in his ear.

"I love you too," he smiled. "And thanks."

I wandered down the hall alone with Billy and closed my bedroom door behind us. I crawled into bed, and she hopped up beside me. I scratched her ears and looked into her big brown eyes.

"This is completely fucked up." I muttered to her. "The two men in my life are out there together and I'm in here alone. Mason is married and my boys are going to find Hayden here when they wake up." I told her shaking my head in disbelief.

I flopped by against my pillows. I was so tired I couldn't sleep. My mind was racing over the night's events. I couldn't make heads or tails out of anything. I really didn't want to leave the boys with my parents for the rest of the week, but I knew if I left them at Lisa's Max would kill me. My parents, especially my mom was going to play twenty questions if I asked her to take care of my boys. And this was not something I was willing to discuss with either of them.

Chapter 5

MY ALARM STARTLED ME AWAKE at six thirty. I was proud of myself for not throwing it through the window as I stumbled to the bathroom. I had no clue what time I finally dozed off, but I knew it wasn't nearly as much as I needed.

This was going to be a very long day.

I woke the boys up and told each of them to keep it down, that Mason and his father were asleep in the living room. They each gave me puzzled looks but I told him we'd discuss it later. They grumbled and moaned as they did every morning they were required to get out of bed and started their morning rituals. I went about my routine as well trying hard not to think about the two men snoring softly in my family room.

"I thought Mason moved back to campus. What's his dad doing here?" Henry asked as he sat down with his cereal at the island.

"Mason showed back up here around midnight and his dad drove down from Chicago. They needed a place to talk." I shrugged slightly and leaned against the side of the island drinking my coffee.

"How ticked is his dad over him getting married?" Max chuckled.

That kid never misses a thing.

"Very." I tried my best not to grin at my son. "But nowhere near where I'd be if you pulled a stunt like that."

"I'm not that stupid." He muttered taking a seat in the barstool beside his little brother.

"Me neither. I'm not ever getting married." Henry added.

"Don't say that. I hope you get married someday — after college and after you get your career going." I smiled at my youngest son.

"Gee Mom, are you sure you don't want him to live with you til he's thirty?" Max giggled.

"You say that like it's a bad thing." I teased.

"Yeah, cause every man wants to live with his momma as an adult. That will do wonders for his love life." Max rolled his eyes at me.

"It's okay. I have no love life." Henry stated bluntly between bites making Max and I laugh.

"We'd better keep it down. We don't want to wake the sleeping beauties in the front room." I teasingly chastised my sons.

"Hey momma, I've got an idea." Max had that shit-eating grin on his face that always meant he was going to say something smartass or sarcastic.

"What's that?" I was almost afraid to ask.

"Well, since Mason's now married and you guys said that the age difference between you was your biggest problem, why don't you just date his dad?" He giggled and I narrowed my eyes at him. "I mean, he's single. He looks a lot like Mason and he's old, like you. It'd be perfect." Even Henry giggled despite his best efforts not too.

"Very cute, Max. You think you're funny, don't you?" I playfully smacked him on the arm.

"I know I am." He stated in his cocky voice.

"But you know now that I think about it. You may be on to something there, Max. Perhaps I will start dating Hayden." I said smugly.

"Good. It's about time you decided to date in your own age bracket — you know, the old one." Max grinned at me between bites.

"Thanks. I love you too." I told him with a smirk and then helped myself to another cup of coffee. "By the way, boys. I may have to run to Chicago for a couple days to help Mason and his father with a few things."

"What? No." Henry pouted.

"If he's man enough to get married, isn't he man enough to fix his own problems? Or does he need you to fix it for him like last spring?" Max glared.

"What do you mean last spring?"

"When you covered for him with his dad about the whole girlfriend crap. He lied to his dad about who you were." Max stated.

"You knew about that?" I had no idea he was aware.

"I live here, and these walls are thin." He told me and Henry nodded. "I can't believe you didn't kick him out for that one."

"I know." I didn't have a defense and we all knew it.

"How long are you going to be gone?" Henry asked.

"Probably the rest of the week. Where would you guys rather stay, at my parents or Lisa's?" I looked between them.

"Lisa's," Henry jumped up.

"No," Max quickly added. "You're not leaving me with Brie for a week. That's just cruel and unusual punishment that I don't deserve."

"You'd rather stay with my parents?" I asked him.

"No, but they are the lesser of two evils. At least no one there would be chasing me around trying to kiss me." He rolled his eyes.

"You're going to change your mind about her in a couple more years." I told him.

"Yeah, and then I'll be happy to spend a week at her house." He grinned.

"Then there's no way in hell I'd let you!" I playfully smacked him again.

"You're no fun." He pushed me back and put his bowl in the sink.

"Get ready, the bus will be here in twenty minutes. And don't forget to brush your teeth." I told them as they wandered out of the kitchen back towards their rooms.

I sat down on the barstool Max had just vacated and rested my head down on the island. All I wanted to do was sleep. I needed another six hours minimum if I was going to function at all and I didn't see that happening.

"You're really wonderful with them." Hayden's voice brought me back from my momentary hazed state.

"I wonder sometimes." I chuckled barely raising my head off the island.

"I heard your conversation. Your oldest is a character." He smiled and fixed himself a mug of coffee. "He has your personality." He took a sip and snickered. "He's you with a penis."

"That's putting it nicely," I laughed.

"Do I get to meet them?" He sat down on the barstool beside me.

"Sure, but only as Mason's dad." I gave him a sly grin.

"Of course, but they did say we should date, ya know, because we're both old." Hayden laughed.

"They are sweet, aren't they?"

"I think they're pretty great." Then he leaned in closer to me. "Just like their momma."

"Hey momma," Max hollered rounding the corner into the kitchen. He came to a halt when he saw Hayden sitting beside me. "Oh, sorry."

"Max, this is Hayden Brooks, Mason's dad. Hayden this is my eldest, Max." I could tell they were sizing each other up. Hayden had of course seen photographs of my sons, but he had never met them until now.

"Hey," Max nodded in acknowledgement.

"Good morning, I hear you're quite a football player." Hayden stated.

"I'm not bad. Mason practices with me a lot." Max took a couple steps closer.

"That's good. I'm glad." Hayden said awkwardly.

"Momma, where are we going after school? Do you want us to take the bus home?" As the words came out of his mouth, Henry walked up behind him and stood silently looking over Hayden.

"That wallflower hiding behind his brother is my youngest, Henry. Henry, this is Mason's dad, Hayden."

"Hi." Henry squeaked.

"Good morning." Hayden greeted him with a smile.

"Momma?" Max shifted his weight from one foot to another, his way of telling me he was quickly getting impatient and annoyed.

"I'll text you once I know. Okay, mister?"

"Whatever." He grumbled.

The three of us took Hayden's car and left Mason's Camaro in my garage. It seemed pointless to drive separately since Hayden planned on us returning on Saturday to spend the night with me. I also think a small part of him didn't want Mason and I to have three plus hours alone on the drive back to talk.

Mason curled up in the backseat with an extra pillow and blanket he'd stolen from my hall closet. We had barely reached the interstate before he was snoring softly again. I envied him in a way because he truly had no clue of the shitstorm he was walking into. I, on the other hand, was a nervous wreck anticipating meeting Kennedy and being introduced to Hayden's world in Chicago.

Granted, Kennedy was the only person who knew the sorted truth about the three of us and Hayden had repeatedly assured me she was trustworthy and would never tell a soul; I still couldn't calm the butterflies in my stomach.

As if he sensed my apprehension, Hayden reached over and took my hand in his. He was always wonderful at the little things; a simple touch, a look, a smile, a hand in mine to let me know that he was with me through it all. He always made me feel special, loved, and secure.

"You okay?" I nodded. "You seem nervous."

"A little. I'm used to sharing my world with you but it's the first time I've walked into yours." I explained.

"Only parts of your world." He smiled over at me before turning his eyes back on the road. "Today was my first encounter with your boys and you've kept me well hidden from your family."

"That's not entirely true. You've met my sister." I said coyly.

"But not your parents."

"Trust me, you don't ever want to meet them. If you don't believe me, ask your son how sweet my mother is." I rolled my eyes.

"You don't think they'd like me?" He squeezed my hand gently.

"Under the circumstances in which our relationship grew, I believe my mother would condemn both of us to hell." I told him with a snicker.

"That's okay, I was heading there anyway. At least we'll be together." A devious grin slid across his shapely lips.

"You're so bad." I shook my head at him and giggled.

"Seriously, my world is not that scary. My ex on the other hand, is going to kill him when she finds out."

"Does she have to find out? I mean it's not like he needs her signature or permission or anything. And if it's only going to cause Mason and her heartache, don't tell her." I suggested.

"Because something like that will come out. It always does whether it's now, five years or ten, she'll find out. She's a mom; they always find out sooner or later." He chuckled.

"And if she finds out about us? The three of us?" I raised my eyebrows over at him.

"Am I supposed to care what she thinks?" He countered.

"But will she tell everyone in your family?"

"Oh definitely." He laughed. "That woman would love to have a piece of juicy gossip like that to hold over my head."

"Wonderful," I muttered not excited at all about the prospect of meeting his ex.

"I don't pay her any attention because that's what she wants." He stated.

"I know what you mean. Danny would have a field day if he knew."

"How do you plan on keeping it from him?" Hayden glanced over at me.

"I don't know, honestly. Either Max or Henry will mention it eventually. It's just a matter of time once we become public." I told him.

"Do you think he'll give you trouble? Try to take the boys?"

"No. Danny wouldn't just because he doesn't want the responsibility it entails. He likes being a part-time dad. Having the boys full time with the daily responsibilities, school, and sports, is more than he is willing to accept. It would cut into his playtime and hell avoid that if possible."

"Is he a workaholic?"

"No. Nothing like that. He enjoys his freedom." I rolled my eyes.

"Does he miss you?"

"No. I believe he misses the idea of me and the boys, but not enough to change his ways. He cheated on me before we were married. Youth and naivety thought I could change him." I snorted. "I was wrong."

"He can't be happy with that lifestyle?" He stated.

"But you've been single for more than twenty years now. You tell me?" I couldn't help but giggle at the pot calling the kettle black.

"I'm a workaholic. Not a whore-dog. There is a difference. I wasn't out running around on my wife. I was building a company and that takes time and dedication. She never understood that." Hayden informed me.

"But don't you get lonely? Don't you regret all the things you missed out on with Kennedy and Mason?" I was curious.

"Not anymore." He squeezed my hand again. "I don't remember ever being this happy. But yes, for years it was not what I would call lonely, but I was alone. I dated occasionally, but never anything serious. I do regret that I missed so much with my kids, but I was trying to leave them something for when I'm gone. I wanted them to be taken care of. My dream was to pass the business onto my children."

"Does Kennedy work for you?" It had never occurred to me to ask, and Mason had never mentioned it before.

"Yes, she started with me right after college. But she also worked for me every summer throughout her undergraduate years, and high school. She is more focused and dedicated than Mason. Mason enjoys being young."

"But isn't that what he's supposed to do?" I tried not to grin.

"Yes, but I wanted him to learn a little discipline also. I tried to instill a strong work ethic in him just as I did with Kennedy, but it didn't seem to take as well with him." Hayden snorted. "He's always been my rebellious child and honestly, he could be a lot worse. Although I believe this stunt is by far his worse, next to his spring break vacation spree."

"He thought he was doing the right thing. You have to give him credit for that one." I reasoned.

"Perhaps he should have paid better attention in health class. Then we wouldn't be in this mess." Hayden rolled his eyes and shook his head at me.

"What I'm surprised about is why he didn't talk to someone; even one of the guys — not that they paid any more attention than he did, but damn, he could have looked it up on the internet or something." Mason sometimes baffled me.

"Seriously;" Hayden chuckled. "He looks everything else up, but not that?"

"I know." I shook my head in disbelief. "It makes no sense." I looked out the window at the snow-covered farms along the roadside. It was so peaceful and beautiful.

"A lot of what my son does makes no sense to me." Hayden muttered.

I dozed off somewhere around Lafayette with my head leaning against Hayden's shoulder. I snuggled up to him and closed my eyes. The hum of the car, the vibration of the tires on the highway lulled me off into dreams of the day Hayden and I would never be apart.

Hayden woke me up as we turned into his business parking lot. He opened my car door and it felt like someone had hit me in the face with an ice shovel. The Chicago air was an easy fifteen to twenty degrees colder than it had been in Indianapolis and the wind whipped right through my clothes.

"Oh, good Lord it's cold." I complained taking Hayden's hand, so I wouldn't slip on the ice that covered the parking lot.

"The wind gets a bite to it coming off the Lake." Mason said walking around the car.

"This is ridiculous." I held on to Hayden's arm as we made our way to the front doors. "Where are we?"

"Chicago," Mason looked at me like I was stupid.

"I know that." I playfully smack his arm as he held the door open for us. "What part?"

"The Gold Coast." Hayden told me.

We walked over to the elevator and Mason hit the button. I was still huddling close to Hayden when this lady in business attire rushed through the door carrying a carrier full of Dunkin's coffee and cursing under her breath.

"Oh, good morning Mr. Brooks." She stammered, clearly embarrassed. "I got chosen to run out for coffee this morning. "Hi Mason."

"I see that." Hayden smiled at her. The elevator door opened and the four of us stepped on. The women hit the button for the fifth floor and the door closed again. I stood there feeling awkward waiting for one of them to say something.

They didn't.

The doors opened onto a landing that broke off into hallways in three directions. I hadn't realized how big the building was. Hayden's office was down the right-side hallway at the very end. It had a large glass window front and glass doors with his business name frosted onto the glass. Hayden held the door open for us and I noticed the receptionist straighten up a bit when she noticed him.

She was a tiny girl who appeared to be in her late twenties. She was an attractive young lady with long blond hair, big blue eyes, and delicate features. She smiled widely and said, "Good morning Mr. Brooks, Mason."

"Good morning, Stephanie." Hayden smiled as we walked past her desk.

The girl with the coffee hurried past us down the corridor. We went by several offices and conference rooms and then came to a big open space with dozens of cubicles. The office was decorated in light grays and marrons with more classic professional appeal. I could tell it was professionally decorated.

It was much larger than I had anticipated, and I was impressed that Hayden had built this all on his own. No wonder he had no personal life. He had poured everything into making his dream into a prosperous reality and he had been extremely successful.

There was a barrage of 'Good morning, Mr. Brooks' and 'Hi Mason' as we passed by the rows of cubicles. Dozens of people were busy typing away, designing something or other; most had headphones on. It was a world I had pictured many times before but, in every version, I always ended up imaging a scene from *Mad Men*.

Hayden's secretary was perched at her desk right outside his office. She looked like she was in her late thirties or early forties. She was a little round woman with stylish brown hair and big brown eyes. She had a kind smile and chubby cheeks.

"Good morning, Mr. Brooks. Here are your messages and coffee." She handed both to him. "And what can I get you two?" She looked at Mason and me.

"Coffee please." Mason and I answered in unison.

"Cream and sugar?" She asked me.

"Yes, please." I smiled. "Thank you."

"Of course, Miss …" She hesitated to look at Hayden.

"Rose." Hayden offered. "Molly, this is my girlfriend, Alexandra Rose." He smiled.

"It's nice to meet you, Alexandra." Molly offered her hand.

"You too. And please call me Alex." I shook her hand.

"I'm expecting Tim shortly. Can you please let me know when he arrives?" Hayden was already sorting through his messages.

"Don't I always?" She laughed. "After ten years, the man still doesn't believe I can do my job." She grinned sarcastically at me.

"Molly, we both know I couldn't function without you." Hayden assured her.

"Damn skippy." She muttered loud enough for us to hear as she took off to get the coffee.

Hayden closed his office door behind us. He set his brief case on top of his desk and his coffee on the coaster. "Make yourself at home." He told me. Mason had already made himself comfortable on the oversized couch.

His office was warm, and cozy done up in brick red and taupe with the furniture in a deep cheery wood. He had a pile of design boards stacked beneath a wall-sized window that had a breathtaking view of Lake Michigan.

"I heard you finally decided to make an appearance." A young lady burst into the office.

"Good morning, Kennedy." Hayden rolled his eyes at his daughter.

"By fifteen minutes." She informed him. "So, you're the infamous Alex." She spun towards me. I immediately stood up from the chair in front of Hayden's desk.

"Kennedy," The warning to behave was clear in Hayden's voice.

"What?" She asked innocently looking at her dad. "I ran into Molly in the break room, and she asked me if this was the mystery woman you disappeared with last summer and I told her I believed it was, wasn't it?" The girl turned back towards me.

"Yes," I nodded.

"Well, it's nice to finally meet you." She shocked me by reaching over and hugging me.

"It's nice to finally meet you as well." She wasn't anything close to what I was expecting.

Kennedy Brooks was slightly taller than me with long blondish brown hair that was naturally wavy, bordering on curly. She had Hayden's green eyes, but the rest of her features must have come from her mother. She was a stunningly beautiful young lady who obviously stayed abreast of the latest fashions from the outfit she was wearing. I suddenly felt underdressed in the jeans, knee-high boots, and sweater I had thrown on for the drive.

Kennedy obviously inherited her mother's beauty, but as soon as she opened her mouth, it was Hayden that came out. She had the same mannerisms, gestures, and laugh as her father. If Hayden could claim Max was me with a penis, then Kennedy was definitely him with breasts.

"So, I'm guessing Tim is on his way in." Kennedy walked over to where Mason was lounging lazily on the couch and smacked him upside the head. "Idiot."

"Stop it," Mason pushed her away.

"I can't believe you! For someone who is so intelligent, you do some stupid shit!" She chastised him.

Hayden's office phone rang, and he picked it up completely ignoring the exchange between his children. "Yes, Molly?" He paused a moment. "Thank you. Send him in." He set the receiver down as a tall thin man in a dark blue suit entered the office.

"Tim. Thanks for coming." Hayden walked around his desk and shook the man's hand.

"I'm not sure what to say. I'm stunned." Tim said pleasantly.

"You're not the only one." Hayden rolled his eyes with a half-hearted chuckle. This is my girlfriend, Alexandra." He motioned towards me, and Tim and I exchanged pleasantries.

"So, you're the one I've been hearing so much about?" Tim said as he sat down beside me in the seat in front of Hayden's desk.

"Don't believe a word of it," I told him with a smile and eyed Hayden suspiciously.

"We have a weekly racket ball game, and I was curious about the lady who suddenly threw a wrench into our schedule." Tim smiled.

"Sorry," I couldn't stop grinning. "I had no idea."

"Well, he'd been making all these mysterious trips to Indy. I figured it was because of someone who was prone to getting into trouble;" Tim looked over at Mason who blushed. "May have been up to something, until he finally confessed, he'd met someone." Tim smiled pleasantly at me before turning towards Hayden. "Given the circumstances perhaps you should have been babysitting someone else."

"In all fairness, this happened in Chicago, not Indy." Hayden glared at his son. "So, how do we get this disaster annulled?"

"It's actually not all that difficult." Tim went on to explain the process while the four of us sat quietly and listened.

It was almost two o'clock before things were wrapped up and Mason had signed the initial paperwork to get the process started. Now it was just a matter of time and the waiting game on dealing with his mother's reactions. Something I knew everyone was dreading.

"I'm starving. Anyone else?" Kennedy announced standing up after Tim had left to file the papers.

It was then that it occurred to me I hadn't eaten all day but had drunk more than my share of coffee which explained my pounding headache.

"I am," I gently rubbed my temples slowly.

"Me too," Mason added.

The four of us headed to a small trendy café in the heart of the Gold Coast district. It was a charming little place and Mason boasted about the cheeseburgers and milkshakes. As cold as it was,

I wasn't about to order one, but he was right about the cheeseburgers.

After lunch, Hayden dropped Mason and me off at his apartment. He and Kennedy had to return to the office for a couple of hours to try to catch up on some work. I followed Mason into the skyscraper and waited patiently as he hit the top floor button on the elevator panel.

"You do realize he's not going to be back before nine, right?" Mason asked as the elevator hummed to life.

"I figured as much." And I did. He was a self-proclaimed workaholic.

The elevator door opened into a small landing that was elegantly decorated with a small table with a crystal vase filled with orchids and large hourglass upon it. Above it was a large mirror trimmed in antique brass. The landing adorned a set of large double doors. "He has the whole floor?" I asked the rhetorical question as Mason unlocked the door.

"Daddy's done well." Mason shrugged casually but I could hear the pride in his voice. "Why do you think I always said I'd never live up to his expectations?" He raised an eyebrow. "That's Kennedy's job. I'm the screw-up child." He opened the door and stepped aside. "I guess we all have our roles to play."

"Mason," I walked past him into the oversized entryway. "You're not a screw-up."

"After the meeting we just had with Tim can you really say that?" He smirked with a raised eyebrow.

"You're a little misguided at times, perhaps, but hey, you did what you did to be honorable, and I believe that is commendable. You just chose the wrong girl to believe in." I lightly touched his arm in a vague attempt to comfort him.

"Yeah, well, I'd been better off and much happier if I'd knocked you up. At least then I wouldn't have lost you to my dad." He stated flatly.

I chose to ignore the comment because here was no response for it and we both knew it. "The view is amazing." I walked over to the wall length windows in the great room and opened the blinds fully. Hayden had a breathtaking view of the Gold Coast and the sweeping shores and waters of Lake Michigan.

"It's cool watching the sunrise over the lake." Mason walked up beside me.

"When have you ever seen a sunrise 'Mr. I sleep til' noon'?" I teased.

"When I roll in at dawn," he laughed. "So, what do you want to do? We've got four or five hours to kill."

The penthouse was much larger than I anticipated and professionally decorated in modern urban décor. It looked almost sterile with its white, grays, and black. The oddly shaped vases and carefully placed knickknacks added a splash of teal and maroon to the cold room. There were only a couple of personal effects and pictures of Hayden's children that said someone lived here and it was not a space for showings.

I couldn't help but think how Hayden's world and home was the exact opposite of mine.

"What do you normally do here?" I turned around scanning over the vast amount of space.

"I don't know. I'm rarely here and it's usually just to sleep or watch movies."

"Okay, do you want to go somewhere? There's tons of museums here."

"Seriously?" He looked at me as if I'd asked him to have a root canal.

"Fine. Then you think of something." I shook my head at him.

Mason flopped down on the oversized sectional and put his feet up on the coffee table. I cringed but said nothing. "I'm cool with just watching a movie."

"Wonderful," I muttered thinking of all the things I could be doing at home instead.

I sat down on the other end of the couch after playfully smacking Mason's feet off the coffee table.

"Or we could have some fun for old times' sake." He flashed me a cheesy grin.

"Mason! I can't believe you!" And this time I smacked him much harder, but he only laughed.

I settled in for a peaceful yet boring afternoon of Mason selection of movies. A part of me wished I was still at home and as exciting as it was to finally see Hayden's world, I couldn't help but wonder where I could possibly fit into it.

Chapter 6

TRUE TO MASON'S PREDICTION, Hayden arrived home just after nine thirty. I had dozed off on the couch somewhere during the third episode of *Bosch*.

"Hey darling, I'm home. Sorry, work took longer than I expected." Hayden woke me with a soft kiss.

"It's okay." What did he honestly expect me to say – the truth?

"Are you hungry?" He asked taking a seat beside me.

"No, not really." I said up a bit still a tad groggy.

"Mason went out with his friends. He left you a note on the island." Hayden placed my legs over his lap and lovingly ran his hands over them.

"Hmm…" I grumbled trying to stifle a yawn. I not accustomed to having so much time on my hands.

"What about a hot shower?"

"That sounds good." I stretched my arms and legs. They were cramped from sleeping on the sofa.

"Or we could climb into the hot tub." Hayden grinned devilishly at me.

"You have a hot tub?" I chuckled.

"Out there on the balcony." He nodded towards the wall of windows.

"It's freezing out there." I looked at him as if he were crazy.

"But it's not in the water." He pointed out.

"But we have to get to the water and there's snow and ice between that hot tub and your balcony door." I stated sarcastically.

"Don't tell me you're that big of a pansy." He laughed.

"Oh, yes I am." I started laughing myself. "And I am not ashamed to admit it."

"Come on," Hayden stood up and pulled me to my feet.

"No," I let him pull me into his bedroom.

I walked over to the French doors that led from his bedroom to the surprisingly large outdoor atrium. The parameter was lined with various shrubs and small trees. The table and chairs sat abandoned alongside the brick fireplace, the frame of the sofa and loveseat that were absent their cushions. All of which were covered in a half foot of fluffy undisturbed snow.

The scene before me was serine. My fingers reached out and touched the frosted glass. There was something in me that did not want to disturb the image before me. It seemed to be a world of cold isolation.

"Whatcha thinking, doll?" Hayden walked up behind me and wrapped his arms around my waist.

"It's beautiful." I whispered leaning back against him.

"Should I turn it on? There's the switch." He nodded to the switch plate beside the door. "We can heat it up. It only takes about ten minutes."

"No. It looks so peaceful out there. I don't want to disturb it." I nestled back into him.

"You're afraid of the cold." He teased.

"No, I don't like being cold." I turned my head to view his profile above me. "Most people don't." I smiled.

"I don't mind the cold as long as I have someone to snuggle with." Hayden leaned down and kissed me.

"You best behave yourself." I teased.

"No promises." He chuckled.

"You are such a tease." I turned around and kissed him.

The faint sound of piano bars — the ringtone I had set for my parents, drifted back to Hayden's room.

"That's my boys." I let go of Hayden and ran back into the family room where I had left my phone on the coffee table. "Hello."

"Hey momma," Max sounded bored.

"Hi, buddy. How are things going?" I tried to sound cheerful.

"When are you coming back?"

"Sunday most likely. We had the initial meeting with the attorney this afternoon," I hated leaving him there.

"Your mother is driving me crazy." He huffed. "She doesn't understand I am not a baby anymore."

"Sweetheart, she doesn't understand that I'm not." I informed him.

"I would rather have Brie chasing me around then deal with her." He admitted.

"I'm sure you don't mean that." I snorted.

"Oh, yes. I do." He scoffed. "She's driving me nuts."

"She has that effect on me too," I muttered.

"I'm serious, mom."

"I know. I understand. And I promise, I will be back as soon as I can. Just hang in there for a few more days, baby."

"Can I please stay with Aaron? I already asked him, and his mom said it's okay." He begged.

"Max. That is putting a lot on Aaron's mom. It's not just a sleepover for one night." I reminded him.

"She knows, mom and she's okay with it. Call her if you don't believe me." I could hear the irritation in his voice.

"It's after ten. I can't call her tonight."

"It's only a little after nine here. There's an hour difference, remember." He pushed.

"You are relentless." I sighed. "Fine. I'll call her and call you right back."

"Thanks, momma. I love you." Max's voice lightened instantly.

"How's Henry?" I asked before he could hang up.

"Tolerating her better than I am."

"That's good at least."

"Let's hope it lasts." Max snickered.

"Be nice," I reminded him.

"Call me back." His anxiety was obvious.

"I love you."

"Yeah, love you too, momma. Bye." The phone went silent.

I shook my head in dismay. I wasn't surprised by Max's eagerness to escape my parents' house. I felt the same way when I was growing up. I scrolled through my contacts and found Aaron's mom, Rhonda number.

"Hello, Alex. I was expecting your call." Rhonda's voice was light and cheery.

"Have they been cooking this up all evening?"

"I believe so. If not before," she laughed. "Aaron said you're up in Chicago for the week."

"Yes. A friend of mine needed some help. I will be home this weekend."

"Max is welcome to stay with us. I promise it won't be any bother."

"Are you sure? I know that puts a lot on you." I felt bad.

"Alex, really. It's fine." Rhonda assured me. "Max can just ride the bus home tomorrow and get off at our place."

"Thanks. I truly appreciate it. Max is bored out of his mind at my parents' house." I told her. "My mom is difficult to handle, and she and Max don't exactly see eye to eye."

"It's okay. I heard." She chuckled softly. "Aaron would be bored to tears stuck with my folks too."

"Please give me a call if Max gives you any grief."

"He'll be fine, Alex. Don't worry. We'll see you when you get home." Rhonda said sweetly.

"Thanks again, Rhonda." I sighed in relief. "Have a great evening."

"You too."

I disconnected the call and sat down on the edge of the couch. I looked around the penthouse and felt so out of place in this world. The room was immaculate. If I didn't know better, I wouldn't have even guessed someone lived here.

My home always looked lived in no matter how clean it was. Our jackets hung on the coatrack by the front door. There was a throw blanket tossed across the back of the couch in case we got cold. Countless photographs of us, our family, and friends adorned our walls. There was usually a pair of shoes lying out or a cereal bowl left in the sink. Our place was not simply a house, it was a home.

But this place, it was so perfect. Except for Mason's things that he had scattered about today, everything was in its proper place. There was no evidence of family on the walls, tables, nowhere. There weren't even the silly personalized magnets on the refrigerator.

I pressed the button to connect me to Max. He must have been holding his phone anxiously waiting for me to call him back because the phone didn't complete the first ring before he answered.

"Mom?"

"Hi Max." I smiled to myself.

"Did you talk to Aaron's mom?"

"Yes, I did. And yes, you can stay with them until I get home."

"Yes!" Max hollered a little louder than he should have.

"Put your grandpa on the phone," I failed to stifle a laugh.

"Okay. Hang on," I could hear Max shuffling about and could picture him going down the hallway from the guest bedroom to my dad's recliner in the front room. "Grandpa. Here. It's mom. She wants to talk to you."

"Alex? Is everything all right?" My dad sounded concerned.

"Yes, everything's fine. How are you doing?" I noticed Hayden coming down the hall.

"Who are you talking too?" He mouthed.

"My dad." I mouthed silently back and held up a finger.

"Good. The boys are good. Did you need to talk to your mom?" My dad asked.

"No. No. I wanted to talk to you about Max." I rolled my eyes playfully at Hayden and smiled as he tried not to giggle aloud. I felt like a teenager again sneaking around with my boyfriend.

"What about Max?" Dad asked.

"He's wants to stay with his friend, Aaron; his best friend that lives down the road. So, I told him he could. He'll ride his regular bus after school tomorrow and get off at Aaron's house." I explained.

"Why? Does he have a school project to work on?"

"No, nothing like that. He's just bored, and mom is well, being mom." I tried to explain.

"I see," he paused for a moment.

"I spoke with Aaron's mom and she's happy to keep Max." I told him.

"But you want me to keep Henry and Billy?" He sounded a bit annoyed.

"Yes, please." I pushed Hayden's hand away as he kept trying to tickle me.

"You know, I don't appreciate this, Alex." His tone turned rough.

"What?" I was dumbfounded.

"You ask us to help at the last minute without giving any thought to what your mother and I may have planned for the week. You just expect us to drop everything for you when you holler. And we do. Every time. And this is how you repay us."

"Daddy," I hated it when he got this way.

"Why don't you have Aaron's mom pick up Henry and Billy as well?" He huffed.

"Are you serious?" I couldn't believe my dad was being such an asshole.

"Yes. Tonight."

"Dad. It's nine thirty." I protested.

"I guess you should have thought about that before you were so ungrateful," he spat.

I would have expected this type of behavior out of my mom, but not my dad. He never acted like this unless he'd been drinking heavily and arguing with my mom. I wished I would have asked Max more about what was going on there when he called earlier.

"Fine. I will have Lisa pick up both boys and Billy tonight. She'll be there shortly. Please get their things ready." I said coldly.

"As you wish" and the line went dead.

"Asshole!" I scoffed and looked angerly at Hayden. "My dad is pissed because Max wants to stay at Aaron's instead of their place. So, he's kicked out both boys and Billy."

"What the hell?" He sat down on the arm of the couch. "I thought your mom was the pain in the ass, not your dad."

"He's usually not unless he's been spending time with Jimmy Beam or mom's cycling again." I shook my head in dismay. "She must have hit another manic phase." I exhaled loudly. "I love having a bipolar mother." I stated sarcastically.

"What do you want to do?" He took my hand in his.

"I've got to call Lisa. I'm sure she's going to be thrilled." I rolled my eyes and hit the button to connect me to her cell. I could only hope she was still awake.

"Hi," She sounded awake, thankfully.

"Hey, I'm sorry to bother you."

"Is everything all right?"

"No," I sighed audibly. "I hate to ask you this but my dad's being a first-class prick tonight. Can you possibly pick up my boys and Billy at my parent's house right now?"

"Um, sure." I could hear her shuffling around. "Erik's here. I can leave him with the kids."

"Thanks. I'm so sorry. Max had asked if he could stay with Aaron until I get back this weekend and I said yes. For whatever reason, it set my dad off."

"That's strange," she stated.

"Yeah. I'm not sure what it was all about. Max didn't say anything about my dad. It was my mom who was driving him nuts."

"Shocker," I heard her keys rumbling and then her car door slam. "I hate to think what she must have said to him."

"Who knows? She loves running her mouth making me out to be this horrible ungrateful child." I smirked.

"Is Max going to stay at Aaron's then?"

"Yes, after tonight. He'll ride the bus home tomorrow and get off at Aaron's."

"And you want me to keep Henry and Billy until this weekend?"

"Please," I held my breath for a second. "I know it's a lot to ask but Mason got himself into some trouble."

"What did the little Beanie Boy do now?" She giggled.

"He married Megan." I blurted out.

"What the fuck!" Her voice was so loud Hayden heard her and started laughing.

"I know," I chuckled.

"How could he be so stupid?"

"We're trying to get it annulled. That's why I'm up here." I explained.

"Is Hayden with you?"

"Yes. We're at his place."

"All of you?" She sounded skeptical.

"Yeppers."

"Wow. One big happy family." Her voice sounded leery.

"You know it." The sarcasm dripping from my voice.

"I can't imagine."

"I can't say I don't deserve it." The truth hurt.

"No one is perfect, Alex."

"I know, but still," Lisa broke my chain of thought.

"I'm here. Let me call you back."

"Tell my boys I love them."

"Will do."

My phone went dark in my hand. I looked up at Hayden and tried to smile.

"They will be fine. Lisa's got them." He took my hand and pulled me to my feet. "Give her a few minutes and call her back. I'm sure everything is fine." He wrapped his arms around me.

"I'm sure it is." I kept thinking of Henry and how confused he must be since it was past his bedtime.

Hayden and I retreated to his room. Our romantic evening had taken a sharp turn into reality where parenthood, disgruntled aging parents, and unexpected tantrums took precedence.

I sat down on the corner of his bed holding my cell phone and willing it to ring. I would have expected this type of behavior from my mother, but I was so disappointed in my dad.

"Perhaps I should take the train home." I said more to myself than Hayden.

"Why would you do that?" He sat down beside me. "The boys are going to be fine."

"But this mess," I shook my head slowly. "Leave it to my parents to pull a stunt like this."

"Let's just wait for Lisa to call back." Hayden placed his hand over mine.

"Okay," I stared down at the floor waiting anxiously.

We sat in silence for several minutes. He gently squeezed my hand, but words failed us both. My parents had a history of running their mouths and spewing half-truths and nonsensical nuances when they didn't get their way, especially my mother.

Ten minutes later, my phone finally rang.

"Hey Alex, it's me. I've got the boys and Billy and all their things." Lisa's voice was a breath of fresh air.

"How are they?"

"The boys? They're good." She assured me. "Your parents, not so much." She giggled. "They were pissed."

"I'm so sorry." I apologized again.

"No worries. You'd do the same for me."

"You know I would. But seriously, thank you for this." I sighed heavily. "I'm glad they are with you."

"Just don't forget to call the school tomorrow so Henry can ride home with Logan." She remined me.

"I promise."

"Oh, Max wants to talk to you. Hold on." I could hear the shuffling of the phone being passed around. "Hey momma, I'm sorry. I didn't mean to make grandpa so mad." My son sounded upset.

"Don't worry about it. I'm sure it had nothing to do with you. Were they arguing before you called?"

"His drinking and smoking. Grandpa snuck out to the garage, and she caught him smoking a cigar." Max chuckled a bit. "Grandma started screaming at him like he was a child."

"She's good at that," I sighed.

"I'm glad you don't do that. I was embarrassed for him."

"I'm sorry buddy."

"I just wanted to get outta there." He admitted.

"I understand. Please behave yourself and have fun. I love you."

"I love you too, momma." His voice dropped an octave. "Here's Lisa."

"Good night, baby boy."

"Night, momma."

"You okay?" Lisa asked.

"I miss my boys." I confessed.

"I'll take good care of them."

"I know you will." I reached out and took Hayden's hand staring into his eyes.

"I'll call you tomorrow."

"Okay. And thanks again."

"Always."

"Love you."

"Love you too."

I set the phone back on the coffee table. Hayden pulled me to my feet and wrapped his arms around my waist. He leaned down and kissed me gently on the forehead.

"Let's go to bed, my love." He whispered softly.

Hayden took my hand and led me down the hallway.

Chapter 7

THURSDAY EVENING, HAYDEN, HIS children, and I were lounging around the family room watching *The Other Woman*, when a knock on the front door surprised us all. Hayden rose to answer it while the rest of us exchanged curious glances at one another. I looked over towards the door when I heard the voice of a young girl.

"Mr. Brooks?"

"Yes," echoed from the foyer.

"Umm," The voice stammered with nervousness. "My name is Tatiana. I'm sorry to just show up here, but I felt I had to. I'm a friend of Megan."

"Okay. Please come in." I could hear the skepticism in Hayden's voice.

"Thank you." The front door shut a moment later. She followed Hayden into the living room and stopped when she saw the three of us. "Hi Mason. I was hoping you were here."

"Tatiana," Mason rose from the loveseat. "What are you doing here?"

Kennedy and I had moved to the edge of our seats piqued with interest.

"Megan told me she was served with the annulment papers yesterday. She was freaking out and screaming how you'd never get away with it." The young blond shifted her weight uncomfortably.

"Yeah, she's been blowing up my phone. I finally gave up and just blocked her, so she's been calling me from all sorts of numbers." Mason told her. "Have a seat." He motioned for her to join him.

Hayden sat back down on the sectional beside me. Kennedy carefully observed the girl with curiosity from the recliner.

"So, what's going on?" Mason asked Tatiana as she sat down looking comfortable.

"Well, this is difficult because Megan and I have been best friends since grade school. Just being here is a betrayal of her trust, but I couldn't let her do this to you." She turned towards Mason. "You seem like such a nice guy who wanted to do the right thing and I can't let her get away with this." Tatiana looked upset.

"With what?" Hayden asked before Mason could.

"Megan found out she was pregnant the week after Halloween. When it was confirmed by the doctor, she was already a month along." Tatiana confessed.

"It's not mine." Mason let out an audible sigh of relief. "It can't be. I was in Indy since August. But then why …?"

"Because she knew you were the type that would do the right thing. She invited you for Thanksgiving with the intention of sleeping with you." Tatiana told him.

"I knew it," Hayden growled.

"Dad, please." Mason looked upset.

"Megan lied about the dates, so you would believe the baby was yours." Tatiana continued. "I told her it was wrong, and I truly didn't think she'd actually do it, but …" Her voice trailed off.

"Do you have any proof of this?" I couldn't help but ask.

"Yes. I kept all her text messages since she first told me she'd missed her period. I'm not sure why I did, but something in the back of my mind kept whispering to me not to delete them." The young girl fidgeted bringing her phone out of her coat pocket.

"May I read them?" Hayden inquired.

"Of course," she handed him her phone after she pulled up the messages.

Hayden sat back and held the phone where I could read along beside him. The texts were damning evidence of her deception. Megan had begun with frantic messages of a pregnancy conceived out of a drunken one-night stand with a nameless frat boy. Then the confirmed pregnancy and finally the plot to entrap Mason because he was the type that would never abandon his child. And she even included that his dad should pay for what he'd done to her career and that she was going to take him to the bank for it.

I watched as Hayden's face got redder. I couldn't recall ever seeing him so upset.

"What a manipulative bitch," I hadn't realized Kennedy was standing behind us reading over our shoulders.

"I'll need a printout of these." Hayden took a deep breath trying to keep his composure. He reached into his pocket and pulled out his phone. "Tim? Hey, sorry for bothering you so late, but can you possibly swing by?" He paused. "Great. See you soon." He put his phone on the coffee table and sat back clearly still agitated.

"This should take care of any legal issues regarding the annulment." I muttered aloud.

"Definitely," Hayden snorted in disgust. "I know this wasn't easy for you but I do thank you for your honesty."

Tatiana smiled a little and nodded. Her doing the right thing would certainly cost her her best friend and she knew it. I was proud of and impressed by her strength of character.

Twenty minutes later Tim arrived and was just as stunned as the rest of us when he read the text messages. Afterwards, he and Hayden disappeared with Tatiana into Hayden's study to print out the texts and get her signature on a statement.

"I can't believe I was so stupid." Mason grumbled.

"You're not stupid, Mason. You believed her and tried to do the right thing. That's admirable." I told him.

"You should have waited until the child was born and had a paternity test." Kennedy shook her head. She was a no nonsense, Type A personality, and a force in her own right.

"I believed her," Mason narrowed his eyes at this sister.

"Well, at least it's almost over." I tried to shift the air in the room before the two of them took it any further.

"Thankfully," Kennedy took one last shot.

Mason, in turn, got up and went into the kitchen. He returned a moment later with a beer and sat down without saying another word on the subject.

"Do you believe everything is going to be all right now?" I asked Hayden snuggling up to him with my head on his chest.

"Tim assures me the texts will have it resolved quickly." He ran his fingers through my hair absent-mindedly.

"That's a relief."

"Yes," he shifted a bit and looked down at me. "So, what do you think of Chicago?"

"It's big and hectic. But I love your home and office. It's exactly how I imagined it would be."

"You know there's plenty of room here for you and the boys and Northwestern is an amazing school." He added.

"Hayden, we've discussed this." I whispered.

"I'm saying maybe over the summer. Not immediately." He explained.

"But my boys and Billy would hate living in a high-rise. They need room to run and play. They spend all their time outside practicing and playing sports. I can't imagine them not being able to do that. And Billy has never even been on a leash. She's never needed one, even when we go on walks" I tried to reason.

"Then I'll sell the penthouse and we'll find us a house in the suburbs." He grinned.

"It's not that simple and you know it." I playfully smacked his chest. "What about their schools, their sports, their friends?"

"I know it will be an adjustment, but I'm fairly certain they do have schools up here too." Hayden teased back.

"You know what I mean."

"I know I want to spend the rest of my life with you." He leaned down and kissed my forehead. "I love you more than I ever thought possible. I want to take care of you and your boys; make you all happy and for us to build a life together."

I looked up into his sparkling emerald eyes, barely visible in the soft glow from the city outside of his darkened bedroom and knew he meant everything he said.

"Hayden, you are the love of my life. And I am going to spend the rest of my life with you, but you must give me some time to break this to my boys. Plus, to be selfish, I want to graduate from my university. We don't know how my credits will transfer between the schools and that could easily delay my graduation." I tried to reason. "It's only another year."

"You graduate in May of next year, right?"

"Yes."

"That's almost sixteen months from now." He pouted.

"I know, but it will give us time to find the house we want in an area we like. I don't know anything about the suburbs around Chicago and," I smiled up at him, "most importantly, it will give you and the boys a chance to get to know each other."

"And if we find an area we like, but not a house, we'll have time to build one." He smiled down at me coyly. "And plan a wedding." Hayden surprised me.

"Wedding?"

"Well, don't you believe it's appropriate?" He asked, but then sat up abruptly, hastily moving me out of the nook under his arm. "You know what …" He tossed the covers back and climbed out of bed. "Fuck that appropriate shit. The last thing I want to do is get married because it's appropriate." Hayden stood beside the bed, naked with his hands on his hips. He looked so edible it was difficult to pay attention to his words.

"Then what do you want to do?" I traced my finger down the center of his chest.

"I want to marry you because you are the most amazing woman I have ever met." A devilish grin slid across his shapely lips. "And your sexy as hell." He pulled me over to the edge of the bed.

Hayden ran his fingertips lightly down the inside of my thighs. I closed my eyes and purred under his touch. He lifted my hips effortlessly and slipped his fingers into my panties gripping my buttocks before sliding them over my legs tossing them onto the floor.

His lips brushed against each of my ankles then gently pushed them apart. His hands glided to the outside of my legs and moved slowly down following the pace set by his lips and tongue glistening warmly down my skin.

Kneeling beside the bed, Hayden used his tongue to part my lips between my legs. His tongue lapped hungerly at my clit. I moaned and nudged my hips closer to him.

Hayden teased me with his fingers before he pushed them deeply into me. He added gentle pressure against my G-spot causing me to squirm and twist in pure euphoric delight.

"I want you." I said breathlessly.

"I know," he smiled up at me for a moment then continued tormenting me.

"Please," I reached up and pulled on his shoulders, but he nudged away from me. "You're so mean." I complained.

"You love it." Hayden raised his eyebrows briefly at me with a cocky grin.

"Don't you mean, you do?" I managed to say through my labored breathing.

"Always," his rough voice responded.

Hayden's fingers probed in and out of me, teasing my G-spot gloriously while his tongue worked it magic tormenting my clitoris. I closed my eyes and let the euphoria engulf me. It spread across my body in rhythmic waves that sent my body into jetted spasms. I groaned loudly and grasped at Hayden, pulling him up to me.

Reluctantly, he climbed up on the bed and skillfully placed my feet upon his shoulders in one smooth motion. He thrust his thick hard cock deep into me sending ripples through my body. I buried my face into his shoulder so as not to scream aloud. My nails dug into his back unintentionally causing Hayden to scream out.

Chapter 8

WE HEADED BACK TO INDIANAPOLIS Saturday afternoon. So much had occurred in such a short time I felt like I'd lived a month in a few short days. I was anxious to see my boys. I missed them dearly and could not wait to wrap my arms around them.

My mind was spinning with all we had discussed. Despite the turn of events with Mason, I still wasn't ready to introduce Hayden to my boys. I wasn't ready for these two worlds to collide despite Max being amendable to it.

Max had been through enough with the emotional turmoil from Danny. He loved Mason although he knew things were over between us. How could I expect my boys to understand something that I was not yet able to?

I leaned against the frosted window and watched the corn and soybean fields covered in their winter blanket, drift by the roadside. The cloud covered sky was a pale grey. The naked trees looked lonely and abandoned in the winter winds.

My head began to ache. My heart wanted nothing more than to spend the rest of my life as Hayden's wife. I loved him dearly. He was everything I had ever dreamt of and more. But the circumstances behind our relationship haunted me and I knew my family would never accept him because of my history with Mason.

~

Classes resumed and life fell back into an uneventful routine. The only noticeable difference was Mason. Although he was no longer living in our home, he continued coming by on Saturday mornings to spend the day with the boys and attend their basketball games.

Our relationship had shifted dramatically. Mason's view of me had shifted as well. I suppose it was fitting since I could no longer look at him as the sweet innocent young man he once was. We still laughed, joked, and teased and tormented each other sarcastically, but it had changed. We rarely touched and when we did it was very platonic. There were no secret looks or stolen kisses, knowing glances, or shy smiles.

I believe in his eyes I had fully transitioned from someone he desired to someone who he had once cared for but was now simply a good friend.

Thankfully, Max and Henry didn't seem to be bothered by the shift and never mentioned Mason's marriage or inquired about his wife. Mason told them things didn't work out with his wife, but never elaborated further than that, at least to my knowledge.

February blew in with harsh winter storms dropping snow and

ice in abnormal amounts. The state declared an emergency and we were banned from leaving our homes for three days due to four inches of ice that coated about six inches of snow. Travel was restricted to emergency vehicles only. Employers and schools across the state had shut down. Even a trip to the mailbox had proven hazardous as evidenced by the bruises on my legs and ego.

Mason was stranded at our home due to a late Saturday Halo battle with Max and Aaron. I was thankful for his presence simply because stir crazy boys had the tendency to bounce off the walls after a couple days.

Wednesday morning, I put the kids on the bus and headed to campus. Mason left an hour before to make his eight o'clock class. The roads were still slush with scattered spots of black ice. I turned up the radio trying to calm my nervous hyperawareness of everyone around me. I hated driving in these conditions.

I had almost made it to campus when my phone rang through my stereo. It was my mother. I took a deep breath knowing if anything was going to ruin my day right at the start it was a conversation with my mother. I hadn't spoken to them since my dad had abruptly kicked my sons out of his house and Lisa had picked them up. By the fourth ring I accepted the call.

"Hello?" I pushed the connect button with irritation.

"Alex? Where are you?" She sounded more annoyed than upset.

"In my car heading to campus," I bit my lower lip trying to focus on the road.

"Where are the boys?" she asked.

"At school. Why?"

"Your dad had a heart attack last night." My mom said bluntly.

"Is he okay?"

"We're at the St. Vincent Cardiac Center in Carmel. He's in surgery." I kept waiting for her to sound concerned.

"What did the doctor say?" I pulled into the campus parking lot.

"There was blockage in the aorta and some value wasn't working properly." My mother exhaled loudly. "You know I don't understand their jargon the way you do. Can you come up here and talk to them?"

"I am teaching a class at 9:30 and I have two classes of my own after that, but I can skip those. I'll email my professors." I parked as close to the building as I could and shut the car off. "I'll be there by lunch. Did they say when his surgery would be done?"

"I don't know. A couple hours or so, I think." She mumbled.

"Did you talk to the surgeon this morning, mom?" I was quickly getting irritated with her lack of concern and information.

"I told you. I don't understand all that medical jargon." She snapped back.

"Did you call Colin and Samantha?" I tapped my fingers on the steering wheel with impatience.

"Colin has been here since last night and Samantha is on her way here."

"Why didn't you call me last night?" I shut the car off and tried to keep my temper under control.

"After the way you treated your father the last time we talked to you, you're lucky I called you now. I wasn't going to, but Colin thought I should since you're the one who has medical training." She scoffed back.

"Thanks, mom. I'll see you in a bit." I hung up the phone before either of us could say anything else.

The car was already getting cold with the heat off, but I wasn't in the mood now to deal with a classroom full of freshman, most of whom were struggling with the course material. I glanced at my watch and decided to call my sister quickly to see if she knew more than what mom had told me.

"Hey Alex," Samantha picked up on the second ring.

"Morning," I immediately felt better just hearing her voice.

"Please tell me you're on your way to the hospital. I don't think I can handle mom alone." She laughed uneasily.

"I have to teach a class first, but I'll be there before lunch. Is Oliver with you?"

"Yeah, I made him." She stated.

"Hello, Alex." Oliver chimed in and I realized her phone was on speaker in her car too.

"Hey Oliver, good luck." I chuckled. "Colin is already there."

"Oh goody," I imagined my sister rolling her eyes. "Is Charlotte there too?"

"Mom didn't say. She was her usual pleasant self." I grabbed by backpack and climbed out of the car. The bitter wind bit sharply at me and I shuttered. "I'll be there as soon as I can."

"Bring a flask," Samantha retorted. "And be careful."

"You too," I said before I disconnected the call.

I stuffed my phone into my coat pocket and as gracefully as I could, navigated my way across the slushy ice-covered sidewalk. The wind whipped around me tearing straight through my clothes. I knew the temperature was already a balmy sixteen degrees with the windchill still in the negative digits.

"Spring can't get here soon enough," I muttered to myself trying to keep my balance as I opened the doors to the science building.

I arrived at the hospital shortly before 11:30. I stopped at the nurses' station on the way to my dad's room to see if I could get an update. My dad's surgery had gone smoothly, and he had been moved back into his room about an hour ago. He was asleep and my mother and siblings had stepped out to grab some lunch.

"Wonderful," I muttered before thanking the nurse and making my way over to my father's room.

My dad was sleeping soundly when I stepped in. He was unshaven and looked old and frail. He had oxygen tubes up his nose and a bundle of wires connected to him monitoring all his vitals. It seemed there were plugs and tubes sticking out of every orifice they could find.

I stood beside the bed and took ahold of his hand. I brushed his hair over his brow and realized how much gray had replaced his sandy blond hair. The tower of strength I had always viewed as my father, now looked so fragile and sickly.

"Hi, Daddy," my voice sounded hollow in the empty room with the echo of machines all around us.

I set my purse on the back of the chair and sat down on the edge of the seat. I stroked the back of his hand with my finger being careful to avoid touching the IV taped in place on top his hand. I had never realized before now how those hands I had always considered so powerful, were now covered with wrinkles from years of hard work — the skin appearing almost transparent and paper thin.

"I'm sorry about our argument, Daddy." I whispered. "The nurse said your surgery was a success and you're going to be fine."

I felt uncomfortable in the cold room with the only sounds coming from the wind howling at the window and the annoying beeping of the machines. I wished my sister was there, but I wasn't overly keen about seeing my mother or my brother.

"Hum," I stood up and walked over to the foot of his bed. "Let's see what the doctors have to say about your heart." I said to my unconscious father.

I flipped open the blue hard plastic cover and glanced over my father's medical history likely dictated by my mother. There was nothing surprising — previous knee surgery from motor cross racing, high blood pressure, borderline diabetic. Information I was well aware of.

My eyes skimmed down the page looking at his blood work that was done upon his arrival. Nothing stood out as exceptional or worrisome until I noticed something strange. My father's blood type was listed as B-. I wracked my brain repeatedly with flashes of my microbiology, physiology, and anatomy classes pounding on the outer recesses of my mind.

"That can't be right," I muttered staring at the chart.

"Excuse me," the petite brunette nurse I had spoken with at the desk was leaning over my dad checking his vitals and monitors. I was so engrossed in his chart I hadn't realized she had entered the room. "Is something wrong?"

"I'm sorry," I mumbled feeling like I had been punched in the gut. "My dad's blood type," I looked up at her. "It's listed as B-."

"Yes," she adjusted his IV bag. "He was typed upon arrival. They do it with every patient. It's standard."

There was no way for her to know the impact of those simple words she said so lightly, had on my life. My head began to spin, and I felt like I was going to vomit. My legs went out from under me, and the world went dark.

"Ma'm, ma'm," I felt eyes boring into me. My head was throbbing.

"I'm fine," I moaned opening my eyes.

"You fainted," the nurse was hovering over me looking concerned.

"Sorry," I pushed myself into a seated position and rubbed the back of my head. "I'm just tired." I lied.

"Can I get you some juice or Sprite?" Her eyes were kind and soft.

"I would appreciate that," I gave her a weak smile.

"I'll be right back," she scurried out of the room as I got to my feet and sat down in the chair beside my father's bed.

I took a deep breath and rubbed my temples roughly. My head felt like it was going to split in two. Surely, I must be misremembering. I was missing something. I wasn't sure what, but something.

"Here," the kind brunette handed me a cold can of Sprite. "Slip it slowly."

"Thank you," I took a refreshing sip and instantly felt my stomach tightened. "I appreciate it."

"Your family should be back shortly. Is there anything else I can get you?" I shook my head. "Some crackers, maybe?"

"No but thank you."

"Your father will be asleep for a while longer. You have plenty of time to get something to eat. The cafeteria is on the bottom floor and there's plenty of restaurants nearby." She smiled kindly.

"I believe I'll do that. Thank you."

I waited for her to leave before I fled the room. I was on the verge of hysterical tears and hyperventilating. My mind was screaming for me to move faster, but my legs felt like lead and couldn't move fast enough. All I knew for certain was I had to get the hell out of there before my family returned.

I reached my car and started up the engine as the world I felt so secure and confident in, crashed in around me. I covered my face with my hands and tried to control my breathing.

"Double check your facts before you have a meltdown." I said to the empty car. "Hysterics are not going to get you anywhere. Think." I pondered over various options and people I knew still working in the medical field.

"Laura," I hit the phone button on my steering wheel. "Call Dr. Johnston's office," and tapped my fingers impatiently as the ringing tone blasted through my speakers.

"Good afternoon, Dr. Johnston's office." A cheery voice answered on the fifth ring.

"Hello, this is Alexandra Rose. Is Laura available?" I closed my eyes mentally crossing my fingers.

"I'm sorry, Ms. Rose. The office is closed until one o'clock for lunch. I can leave her a message and have her call you back." I gritted my teeth and swallowed hard trying not to snap at the sweet receptionist.

"I understand," I managed to squeak through my dry throat.

"Um, hold on." She mumbled sounding like she had dropped the receiver.

"Hi, Alex. This is Laura. How are you?" The familiar voice sounded heavenly in my ears.

"I'm sorry for interrupting your lunch."

"No worries. I was finished eating and you saved me from devouring a bag of Oreo's." I could hear the chuckle in her voice. "I heard Tracy say your name so," her voice trailed off.

"I hate to ask you this, but I need a huge favor and I'm praying you can help me." I tried to wrack my brain on how to get around the damn HIPAA law, but I couldn't think of any.

"Of course. I'll do what I can." Her warm voice filled my car.

"Can you please check my chart. I believe my blood type is O+, but I need to be sure. My father is in the hospital for heart surgery." I added.

"Oh, were you thinking of donating blood to him?" I could hear her fingers typing in the background. "Let me see," she mumbled. "Yep, it says here you are O+."

"That's what I thought. Thank you for checking for me."

"I hope everything goes well for your father. I will keep him in my prayers." Laura responded kindly.

"Thank you. I appreciate that." I sighed heavily.

"Take care, Alex."

"I will. You too, Laura. And thanks again."

"Bye," I heard her say before she disconnected the call.

I sat there a moment longer before putting my car in gear. I knew Samantha was going to be upset that I was not there when she returned, but I knew I couldn't stay. I pulled out onto Meridian Street and navigated my way through the heavy traffic. All I wanted to do was get home safely before I completely came unglued.

Samantha called as I exited the interstate and headed towards town. I was hoping I would make it home before this call came, but no such luck.

"Where are you?" she demanded before I could even say hello. "You better be pulling into the parking lot." She sounded agitated. "Mom is driving me nuts."

"I was there, but you guys were out to lunch. I waited with dad for a half hour, but you guys didn't show." I explained.

"We went to Cheddar's for lunch. It was hell. Are you coming back?" Her voice turned whimsical.

"Hey, you donated blood when Mom had her back surgery, right?" I switched the subject.

"Yeah, why?"

"Do you remember her blood type?"

"A-. Same as mine. Why?" Samantha sounded curious.

"I need you to come over."

"What's going on, Alex?"

"Just please," I struggled to keep my breathing even and my eyes on the road while fighting back tears. "I need to you come over right now."

"Okay," I could hear the anxiety in her voice. "We're on our way. Let me tell mom."

"Text me when you're on the road."

"All right," I disconnected the call on my steering wheel noticing my hands were shaking uncontrollably.

I felt the tears splash down on my neck. I hadn't realized I was already crying. I hastily brushed them off my cheek with my gloved hand trying to get myself in control.

"You're almost home," I said aloud. "You're almost home. Only two more miles, Alex. You got this."

But I didn't. The tears wouldn't stop. I strained my eyes to see the icy roads. Everything I had ever known, believed, lived had all been a lie.

I pulled my car into the garage and shut the engine off. I left my backpack in the car and the garage door ajar. Billy jumped on me when I opened the door.

"Down, Billy," I chastised her and went straight for the back door. I opened it and let Billy out. I knew she wouldn't wander beyond our yard.

I put my phone on the island before removing my gloves and coat. I draped them over the top of the bar stool instead of hanging them up. I paced the kitchen anxiously. It felt like forever instead of five minutes for Samantha's text to come through. She was on her way.

I stared at her words knowing what I needed to do. I was so angry, confused, and hurt I wanted to reach out and punch someone — namely my mother.

I poured myself a glass of wine and drank it quickly. I scrolled to my list of favorites in my contact list and pressed the icon for my mother.

"Alex? Where are you? The nurse said you were here but weren't feeling well." My mother's voice lacked any trace of genuine concern.

"I'm fine," I said nonchalantly.

"She said you fainted. Are you pregnant? Did that boy you're sleeping with get you pregnant?" Irritation mixed with condemnation rang clearly over the phone.

"No, mom. I am not pregnant." I said hotly. "But I have a question for you."

"What?" she asked impatiently.

"I was looking through Dad's chart when I was up there," I began, but was quickly interrupted.

"And?"

"And I noticed dad's blood type is B-."

"So," I heard her huff.

"Yours is A-."

"I know," she scoffed back at me.

"Well, I'm O+." I stated through my teeth.

"Okay. And your point?" I could envision her standing there with her hand on her hip rolling her eyes impatiently.

"My point is an A- and B- couple cannot produce an O+ child. Dad is not my biological father." I seethed.

"Good Lord, Alex." She spat back. "Like it really matters."

"It matters to me," I screamed into the phone. "Who is my biological dad?"

"I am not having this conversation with you here." She said abruptly.

"I want to know!" My jaw felt locked in fuming anger.

"It is none of your damn business, Alex."

"What?" I gasped. "Are you kidding me?"

"We are not going to discuss this." My mother stated pointedly.

"I have a right to know!" I demanded.

"It is none of your damn business. The past is in the past," she stated hotly.

"But," I barely got out before she cut me off.

"I am never going to tell you and I do not want to discuss it again." She shouted before disconnecting the call.

I tossed my phone onto the island sending it sliding across to the other side and crashing onto the floor. I stormed over and picked it up only to find a horizonal crack across the screen.

"Damn it," so much for the fifty-dollar guaranteed to protect my freaking phone cover. "Perfect," I walked into the living room and threw myself down on the couch.

Chapter 9

MY BODY FELT DRAINED, NUMB, and livid. My mind raced over numerous recollections from my childhood of my cousins teasing me, calling me the mailman's kid because they all shared similar traits — none of which I obtained. They were all various shades of blond, tall, with blue eyes. My female cousins were small chested with bigger bones. Whereas I was the shortest of the group with long dark hair and eyes such a dark brown that appeared almost black.

When I had cried about it to my mother after being teased, she would dismiss it and say I looked like one of her aunts or some other distant relative.

I looked up when I heard a car door slam shut. Through the front window I saw Oliver and Samantha making their way up my front walkway. She was holding onto his arm for support. I opened the door before they reached the porch and held the screen door open for them.

"What in the world is going on?" Samantha removed her gloves and stuffed them into her pockets before taking off her coat and hanging it on my coat tree in the foyer. "You sounded like you were hysterical." She took Oliver's coat from him and hung it beside her own.

"Just about," I shut the door behind them. "Wine?"

"Sure," Samantha glanced over at Oliver who shook his head.

"Do you have any coffee?" He asked stomping the snow and slush off his shoes on the matt.

"I'll brew some," I turned to my sister giving her a look to follow me to the kitchen.

"So, what's going on?" She leaned against the counter as I started a pot a coffee for Oliver.

"You're never going to believe this," I hit the start button and then got her a wine glass out of the cupboard. I was struggling with keeping my voice steady and not slam everything I touched. "I should have freaking known!" I seethed. "That fucking whore!" I grabbed the wine from the refrigerator and filled both our glasses.

"What are you talking about? Who's the whore?" My sister's eyes widened with curiosity as Oliver joined us in the kitchen taking up residency on one of the barstools.

"Our mother!" I nearly shouted thrusting her glass at her.

"Shocker," much to my astonishment, my sister was laughing. "I could have told you that."

"Why didn't you tell me?" I stared at her with disbelief.

"I thought you knew," she declared taking a sip of her wine.

"Explain," I demanded.

"Sonny Robertson," she rolled her eyes. "Do you remember him?"

"Who's Sonny Robertson?" Oliver asked helping himself to a cup of coffee.

"A guy who used to work with our dad. I vaguely remember him," the imagine of a balding narcissistic man with enough hair on his chest and back that he could have been a gorilla. "What about him?"

"The Holiday Inn in Lebanon?" Samantha raised her eyebrows pointedly.

"Oh my God," I slumped back against the counter. "I had completely forgotten about that."

Sonny Robertson was a friend or coworker of my dad's. Our families used to hang out together when we were young, but then they sort of disappeared out of our life when I was around seven. I never knew what had transpired between them to end their friendship, but it all suddenly made sense.

Sonny was married to a prudish homely woman named Nadine and had two children. His eldest was a creepy brutish boy named James that was Colin's age and a daughter, Maureen that was a year older than Samantha. I remembered them living in an older home in the historic district that looked like it hadn't been updated since the 1920s.

Our families used to get together on the weekends for cookouts and such. I remembered watching scary movies in the family room while our parents played Euchre at the kitchen table. We also took several trips with them to Kings Island and camping by the lake.

"I remember catching mom and Sonny kissing in the hallway at the Holiday Inn," I could still see the image burned in my memory. "I remember mom yelling at me and making me promise never to tell dad," I locked eyes with my sister. "I never did." I confessed.

"He found out anyway," she shrugged. "Don't you remember mom taking you and me with her up to the Holiday Inn on Saturday afternoons." She jogged my memory. "She would tell Dad she was taking us shopping. Colin never came with us because he would talk. She would leave us in the pool with Maureen and James and the two of them would sneak off for several hours."

"Oh, my God!" It all came rushing back. "I can't believe her." I stood there numb shaking my head.

"I can't believe you didn't know," she took a long sip of her wine. "That's why they split when we were little." She looked at me like I was stupid. "Mom told us Dad's work was on strike and he had to live there."

Horrible memories of the time of living with our mother without our dad as a buffer flooded my mind.

"Where did dad go?" I felt like a small child learning that Santa Claus wasn't real.

"His parents," my sister looked almost sad. "I can't believe you didn't realize it."

"I was five, Sam. I didn't know." I was dismayed by the level of betrayal my entire childhood had been.

"It wasn't like it was the first time she cheated on him," I waited for her to confess knowledge of my recent discovery. "The blood tests when they got married."

"What do you mean?" I finished off my glass of wine not sure if I was mentally prepared to hear this one and refilled my glass.

"Back when you had to get blood tests before you got married," Samantha climbed up on the barstool beside Oliver and refilled her glass. "Do you remember mom ever saying anything about her parents boycotting her wedding?"

"I remember grandma mentioning it, but she never clarified why. I figured they didn't approve of her marrying Dad although they always seemed to like him."

"No. It had nothing to do with dad," my sister smirked knowingly. "When mom and dad had their blood tests done at the Health Department, they contacted you only if there was something umm, shall we say, amiss," she giggled. "Dad's mom was standing there when they called the house and told Dad that his texts were fine, but mom's bloodwork revealed she had syphilis."

"What! You're kidding," I busted out laughing. "Miss Holier Than Thou, I was a Virgin when I got married, had syphilis!"

"Yep," she and Oliver were laughing so hard they had tears glistening in their eyes. "Oh, you can imagine how pissed Dad was and how long it took grandma, Mary to call grandma, Peg."

"That explains why grandma, Mary hated mom all these years. I wouldn't want my son to marry some whore either." I sympathized with the woman who had treated me like the red-headed stepchild all my life and never like her grandchild. She must have known about me all along. "How did mom get her parents to attend the wedding?" I had seen pictures of my grandfather walking her down the aisle, so I knew they had attended.

"Oh, you'll love this," Samantha took another sip of her wine before she continued. "Mom claims she has this rare blood type and that's why it showed up positive for syphilis."

"There's no such thing," I looked at her dumbfounded.

"I know," she couldn't stop laughing. "She still claims that — like we're honestly that stupid."

"Our mom's a whore," I pulled myself up on the counter to sit. "A nice little side effect of her Bipolar and Borderline Personality Disorder." My sister nodded in agreement.

"So, what got your panties in such a bunch today?" Samantha wiped the tears of laughter off her cheeks and attempted to recompose herself.

"I saw Dad's chart," I took another long drink for courage before I continued. "Or rather I saw Dad's blood type."

"So," she raised her eyebrows waiting for me to continue.

"Dad's B-, Mom's A-, I'm O+," I waited for the significance to register, but the look on Oliver's face immediately told me he got it when my sister didn't.

"And?" she looked irritated when she realized Oliver got it and she didn't. "Explain."

"It's genetically impossible for an A- and B- couple to produce an O+ child. Your father is not her biological Dad." Oliver and I watched the words sink in and the expression on my sister's face chance to complete shock.

"What a whore!" Samantha declared.

"Pretty much," I agreed.

"Are you going to confront her?" My sister drained her glass and refilled it.

"I already did, while you were driving over here." I tilted my head with a smirk.

"I bet she denied it emphatically," Samantha shook her head.

"You know, I truly expected her too, but she didn't. She said, like it matters."

"What?" she looked as stunned as I felt.

"Who is your biological father?" Oliver pipped in.

"She told me it was none of my damn business," I said hotly. "She said it was in the past and she is never going to tell me." I felt the anger boiling back up inside me.

"But you have a right to know," Samantha looked bewildered. "What a bitch."

"Precisely." I pinched my lips together in anger. "I will never forgive her for this. My entire life has been a lie."

"Grandma Mary knew," Samantha slowly shook her head. "Remember how mom always claimed that Grandma didn't like you because you looked like her side of the family and had said that when she came to the hospital when you born that she took one look at you and said, 'this is not my grandchild', and left. Now it makes sense. Grandma Mary knew you weren't dad's child."

"That explains why she treated me like shit my whole life," I rolled my eyes.

"Your grandmother treated you like shit? It wasn't your fault," Oliver looked at me sympathetically.

"The woman gave me clothes pins for Christmas one year." I laughed at the painful memory from my ninth Christmas.

"That's horrible," he declared. "I can't imagine doing that to a child."

"Oh, but she loved Samantha."

"Yeah, she spoiled me," she looked over at Oliver. "I look a lot like my dad."

"So, what are you going to do?" Oliver turned his attention back to me as he got up to get another cup.

"Nothing," I shrugged. "Get drunk." I laughed humorlessly.

"Are you going to ask dad? I'm sure he knows who your father is." My sister finished off her wine. "I wonder who it is?"

"I can't ask dad," I traced the rim of my glass picturing the unconscious man I had just seen lying in the hospital. "Can you imagine how much that would hurt him? For all intents and purposes, he's been my dad — genetically or not. He is my dad. He raised me even though he must have known I wasn't his." I suddenly felt sorry for him.

"I wonder if that's why he stayed with her all those years?" my sister speculated. "You remember when mom would go off on her little tantrums and she'd pack up her stuff and yours, but she would always leave me and Colin with Dad?" I nodded. "When I asked her why one time, she told me that you were her kid, and Colin and I were Dad's." my sister's expression looked far away as if she was lost in some distant memory. "I always thought it was because Colin and I *looked* more like dad than you, but I supposed she was actually telling me the truth for once."

"I remember several times walking into the room when they were fighting and her screaming at me that I'd ruined her life and it was all my fault. I never understood how, as a little kid, I could have ruined her life, but it makes sense now." I felt a terrible ache in my heart. "I guess that was her way of telling me I wasn't his."

"Your mother is an evil woman," Oliver rubbed his temple in disbelief of all that he was hearing. "Your family makes mine look like *Ozzie and Harriet*." He offered us a weak smile.

"Are you sure you want to marry into this craziness?" my sister bumped him playfully.

"Yes, but your mother is never going to be alone with our children." He stated seriously. "I don't trust her."

"Agreed," my sister put her arm around him and kissed him on the cheek.

"Does that mean you two have set a date?" I said hopefully.

"Not yet," Samantha smiled. "But soon."

Knowing how scared my sister was of taking the plunge, as she put it, soon could mean anytime within the next three to five years. I decided not to push her on it and let the subject drop.

"Are you going to tell the boys?" she asked.

"I believe I have to at some point," I hated the thought.

"I still think you should talk to dad," Samantha poured the remainder of the wine into her glass.

"I don't know what to do," I confessed noticing the time. "The boys will be here soon." My head was spinning from both the wine and the reality I found myself in.

Oliver and Samantha stayed until after the boys were in bed. Our mother had called Samantha twice, both calls she let go to voicemail, but mom never left a message. We agreed that if it had something to do with dad she would have. She was trying to confirm Samantha's whereabouts and checking to see if I had shared my little discovery with her.

Oliver had been kind enough to pick up a pizza for us for dinner since Samantha and I were in no condition to drive or cook. We explained to the boys that grandpa had heart surgery and was in the hospital but assured them he was going to be fine. They didn't seem to be bothered by it after they way he had treated them the last time they had seen them.

I crawled into bed with Billy, once again clear headed and heartbroken. The house was quiet and lonely, and I wished Hayden was lying beside me. I wanted to feel the strength of his arms around me and know that he loved me regardless of my family drama.

I picked up cell and called him needing desperately to hear his voice.

"I was just thinking about you," Hayden answered on the second ring sounding warm and cheerful.

"Hi sweetie," my voice cracked at the sound of his voice and the flood gates reopened.

"What's wrong," I could hear the concern echoing across the miles.

"My mother's a whore," I sobbed.

"What?" he quipped.

I spent the next hour detailing him all that had transpired from the moment I arrived at the hospital until Oliver and Samantha pulled out of the driveway. I was emotionally spent, my pillow soaked with tears, and the anger from years of betrayal seethed on the outer recesses of my brain.

"I agree with your sister. You should talk to your dad."

"I wish you were here," I ignored his comment.

"I wish I was too."

"I'm so mad," I sniffled. "I hate her."

"Rightfully so, but you have to admit, your dad must have loved you a great deal. If he has always known you were not his biological child, but he raised you like his own. He loves you." Hayden reiterated.

"Which is precisely why I cannot talk to him. As mad as I am for what he did, he's still my dad and I love him. I don't blame him." I explained.

"Do you think that's why he never divorced your mom? You've said numerous times how miserably married they are, but your dad always came back. Do you think she used his love for you as a way to keep him?" I heard him exhale loudly. "I mean, she could have proven you weren't his and kept him from being a part of your life."

"Perhaps," I considered it for a moment. "It sounds like something she would do, but that doesn't explain why they're still married. It's been quite a while since I turned 18 and he's still with her."

"Maybe he's a glutton for punishment," Hayden chuckled. "Afterall, it's cheaper to keep her."

"Oh, and she would take him for every penny she could. I have no doubt about that." I added. "She is a money-grubbing heartless bitch."

"Gee, I can't wait to meet this woman." Hayden said sarcastically.

"I don't believe you'll ever have to worry about that one. I never want to see or speak to her again." I declared.

"And your dad?"

"I just don't know."

"Get some sleep, darling. It's getting late." I glanced at the clock and saw it was after one in the morning.

"Sorry for dumping all this on you." I felt bad for keeping him up so late.

"We're in this together. I love you."

"I love you too."

I kept my cell next to me after I disconnected the call. In some small silly way, it kept Hayden closer to me. I closed my eyes and thought about lying in his arms with my head on his chest listening to his heartbeat as I drifted off to sleep.

Chapter 10

MY SCHEDULE FOR THE SPRING semester was hectic and overwhelming. My classes were more challenging and required longer hours reading textbooks, writing papers, and pouring over notes. Most nights I felt fortunate to get three or four hours of sleep. I was functioning almost solely on caffeine and the occasional protein bar. It wasn't that I was trying to lose weight, it was simply my forgetting to eat amongst everything else I had on my plate.

Valentine's Day came and went, and I had still not seen Haydon since our Chicago adventure. It was becoming more and more challenging to find the time. He was consumed with work and my time was spread thin with classes, teaching, my boys, and their never-ending basketball practice and game schedule. I was afraid Hayden was forgetting about me. Two or three days would drift by without a call or a returned text.

I missed our winter wonderland before our world imploded. I missed his touch, his kiss, the warmth of his skin, falling asleep in his arms. The distance between us was disheartening. But there was nothing else we could do about it right now.

I clutched my backpack and fought my way down the crowded hallway after my last class. It was half past two in the afternoon, and I was feeling like the clingy rejected girlfriend. I had left Hayden two voicemails and he hadn't called or texted. I felt torn between heartbroken and pissed.

"Alex?" Michelle walked up beside me. "Have you got a minute?"

"Sure." I followed her silently around the corner to her office.

I moved a stack of papers off her extra chair and sat down. She closed her door and walked around to her desk chair.

"I will be so happy with this semester is over." She flopped down in seat and tossed her glasses on her desk. She looked exhausted. "I don't know what the hell I was thinking when I took this job." She shook her head, and I noticed the dark circles under her eyes. "Truthfully, I am considering returning to counseling full time."

"Seriously?" I looked at her with a quizzical brow.

"Yes. The patients aren't nearly as whiney as my students," she laughed. "Or have as many excuses."

"Happy Valentine's Day." I snorted.

"Screw you." She smirked and tossed a small box of chocolates at me. "I got you a little something to say thanks for all your hard work. I honestly don't know what I'd do without you."

"Awww . . . thank you." I blew her a playful kiss.

"Yeah, right back at ya, babe." Michelle grinned. "Any big plans for tonight?"

"Just a date with a half-gallon of cookie dough ice cream and a lonely bottle of wine after the boys go to sleep." I slumped back in my seat.

"Still no Hayden?" I hated the pitiful look on her face.

"Nope." I sighed heavily. "I've called him twice today and he hasn't even had time to text me back." I shook my head in dismay.

"What an asshole." She stated flatly.

"And your night?" I looked up at her hopefully.

"About the same as yours." She shrugged. "Aren't we the fabulous duo?"

"Pretty much," I stood up and gathered my things. "Well, I'd better get going if I'm going to beat the bus home. Thanks again for the chocolates. Have a good evening." I smiled and opened the door.

"Thanks. You too." I closed the door behind me.

I pulled into the garage ten minutes before the buss was due. I dropped by things on the island and dug my phone out of my purse.

No missed calls, no messages.

I blinked a couple times trying to keep the tears from falling. Then I felt stupid for getting so worked up over a commercialized made-up holiday.

"Hey momma," Max's voice rang through the house.

"In the kitchen." I hollered back.

"Were you going to just leave these on the porch?" He held out a long slender box with a clear window on the top tied shut with a large red ribbon.

"I didn't know it was out there?" I took the box from him. "I parked in the garage."

"You should glance at the porch once in a while." He set down his backpack beside mine.

"Who are they from, momma?" Henry came bouncing in the kitchen.

"Where's your backpack?" I inquired trying to change the subject.

"By the front door." He headed straight for the refrigerator.

"Momma," Max shifted his weight from one foot to the next impatiently. "The flowers. Who are they from?"

"I don't know, Maximillian." I set them on the island and opened the box.

"Wow," Henry climbed up on the barstool and peeked over my shoulder. "Those are pretty."

"Yeah, pretty expensive." Max leaned across the island.

"Mind your own business." I lightly, playfully smacked him in the top of his head.

"There's a card?" Henry pulled out the small pink envelope tucked in the corner of the box and handed it to me.

"Well," Max said impatiently.

I walked away from the island and leaned against the sink opening the envelop. The card had two champaign glasses on top an elegant candlelit table. Above it inscribed in gold letters read; Be My Valentine. I smiled opening the card.

"Mom?" Henry bounced impatiently in front of me. I waved him off lost in card.

Hayden had written, or rather had someone at the floral shop scribble down his words. *Happy Valentine's Day, my love. I wish we were back on the beach in Duplin walking in the sand. I promise we shall be there together again. I love you and miss you. See you soon. Love Always, Hayden.*

I smiled to myself and closed the card.

He remembered.

"Annnnnnd got it . . ." Max yanked the card out of my hand and ran around the kitchen table laughing.

"Give me that." My lovely thoughts of the beach brutely interrupted.

"Hayden?" A devilish grin slid across his face.

"Never you mind." I leapt over and grabbed the card from my son. "Nosey little shit." I made a goofy face at him making Henry laugh.

"Is he your new boyfriend?" Henry asked.

"I don't know what he is." I tucked the envelope and card into my backpack. "Who's hungry?"

"Nice try, momma." Max smirked. "Are you going out to dinner this evening to celebrate Valentine's Day?"

"No."

"No?" Henry looked puzzled. "Why not?"

"Because he's in Chicago. And I don't know what we are and until I can figure that out, I'm keeping my mouth shut." I explained as vaguely as I could.

"It seems like he's figured it out." Max stated as a matter of fact.

"Let it go." I raised my eyebrows at him as a warning.

"Whatever," he murmured. "All I'm saying is this guy seems to make it pretty clear where he stands. This is the same guy who took you to Europe."

"Really?" Henry brought his attention back to me. "Wow, momma."

"Boys, please." I picked up my things and carried them into the living room setting them on my desk. "I don't want to discuss this any further."

"But mom," Max interjected.

"Max, I'm serious. I don't want to talk about it. I will let you know when there's something to know." I tasseled Henry's hair. "Why don't you guys help me put dinner together?"

"Fine." Max moped into the kitchen.

"Okay," Henry bounced after his big brother.

After the dishes were done and Henry was tucked in for the night Max came over and sat down beside me on the couch. I was watching *Supernatural* on Netflix. It was a show we both loved.

"When are you going to tell Henry about Hayden?" Max asked casually.

"You are quite the little actor." I grinned over at him.

"I try." He shrugged. "But don't you think you should tell him?"

"I don't know if he'd understand." I answered honestly.

"Henry will like him if you like him." Max reached over and took my hand, a real rarity in the last year since puberty kicked in. "And anyone who can make you smile like that," my handsome young man who suddenly seemed so grown up smiled and squeezed my hand gently, "I am sure we will both approve of."

"Who are you and what have you done with my son?" I laughed leaning over and wrapping my arms around him. "Thank you, Max. That means a lot to me."

"Happy Valentine's Day, Momma."

"Happy Valentine's Day, buddy."

"I'm gonna go play some video games before I turn in." He hopped up and headed to his room.

"Not too late." I called after him.

I sighed and curled my feet beneath me wrapping the couch blanket snugly around me. I felt so proud of Max and the young man he was growing into. I still wasn't sure whether I was ready to intermix my boys with Hayden, but we were moving steadily in that direction.

I closed my eyes and tried to not think about Hayden. It was impossible. I missed him terribly and wished I could at least hear his voice. As much as I loved the roses, they didn't mean as much to me as if I had gotten to hear his voice. It was out of character for him not to call on a special occasion and I couldn't figure out what was wrong.

I was finally drifting off to sleep when my phone started ringing loudly as I'd forgotten to put it on vibrate. Startled, I shot up in bed startling Billy. She barked once at me and jumped onto the floor as I groped around in the dark for my phone.

"Hello," I couldn't keep the smile off my face despite my slight intoxication. "Happy Valentine's Day."

"Alex?" Hayden sounded tired.

"Yeah?"

"Are you drunk?"

"A little bit." I admitted.

"How much did you drink?"

"Just a smidgen," I glanced at the bottle of wine I'd opened after the boys went to bed. There was only about two inches left in what started out as a new bottle.

"I know you're a light-weight Alex, and you've had more than a smidgen." His voice lightened a bit, and I could picture his dimples as he smiled.

"Fine. I may have finished about 80% of a new bottle." I confessed.

"Is that all?" He laughed.

"And I may have finished off a tub of cookie dough ice cream." I realized how pathetic I sounded.

"Was your Valentine's Day that bad? Didn't you get my roses?" His voice dropped a bit.

"Yes and thank you. They were gorgeous. I love them." I said apologetically. "It's just that . . ."

"That you wish we were together." He finished for me.

"I know. It's silly." I felt like a fourteen-year-old girl pondering on her first crush. "It's pathetic."

"No. It's sweet. I wish I were there too." He sounded sincere. "I wish I were lying beside you, holding you in my arms, kissing you." His voice trailed off.

"You are such a tease. It isn't fair." I pouted.

"I thought you liked it when I tease you." I could almost see the coy smile across his shapely lips.

"Physically, yes. But mentally no, especially when your three hours away. That's just cruel." I complained.

"What if I promise to make it up to you?" He offered.

"And how do you propose to do that?" I laid back against my pillows enjoying toying with him.

"I have something special in mind." It was obvious he was enjoying the game too.

"Really? Like what?"

"When is your spring break?" Hayden inquired.

"The second or third week of March. I'm not sure. I'd have to check. Why?"

"I may have something up my sleeve." His voice sounded as smooth as honey and warm as chocolate.

"Darling, I wish I could. But I can't. I have the boys and their spring break never aligns with mine. And even if it did, I'm not sure they're ready for this." I closed my eyes and felt defeated.

"I'm sure we can figure something out." His voice remained smooth and comforting.

"Okay." Although I wasn't nearly as optimistic as he was.

Chapter 11

LISA WAS WAITING FOR ME just inside the gymnasium doors when I arrived with the boys early Saturday morning for their basketball games. The gym was bitter cold this early in the morning and felt only slightly warmer than the air outside.

She grabbed my arm as soon as we crossed the threshold. She was grinning ear to ear and bouncing from one foot to the next.

"What?" Her unexpected grip on my arm startled me.

"Where have you been?" Anticipation radiated off her.

"We're on time." I glanced up at the clock on the wall. "Five minutes early actually." I tiled my head and looked at her with confusion. "What's got you all riled up?"

"You're never going to believe this." Lisa held onto my arm and dragged me towards the bleachers.

"Okay," I muttered stumbling along behind her.

She pulled me halfway up the bleachers behind the bench where Henry and Luke's team were sitting. She was way too excited, and I had not had enough coffee in me yet to muster much enthusiasm.

"Sit." She plopped down on the wooden bleacher and dropped her purse at her feet.

"What in the world has you in such a tizzy?" I sat down beside her nursing the hot coffee in my travel mug.

"You'll never believe what Erik did." Lisa twisted towards me.

"Good or bad?" I smirked.

"Good." She playfully rolled her eyes.

"Sorry," I was having fun giving her a hard time.

"I came home last night after work and there were dozens of candles lit in the family room and the fireplace was going. The house smelled heavenly."

"So, your perfect little boyfriend made you a romantic dinner for Valentine's Day?" I smiled. "Must be nice." I nudged her.

"The man can definitely cook."

"Where were the kids?"

"It's Brian's weekend. They rode the bus to his house after school."

"I'm jealous." As much as I dearly loved my boys, sometimes I wish I had the benefit of having a weekend off. But with Danny fifteen hundred miles away, I was simply out of luck in that department.

"Danny's a prick." Lisa stated.

"I know." I shrugged.

"Anyway, Erik fixed lasagna from scratch."

"Seriously? Damn. I am jealous." I admitted.

"It was fabulous." My dearest friend could not stop smiling and I knew what was coming.

"Good."

"Anyway. We had champaign and dinner by candlelight. Then he served us some Raspberry gelato from my favorite little bistro in town."

"The one off main street?"

"Yep." Lisa squirmed in her seat and held out her left hand. "And look what was in the bottom of the dish." She was sporting a gorgeous white gold diamond ring with a large rock in the center.

"Oh, my God!" I grabbed her hand and examined her new accessory more closely. It was truly exquisite. "That's gorgeous!" I proclaimed.

"I know!" She squealed.

"I'm guessing you said yes?" I hugged her.

"Of course."

"I'm so happy for you!"

"Happy about what?" Our friend and fellow mom, Kim approached us.

"I'm engaged!" Lisa held out her hand across me to show Kim her new ring.

"Wow!" Kim smiled and sat down beside me. "That's gorgeous! Congratulations! When are you getting married?"

"This summer."

"That's great." Lisa deserved to be happy, and Erik was an incredible man.

"Have you picked a place?" Kim inquired.

"No. We haven't discussed all the details yet. Only that it will be in August." Lisa picked up her phone from her purse and pulled up the calendar.

"August?" I wrinkled my forehead. "The hottest month of the year?" I questioned her sanity.

"Well, we both want a summer wedding and August is the only month that we don't have a previous anniversary with an ex or a kid's or ex's birthday." Lisa rolled her eyes. "The joys of a second marriage and blending two families."

Kim and Lisa sat there discussing the various aspects of wedding preparations while I half watched the game considering the true ramifications of blending my small family with Hayden and his children.

Kennedy would be more like having a younger sister than a stepdaughter and it was almost creepy to think of Mason as my stepson. Still, Hayden seemed jubilant about the prospect of being a stepfather. It was almost like he wanted to do with my sons all the things he had missed out doing with Mason like coaching their sport teams, family vacations, and teaching them how to work on cars. While the thought was pleasing enough, I could not help but think of how it would be perceived by Mason who often complained about his absent father. Certainly, watching his dad do all the things with my boys he had longed for him to do with him throughout his formative years would upset him.

Then again, knowing my sons dealt with the same absentee father he had grown up with, he may not begrudge them Hayden's love and attention, especially since he loved my boys so much.

The not knowing and speculation was the worst part of it. I had considered talking to Mason about it, but we were still building our relationship on this new foundation, and I did not want to upset him about something that was still years away or at least until I graduated.

"Sorry, I'm late. I overslept." Mason plopped down behind me. "How are they doing?"

"We're up by six." I leaned back and told him. "Henry's made three baskets." I smiled.

"He keeps going like this, he's going to be outscoring Max at his age." Mason spent countless hours shootin' hoops with Henry — each of them determined to compensate for Henry's smaller stature.

"I wasn't sure if you were coming or not." I said over my shoulder.

"I promised them I'd be here." Mason leaned forward smiling. "I couldn't go back on my word."

"I appreciate it." I grinned.

"Look," Lisa thrust her hand over my shoulder.

"Engaged?" Lisa nodded. "Congratulations. Erik is a lucky man."

"Thank you." Lisa beamed.

"Where's Max?" Mason turned his attention back to me.

"He's down there with Aaron and Tyler." I pointed towards the far bottom of the bleachers.

"I'm gonna go say hi." Mason stood up and headed back down the bleachers.

"I thought you two stopped seeing each other?" Kim watched him descending the steps.

"We did."

"What a shame. He is edible." Kim shook her head slightly.

"We're still good friends." I pointed out.

"Friends with benefits? I was wondering why he was still around." Kim giggled.

"No. We're not friends with benefits. Just friends." I corrected her.

"Seriously?" Kim raised her eyebrows at me.

"Sadly, it is." Lisa chimed in.

"Are you seeing someone else?" Kim smiled deviously.

I nodded but remained silent. Lisa giggled arousing Kim's suspicion.

"Really? Who are you seeing?" Kim looked at Lisa for an explanation. "I'm guessing you've met him."

"Yes, last summer when it started." I elbowed Lisa in warning.

"Oh, it must be good." Kim laughed.

"It's complicated." I stated glaring at Lisa.

"I'll say." Lisa just smiled back.

I rolled by eyes at the two of them and turned my attention back to the game.

It was past one by the time we walked out of the gym. My body was stiff from sitting so long on the wooden bleachers and I was starving. The sun had decided to make an appearance but held little warmth. Its reflection was glaring off the snow causing me to immediately start digging through my purse for my sunglasses.

"Who's hungry?" Mason asked when we hit the parking lot.

"Me." Henry bounced around beside me.

"I'm starving." Max turned his back to the wind blowing in his face.

"Pizza King?" Mason looked over at me.

"I could go for a strom." My mouth watered just thinking of it and my stomach rumbled.

"Great. I'll meet you there." Mason took a couple steps towards his car parked across the lot from mine.

"Can I ride with Mason?" Max spoke up causing Mason to turn.

"Fine with me." Mason shrugged.

"Please," Max implored me.

"All right," I sighed. "Just be careful." I warned Mason.

"Here," Max tossed his gym bag at me without thought and took off after Mason.

"Thanks. I guess I'll take care of this." I hollered after him.

"Sorry. Thanks, Momma." My eldest smiled back at me over his shoulder.

I grinned and shook my head at him. He was turning into a teenager at a rapid rate, and I had mixed feelings about it.

I put the boy's gym bags in the trunk of my car and slammed it shut. "Ready?" I smiled at Henry.

"I'm starving," he climbed into the back seat.

"Me too" I shut the door behind him.

Chapter 12

S T. PATRICK'S DAY PASSED WITH little recognition due to it landing the same week as midterms. My brain had turned to mush, and I could not think straight. Thankfully, next week was the university's spring break which, per usual, did not line up with my boys' school district. Their spring break was a week afterwards making it impossible for us to do anything.

I got the boys off to school and sat down at my desk in a pair of sweatpants and hoodie. My hair was pulled up in a messy bun and I hadn't bothered to put any makeup on. I had two more finals tomorrow and I had planned on studying all day.

I stared out the front window enjoying the early signs of spring. Little buds were breaking through in my flowerbeds and sprouts were popping out on the trees. The sun was shining brightly in the nearly cloudless sky but offered little warmth. The weatherman called for a high of 65 and after the long harsh winter, it sounded heavenly.

I was on my second pot of coffee and charting neuropathways when I heard a car door shut. I peered out the front window and felt my stomach drop. My dad was walking up the pathway to my front door. I looked back at his truck in the driveway to make sure my mother was not with him.

I had not spoken to either of them since early February after my father's surgery and history lesson. My mother had not bothered to reach out to me but was relentless in her pursuit to reach Samantha. She had told me that mom was calling her every two or three days but had yet to leave a message. Samantha continued to dismiss her calls and refused to speak to her.

The sound of the doorbell jolted me out of my thoughts as I rose to answer the door.

"Hello, daddy," I greeted him. "You look better. How are you feeling?" I stepped back and allowed him to enter.

"Good," he unzipped his jacket but did not remove it.

"What brings you by?" I tried to sound casual as I stood there awkwardly in my foyer.

"I just wanted to see you," he finally removed his jacket and hung it on the stand beside the door. "I went to see an old friend across town and was on my way home."

"Oh," He followed me into my living room. "Who did you go see?"

"Just an old friend. We had a long overdue conversation about the past." I was intrigued by his vagueness.

"Anyone I know?"

"That's not important." He sat down on the edge of my couch. "Do you have anything to drink?"

"Coffee, water, soda?"

"I'll take a soda," he leaned back and made himself comfortable.

I walked into the kitchen with my brain racing with a million questions I wanted to ask him.

Did mom tell him about our confrontation? Does he know who my biological father is? Was that who he went to see? Does my biological father know about me? Why hasn't he ever tried to reach me after all these years? Does he even care that he left me in the care of an alcoholic father and a bipolar mother with borderline personality disorder who was extremely verbally, emotionally, and physically abusive?

I handed him a soda and sat back down in my desk chair across the room from him.

"Thank you," he popped it open and took a sip. "What'cha working on?"

"Neuroscience," I held up my notebook and nodded at the open textbook on my desk. "I have midterms this week."

"How is school going?" He uncharacteristically asked me.

"Good. My classes are challenging this semester," I shrugged and set my notebook back down on my desk. "Is everything all right?" I asked hesitantly.

"Yeah," his refusal to elaborate was aggravating.

"Okay," I said uncomfortably.

"Go ahead and study. I don't mean to interrupt you. I'm just gonna sit for a minute and relax if you don't mind."

"Can I get you anything else?" I offered before I got back to work.

"No, I'm fine." My father smiled broadly, but it did not reach his eyes.

I turned back around to my books and felt his eyes boring into the back of me. My brain kept screaming at me to turn around and confront him, to demand answers as to why my entire life had been a lie.

But my heart wouldn't allow me. It screamed that it didn't matter. Regardless of blood type, he was my father. He was the man that raised me. He taught me to ride a bike, play softball and basketball. He was the one who got me a basketball goal for my eighth birthday and took me to the father daughter dance. The other man did not matter. For better or worse, he was my Daddy. He had stepped up and raised me as his own.

And that was all that mattered.

An uncomfortable and painful hour slowly crept by in silence as this man sat and watched me study. I had reread the same page three times and took meticulous notes, but still had not comprehended a single thing. The agony of the silence between us was unbearable.

"Well, I guess I should let you concentrate." My dad stood up and walked into the kitchen to throw away the empty soda can.

"Are you feeling okay?" I got up and met him in the foyer.

"Yeah, I'm good. The doctor said I'm fine." He grinned and opened his arms to me. "Don't worry."

"Okay," I wrapped my arms around him hugging him.

"I don't care what anyone says, you're *my* little girl." I felt my body stiffen and tears rose to my eyes.

"Of course I am, Daddy," He kissed me on the cheek and took a step back with his hands still on my shoulders and looked me in the eye.

"You are *my* daughter and I love you." I could see the tears brim in his eyes.

"I love you too, Daddy." I couldn't remember the last time I had called him Daddy, but I felt he needed to hear it as much as I needed to say it.

He smiled at me as a tear fell from the corner of his eyes. Without another word, he walked out the front door closing it softly behind him.

I stood there rooted to that spot until after I heard his truck pull away.

He knew.

I was heartbroken for both of us, and so thankful that my heart had won the argument over my brain. I knew I had made the right decision not to confront him. He had been through enough.

I dropped my bag on the island and grabbed a bottle of water

out of refrigerator. It was Thursday afternoon and I had just finished my last midterm. All I wanted to do was curl in in bed and let the world drift away.

Unfortunately, that was not an option because the boys would be getting off the bus in a half hour and would at some point this evening, expect dinner.

I flopped down on the couch, kicked off my sneakers and put my feet up on the coffee table. I closed my eyes and felt every muscle in my body melt into the couch. I didn't want to move. I started drifting off when I felt my phone vibrate in my back pocket. I groaned and reached for it.

"Hello," I tried to sound awake.

"Alex?" A women's voice sounded too cheerful. I recognized it immediately and felt a knot in my stomach. "This is Marian. Danny's mom."

"Hi, what can I do for you?" This woman never contacted me unless she absolutely had too. We didn't get along when I was married to her son and things had gotten worse since the divorce. She was a prissy little snob who believes no one is good enough for her son and that her little angle never did anything wrong.

"Philip and I wanted to see if you had any plans with the boys for spring break." Her pleasantness sounded so fake I was happy she couldn't see me roll my eyes.

"Why?" My guard immediately went up.

"We wanted to visit Danny and thought it would be fun to take them with us." She said sweetly.

"I would have to talk with the boys and Danny first." I rubbed my eyes just trying to end the conversation.

"Why?"

"Excuse me?"

"Why do you need to talk to the boys first or Danny?" She asked abruptly.

"Because Danny is their dad, and the boys are old enough to have a say in what they do." I explained.

"Danny has rights to see his sons." Her voice got edgy.

"And he exercised those rights over Christmas break and therefore, I have them for spring break." I fired back.

"You see the boys every day. Danny has not seen his sons since Christmas. Do you really think that is fair?"

"Perhaps you should have asked your son that before he moved to Arizona." I shot back.

"He moved for his career." Marian spat back.

"I'm not going to discuss this with you. You didn't even bother to see your grandsons for Christmas or their birthday's and now you want to take them across the country? You know what, Marian. You're right. I don't need to talk to the boys or Danny. The answer is no. You cannot have my sons for their spring break and now, thanks to you, neither can Danny." I hit the off button and tossed my phone on the cushion beside me.

That woman!

I wanted to scream.

Danny's mother gave my mother a run for her money in many ways. She was one of those people who simply believed she was better than everyone else and had no consideration for anyone other than herself. Another true blessing that came out of our divorce was the removal of that woman from my life. Thankfully, Indiana did not have grandparent rights, so I was under no obligation to let her near my boys. And considering how she treated them, I felt zero guilt for it.

I enjoyed another ten minutes of peace and quiet, before I heard the boys running up the front yard and banging the screen and front doors open.

"Hey momma," Max dropped his bag in the foyer and headed straight for the kitchen.

"Hi momma," Henry dropped his beside Max's and plopped down on the couch beside me. "Can I stay at Logan's on Saturday?" He was out of breath and sweaty.

"Breathe," I laughed at my little man. "I will call Lisa and talk about it. Okay?"

"Okay," he smiled and headed off to the kitchen.

I got up and dragged myself in after them to see what they were into. Max was sitting at the table with a bag of Doritos' while stuffing the last of a honey bun in his mouth.

"Put the chips up." I told him. "And only one Little Debbie." I told Henry as he dug through the pantry. "I'm going to start dinner shortly."

"Fine," Max muttered. He went back to the panty and put the bag back. "What's for dinner?"

"Tacos." Always a favorite.

"That sounds good." Max wandered back into the living room.

"Do you have homework?" I hollered after him.

"Yeah," he responded from around the corner.

"Get started on it, please."

"Okay."

"What about you little man, any homework?" I turned towards Henry.

"Nope." He finished off his cupcake. "Can I watch tv?"

"All right," He disappeared into the living room, and I started getting things out for dinner.

I started browning the ground turkey and pulled out the chopping block to cut of the tomatoes and lettuce when Henry returned with my phone as it continued to vibrate.

"Momma, it's dad." He handed it to me.

"Wonderful," I muttered, expecting his call.

"Hello," I turned the stove down and walked out onto the back deck for some privacy.

"Seriously, Alex?" Danny sounded annoyed.

"Don't start. I'm not in the mood." I informed him.

"I'm not concerned with what kind of mood you're in. My parents wanted to do something nice for me and my sons and you had to be a complete bitch to them about it. Why?"

"Woah, wait a minute. Don't put this on me. You know how your mother is. She immediately jumped on me when I told her I had to talk with you and the boys before I gave her an answer." I informed him.

"I know she can be difficult." I snorted.

"That's putting it mildly." I retorted.

"She hasn't seen the boys in over a year."

"Danny, she hasn't seen the boys in almost three years. They don't even know your folks and they live twenty minutes from us."

"Has it been that long?" He questioned. "I hadn't realized."

"Why would she think I wouldn't talk to my sons first and you? I realize we don't have the best of relationships, but when it comes to the boys, we do better than most." I told him.

"I agree," Danny exhaled loudly. "I believe we both try to do what is in the best interests of our boys. I realize I haven't been the best dad, but I am trying to do better."

"And I appreciate that." I said honestly.

"Do you think the boys would want to come down for spring break?"

"I don't know. I haven't talked to them about it."

"It would mean a lot to me."

"Danny, I'm not trying to be a bitch, but you had them over Christmas which means I get them for spring break." I explained.

"I understand that." I could hear him fidgeting with something which was unusual for him, and I couldn't understand why he was so nervous and hesitant to talk to me.

"What's going on, Danny? You're not telling me something. Are your parent's sick or something? Are you?"

"No. No. Everyone is fine." He paused.

I impatiently returned to the kitchen and stirred the meat. I turned the burner down to its lowest setting and slipped out back to the deck.

"Look. I've got dinner cooking and I'm trying not to burn it. Can you please be honest with me?"

"I really didn't want to do this on the phone." He was reluctant still.

"Okay, but it's not like we can talk in person." I was trying not to lose my patience.

"I'm getting married in a couple weeks." He blurted out.

"Oh," that was the last thing I expected to hear about of him. "Congratulations." I stumbled

"Thanks," Danny's voice was low.

"Amanda?" I sat down on the swing and blinked back the tears.

"Yes."

"I'm happy for you." I hastily brushed the tears off my cheeks. I was angry at myself for getting so emotional.

"Thanks, Alex." A silence fell between us that seemed to last forever. "So, can I have the boys?" The hesitation in his voice was evident.

"Do they have any idea about this?" I couldn't believe they did without me hearing something about it.

"No. I haven't told them." He admitted.

"And you're going to drop this bomb on them when they get there? Danny, you're asking for trouble. Have you met Max?" I could only imagine how well this was going to go.

"Can you talk to them?" The coward inquired.

"Are you serious? Danny, this is your news to share with them. Not mine." I pointed out.

"It's not exactly what I want to tell my boys on the phone or over Skype."

"You are such a coward." I was so disgusted.

"Thanks."

"Yeah, right back at ya." I disconnected the call and tossed my phone on the cushion beside me.

I closed my eyes and dropped my head between my knees. Images of me in my wedding gown standing at the back of the church holding onto my dad's arm and looking up the aisle at Danny standing up at the alter flashed through my mind. He looked so handsome, so nervous, so young.

I could still feel the butterflies in my stomach as my dad and I began our accent. I was terrified. But I also knew I loved Danny more than anything in the world and I couldn't wait to be his wife.

It was a time when I was naïve enough to believe in happily ever after and that love could conquer all.

I hated myself for crying. What did I care if Danny got remarried?

I knew I cared because I was stupid enough that day to believe in him as we recited our vows. I believed he would be faithful, love me, and always be with him until death do us part.

I was so wrong.

I brushed the tears away and hated myself for the rush of memories that continued to flood my brain. The look on Danny's face when I told him I was pregnant with Max. Seeing him holding Max for the first time and the pure joy on his face. He was so proud of his son. And then the same with Henry.

A lifetime of what if's and what should have been consumed me. I wrapped my arms around my body sobbing. I couldn't explain it or even understand it myself. Danny's news should not have this effect on me.

But Danny was my first. My first love. My first lover. The father of my children. At one point, he was my best friend. We spent years sharing secret smiles, looks, touches, private jokes, and the little things that only someone who is a part of you knows.

And our boys — these two perfect little human beings that would not be here if it hadn't been for us. We made them and they were conceived in love. They were the living proof that Danny and I once loved each other very much.

There's always something about the first that touches your soul and changes you forever. A part of me would always love Danny and there was nothing or no one that could ever change that.

"Mommy, why are you crying?" I felt Henry's hand on my shoulder.

"I'm okay," I quickly wiped my face off with my shirt and stook up. "Let's go check on dinner."

Henry didn't say anything but put his hand in mine and followed me back into the house.

Henry kept his eyes on me carefully watching my every move as I finished preparing dinner, but he never said a word and only nodded when I asked him to go tell Max dinner was ready.

Max rambled on through dinner about Spring Break yammering about all the things he and Aaron have planned. With each word, my heart broke a little more and I dreaded the thought of telling him that he wasn't going to be doing any of the fun things they have planned and that he was going to be down in Phoenix at his dad's wedding.

Danny's wedding.

The words were wedged in my throat. How could I explain it to them? I knew they really did not like Amanda although neither had given me an explanation as to why? But knowing them and their ability to get along with just about anyone, it did concern me — especially with Henry. He was my sweet boy, and everyone adored his kind and loving nature. Max could be a little more challenging only because he had learned, unfortunately, to be more cautious in putting faith into people — thanks to Danny letting him down so often in his young life.

Max was so excited and seemingly oblivious to my red eyes and lack of rapport. Henry — silent. He knew something was wrong and I could see the apprehension in his big brown eyes. He was waiting for the bomb to drop.

The boys helped me clear the table and load up the dishwasher. I wiped off the table and rinsed out the dishrag. Henry was standing so close behind me I almost tripped over him when I turned around.

"Oh, sorry buddy." I smiled and patted his shoulder.

"What's going on, momma?" He asked in a small voice.

Max, pushing in the last of the chairs, stopped with his hands still on the back of the chairs and looked at me like I had smacked him across the face.

"Boys, we need to talk." I swallowed the lump in my throat.

"Let me guess. Dad called." Max started chewing on his lower lip — a habit I learned he did when he was fighting not to say what he truly was thinking.

"Yes. So did your grandma, Marian."

"Seriously?" Max gritted his teeth as I nodded. "What did she want?"

"Dad's mom?" Henry looked up at me.

"Yes," I placed my hand on his shoulder. "Let's go sit on the couch." I took a step toward the living room, but Max spoke up.

"Just say it, Momma. Our spring break is ruined, right?"

"Max," I started, but he interrupted me.

"I knew it." He shook his head. "I'm not going to Phoenix. Our winter break was horrible because we had to go down there and put up with that woman and her brats. I'm not giving him spring break too."

"Can I please explain?" I took a deep breath.

"You said Dad could only take us every other holiday or break. If we had to go on Christmas, doesn't that mean we get to stay here for spring break?" Max inquired.

"You're right, but."

"No but's. I'm not going. And Danny can't make me." That was the first time he had referred to his dad by his name and I knew this was only going to get worse.

"Your Dad is asking you to come down for your spring break because he is getting married." I figured I might as well go for broke because there was no sugar coating this one as upset as Max already was.

"He's marrying that Bitch!" Max shouted.

"Language!"

"That's what she is!" Max spouted. "She's horrible. She was so mean to Henry over Christmas and called him a baby and both of us spoiled brats. I hate her."

"And you?" My eyes turned to Henry who stood silently beside me with big tears rolling down his cheeks.

"She's mean." He replied in a small voice.

"I don't know what to do, boys." I told them honestly leaning against the counter. I felt exhausted and heart-broken for them.

"Tell him no." Henry said simply, his eyes pleaded with me.

"I'm afraid it's not that simple, buddy."

"Yes, it is." Max quipped up.

"If I were getting remarried, I would want you both there. In fact, I wouldn't get married without you boys there." I told them.

"You would never marry someone who didn't like us." Max stated.

"Momma would never marry someone who didn't love us." Henry turned to his brother.

"You're right. I wouldn't. And I don't believe your dad would either." I wanted desperately to believe I was right in that.

"Ha," Max rolled his eyes.

"Dad was the one she called us spoiled brats to. Dad said it wasn't his fault that you had made sissy's out of his sons." Henry told me in a low voice.

"What?" A fire ignited in my stomach.

"She told her kids Henry was a baby." Max tossed in. "She thought we were out of ear shot, but I don't think she really cared if we heard her or not." I saw him gripping the back of the chair.

Every fiber of my being wished Danny were standing in front of me so I could punch him dead in the face for making my son's feel this way.

My boys were anything but spoiled brats, let alone sissy's.

I was pissed!

"I'm sorry." I put my arm around Henry. "You know none of that is true, right?"

"I know," but the doubt was prominent in his big brown eyes and I struggled to keep my anger at Danny under control so I would not say something I knew I shouldn't.

"What did Marian want?" Max finally asked. He never called her grandma because she had never been one since the divorce.

"She asked if you and Henry could fly out with them."

"No," Max shook his head angrily. "Absolutely not!"

"I don't want to fly with them." Henry shook his head.

"Okay," I exhaled slowly. "That's fine with me."

"Do we have to go to the wedding?" Henry brushed the tears off his and his runny nose with the back of his hand.

"Here, baby." I handed him a napkin off the counter. "Blow your nose and wash your hands."

"Do we?" Max watched his brother over at the sink.

"Your dad would be so hurt if you weren't there."

"I don't think he'd notice." Max rolled his eyes. "We're nothing more than decoration for his ego anyway."

His words stabbed directly into my heart. There was no hiding the realization that my son was no longer the innocent little boy who I could protect from his father's true nature. Instead, a young man stood before me fully aware that he was nothing more than a prop used by his dad to make his father appear to be something he's not to those too ignorant to know any better.

"I wish I could change things for you both." I admitted.

Max closed his eyes and took a deep breath slowly shaking his head and rocking back on his heels deep in thought.

"Fine," he finally said. "Tell Danny that Henry and I will go. But we are not flying out there with his parents."

"Okay," I mistakenly thought he was finished.

"And," Max exhaled loudly. "You make it clear to Danny that this is the very last time I will go to Phoenix to see him. If he wants to see me again, he has to come here without her and her kids."

"Max," he abruptly cut me off.

"I am old enough to decide." My son's eyes narrowed. "I checked and I now have a say and I am not going back out there again. If he can't come visit me without his *new* family, that's fine with me. He can force Henry to spend time with him for the next couple of years, but I'm done." Max's voice wasn't angry, it was hurt. "And you can tell him that Mason has been more a dad to me and Henry than he ever was." He looked at me sadly for a moment and walked out of the kitchen. A moment later I heard his bedroom door close.

A tear fell from the corner of my eye.

"I agree with Max." Henry stood beside me still holding the hand towel. "This is my last trip. I don't want to see him again."

The tone of his voice made him sound so much younger than he truly was, and it ripped at my heart.

"Henry," I bent down and hugged my little man.

"He can ask the judge to see me, but I don't think he will. He has a new family now."

"Your daddy loves you." I tried to assure him.

"I know better, momma." Henry shrugged in a defeated manner that served as icing on the evening.

He dragged his feet as he walked out of the kitchen to his room. I leaned back against the cabinets and closed my eyes. I knew the relationship they had with Danny had deteriorated over the years, but I had not realized it was to this degree.

It was heartbreaking to think that a 21-year-old kid who entered our lives had been a better father and role model to my young sons than their own father. I was so grateful to Mason and his relationship with my boys and even though things between us had changed drastically, his love for them never wavered and he continued to be a big part of their lives. Mason was truly an exceptional man — just like his father.

Even though I knew eventually Hayden would be the stepfather my sons truly deserved, and Mason would shift into the big brother role, the relationship they shared would be one that would never falter.

I sat down on the swing with a large glass of wine and hit the button on my cell that would connect me with the man that had not only ripped the heart from my chest but had destroyed my son's faith in others and robbed them of the father they should have had.

Would there ever be a day when Danny's behavior did not shatter the hearts of my family?

"Alex, how did it go?" The chipper eagerness of his tone made it all the worse.

"Not well."

"I figured they might be surprised." He laughed.

"That's an understatement." I muttered.

"Let me guess, you're not going to let them come." Danny voice sharpened.

"No. They're coming to your wedding." I paused long enough to take a long drink of wine. "But they have some concessions."

"Bribes?" Danny laughed. "What do I have to buy them?"

"Are you kidding me?" I heard a female voice snap in the background and instantly I went to fierce recalling what this woman said about my sons.

"Tell her to shut the fuck up!" I snapped at Danny. "My boys are of no concern of hers."

"Whoa, Lexie. Calm down. She was just asking." Danny spoke up.

"Go outside or somewhere I can talk to you without an audience." I requested, knowing he had me on speaker.

"Wherever you need to say to me you can say in front of Amanda. We have no secrets."

"Okay," he asked for it, I thought. "The concessions given by both your sons is that they will stand up with you at your wedding, but this is the last time they will ever fly out to see you."

"What? Why would they say that?" Danny sounded shocked.

"They both hate Amanda and her kids." I stated.

"I never did anything to them. Neither did my children." Amanda spoke up angerly.

"I'll handle this." Danny assured her. "What did they say?" He directed back at me.

"Well, Amanda called them spoiled brats and you said it was not your fault I had turned them into sissy's and Amanda referred to Henry as a baby to her children who did nothing but be mean to both boys during Christmas break. The boys were miserable." I concluded.

"I didn't mean for them to hear that." Danny defended himself.

"I understand that, but they did. Imagine how you would feel if you were them and heard your dad say your mom had turned you into a sissy. Plus, being called a spoiled brat and a baby did not exactly make the boys a fan of Amanda." I informed him.

"Blending two families is not easy." Danny quipped.

"I realize that, but that's something you won't have to worry about."

"You can't keep me from seeing my boys." Danny got angry.

"Just take her to court." Amanda spoke up. "We can get custody of them."

"You can try." I spat. "Good luck with that." I laughed taking another drink.

"You're a single mom and a full-time student. It would be a no brainer for the judge." She cackled.

"Go for it, bitch." I chuckled.

"You know I'd never do that." Danny spoke up. "I wouldn't do that to the boys or you."

"We should," Amanda spat. "Perhaps then she'd learn her place."

"My sons would never forgive me if I tried that." Danny assured her.

"Like you said, they're sissy's — little momma's boys!" Amanda ranted.

"Bitch, you don't know my boys or anything about them. You worry about your own children and leave mine alone." I hollered back.

"They're mine now." She laughed.

"The hell they are! They are my sons, not yours!" I gripped the edge of the handrailing. "Danny, you best set this bitch straight before I show up at your wedding and educate her."

"Enough!" Danny shouted. "Give me a minute." I heard him shuffling and moving around.

"Where are you going?" Amanda shouted from a distance.

"Let me handle this." He hollered back.

I emptied my glass of wine. Stood up, wavering just a bit, and staggered into the kitchen for a refill. Returning to the swing on the porch, Danny finally spoke up.

"Are you still there?"

"Yes," I exhaled leaning back against the cushion.

"What was all that for?" He asked.

"I didn't start that. You need to put a muzzle on that bitch." I snorted.

"Lexie," he huffed. "Seriously?"

"Seriously? I can understand why my son's hate her so much." I retorted.

"They are my son's too." Danny shot back.

"You should remember that." I laughed.

"I do," he fired. "Why do you think I want them here."

"What did Max say — they're nothing more than a decoration for your ego." I bit my lower lip so I wouldn't laugh.

"Bullshit! My son would never say that."

"But he did."

"I don't believe you."

"I don't care if you do or not." I took a sip of my wine. "What did you honestly expect, Danny? They heard you call them sissies. I mean, damn Danny. You let her badmouth your boys and you took part in it. How could you do that do them?"

"Max took it the wrong way." He back peddled.

"There's no wrong way to take that one and you know it. You really hurt him. And so did she. The boys really don't like her."

"I got that." Danny exhaled loudly into the phone. "So, what are these concessions they came up with?"

"They will come to your wedding, but this will be the last time they will fly to Phoenix. If you want to spend time with them hereafter, you have to come here — alone."

"Are you serious?"

"Yes."

"This is not what I wanted." He sounded defeated.

"I'm sorry."

"Yeah, I bet." He huffed.

"I'm serious. I'm not enjoying this anymore than you are. I hate being put in the middle of this."

"I am entitled to every other holiday and 2 weeks of their summer vacation. I can force you." The edge in his voice returned.

"Max is old enough now to have a say if you take me to court. And do you really want to force Henry to visit you when he is mistreated by Amanda and her kids?"

"She doesn't mistreat him. She's never hurt him." He spat.

"Maybe not physically, but emotionally she already has. And if anything, it's going to take some time before their opinion of her is going to change. She's not endeared herself to your sons."

"Fine," he breathed heavily into the phone. "Whatever. I give up. I'll have my mom call you with the flight info."

"Oh. That's another thing."

"What is?"

"They refuse to fly out with your parents."

"Damn it, Lexie. I'm supposed to pay for the chaperone as well when they could just sit with my parents. This is ridiculous. What am I supposed to tell my parents?"

"That their grandsons don't want to be stuck on a plane with them for five hours." I smirked.

"Nice," he snorted.

"They don't know them, Danny. What did you expect?"

"Fine. I don't care anymore." He sounded exhausted. "I'll book them on a different flight."

"Thank you." I wasn't sure what to say. He'd made his decision and now he was having to face the consequences and I couldn't bring myself to feel sorry for him.

"I'll email it to you."

"All right," I sighed.

"Good night, Lexie." With that the line went dead.

I set my phone aside and picked up my glass of wine. I kicked off my shoes and stretched out across the swing rocking slowing. Our life had been turned upside down in one evening. All three of us had been thrown on an emotional rollercoaster and were left scrambling for the exit.

Danny had turned into a man I no longer knew or recognized. Occasionally, I would get a glimpse of the man I had once loved, but those moments were rare and when they appeared, it only served to leave me heartbroken.

I stared out over the vacant backyard. The crescent moon hovered over the blackened outline of the trees giving them a luminous quality that was both beautiful and eerie. I swung my feet back and forth enjoying a moment of peace after the emotional turmoil surrounding our evening.

This spring had left me emotionally exhausted. I had not heard anything from either of my parents since my father's surprise visit. I found it humorous since my mother was still intent on reaching Samantha but did not find it necessary to contact me. I knew I was her least favorite, but now it felt as if I had become orphaned.

Chapter 13

I PUT TWO ANGRY BOYS ON THE 4:10 PM flight to Phoenix. Max had grumbled all the way to the airport, but my poor little Henry sat silently in the backseat simply staring out the window. His thoughts were written plainly across his face and my heart ached for him. I wanted so badly to keep them both with me and tell Danny he could go to hell. But I just could not bring myself to do it. I knew if I were ever to get married again, I would want my boys there and I could not deny Danny that even if he was marrying a detestable shrew.

Max barely said goodbye to me as I signed them over to the watchful eye of the flight attendant. But Henry hung on to me for dear life. I felt horrible putting them through this, and as horrific as it sounded, I was happy they were not blaming me for ruining their spring break. Danny had accomplished that on his own without any assistance from me.

Hayden was waiting for me when I pulled in the driveway. He looked stunning in his business attire. I smiled thinking that he had left straight from the office to see me.

"Hello sexy," I eagerly went to his awaiting arms. "How are you?"

"Don't ask." I muttered into his chest.

"That good, huh?" He tucked my hair behind ear.

"I hate this," I looked up into his deep green eyes.

"I know," Hayden kissed the top of my head.

"Max looked ready to tear something or someone apart and my poor little Henry was struggling to be brave, but I could tell he was ready to cry. If Max hadn't been there, he would have." I released him and walked towards the house.

"I'm sorry, darling." Hayden picked up his overnight bag and followed me into the house.

"You know what Max told me after he found out about the wedding?" I dropped my purse and flopped down on the sofa.

"What?" He sat down beside me.

"He told me to tell Danny that Mason was more of a father to him and Henry than he was." I slowly shook my head in dismay.

"Ouch!" Hayden wrapped his arm around my shoulder and pulled me close to him. "That makes me strangely proud of my son." He smiled. "Did you tell Danny?"

"Hell no," I chuckled. "Can you imagine the fallout if I told him that?"

"The truth hurts." He smiled broadly.

"Unfortunately, this time it would hurt my sons. This week is going to be challenging enough for them, I wasn't about to make it ten times worse." I snuggled into him.

"Most likely," Hayden absentmindedly played with my hair. "Are you hungry?" I nodded. "What would you like to do for dinner?"

"Are you in the mood for anything in particular?"

"Not really. Would you prefer to order something and pick it up or go somewhere and eat?"

"Pick up." I reached up and kissed him softly. "That way I get more time alone with you."

"Sounds good to me." He reached for his phone and typed in restaurants near me and began scrolling. "There's Boulder Creek, Brickers Pub, Pit Stop BBQ & Grill, Dawson's Too, Green Street, or B Squared Bar & Grill?" I wrinkled my nose. "Okay, how about Papa's Pizzeria or Sal's Famous Pizzeria or what about Tequila Sunrise?"

"Oh, Tequila Sunrise sounds good." I looked up at him. "They have the best seafood nachos and carne asada tacos in town."

"Sounds good," he placed the order online. "It should be here in about an hour give or take." He placed his phone on the coffee table.

"An hour?"

"It's Friday night," he shrugged.

"Right." I reached up and kissed him again. "What would you like to do to kill time?"

"Hummm, I'm sure we can think of something." Hayden pulled me closer to him kissing me passionately.

"I believe we can." He scooted to the edge of the sofa and started to lift me, but Billy had other ideas.

She trotted over to us carrying her leash in her mouth and nudged Hayden's arm. She dropped it on the floor beside us, sat down, and wagged her tail.

"Care to go on a walk first?" I laughed.

"Do we have a choice?" Hayden smirked.

"Not really," I pursed my lips together. "She can be insistent."

"Of course, she can. She's a female." He laughed.

"Asshole," I nudged him playfully.

"But you love me anyway," he kissed my forehead.

"God only knows why."

I put the leash on Billy and the three of us headed out. The neighborhood was active with people mowing their yards before the weekend set in, children riding bikes, playing basketball, and running around. It was a neighborhood that I loved. A small community where people looked out for each other and took care of each other.

I had lived here more than a decade. The boys and I felt safe here. It was home.

A cool breeze drifted around us as we walked hand in hand down the sidewalk. Flowers were starting to bloom, and the trees were sprouting leaves after their long winter slumber. The warmth of the day's sun was just starting to fade as the spring twilight began to set in.

I held Billy's leash although she really did not need one. She was well behaved and although she looked intimidating, everyone in the neighborhood knew her well and knew she was friendly and loved children.

My neighbors waved as we passed and called out various greetings. Hayden waved alongside me but chuckled as the behavior continued one street after another.

"I feel like I'm stuck in an episode of the *Wonder Years*." He sarcastically stated.

"What do you mean?"

"Neighbors waving, asking how you're doing, being friendly. I keep waiting for them," he nodded towards a group of men sitting in lawn chairs enjoying a beer and talking, "to break out the grills and their wives to bring the jell-o salad and brownies."

"There's a strong possibility of that." I smirked. "You act like that's a bad thing." I looked up at him after waving to the group and saying hello.

"It's just strange is all. I've lived in my building for years and I barely say good morning to my neighbors in the elevator. I couldn't tell you their names or anything about them." He admitted.

"That's sad," I look back up at him. "I can't imagine being so impersonal in a place I call home. I love our little *Wonder Years* lifestyle here. "

"I can see that with the boys. My ex-lives in a neighborhood like this and it was much better for my children than my penthouse." He confessed. "I'm happy she was able to provide this lifestyle for them."

"I know we talked about living together in the suburbs outside Chicago, but honestly I hate the idea of taking my boys away from a life and school and friends that they love."

"I understand that, but my business is in Chicago. I can't exactly change that."

"I know." And I did, but it still did not make me want to move up to that god-awful violent hellhole of a city although I could not bring myself to say it to him.

Our dinner arrived shortly after we returned home. It was as delicious as I remembered, and Hayden fell in love with it also. We sat in the swing on the back deck enjoying our feast and watching the sun make it final decent behind the trees.

The sky was aglow in a vast array of orange, pink, and purple hues. I finished off the last remains of my tacos and snuggled up to Hayden attempting to steal some of the heat from his body. He licked the sour cream off his fingers and wrapped his arm around me. I took a sip of my wine and snuggled back against Hayden.

"I love this," he remarked in a soft voice. "I wish every evening could be like this."

"Me too."

"I realize you want to finish school here, but I hate waiting for our life together to begin." He admitted.

"I promise, I will be worth the wait." I smiled up at him.

"I know you are." Hayden leaned over and kissed the top of my head. "It's just like when you know what you want, you want it now." He let out a small laugh. "But I understand your position because of your school and your sons."

We sat silently holding on to each other rocking softly and loving the time allotted to us. Each lost in our own thoughts about the future, what it held, and how we were going to combine our lives with the least amount of impact on my sons.

I knew it was not going to be simple. Nothing in life worth having ever is. But I wished I could make Hayden see how important it was to me and my sons, to live a humble little life in this small close-knit community.

I slipped into a long, sheer red teddy with spaghetti straps and brushed out my long dark hair until it glistened in the light. I brushed my teeth and spun around in the bathroom mirror admiring the way the teddy enhanced my figure in all the right places.

Hayden was already in bed when I opened the bathroom door. The sheet was casually draped over his midsection with his chiseled chest and one muscular leg uncovered. One arm was resting behind his head, his other hand cradled the remote as he flipped through the channels. A devious smile spread across his lips when he noticed me return.

"Hello gorgeous," he reached out his hand. "Join me."

I walked slowly towards him with a Cheshire cat grin on my face. Hayden giggled softly as I climbed up the foot of the bed and crawled up to him. I pulled the sheet off his midsection exposing his defined abdomen and throbbing cock.

I smiled mischievously into his emerald, green eyes and languidly wrapped my fingers around the base of his quivering member. It twitched eagerly in my hand. Droplets of precum glistened on the head. I lapped them up leisurely. Hayden groaned and arched his hips towards me.

Lounging against my pillows, with his hands tucked comfortably behind his head, Hayden smiled down at me with a look of pure pleasure on his face while I slipped his cock down my throat. I loved the way he looked at me that way. I loved being responsible for putting that expression on his face.

"Climb on up, darling. I'll be fun." Hayden winked and I giggled as he reached for my shoulders and pulled me to him.

"You're such a dork," I climbed up on him, straddling over him, and slide down his thick cock.

I leaned back, closing my eyes, feeling totally euphoric as it filled me up. His hands massaged my breasts and his fingers pinched and teased my nipples. I was in heaven.

I rocked my hips over him riding him to my heart's desire. His hands glided down my body gripping my hips increasing our speed and keeping our rhythms matched. It was a dance we had perfected as our bodies fit perfectly together in unison.

Our breathing synchronized, increasing as the euphoria spread throughout of bodies. My legs went numb as the organism rippled through me. I gripped his pecs and grinded into him feeling him explode deep inside me.

I collapsed upon him, breathless and spent. He wrapped his arms around me, our breathing still in unison. I leaned up and kissed him passionately, my tongue dancing in perfect harmony with him.

"You are amazing," Hayden smiled broadly.

"I love making love to you."

"I can tell," he brushed my hair away from my face.

"There is nothing wrong with a lady having a healthy sex drive." I smirked.

"I'm not complaining." He brought his lips back to mine.

I fell asleep a short time later wrapped in his arms, my head resting comfortably on his chest letting the lullaby of his heartbeat carry me off to a place where every night was spent like this.

Chapter 14

THUNDERSTORMS HAD MOVED IN during the night. The world turned cold, wet, and gray in the span of a few hours. The small gap I had left in the window last evening now flooded the room with the fragrance of fresh rain and spring air.

I rolled over and looked at the man snoring softly beside me. Hayden's hair was tasseled in a way that made him appear much younger than his true age and I hated to admit that it also made him look a lot like Mason. Still, the scruff on his face, the few scattered traces of gray hairs, and the slight laugh lines offered evidence to his true age.

I got out of as quietly as possible trying not to disturb him. After freshening up in the bathroom, I started the coffee and let Billy out the back door.

Coffee in hand, I stepped out on the back deck. The drizzling had ceased, but there was still a fine mist that clung to the air. I took a sip and leaned down over the railing looking out over my large backyard. Billy was sniffing each blade of grass enjoying all the new scents the storm had kicked up. Birds were peeking out of trees calling out to each other across the yards.

But the clouds littered the sky. There was no trace of the sun as if it had a chance of penetrating this thick coverage. Rather, the clouds looked as if they were taking a small break but were going to start unloading their heavy burden upon us at any moment.

"What'cha doing, doll?" I heard his footsteps approach and then his arm slip around my waste.

"Enjoying the morning," I whispered leaning back against him.

"Did you hear from the boys?" He lifted the mug from my hand and took a sip before handing it back.

"Danny texted a little after midnight that they made it and he was sorry he forgot to text."

"I'm surprised the boys didn't text."

"I'm sure they will today."

"Hungry?"

"Starved." I smiled up at him.

Hayden fried the bacon while I scrambled the eggs and made biscuits. It amazed me how easily and effortlessly we fell into roles perfectly complimenting each other. It was so hard to imagine a relationship that fit so well together, that didn't require the constant grind of worry and trepidation that seemed to surround my relationship with Danny. With Hayden, it was easy, simple, and peaceful. I never believed in soulmates before, but with Hayden, he truly was the other half of me and together we balanced each other beautifully.

After the dishes were done, we jumped into the shower. The bathroom quickly filled with steam and Hayden was in a playful mood. He turned on the playlist on his cell and set it on the counter. *Demons* by Imagine Dragons blasted through my bath.

Hayden flicked me with his t-shirt as he danced around my bathroom doing a striptease. I leaned against the counter and laughed at him. He looked so silly and carefree.

He took my hand and spun me around. He dipped me low with a devious grin on his face kissing me firmly.

"Today is going to be a wonderful day." He announced spinning me back around.

"I'm almost afraid to ask what you have in mind." Hayden let go of my hand and wiggled his hips to the music shimmering out of his boxer briefs.

"If I tell you what I want to do, you can't laugh at me."

"Fine. I won't laugh." I put my hand over my mouth stepping into the shower.

"I thought since it was raining today, we could visit the Children's Museum downtown." Hayden stepped in behind me.

"Why would I laugh at that?" The Children's Museum was not the response I was expecting.

"I don't know," he shrugged reaching for the shampoo. "I know the one downtown is the largest Children's Museum in the world and I've always wanted to see it."

"It's phenomenal. I love it. I've been there many times growing up and with the boys." I playfully bumped him out of my way. "Plus, we can grab some dinner downtown afterwards."

"Hopefully, it will stop raining by then."

"Oh, I hope not. I love the rain. It's so romantic." I stood on my toes and kissed him quickly. "I'm sure we could think of something to do on a rainy night."

"I see the wheels turning," he laughed. "What are you thinking?"

"That after dinner, we can come back here, start a fire, set up our own little haven in the living room." I wrapped my arms around his neck and kissed him again.

"Perhaps we should skip the museum." He wiggled his eyebrows at me in a devilish manner.

"No way, mister." I playfully pushed him away. "We are going to enjoy every aspect of today," I ran my fingers over his sculpted chest. "And tonight."

A light drizzle stuck to our hair and clothes as we crossed through the large parking lot. It was just enough to make my clothes stick to my skin and feel grimy. I hated drizzle. A downpour was fine, light rain too, but a drizzle does nothing but ruin your hair, makeup and clothes and make you feel icky.

Hayden seemingly didn't notice or didn't care. He squeezed my hand like an excited child when passed the enormous dinosaur by the entryway. Then he stopped before we reached the cashier.

"Is that a water clock?" I nodded. "I love it. I wish I could put something like that in my office." A grin stretched across his face.

"I don't believe it would fit." I couldn't help myself.

"I said something like that, not that one." He nudged me and rolled his eyes. "I just think it would look fabulous in the lobby."

"Of the building, but not the office. It wouldn't look right."

"I can dream," Hayden made his lower lip more prominent like a pouting child.

"Oh, good grief," I chuckled grabbing his arm. "Come on."

After we paid a ridiculous amount for admission, we wandered through each floor looking at all the different activities for children, the works of art, the science exhibits, and games until finally we reached the carousel on the top floor.

Hayden paid the dollar each for us to ride. We descended on the jumpers, which Hayden quickly discovered he was no longer eligible to ride due to the weight limit. So, he settled for an elephant next to my lion and snapped a picture of me on his phone.

"Let me take one of you." I reached for his phone, but he twisted away from me.

"No," he snickered like a child.

"Fine," I pulled my phone out of my bag and snapped a couple pictures of him.

Hayden turned coyly, smiling, sneering, acting like he was a model at a photo shoot. The final shot I got was of him sticking his tongue out at me.

We completed our tour with a stop at the Reuben Wells steam engine from the 1890s. During its heyday, this 35-foot-long, 55-ton steam engine was considered the most powerful locomotive in the world. Hayden walked through it with a look of complete awe on his face. His fingers lightly ran over the various surfaces like he was touching something truly sacred.

I never understood the male's preoccupation with planes, trains, and automobiles. Perhaps it is special protein only created within the male species of their DNA. I was not sure because the fascination befuddled me.

Granted, ever since I was a teenager, I have been in love with the late 60s Corvette. But still, I could not fathom spending the ridiculous sums of money some men did to obtain their *dream car*. Hayden apparently had an affinity for trains as well.

I guess the little boy in them never truly grows up.

We left the museum a little after four in the afternoon. The rain had finally stopped but the air was chilly and damp. There was still no trace of the sun penetrating through the thick cloud coverage that threatened to break loose at any moment. I pulled my jacket tighter to me and snuggled closer to Hayden as we fought our way through the surprisingly busy city sidewalks.

We walked over to Circle City mall and decided to dine at St. Elmo's Steakhouse. The atmosphere was warm and inviting — a welcomed change experienced by not only us but the dozen or so people waiting around for an open table.

Still, even with the 45-minute wait, the day was perfect in every way. Bloated and happy, we jogged through the rain after dinner in search of our car. Hayden had parked near the mall, but in a garage I was unfamiliar with. I was a creature of habit, I always parked in the same garage on the same floor (if possible) whenever I came down here simply to eliminate this issue. But Hayden had his own system and I learned not to mess with it.

My purse began to vibrate when we reached the shelter of the garage. I fumbled around in my purse hoping it was my boys. It wasn't.

"Hey girl," I shivered at the cold breeze whipping through the elevated air.

"Hello, what'cha up to?" Lisa's cheerful voice came booming through my phone.

"Freezing," I followed Hayden over to the stairs.

"Freezing? Where are you?"

"Downtown. Hayden wanted to see the Children's Museum and then we had dinner at St. Elmo's."

"I love that place. They have the best prime rib in the city."

I know. I'm stuffed." I groaned.

"Bitch," she laughed. "I don't feel sorry for you at all."

"Thanks. I appreciate that."

"I can't believe you didn't invite me."

After trapsing up four flights of stairs I followed Hayden to the far edge of the garage to his car. I was cold, soaked, and tired from running in the rain in my boots which were not conducive to running marathons.

"I'm sorry. I will make it up to you, I promise."

"You bet your sweet ass you will," she laughed. "Tomorrow."

"Huh?"

"Tomorrow," she repeated.

"What tomorrow?" I jumped in the car quickly. I put Lisa on speaker and set the phone in my lap rubbing my hands together.

"Good God, Alex." Hayden grinned and started the car. "You act like it's 30 degrees outside."

"It feels like it," I complained.

"Hi Hayden. How are you?" Lisa's voice rang through the car.

"Doing great. How are you?" He fastened his seatbelt. "Oh, congratulations! I hear you're getting married."

"Yes, thank you. You had better be there." She teasingly warned him.

"I will as long as you promise to teach Alex how to say yes?" He looked at me coyly.

"Shut up," I smacked his arm playfully.

"Huh?" Lisa sounded confused.

"Nothing. Hayden keeps trying to convince me to marry him." I stuck my tongue out at him.

"You proposed?" She sounded excited. "I can't believe you didn't tell me!"

"No," Hayden and I answered in unison.

"Not yet, but we're talking about it. I'm trying to convince her. Plus, a man's not likely to propose without a good indication of acceptance." He laughed.

"I want to finish school." I added.

"I know," he muttered backing out of the parking spot.

"Ouch," Lisa echoed through the car.

"Anyway," I wanted to change the subject quickly before our perfect day turned into a heated debate. "So, what did you have in mind for tomorrow?"

"Right. So, tomorrow you two are going to join us for brunch at my place. Erik and I would like to talk to you guys about some of the wedding details."

"Sounds good." I smiled and took Hayden's hand in mine. "What time?"

"11:30."

"We'll be there." Hayden told her.

"Wonderful. See you then. Be careful going home. Love you." Lisa's cheerfulness was contagious.

"Love you too, darling. Have a fabulous evening."

"You too."

I disconnected the call and grinned over at Hayden waiting to hear his thoughts. I knew him well enough to know the wheels were turning.

"Say it," I smirked.

"She's going to put me in a penguin suit." It wasn't even a question.

"I believe so," I squeezed his hand. "And you're going to be the most handsome man there." He typically was everywhere we went.

"Right," he rolled his eyes. "You know I'm only doing this for you."

"And I love you for it."

"You'd better," he laughed. "You owe me."

"I'm good with that." I raised my eyebrows briefly at him.

"Tease," he squeezed my thigh with a wicked grin.

Chapter 15

THE PATTER OF LIGHT RAIN ROUSED ME out of a deep sleep early Sunday morning. Hayden was spooned up behind me, his leg and arm draped across my body. I could feel his breath on the back of my neck.

I tried to slide out from beneath him, but as soon as I moved his grip tightened around me. I felt his lips brush against my bare shoulder.

"Where do you think you're going?" he whispered.

"To the bathroom." I attempted once more, but he held me tighter.

"Say please," He teased and tickled my sides.

"You're going to think you're really funny when I pee on your leg." I squirmed against him.

"I can shower, but you'll have to change the sheets." He giggled.

"You're an ass!" I reached back and playfully smacked his ass.

Hayden laughed as I stumbled into the bathroom. I completed my morning routine and finished with pulling my hair up in a French twist. I grabbed my robe off the back of the door and headed towards the kitchen. I was in dire need of some coffee.

With an oversized mug in each hand, I walked back into our room. Haydon was sprawled out across the bed with just the sheet covering his rear end. He looked adorable.

I set the mugs down on the nightstand and climbed up on the bed. I straddled over him, sitting on his rear end. I leaned down and kissed him on the cheek.

"That coffee smells like heaven." He stretched and yawned flipping me off him. I giggled and rolled to the side.

"I made it just for you."

"Is it Irish?" He raised his eyebrows with a smirk as he picked up his mug.

"Afraid not." I rolled my eyes at him. Hayden's phone buzzed on the nightstand. "Someone's calling." I nodded in the general direction.

"Hum," he grumbled reaching for it. "I don't recognize this number." He glanced and put it back down. "I don't answer numbers I don't know. It's always solicitors."

"I don't either." I agreed.

Before he could say anything else, his phone started buzzing again. "Damn," he reached for it once more just as it stopped. "That's strange." He flipped through his call log.

"What?"

"I have six missed calls from the same number. It's a Chicago area code, but they didn't leave a voicemail." His forehead wrinkled.

"That's odd."

"Oh well. It couldn't be that important or they would have." He tossed his phone aside and took another drink. "So, what would you like to do today?"

"We're having brunch with Lisa and Erik, remember?" I shook my head and smirked in disbelief at him.

"Oh, yeah," he snorted. "My bad." He took another drink and set his mug on the nightstand. "I'm afraid I've had other things on my mind." Hayden laughed and pulled me to him.

"Hey, be careful." I expertly balanced my mug. Thankfully, it was almost empty otherwise I would have spilled coffee all over my bed.

"Sorry," he snickered.

"You realize sorry doesn't count if you're laughing when you say it." I smacked his thigh as his phone began buzzing once more. "You're being bellowed." I turned hearing pounding on my front door. "Who in the hell?" I kicked my feet over the side of the bed and headed to the front door while Hayden gave in and answered the mysterious caller.

I figured it was Diane. She was most likely making Mark breakfast and forgot something. It certainly wouldn't be the first time we'd raided each other's refrigerators.

I was shocked to discover the comic relief trio in the form of Jared, Josiah, and Nick at my door at seven in the morning. Standing in the early morning sunlight, they looked worse for the wear.

"Alex. Oh my God. Thank God, you're home." Nick walked in before I had the chance to say anything. The other two followed him into my family room. "I don't know what happened. Have you heard anything?"

"It was just a joke. And it was Mason's idea. It just went all wrong." Josiah was flustered and babbled on without making any sense.

"Whoa, whoa, whoa." I closed the front door behind them. "Hold it. What are you talking about?"

"Mason wanted to get her back for screwing him over. So, he set up the camera just to humiliate her. It was his idea. I told him not to do it." Nick rambled.

"Megan?" I asked.

"Yes," Jerad and Josiah answered in unison.

"What did the idiot do now?"

"Mason's dead." Hayden's voice was hollow.

I spun around and saw him standing in his boxer briefs at the end of my hallway leaning against the wall. His cell phone was still clutched in his hand.

"What?" My body went numb.

"That was Detective something with the Chicago police department. Mason was found dead at my place." Hayden sounded distant; his eyes were glassed over.

"I, I, I . . ." I searched the faces of the three young men staring at me with disbelief. "Oh, God." I rushed over to Hayden and put my arms around his neck.

He dropped his phone and wrapped his arms around me so tightly I thought he crushed my ribs. Then this horrible sound escaped from somewhere deep inside him. It was the sound of pure unimaginable pain. His body went limp in my arms, and we slid together onto the floor where Hayden wept in my arms.

I held his head against my chest. His tears soaking through my robe. His arms crushed me to him. I ignored my own tears that were pouring down my face and rubbed his hair gently.

There were no words.

Hayden moved in a fog. It took almost an hour for the boys and I to get him onto the couch. I hadn't been able to piece together exactly what had occurred, only that a piece of me was gone forever.

"What did the detective say?" I sat down beside him and took him hands in mine.

"My son is dead." Hayden muttered.

"How?" I inquired.

"He was beaten to death in my home, blunt force trauma." The flat tone of his voice matched the far-off stare in his eyes.

"Was there a break-in?" Out of the corner of my eye, I saw the three young men fidgeting on my loveseat and looking uncomfortable.

"It was a girl. They are trying to find out who it was." Hayden stated.

"It was Megan." Jerad squeaked in a low voice.

"Excuse me?" I asked turning towards him.

"What?" Hayden's voice raised a couple octaves. "Why do you say that?"

"Because Mason went out with her last night." Josiah mumbled.

"And then turned on his computer video in his room when they got back to your place." Nick added.

"And we sort of saw everything." Josiah admitted.

"You're kidding?" I could not believe what I was hearing.

"I wish I was." Josiah looked down at his hands.

"Are you telling me you saw Megan murder Mason?" I shook my head slowly at them.

"And you did nothing?" Hayden started to get up, but I pushed him back.

"We were in Indy. What were we supposed to do?" Nick asked.

"We did." Jared pipped up. "We called the police. We gave them your address. We sent the ambulance to your place. We tried." His voice cracked as tears broke free once more.

"We also brought a copy of the video for you to give to the police." Nick held up a flash drive.

"My God," I reached over and yanked it out of his hand. "You videotaped it?" I almost shouted.

"Well, that wasn't exactly how things were supposed to go." Nicked mumbled. "There's other things on it as well and Mason wanted me to record it." He looked embarrassed.

"We need to give this to the police." I looked over at Hayden. "And you three are coming with us." I informed the moron triplets.

"Okay," Nick said and the other two nodded.

I got Hayden into the shower with me and cleaned him up. He let me wash him and dress him. He went through the motions but was more robotic. My heart was breaking, but I could not bring myself to feel anything. The man I loved had just lost his only son. Now was the time to focus on him, and him alone. I could grieve for Mason for myself later.

The long drive to Chicago felt twice as long as it usually did. Hayden sat in the passenger seat and rested his head against the window. He never said a word. The boys sat in the backseat in silence as well.

We arrived at Hayden's building to find police cars still parked out front and in the side parking lot. I wasn't sure what the protocol was or even if we were going to be able to get into the apartment.

A uniformed officer stopped us in the landing before we could enter the apartment. The front door was open, and I could see several people milling about. Two men in professional attire with badges on their belts and sidearms were talking softly in the corner.

The uniformed officer asked us to wait. He stepped inside and motioned towards the detectives. The taller of the two men approached us.

"I'm Detective Jack Rasmussen. I am sorry for your loss." He reached out and shook my hand.

"I'm Alexandra Rose. This is Hayden Brooks, Mason's father. This is his apartment."

Detective Rasmussen must have been six and a half feet tall. He appeared to be in his late thirties or early forties. He was too stylishly dressed and groomed for a homicide detective, like his wife bought too many GQ magazines. He was handsome but had an arrogant quality about him that was off-putting.

"I have a few questions I need to ask you about your son." The detective tried to make eye contact with Hayden, but nothing was registering with him.

"I can help you with that." I stepped forward a bit. "Nick?" I nodded at Hayden and reluctantly let go of his arm as Nick took his other one to make sure Hayden stayed upright.

"How did you know Mason?" the detective asked as we walked to the opposite end of the foyer.

"We met in college a couple years ago." I failed to elaborate.

"You teach?" He raised his eyebrows at me.

"No. I went back to school after I got divorced and my youngest started school full time."

"I see," he scribbled something down on his little notepad. "And now you're involved with Mason's father?"

"Mason introduced us last spring." That much was true.

"Did you know Mason well?" the detective asked.

"Yes, I did." I brushed the tears off my cheeks.

"What can you tell me about him?" He leaned against the wall with pencil in hand.

"Mason was kind, loving. My sons adored him." I choked on the words. "He was the perfect big brother to them. He played video games and practiced sports with them." I sobbed heavily fighting to keep my grief as quiet as possible for Hayden. "Mason was going to graduate in May and move back up here to work at his dad's firm."

"I see," Detective Rasmussen jotted down a few more things. "And can you think of anyone who would want to hurt him?"

"Megan. Megan did this." I blurted.

"Megan who?" He looked confused.

"Mason's ex-wife. I don't know her last name." I sighed. "I thought you saw the video." I looked over at the boys. "I thought you said they had the video."

"No. We brought a copy of it." Jared explained handing the Detective a flash drive.

"Is it on your phone?" I searched the faces of the three of them.

"I have it." Josiah pulled his phone out of his jacket pocket. "It's in my email." He walked over to us.

"Pull it up." I told him.

"Okay." Josiah typed in his code.

"And you are?" the detective asked him.

"Josiah Wright. I share a dorm room with Mason." Josiah handed Detective Rasmussen his phone.

"What's this?" the Detective took Josiah's phone. "Is this the same thing on here." He nodded towards the flash drive in his hand.

"Yes, sir." Josiah looked as if he wanted to floor to open up and swallow him whole.

"Okay," the Detective hit play and suddenly Mason's voice filled the atrium.

"Detective?" I nodded in the direction of Hayden.

Mason's voice ceased immediately. "Follow me, please." Josiah and I followed him into the penthouse over by the kitchen island and out of earshot of Hayden.

Detective Rasmussen set Josiah's phone on the island not realizing what he was about to witness. I wanted to move away, but my feet were rooted where I stood.

Mason suddenly appeared on the six-inch screen and Josiah grabbed a hold of my hand. His voice relaxed. He was casually walking around his room, picked up a pen off his desk to fiddle with while unbeknownst to Megan also flipped on his video camera. Megan was seated on the edge of his bed across the room in a short little dress and heels. Her legs were crossed at the knee and one of her heels was dangling off her foot.

I had never seen Megan before or even a picture of her. She resembled nothing of the image I had of her in my head. I guess I had assumed she was a brunette and petite since that seemed to be Mason's type, but she was nothing of the sort.

Megan had long, wavy, blond hair, an angelic face, legs up to her armpits and a figure that any woman would be envious of. She was beach bunny gorgeous. She looked as if she should be lounging on a beach covered in coconut oil.

Mason stood to the side of her twirling the pen between his fingers clearly providing optimal viewing for the moron triplets across the airwaves. Their voices were light for the first few minutes. Then Megan reached up to Mason and ran her fingers longingly down his chest with a seductive smile on her face.

"Come here," she teased him. "Let me show you how sorry I am."

"And how sorry are you?" Mason quipped.

"Very," she slid off the bed and onto her knees in front of him.

Megan obviously knew what she was doing and both men next to me shifted their stance as the show continued. Several minutes later, Megan stopped and looked up at him.

"What's the matter?" she asked.

"Nothing," I could tell by his expression Mason wasn't enjoying her technique.

"Something's bothering you. You're barely hard." She stated the obvious.

"Ummm . . ." Mason rubbed his chin as if searching for a response.

"Or are you still fucking the whore that's fucking your dad." The Detective's eyes suddenly flashed on me.

A female detective who disparaged every stereotype of female detectives due to her delicate features, long dark hair and big doe eyes had joined us and was leaning on one of the island barstools. A wide grin spread across her face as she smiled at me.

"Can't blame ya for that one," she said under her breath.

A stout Detective with a shaved head, who had wandered over several minutes before to view the video standing next to Detective Rasmussen, tried to cover an unintentional outburst of laughter with a cough, but kept his hand over his mouth as his entire head turned beet red and his body continued to shake with laughter.

"Jealous, Jen?" the stout detective choked behind his hand.

"Hell yeah, my husband doesn't look like either one of them." she smiled and shrugged.

"Where were you when I was 22?" Detective Rasmussen said in a low voice more to himself, but the other two snorted back another laugh causing Rasmussen to have to rewind the video.

I rolled my eyes at Josiah who offered me a gentle squeeze of my hand to show his support despite my humiliation.

"She is not a whore!" Mason's voice grew angry.

"The only thing that makes her not a whore is she's not getting paid." Megan stood up to face Mason in her bare feet. "That just means she's just a skanky slut!"

"Alex has more class, intelligence, and heart than you ever will. You are nothing but a cheap piece of ass and you're not even talented enough to give me a hard on!" Mason took a step back and fastened his pants. "Get out of my house you manipulative, back-stabbing, bitch." Mason turned his back on her and approached his desk. He rolled his eyes at the camera indicating the presence of his audience.

"I hate you!" Megan's voice roared in the background and in a flash, the marble end of one of Mason's sport trophies came crashing down on the side of his head.

A gush of air escaped my lungs and I physically jumped.

Mason fell out of view.

"You son of a bitch! I hate you! You ruined my life. You think you're too good for me. Fuck you!" Megan's face was distorted in a rage as she hit Mason repeatedly. Thankfully, it was not caught on screen.

But the blood.

Blood splattered up on her face, her clothes, her hair, and everything about the room.

Then reality set in.

Megan realized what she'd done. She started shaking and dropped the trophy to a loud thump on the hardwood floor.

"Oh, my God!" She rubbed her face smearing the blood in a grotesque fashion. "Oh, my God!" Her eyes scanned the room. "I've got to get out of here." She ran her hands down the front of her dress and it was only then that I noticed the small baby bump starting to become more prominent.

"I can't go out like this," she muttered to herself disappearing off screen, but the distinctive sound of water running a moment later could be heard presumably from Mason's bathroom.

Megan crossed the screen — naked and wet from the shower. She went to his closet in the distant corner and began sorting through Mason's clothes. We stood there in disbelief as she tried on his clothes and tossing them aside carelessly until she found a pair of gym shorts and a *Deadpool* t-shirt that Mason loved. It was the shirt I had bought him on our trip to Brown County with the boys. A tear rolled down my cheek and I fought the urge to scream out.

She disappeared once more only to return a few minutes later with cleaning supplies. She didn't seem to care about the blood or the fact that Mason's lifeless body was lying on the floor. She seemed to be focused on wiping everything down in hopes of removing her fingerprints.

With her bloody dress and shoes in a trash bag, she stood in the middle of Mason's room and surveyed the results. Satisfied, she threw on one of Mason's sweatshirts, picked up her things and exited the picture looking like a young girl in her oversized casual clothes, hair in a messy bun, and stocking feet.

I wanted to rip her face off.

"Do you know who the girl in this video is?" Detective Rasmussen asked Josiah.

"Yes, that's Megan Selvius. I don't know her address, but I know she's a student at Northwestern."

"She did her internship at Mr. Brooks' firm last summer. That's how they met." I added.

"I see," The detective scribbled down some notes. "And do you know if they had been fighting lately?"

"Well, he did just have their marriage annulled after he found out she lied about the baby being his." Josiah said with hesitation.

"Are you serious?" The female detective, Jen pipped in.

"Afraid so," I shrugged.

"I'm guessing she was unaware that she was being recorded." The stout detective asked.

"No, that was the for the benefit of the moron triplets." I narrowed my eyes at Josiah.

"I think I like being called the comic relief trio better." Josiah muttered.

"Seriously?" My mom voice rang through shutting the young man up immediately.

"Would you have Megan's cell number by chance?" Jen asked.

"No. I'm sorry I don't." I replied.

"We'll get it. Thank you for your help." Jen motioned another detective over to her passing along information.

"Do you have somewhere else you can go for now?" Detective Rasmussen asked.

"I believe so," I tried to think of a hotel nearby. "Have you notified Mason's mom or his sister?"

"No. We only reached out to his dad because it's his place." He responded. "We should be out of here by tomorrow morning. Will Mr. Brooks be with you?"

"Yes," I nodded.

"Can I get your number so I can contact you when we're done and keep you updated." Detective Rasmussen asked.

"Sure," I gave it to him quickly and he walked us to the door. "What happens now with Mason's body?"

"The medical examiner will take care of him." Detective Rasmussen assured me. "I will be in touch."

I didn't turn around and look down the hallway towards the bedroom. I didn't know if Mason was still in his room or if the medical examiner had removed him already. I didn't want to know.

I swallowed the lump in my throat before I walked over to Hayden who was still sitting on the floor. I reached into his pocket and took his cell phone. Hayden didn't acknowledge anything.

I scrolled through his contacts list and found Kennedy's number. The last thing I wanted to do was make this call. I slide down the wall beside Hayden and took his hand in mine.

"Sweetheart," he barely looked over at me with red swollen eyes. "We need to leave for a while. They have to finish processing things here." He nodded slightly. "We need to tell Kennedy and Mason's mom." I said in a low voice. "Do you want me to call Kennedy?"

"Would you?" I nodded. "Have her meet us at her mom's. Don't tell her why. She's going to need her mom when she finds out." He climbed to his feet and reached his hand down to me pulling me to my feet.

Using Hayden's phone, I sent Kennedy a text telling her to meet us at her mom's asap. She replied with a simple K. I tucked his phone into my jacket pocket and entered the elevator with Hayden and the boys.

News crews were gathered on the sidewalk in front of the building. The doorman rushed to our side before the elevator door was fully opened.

"Mr. Brooks," his hand outstretched to Hayden who took it. "I am so sorry for your loss. Mason was an incredible young man."

"Thank you, Carl." Hayden's voice was solemn.

"Please, exit through the parking garage. Vultures have gathered out front trying to find out the identity of the victim." Carl ushered us towards a side door.

"Please don't let them release anything yet. I'm on my way to tell his mom and my daughter. I don't want them seeing it on the news." Hayden hastily brushed a lone tear off his cheek.

"My deepest condolences, sir." Carl bowed his head respectfully.

"Thank you," I shook his hand on our way past the leaches.

Chapter 16

THE SUN REMAINED HIDDEN AWAY, and the rain clouds from the previous day had decided to stick around. The lakefront air stampeding us off Lake Michigan felt artic. I shivered next to Hayden across the garage with the three years boys right on my heels.

It felt so strange being with them without Mason. Everything felt wrong. I was numb, moving about on autopilot in an extended suspension of disbelief. I reminded myself again that I was not allowed to fall apart. This was not about me losing the young man I had loved for the last two years. It was about the man I loved losing his only son and the giant crater that just ripped his world in two.

It took me several minutes to find Hayden's ex-wife, Marcie's address in his contacts and set his car's GPS for our destination. We drove in silence the entire 40-minute drive. Each mile felt like an eternity, and I dreaded reaching our destination. I could not imagine being in this woman's shoes today. It was my greatest fear — losing a child. She had no idea that in less than an hour her world would be shattered forever.

We pulled into a neighborhood that resembled every small suburban neighborhood across America. Cute little stylish homes with wide yards, mature trees, manicured lawns, and basketball goals littered the horizon. It was exactly what both Mason and Hayden had described.

Mason's moms' home was a beautiful two-story house with a wraparound porch and gorgeous flower beds in full bloom. There was a small girl, probably six- or seven-years old swinging on a rope swing with a plain wooden seat on the huge maple tree in the front yard when we pulled up.

I shut the car off but didn't move to open the door hoping Hayden would take the lead. He didn't. I placed my hand over his and squeezed it gently.

"Hayden, we need to go in." I said softly.

"I know," he brushed a tear off his cheek and nodded his head opening the door.

"We'll wait out here," Nick reached over and laid his hand on my shoulder.

"Okay," I smiled back as best as I could at them.

"There's a coffee shop and burger joint called Gus's that's about a mile or so from here." He handed Nick the keys and a fifty-dollar bill. "Go get yourselves something to eat and we'll text you when we're ready."

"Yes, Mr. Brooks. Thank you." The boys seemed relieved, and I hated to admit that I desperately wanted to go with them — go anywhere other than here and be a part of the worse moment in this mom's life.

I swallowed hard and climbed out of the car with Hayden.

Kennedy answered the door with a bright smile that evaporated immediately.

"What's wrong?" She demanded.

"Kennedy," she stepped back allowing us to cross the threshold.

"Darling, where's your mother?" Hayden stepped up.

"In the kitchen. What's going on?" His daughter demanded again.

"And Tony?" Hayden took off his jacket but held onto it.

"In his office. Dad?" Kennedy looked flustered. She did not like being kept waiting.

"Please go get them." He walked over and sat down on the living room sofa.

Kennedy and I both watched him nervously, but he was holding it together remarkably well. I didn't know much about Hayden's relationship with his ex-wife, but I was surprised to see him make himself at home in her house. I knew I could not do that in Danny's place now that he was marrying the shrew.

"Hayden?" a stunning looking brunette walked into the room wiping her hands on a dishtowel. "This is unexpected. What are you doing here?"

Marcie Penn was a bit taller than me with soft delicate features, Mason's beautiful blue eyes, and a nice figure. She had a pleasant aura about her like she was someone, under different circumstances, I would have easily been friends with.

I struggled to make eye contact with her and stood there awkwardly in her foyer waiting for Kennedy to return with her stepfather, Tony. I felt like such an outsider invading on this family at what was about to be the worse day of their lives and I hated it.

"Hello Marcie," Hayden lifted his eyes in my direction. "Alex?" He patted the vacancy beside him. "This is my fiancé, Alexandra Rose."

"It is nice to meet you. Hayden has said some wonderful things about you." I took a couple steps and shook her delicate hand before sitting down next to Hayden.

"It's nice to meet you too," Marcie appeared rightfully confused.

Kennedy and Tony walked in behind Marcie with apprehensive expressions. Tony was a handsome man with short brown hair and a little scruff on his face. He was dressed casually in jeans and a polo shirt, and I tried not to think about how Marcie and I have similar taste in men.

"Hayden," Tony rested his hand on the back of his wife and led her over to the loveseat. "What brings you by today?"

"I don't know how to do this," Hayden said in a low voice and reached for my hand. Noticing, Kennedy sat down on the other side of her dad.

"What's happened?" She reached for his other hand. "Daddy?" he looked up at his daughter with huge tears in his eyes. "I thought you were spending the week at Alex's?"

"I was. I got a call this morning from a Chicago Homicide Detective." His voice was barely above a whisper.

"No," Marcie squeaked in a helpless voice. "No." She reached for her husband's hand.

Tony wrapped his arms around his wife with tears running down his cheeks. "How? Who?"

"He was supposed to be at school." Kennedy stated with a stone face of denial and confusion. "You said Chicago police called you? He was here?"

"I thought he was on campus. I guess he drove up sometime yesterday. He was at my place." Hayden told her.

"This happened in your home?" Tony interjected. "I thought you lived in a penthouse with a doorman and all kinds of security."

"I do. Mason let her in." Hayden looked over at Tony.

"Her?" Marcie sobbed.

"Megan Selvius." Hayden told her.

"The intern he met at your office?" She asked.

"I'll kill her," Kennedy's face turned red.

"The police are already looking for her." He put his hand on his daughter.

"How do they know it was her?" Tony wondered.

"It was caught on video." Hayden admitted.

"What?" Marcie stood up. "Are you serious? My son's murder was videotaped?" Hayden nodded. "How?"

"Mason and his dumbass roommates on campus set it up to humiliate her and it backfired. It was Mason's idea as payback for what she'd done to him." Hayden admitted.

"So, childish antics got my son murdered?" Marcie growled.

"I have no idea what Mason was thinking." Hayden informed her.

"Did he know you were coming down to Indy?" Kennedy asked.

"My son, Max talked to Mason on Thursday evening. I knew Max had called him because he was upset and about his dad getting remarried. He must had told him they were flying down to Phoenix Friday for their Spring Break. I guess Mason figured you'd be coming down." My eyes rested on Hayden who nodded in agreement. Mason knew if my boys were gone then Hayden would be come down since we hadn't seen much of each other lately.

I tried to push my boys out of my mind. They were going to be devastated and there were so many unanswerable questions on that end — Danny's wedding verses Mason's funeral. How to tell the boys. Bringing them home for the funeral. Exposing them to harsh realities that would shatter their world and deny them forever the one constant man in their life that they both could always count on, admired, and loved dearly.

"Mason was close to your son?" Marcie looked at me for the first time.

"Yes, very much so. Both of my boys love him very much. Mason has spent the last couple years practicing sports with them, attending their games and practices. He's been an amazing role model for them, and they both look up to him." I confessed.

"Where are your son's now?" She asked.

"They left Friday evening for Phoenix. Their dad lives there and is getting remarried. My eldest was really upset about it and called Mason."

"How old are your boys?"

"Thirteen and nine." Marcie nodded.

"Mason was always wonderful with his younger siblings, even when they were driving him batty." Tony smiled weakly and brushed the tears off his cheeks.

"Yes, he was." Marcie sat back down and leaned against her husband.

My phone vibrated loudly in my purse. I reached down to silence it. It was the third time Lisa had called and I felt horrible for standing them up for brunch.

"It's Lisa. I need to call her back." I whispered to Hayden. "Please, excuse me for a moment." I took my purse and stepped outside calling Lisa back. She picked up almost immediately.

"You'd better have a damn good excuse for the no show." The anger in her voice was obvious.

"Mason's dead." I sunk down into one of the rocking chairs on the porch.

"What?"

"Mason's dead." I repeated.

"How?" Her voice dropped to almost a whisper.

"He was murdered in Hayden's penthouse last night. Hayden got the call this morning from a Chicago Homicide Detective, so we drove straight up here."

"You're there now?"

"Yes, at his mom's house. We just told her and Kennedy."

"Dumb question. How is Hayden?" I knew Lisa was like me — the thought of losing a child terrified her to her core.

"Numb. Not well. There's nothing I can do for him. I want to scream at God and kill that skanky bitch with my bare hands." Fresh tears streamed down my face.

"Huh?"

"Megan."

"She's the one who did this?" Lisa sounded shocked.

"Yes."

"Are you sure?"

"Yes. It's a long story that I'll tell you later, but Mason decided to get even with her for what she did to him by humiliating her and he videotaped it." I sat there shaking my head in disbelief.

"I guess she didn't know she was being recorded?"

"No."

"Damn," she exhaled loudly. "Did the police tell you it was videotaped?"

"No, the moron triplets did. They were watching it live and recording it."

"Oh shit!"

"I know."

"What are you going to do about your boys?"

"I don't know. I'm gonna have to bring them home. They will never forgive me if they don't get to go to his funeral." I explained.

"How are you going to tell them over the phone?" She sounded as worried as I was about it.

"I honestly don't know." I admitted. "There's no good way to do any of this and Danny is going to be so pissed."

"Fuck him," Lisa scoffed. "If he'd been any type of father to those boys, they wouldn't have idolized Mason so much."

"I agree."

"Please give Hayden our love and condolences." Her voice softened. "I cannot fathom what he is going through."

"I know, me neither. I just want my boys' home so I can hold them." I admitted brushing more tears aside.

"Call Danny now and get them on the next flight. If you need us to get them before you get here, we will."

"Thanks darling. I love you."

"I love you too."

I sat there for a few minutes trying to figure out how I was possibly going to tell my boys. There was no easy way to lessen something like this for them and I hated it. I took a deep breath and hit Danny's icon on my phone.

"Hey, Alex. What's going on?" A cheerful voice greeted me.

"Hi, Danny. How are the boys?" I sniffled wishing I had a tissue.

"Grumpy," he chuckled. "They have been fighting nonstop with Amanda's children.

Ordinally, I would have cared, but right now it was the least of my worries.

"Danny, hold on a sec. I need to put you on speaker." I switched my phone to speaker and pulled up their airline on my phone to check departure times from Phoenix. "Okay, sorry."

"Sure," he turned his head. "I don't care who started it. I said stop it or you're going to spend the rest of the day with no tv or internet." Danny cleared his throat. "Damn. I'm sick of them fighting. It's been nonstop since the boys arrived."

I considered forging sympathy for him but couldn't muster myself up to do it.

"Danny, I need to tell you something."

"What's going on?"

"Mason was murdered last night in Chicago." I struggled to put the words together.

"Ah damn, Alex. I'm sorry to hear that. How are you?" He actually sounded concerned.

"Not good." As soon as the words passed my lips the damn broke.

"I'm so sorry, darling." He paused while I continued to sob. "I will change the boys flight and get them home tonight. Will you be able to pick them up?"

"Yes."

"Do you want me to tell the boys?" Danny offered.

"What other reason could you give then for sending them home before the wedding?" I asked.

"That I'm sick of the fighting," he half chuckled. "Which isn't too far from the truth."

"You can't tell them that because then you're essentially choosing Amanda's children over them, and they will never forgive you for that."

"Do you really want to tell them right before I put them on a plane for five hours so they can sit and stew over it? Perhaps it's better for them to hate me for a few hours and once they know the truth hopefully, they won't hate me." He reasoned.

"They won't." I assured him.

"I just don't want to put them on a plane alone for five hours after losing someone they love," he sighed. "And as much as I hate to admit it, my son's loved Mason very much and I know he spent a lot of time with them over the last couple years and they were close with him."

"Yes, they were," I sobbed. "Thank you, Danny. I know this isn't fair to you, and I truly appreciate you doing this."

"Alex, I know I'm not the best father and I know they deserve better. You all deserved better. I like to think I'm getting a second chance to do things right and be a better husband and father." My ex-husband painfully confessed.

"Well, don't screw this one up. I do wish you the best, Danny and I hope she makes you happy."

"Thanks. I'll text you with the flight information as soon as I get it straightened out."

"Thank you," I sniffled again.

"And Alex, I am truly sorry you and the boys are going through this. I know how much he meant to you all."

"Thanks, Danny." I disconnected the call feeling a bit relived. I couldn't believe Danny was being so human about all this.

"You're very fortunate." Marcie's voice caught me off guard. "Mason mentioned your boys before in passing but I had not realized exactly who they were." She sat down in the rocker next to mine. "My children never discuss their dad with me, and I don't ask about his life, but it makes sense now why he would attend your boy's games and such. I remember him mentioning you as well."

"He told me you'd remarried and had children with your second husband." I told her. "I know he had a somewhat difficult relationship with Hayden, and he said Tony was more of a dad to him. We had discussed it a couple times." I conveniently left out the context of how I'd learned so much about her family.

"Hayden loves his children and would do anything for them, but he wasn't exactly there for them growing up. Kennedy is more forgiving and understanding than Mason. She has his ambition and drive. Mason is more like me. He wanted a wife and children more than career success." She looked out over her front yard lost in her own thoughts and memories brushing the constant flow of tears off her cheeks.

"Mason was an incredible young man. You raised him well. My boys looked up to him a lot and loved him so much." I told her.

"I'm very proud of him," Marcie said in a low voice still loving out over the lawn.

Our comfortable silence was interrupted by my vibrating phone. Thinking it was Danny, I instinctively answered without looking at the number.

"Hello?"

"Ms. Rose?" a masculine voice inquired.

"Yes."

"This is Detective Rasmussen. I wanted to let you know that we have arrested the suspect and she is in custody."

"Good," I closed my eyes for a brief moment of solace. "Thank you for letting me know."

"You may want to let Mr. Brooks know that the press is all over this because of his position." Detective Rasmussen stated.

"I'm not surprised," I muttered.

"Also, we do not normally do this, but considering the circumstances we sent a crew to clean up the penthouse. You should be able to return by tomorrow. I can text you when they leave." He offered.

"Thank you," I noticed Marcie following our conversation closely.

"Again, I am sorry for your loss. I will keep you updated on our case."

"I appreciate your time. Thank you, Detective." I disconnected the call and turned towards Mason's mother. "They have Megan in custody, and she's been arrested."

"That's something," she sighed. "What is she charged with?"

"He didn't say and I'm sorry, I didn't think to ask. I don't know if they even formally charge them until they are arraigned." I speculated.

"I'm not sure either," she admitted.

"He did say he would keep us updated."

"Did he say when his body would be released so I can make the funeral arrangements?" Her bottom lip quivered, and the tears started again.

"No, but I believe they have to do an autopsy on every homicide." The thought ripped my heart out.

"I hope not." Marcie said in a small voice.

Chapter 17

THE BOYS ARRIVED IN INDIANAPOLIS a little after nine o'clock. I dropped Nick, Jared, and Josiah off on campus and Hayden at my house before I headed to the airport. I was not sure what to expect when I picked them up, but I knew it wasn't going to be good.

I could tell by his expression how angry Max was when I saw him off in the distance approaching me. Henry simply looked sad. I embraced them both and held them tightly.

"Mom. Enough. We were gone not even three days. Gee whiz." Max wiggled away from me.

"I'm glad we're home." Henry held my hand as I picked up his duffle bag.

"I'm happy your home too, buddy." I smiled.

"Can you believe Dad did this?" Max's face was distorted in anger. "He said he was tired of listening to us fight and that since we couldn't behave for his wedding, he was sending us back to you until we learned to behave." He rolled his eyes. "Fat chance," I heard him mutter under his breath.

"Max?" I reached out to him, but he pulled away.

"No. I'm done. He made his choice." Max stated angrily.

I wanted so badly to stop right there in the airport garage and tell him his Daddy loves him very much and would never choose Amanda's children over his own. But I couldn't just yet. He would understand soon enough. I just had to hold it together long enough to get them home.

I walked through the parking garage to Hayden's car. I had been so busy trying to drop everyone off and get to the airport before their plane arrived that I hadn't switched cars at my house.

"What are you doing?" Max stopped short of Hayden's car when I stopped.

"Did you get a new car?" Henry as I unlocked the door.

"No. It's my friends."

The boys didn't say anything else, but climbed in.

"I like this car." Henry fastened himself in the backseat.

"Me too," I smiled at him in the rearview mirror.

Max rambled all the way to the house about how horrible Amanda and her children were. He complained about his grandparents who were virtually strangers to them and kept trying to suffocate them — even Henry jumped aboard that one. It sounded like they had been miserable since the plane landed.

I parked Hayden's car in the driveway and took a deep breath. The boys were still chattering away as they climbed out of the car. Max punched in the garage code and hurried into the house.

The light over the stove was on, but the rest of the house was quiet. I checked the living room while the boys dropped off their bags in their rooms. I crept into my room and found Hayden asleep in my bed.

I closed my door as quietly as possible and held my finger up to my lips to both boys in the hallway.

"I need to talk to you guys. Come in the living room." I whispered.

"Who's here?" Henry asked following me down the hallway.

"Shhh. . ." I sat down on the couch. "Have a seat, guys,"

"What's going on, momma? Who's here?" Henry asked again.

"Hayden."

"Mason's dad?" Max raised his eyebrows with a smirk.

"Yes."

"Why is Mason's dad here?" Henry wondered aloud.

"Guys," I started fumbling with the corner of the blanket until Max placed his hand over mine.

"Momma?" Max was growing impatient with me.

"I don't know how to tell you this," my eyes pleaded with my boys.

"Just say it, good grief." Max snapped at me.

"Stop," I glared at him for a moment. "Mason was killed last night in Chicago."

"What?" Max said loudly.

"Mason's dead?" Big tears poured over the edge of Henry's big brown eyes.

I wrapped my arms around Henry and reached for Max, but he pulled away. His face was red, and his expression couldn't have been more shocked than if I had slapped him across the face.

"Yes, baby." I squeezed him tightly.

"How?" Max's lips pinched together.

"Max," I didn't want to give him details. "He was killed by Megan."

"His ex-wife?" Max's lower lip became to quiver.

"Yes," my eyes filled up with tears.

"Why?" Henry squeaked in a low voice.

"They had a disagreement." I held him close to my chest.

"What a bitch!" Max growled through his tears.

"Yes, she is." Hayden's voice startled us from the hall.

The boys jerked towards the sound of the foreign male voice in our home. Henry's eyes grew wider with curiosity, but Max seemed almost relieved to put a face with the name.

"Max. Henry. This is my boyfriend, Hayden." I tried to keep my voice cool.

"You look a lot like Mason." Henry remarked.

"It's nice to meet you both." Hayden ignored the comment and sat down on the loveseat.

"I'm sorry about your son," Max chocked on the words as the tears overflowed.

"Thank you," Hayden's voice wavered a bit.

"I'm gonna miss him so much!" Henry stated. "He never missed our games and he practiced with me all the time."

"I know he really loved you both," Hayden assured my little one.

"Can I go to my room now?" Max turned towards me.

"Max," I reached for my son again.

"I just need to be alone." He stood up. "Just for a while."

"I'm here," I squeezed his hand.

"I know," he nodded and squeezed mine back. "I love you, momma."

"I love you too."

Max disappeared down the hall and a moment later I heard his door softly close. Henry's tears continued, but silently as I held him close to me. Hayden sat there quietly, starring off into space. His expression was almost vacant as if he was still moving in an unreality.

I imagine he was.

The next couple days were a fog. Marcie was handling the funeral arrangements and my only job was taking care of the three heartbroken men in my life. With my mind consumed with them, it was impossible for me to think about Mason or fall apart.

I emailed my professors and called Michelle Monday morning explaining what had happened. I knew I wouldn't be able to teach that week or attend any other my classes. Michelle was astonished and told me not to worry, she would cover my classes for me. The rest of my professors were just as kind and understanding. I was thankful to bury myself in my schoolwork when the boys were focused elsewhere. It was a welcomed distraction.

Tuesday evening after everyone had fallen asleep, I drove over to Lisa's house. I was holding on by a thread and needed the chance to let it out. I hadn't allowed myself to break down because Hayden was a basket case. I couldn't let him see me that way.

Erik answered the door dressed in dark grey pajama bottoms and long-sleeved white t-shirt. He was a handsome man and looked perfectly natural in Lisa's home.

"Hi, Alex. How are you?" he held the door open.

"I'm smiling." I hugged him briefly.

"I'm so sorry, Alex. I can't imagine what you and Hayden are going through. Mason was an incredible young man."

"Yes, he was." Tears started welling up in my eyes.

"How is Hayden holding up?" Erik gently squeezed my arm.

"Not well," I admitted. "He's been in bed mostly, but not sleeping. He just stares at the walls."

"Oh darling," Lisa came around the corner wiping her hands on a dish towel. "How are you doing?" She wrapped her arms around me, and I broke.

That thin piece of scotch tape that had been holding me together gave way and I collapsed. Erik and Lisa guided me over to the couch and sat down on either side of me. I rested my head on Lisa's shoulder and sobbed. The pent-up emotions, grief, and sorrow I held at bay poured out like a busted dam.

My body shook as the imagines of that horrid video replayed repeatedly in my mind. I kept seeing her raise that trophy and hearing it cracking Mason's skull as he dropped to the floor. The picture was burned on my retina's and would haunt me for the rest of my life.

Erik rubbed my back gently as Lisa held me tight. Time passed but it did not matter. Nothing mattered. Mason was gone and I would never see his crystal blue eyes again or hear him laughing. I would give anything to hear him say 'I love you' just one more time.

I pictured our first encounter, his curls escaping the beanie, eyes closed, feet propped up — I thought he was sleeping. Our study sessions, the day we spent fulfilling our charity obligation for class and how much fun we had helping others and getting to know each other. The sight of him walking towards me in the parking lot carrying coffee on the early spring morning.

And his 21st birthday — lemon drop shots and our first time together. Clumsy and awkward, he was so naïve and innocent.

Mason was a huge part of my life and the lives of my sons for the last three years. And now he was gone.

It didn't feel real. It had to be a nightmare. I just wanted to wake up. I wanted to open my eyes and find him sitting beside me on the deck swing watching the sunset and complaining about my wine selection.

But I would never again look out my window while doing dishes and see Mason patiently working with Henry on his batting techniques or throwing the football with Max.

All I had were the memories of a young man I had dearly loved. I felt fortunate to have experienced his transition into a man, one that wanted so desperately to step into shoes years to mature and responsible for him to fill, but he tried. He tried with everything he had, and I was so proud of him.

"Alex, honey," Lisa patted me soothingly on the back. "You're on the verge of a crying jag." She tried to smile, releasing me, and handing me a tissue.

"Sorry," I muttered wiping my nose. "I haven't allowed myself to lose it because I didn't want to fall apart in front of Hayden and the boys."

"You haven't cried yet?" Erik looked surprised.

"Yes, I cried, but not fallen apart like this." I reached for another tissue and wiped my nose again. "Hayden is a basket case, and my boys aren't much better. Henry cries every day and Max barely speaks." I shook my head.

"That's normal," Erik remarked sympathetically.

"Of course, it is. This is their first real experience with death, and they loved Mason very much." Lisa added.

"I know," the tears continued to fall, but I was regaining my composure. "I hate that I don't know what to say to them — any of them."

"Sweetie, there's nothing you can say. Nothing is going to make this better." I knew she was right, but her words left me feeling even more helpless.

"When is the funeral? We'd like to attend if that's okay." Erik returned from the kitchen with a glass of water handing it to me.

"Mason would like that. It's Thursday, but it's in Chicago." I told him before taking a drink. My throat was parched.

"That's okay. My mom is going to watch the kids." Lisa mentioned.

"I'll text you the address. I wrote it down last night after Marcie called with the details."

"How is she doing?" Lisa inquired.

"Much better than I would be. She's an amazing lady. I can see why Hayden was attracted to her." I admitted.

"You'd never hear me say that about Erik's ex." Lisa chuckled for the first time relieving some of the tension in the room.

"That's because there's nothing amazing about her except perhaps her drug addiction." Erik rolled his eyes.

"I don't know how she's holding it together. We talked for over an hour, and she kept saying she wanted everything to be perfect for her son." I brushed the tears off my cheeks with the back of my hand. "Marcie asked me how Hayden was doing. When I told her, she said he was the same way when his father passed away. It's his way of processing. She advised me to just be there for him but give him space to come to terms with it on his own."

"Is he moving back to the penthouse after the funeral?" Erik asked.

"I don't know. He hasn't mentioned it." I fumbled with the tissue. "He gave me his credit card yesterday and asked me to go buy him and the boys suits for the funeral and to pick myself up a dress or whatever I needed."

"That was generous." Lisa remarked.

"Hayden's always been very generous." I agreed. "I just wish there were something I could do for him. He just stares at the wall and occasionally scribbles in a notebook I'd left on the nightstand for school."

"Have you looked at what he's writing?" Lisa questioned.

"No," I took another drink.

"I would," she admitted. "It may give you some insight into how he's processing things."

"I know, but I was trying to respect his privacy." I shrugged.

"Now may not be the time for that." Erik added.

Chapter 18

ERIK'S WORDS FRIGHTENED ME when I drove home later that night. I wondered if I should sneak a look at what Hayden was writing. Even though Erik never said it, his tone left no doubt to his meaning — what if Hayden is suicidal and I didn't catch it, and something happened? I would never forgive myself.

The house was quiet when I returned. No one realized I had stepped out for a moment. I quickly texted Lisa the address to the church where Mason's funeral was to take place before I forgot.

I looked in on the boys and found them each sleeping peacefully. I lingered in their doorways longer than normal saying a silent prayer over them and that I would never experience the hellish nightmare Hayden was now engulfed in. I kissed each of my sons on the forehead and pulled their blankets up around them.

They were the most precious people in the world to me and I could not fathom a life without them in it. The thought of it terrified me to the core of my being.

Hayden was sleeping restlessly when I opened my bedroom door. He tossed and turned, mumbled, and kicked at the covers, but never opened his eyes. I brushed my teeth and changed into my pajamas keeping an eye on him as he fought through whatever was haunting his sleep.

Before climbing into bed, my eyes rested on the notebook and the implications of not looking took over my respect for Hayden's privacy. I checked to make sure Hayden was still asleep before I picked it up and took it into the living room.

My hands were shaking as I opened it. He'd only written a single page that was smudged by his tears. The other pages were nothing more than meaningless doodles and scribbles amidst the tear-stained sheets. I turned the pages back to see what he had written.

> *I am numb. I have no desire to get out of bed. I could care less about my company, Alex, my home, family, or living. My only son, my pride, my joy, my legacy has been stolen from me.*
>
> *All I can think about are those times I was too busy with work and missed my son's ball games. The times I should have been practicing with him but was attending business meetings instead. How many birthdays did I miss? Most. All the weekends I should have picked him up but didn't. How stupid I was that I too busy playing golf with a prospective client trying to build my empire for him instead of spending time with him. Now it was all for nothing.*
>
> *I thought there would be time. Time for us to get to know each other. Time to do things together — an endless amount of time to make it all up to him for being a lousy father. But somehow, we ran out of time.*
>
> *Every time I close my eyes I see him as a small boy, messy blond curls, running after me begging me to take him with me and me tell him no. It's haunting me. All I see is his little tear-streaked face with his little arms reaching for me.*
>
> *I just want to die.*

Tears poured down my face — the unimaginable regret, guilt, and pain were consuming the man I loved. He was on the verge of entering a very dark place and I wasn't about to let him. I could not lose him too.

I wiped my tears aside and blew my nose. Returning to my room, I set the notebook back in the same position I'd found it on the nightstand. I crawled beneath the covers causing Hayden to roll onto his side with his back towards me. I scooted over to him and wrapped my arms around his warm body.

"I love you," I whispered resting my head on the pillow behind his.

"Hum," his groggy voice responded.

"You are not alone, darling. I'm here. I'm always going to be here." I squeezed his body tightly to my own.

"I know," he patted my arm before rolling over to face me. "I feel lost." I could see his eyes glistening with tears in the moonlight coming in from the windows. "I don't know if I can do this."

"You can," I reached up and touched the side of his face. "I need you. Kennedy needs you. My son's need you."

"I wasn't there when my son needed me." He sighed heavily. "I was here with you. If I'd been home, my son would still be alive."

Hayden's words slapped me across the face. He looked at me for a moment before rolling back over and putting his back to me.

He blamed me. I could not believe it. I felt frozen in place — utter disbelief fell over me like a cactus blanket pricking every part of my body.

I wanted to react by lashing out. I wanted to scream at Hayden for insinuating I was somehow responsible for Mason's death. I wanted to slap him for saying something so horrific to me when I was hurting as well.

But I didn't.

I didn't do anything. The rational side of my brain, the side that had almost 3 years of psychology classes knew Hayden was deflecting his anger towards me. I knew he truly didn't blame me but, that he needed to release some of the pain that was destroying him, and I was an easy target.

Despite knowing that, his words still shattered my heart. I brushed the tears off my cheeks and wiped my nose with the back of my hand. I rolled over and scooted to the edge of my mattress.

A part of me wanted to roll over and cling to Hayden. I needed to feel the warmth of his body against mine. I longed for the comfort it always brought me. But tonight, his words had created an ice rink between us, and I was powerless to skate across it.

I felt so alone.

I dropped Billy off Thursday morning at Aaron's before the four of us headed back up to Chicago. The boys were wearing suits and I had packed an overnight bag although I wasn't sure where we would be spending the night.

Hayden hadn't been back to his penthouse since that horrible morning. I knew everything had been cleaned up, carpet replaced, but just the knowledge of Mason being murdered there was keeping Hayden away.

I couldn't blame him. I didn't want to walk into that place again. I couldn't imagine Hayden did. As a parent, I would sell immediately, but maybe that was just me.

Thick gray clouds hovered over us along our journey north. My sons sat in the backseat of Hayden's car, each staring out the side windows. They never uttered a word or asked their infamous 'are we there yet'. Their silence only verified their broken hearts. Every now and then I would hear one of them sniffle, but they never said anything.

I had offered to drive separately since I wasn't sure what Hayden's plans were in the days following. I had no idea what was going on with his company or who was taking care of things. I had spoken briefly to Kennedy, and I knew she was sporadically attending to work issues when necessary. She had told me the office was closed today and tomorrow for the funeral and burial to which I imagined everyone in the company would attend.

But Hayden insisted we take one vehicle, and I wasn't about to argue with him. We had barely spoken the last two days and he never mentioned his accusation of his perception of my role in Mason's death. And I didn't have the heart to bring the subject up. However, he still wasn't holding me like he used to when we went to bed, and it made me feel even more isolated from him.

We arrived at the church an hour before the showing was scheduled to begin. Marcie and Tony along with their children were already there. The children sat in the pews while their parent's spoke with the priest over last-minute details.

My boys huddled close to me as we stood awkwardly in the back of the sanctuary. Henry took my hand and squeezed it hard when he saw the casket sitting up by the alter. Thank goodness it was closed.

"Is Mason in that box?" My little man looked up at me with tear-filled eyes.

"Yes," I whispered.

He barely nodded but couldn't seem to take his eyes off the mahogany casket with gold handles.

I couldn't help but think how much Mason would hate it. It didn't reflect his personality at all and seemed wrong somehow. I imagine his mother selected it and didn't want to think about how others might share my opinion. Afterall, there comes a time in a child's life when their friends know them so much better than their parents. I wasn't sure exactly when that occurred, but I knew Max was probably closing in on it if he hadn't already reached it.

"How is he doing?" Kennedy's voice brought be back.

"Not well," I hugged her tightly. "How are you holding up?"

"Best to be expected, I supposed." She offered me her best smile. "And these must be Max and Henry." She hugged each of my boys. "I'm Kennedy, Mason's older sister. I've heard so much about you both." She reached over and tasseled Henry's hair making him smile for the first time in days.

"Mason talked about you too," Henry grinned. "I miss him." He stated before looking down at his feet.

"Me too," I noticed tears welling up in her eyes. "He really loved you three." She gently squeezed my arm, but it felt more like a dagger through my heart.

"We loved him dearly. Mason was an important part of our family." I brushed the fresh tears off my cheeks. "How is your mom and Tony?"

"Furious, grief-stricken," she sighed. "Mom wanted to go down to the jail and confront Megan, but Tony wouldn't let her. She's scheduled for arraignment on Monday, and I know my mom's gonna be there just to have her say if she can."

"I got a call from the Detective about it, but I didn't tell your dad. He hasn't been outta bed since we got to my place, and I didn't have the heart to say anything about it." I told her.

"It's probably for the best," she agreed.

"What's an arraignment?" Henry asked.

"It's where Megan is formally charged and bail is set, right?" Max spoke up.

"Who told you that?" I was surprised.

"I looked it up," he said casually with a shrug of his shoulder.

"Oh," I wasn't sure what to say. "You're brother's right." I squeezed Henry's arm gently.

"Are we going?" Max inquired. "I think we should."

"I don't think it's an appropriate place for you guys." I wasn't even sure how I felt about going to it.

"Are you going?" Max turned to Kennedy.

"Yes," she smiled nervously at me.

"Can I go with you?" Max looked at her.

"Me too," Henry piped up.

"Why do you guys want to go?" I questioned.

"Because I want to see the girl who decided to take away my best friend forever." Big tears rolled down Henry's cheeks.

I knelt in front of my little man and took a tissue out of my purse wiping them away.

"Sweetheart, that's not going to change anything." I told him.

"But I want to ask her why? Why did she have to kill him? I want to know why she took him away from us." His tears continued to fall, and I wiped his face again before pulling him to me.

"I know, baby. I understand." I assured him.

"I know exactly what you mean." Kennedy informed him. "I would love to know those answers too."

People started arriving and Kennedy walked us down front and showed us the pews that were reserved for us and Hayden. I looked around not sure where he had disappeared too.

"Kennedy?" I touched her arm stopping her as she started to walk back to the front to greet people. "Have you seen your dad?"

"No," she glanced around the room. "Would you mind looking for him? I need to go represent." She smirked slightly.

"I'll find him." I smiled at her before she left us, and I turned to my sons. "I need to go find Hayden before more people show up."

"Okay, we'll wait right here." Max shuffled in his seat.

"And Max," I started.

"I'll watch Henry." He rolled his eyes at me.

"Thank you," I smiled at my new teenager.

I walked back up the aisle scanning small groups of people trying to find the familiar face that I loved. But he was not there. I wandered out into the hallway, foyer, front steps, and out into the parking lot. Hayden had simply vanished.

I walked back through the front doors when a voice called out to me across the foyer.

"Alex," I walked towards Marcie. "Have you met Hayden's sister, Lauren?"

"No, I've not had the pleasure." I extended my hand. "I am pleased to meet you." She took my hand and pulled me into an embrace.

"I'm so happy to finally meet you. I just wish it were under different circumstances."

Lauren was a little taller than me with stylishly bobbed blond hair and the same emerald, green eyes as Hayden. She was wearing a tailored black suit with delicate heels and a white gold chain with a cross on it. She had an infectious smile and I liked her immediately.

"Where is my brother?" she asked.

"He's taking a moment alone." It was the simplest thing I could think of without admitting I couldn't find him. "I was just going to tell him that people are arriving."

"Of course," she patted my forearm. "I'll see you both inside."

"Please, excuse me." I smiled quickly before turning away.

I wandered down a long hallway where other rooms broke off with doors closed trying to figure out where he could have disappeared too. Then I noticed a door that was opened just a crack and peeked in. Hayden sat there on a folding chair with his elbows on his knees, head in hands. His back shook as he sobbed relentlessly.

I quietly entered the room and shut the door behind me. I knelt beside him and gathered him in my arms. Hayden wrapped his arms around me and buried his face in the nap of my neck.

"I can't do this," he cried. "I can't."

"Yes, you can." I rubbed his back. "Hayden, you are the strongest man I have ever met with the biggest heart I have ever encountered. Kennedy needs her Daddy if she is going to get through this. You must do this for her."

"I can't," he sobbed.

"You can. I know you can." I pulled back and cradled his face in my hands. "She needs her Daddy, and you need her." I whispered through my tears. "Do this for her."

Hayden nodded and got to his feet. I kept my arm around him guiding him to the door. His steps were sluggish as if he had been drinking all day despite not having a drop. He leaned heavily against me down the hallway and barely acknowledged those who tried to speak and offer comfort to him.

We entered the sanctuary, and all the pews were filled save the two spaces waiting for us up front beside Kennedy, Marcie, and

Tony. My sons were seated behind them with the rest of Marcie and Tony's children. People were standing across the back several rows deep and along the sides of the room.

I recognized a few of the faces of people I had seen Mason talking to on campus. Nick, Jerad, and Josiah were seated a couple rows behind us along with their girlfriends. I recognized Emma and Tricia, as Jerad's and Josiah's girlfriends, but I did not recognize the girl with long auburn hair that accompanied them assumingly with Nick.

We took our seats shortly before the priest began the services. Max reached up and put his hand on my shoulder. Tears welled up in my eyes and I placed my hand over his. Hayden sat beside me stiff as a board and expressionless. Marcie cried quietly as did Kennedy. Both ladies showed grace over devastating emotions that I knew was masking a shattered heart.

The priest concluded and Garth Brooks' song, *The Dance* began to play softly. It was a favorite song of mine and I couldn't think of a better song Kennedy could have chosen as an anthem for her brother. On the overhead screen, a slideshow of Mason's time on earth played out in a display of photos. I watched the majestic chronological exhibit from Mason's first photograph to the final one of him with Nick, Josiah, and Jerad laughing and being silly in their dorm room. It was heart wrenching and beautiful.

We waited patiently watching the procession of mourners make their way by the barrage of photos that documented Mason's short life, whispering memories, and sharing stories of good times spent with him. They lovingly touching his casket and said their goodbyes.

Lisa hugged Hayden and me when she and Erik passed us by. Behind her, Debbie and Mark also paused for a moment to offer Hayden their condolences. I had not realized Lisa had contacted Debbie and the four of them had made the journey to Chicago together. But I was touched by their love and friendship, and it meant everything to me to have them here.

Slowly, the room emptied and soon there were only Marcie, Tony, Kennedy, Hayden, and I left. Nick had offered to take my son's outside for some fresh air to which I was grateful. Henry and Max had never experienced a loss of someone they loved. It broke my heart to see the sorrow on their faces and know there was nothing I could do to erase it.

I walked with Kennedy to the front of the room. The first easel held a collage of photos of Mason from infancy through his elementary years. His formative years and sports were displayed in the second collection followed by prom, graduation, and shots of various holidays spent with family and friends. It was a heartbreaking display of the young life not fully lived.

Mason's short life was one filled with laughter, love, and time spent with family and friends. His mother had carefully documented every achievement and accomplishment he had ever made. It also pained me to notice how despite my years with Mason, any image of me and my sons with him were absent from the displays. I understood why — no one other than Kennedy and Hayden in Mason's immediate family knew the history of our sorted love triangle — for which I was profoundly grateful. Still, it pained me to realize that an important element of the last years of Mason's life were somehow eliminated. My son's, whom Mason loved dearly, were nowhere.

And while his mother and Tony knew Mason had been an important part of their young lives, they only knew a smidgen of the impact he had truly had on my sons and what his example and love had done for them. It saddened me to think of all the things running through my mind that I could never say, except for in the presence of Lisa.

Kennedy hugged her parents and made her way to the doors in the back of the room. Her footsteps echoed loudly off the walls of the empty room reminding me how alone I felt. I reached over and took Hayden's hand in mine squeezing it lovingly.

His eyes remained forward, unfocused, red, swollen, and tear-filled. I wiped off his face and kissed him softly on the cheek.

"Darling," I whispered. "It's time." The pallbearers comprised of Mason's Uncle's, and cousins who had quietly entered the room and stood along the back wall patiently.

Hayden nodded but made no effort to move. I put my arms around his shoulders and noticed that Tony was struggling with Marcie as well. Heartbroken as I felt, I could not fathom the unbearable pain and anguish of losing a child. And Hayden was living my worst nightmare.

I wanted more than anything to ease his pain, but I could not. It was a pain unlike anything in this world and I hated watching the man I had always viewed as a pillar of strength, collapse beneath of the weight of it. I pulled him closer to me and embraced him. His tears ran down my neck soaking my blouse, but I did not notice nor care. I simply wanted to hold him forever. It was all I could do for him.

Time passed without meaning and neither parent had moved. The priest walked to the side of the room and cleared his throat rudely letting us know it was past time for them to carry Mason out.

Marcie slowly rose to her feet and turned towards Hayden. In a gesture of parental solidarity, she reached out her hand to her ex-husband and the father of the son she had just lost.

Hayden wiped his face briefly, stood, and took Marcie's hand. Together they walked hand in hand up to the side of the cherry wood casket that held their child. Marcie wobbled and I watched as Hayden wrapped his arm around her waist steadying her. She leaned against him, weeping on his shoulder. He wrapped his arms around her and kissed the top of her head lovingly.

It was a sweet and kind gesture shared by two people who truly felt what the other was experiencing in a way that neither Tony nor I could. For some, I am sure, would not appreciate or perhaps even be upset by this display. But Tony and I both understood. We were parents. And we both knew that was a bond shared that could never be broken despite all the petty grievances, fights, or anything else.

I knew if, heaven forbid, I was standing in their shoes I would want Danny — I would need Danny beside me and as much as I love Hayden, the loss of a child would be something only Danny would feel as intensely as me. I physically shuttered at the imagine and quickly said a silent prayer.

Tony stepped back next to me and let the pallbearers through. They lifted Mason effortlessly and began descending the center aisle. Hayden and Marcie followed still leaning heavily upon each other. Tony took my hand with somber eyes as we stepped in behind them.

The hall and parking lot were lined with people as we passed and placed Mason in the long black hearse. Family members gathered the flowers and the pictures carrying them out to their cars to take them to the cemetery.

Tony and I climbed into the limousine behind Hayden and Marcie. Kennedy leaned in hugging her parents.

"I'm going to ride in the second limo with the kids." She told him. Her mother nodded in acknowledgement. "Your boys are with my siblings." She squeezed my hand briefly with a comforting smile.

"Thank you," I choked on the words.

"We're family." She leaned down and kissed me on the cheek. "We take care of each other." She whispered before disappearing and closing the door behind her.

Chapter 19

THE GRAVESIDE SERVICE WAS SHORT. I sat next to Hayden with Marcie and Tony on his other side and Kennedy beside me. The row behind us was filled with their children and my sons. The number of people present was a true testament to Mason's character and how much he had touched so many lives during his short time with us.

We remained in our seats long after the service was over and most of the mourners had left. I barely remembered Lisa and Debbie speaking to us before they left. Hayden had invited them to join us afterwards at Marcie's home, but they felt it should be just family.

I was disappointed and wanted to insist, but I didn't feel it was my place since it was being held at Mason's mother's home. I wanted to tell them I felt so alone, brokenhearted, scared, and uncomfortable, but I couldn't. It was not about me. This was for Hayden and his son — two men I loved dearly.

Kennedy took all the children and went back to the house to take care of things while the four of us stayed behind. Tony and I lingered in the background as we watched the people we loved say their final goodbye to the son they shared.

We rode to Marcie and Tony's house in silence. Hayden put his arm around me, but never uttered a word. His face was expressionless and a part of me wished I knew what he was thinking.

A short time ago I could almost anticipate his thoughts, his words, his behavior. But over the last week, he had turned into someone I did not know. His actions lately frightened me, and his words were not always kind. I tried to dismiss them as simply the grief and not him talking, but it was getting more difficult to do.

The street was lined with cars and people milling about the front yard when we arrived. The sky remained overcast threatening to rain, but no one noticed. The air was chilly with a bite of winter clinging onto the breeze when I climbed out of the back of the limousine.

I took Hayden's hand and noticed my son's sitting together on the double porch swing. Their solemn faces told me everything they were feeling. I squeezed Hayden's hand and leaned into him.

"I'm going to check on my boys. I'll be right back." He barely nodded as I let go of his hand and made my way through a sea of strangers to my sons.

Henry was clinging to his older brother. I could not recall a time when I had seen the two of them sitting so close to each other. I knelt in front of them and took each of their hands.

"Hey boys," I said softly. "How are ya holden up?" It felt like a trivial question.

"Can we go home now?" Henry asked in a small voice.

"Soon," I assured him. "It's been a long day. Are either of you hungry?"

"No," they replied in unison.

"Alex?" Hayden's voice came from behind me.

I stood up and turned towards him as he handed me an envelope.

"What's this?"

"Tickets," his voice was sharp. "I should have let you drive your car."

"I'm confused," I opened the envelope and removed three plane tickets.

"I called an Uber to take you to O'Hare."

"What?" Kennedy took the tickets out of my hand. "You're sending her home? Are you serious?" There was no mistaking the anger in her voice.

"I just think it's best," there was no emotion in voice.

"Alex has been taking care of you since Mason was taken from us. She's put everything on hold for you just to be here for you and this is how you repay the woman you claim to love?" Kennedy huffed at her father. "She loves you and you're asking her to leave?"

"It's fine," I stated before Hayden had the chance. "My sons are tired and flying will be faster than driving." Although, we all knew it was bullshit with check-in and security scans, driving was preferable.

"No, it's not fine. It's rude." Kennedy's eyes narrowed at her dad.

"Boys, are you ready?" I reached for the tickets she was holding, and Kennedy released them to me. I glanced at our departure time and then my phone — ninety minutes. "We need to get going."

"I'll drive you," Kennedy continued glaring at her dad.

"Can I have your keys? I would like to get our things out of your trunk." I asked Hayden.

"I have them. I drove his car back here from the funeral home." Hayden never uttered a word as she handed me his keys. He simply stared at the ground.

"Thank you," I headed towards his car parked in Marcie's driveway.

I expected him to follow me, to give me some sort of explanation for this treatment. But when I opened the trunk, only my boys had followed me.

"What an asshole." Max muttered under his breath.

"Max," I placed my hand on his shoulder. "Language."

"Well, he is," I could tell he was struggling to hold his temper in check.

"I agree," Kennedy approached us. "My car is over here." She reached down and grabbed Henry's backpack.

"We can take the Uber." The boys and I followed her down to the curb. "I don't want to take you away from your mom right now."

"No worries," She smiled at me opening the back of her SUV and placed our bags inside. "My mother has her hands full with my younger siblings and relatives."

"Thank you," I climbed in the passenger side after my boys got buckled in the backseat. "I appreciate this."

"I don't know why he's being such a dick." She shut her door and fired the engine.

"I do," I looked out the side window at Hayden still standing on the front porch. He didn't wave, nod, or make any gesture. I swallowed hard watching the love of my life slip away as Kennedy pulled away from the curb. "He blames me for Mason's death."

"What?" She huffed. "That's absurd. Why?"

"He told me it was my fault because if he had been home and not at my place, his son would still be alive." I told her Hayden's logic of the situation.

"He said that to you?" She glanced over at me while speeding up to the flow of traffic on the interstate.

"Yes," I sighed heavily.

"Max," Kennedy looked at my son in her rearview mirror. "You were right. He's definitely an asshole."

"I don't like him." Henry said in a low voice. "He's nothing like Mason."

"Well, I'm nothing like my dad either." Max declared. "Just because you're related doesn't mean you have to be the same. Right mom?"

"That is true," I smiled at my sons over my shoulder.

"I don't want to be like Hayden or my dad." Henry declared.

"I guess I'm more like my dad than my mom." Kennedy added turning towards me. "What about you?"

"I've spent my life trying to be nothing like either of my parents." To which both of my sons laughed.

"I wonder why," Max laughed easing the tension.

"Mason told me your mother was difficult." Kennedy smiled. "I guess she didn't approve?" She raised her eyebrow.

"That's an understatement." Max leaned forward. "She was rude to him every chance she got."

"And I haven't spoken to them in months." I reminded him.

"Don't you miss them?" Kennedy asked switching lanes.

"Sadly, not really." I shrugged. "Life is easier without all their drama and criticism."

"I can appreciate that." Hayden's daughter smiled at me. "My mom wasn't overly enthusiastic about me working for my dad after I graduated college. I think she liked to believe the reason he never remarried or got seriously involved with anyone was because he was still in love with her. She would try to be all casual about it when she would ask me questions about his personal life." She checked her mirrors and changed lanes again. "I never had the heart to tell her he never asked about her. She loves Tony. I know she does. But I don't believe she's ever gotten over my dad. He was her first love." She smiled.

"I understand. I have an ex-husband too." I sympathized.

"My dad got remarried last weekend." Henry pipped up.

"Really?" Kennedy raised her eyebrow again at me. "Do you like your new stepmom?"

"No," Henry answered immediately. "She's mean and her kids are brats." Kennedy giggled looking over at me.

"I've never met her." I raised my hands defenselessly.

"She's a dragon lady. I hate her." The disdain was evident in Max's voice.

"That's a bit harsh, isn't it? I mean, your mom will be my stepmom when she marries my dad." I immediately bit my bottom lip and closed my eyes. I knew she didn't know I had not discussed the possibility of marrying Hayden with my boys.

"What?" Max shot up straight with both hands on the console between us.

"You're getting married, momma?" Henry sounded like he was going to cry.

"Oh," Kennedy's hand went up over her mouth. "I'm so sorry. I thought they knew." She said in a low voice.

"Um, no." I inhaled deeply. "I hadn't talked about it with them yet because nothing is going to happen until after I graduate next year." I assured my boys.

"Hayden proposed?" Max held his breath and narrowed his eyes at me.

"Yes, we've talked about it. But as I said, nothing is going to happen until after I graduate next year. There's a lot of things to consider." I tried to explain.

"Such as," Kennedy waited for me to elaborate more.

"We live in two different cities, states even." I wasn't prepared to have to defend my position. "Our lives," I motioned towards my sons. "Are in Indiana. I love our small town. The boys are doing great in school. All their friends are there. My friends are there. Our lives are there. The boys' sports, and my school." I caught myself rambling. "We're not made for the city life or living in a penthouse. We need a yard. Billy's never even been to the city."

"Who's Billy?" Kennedy questioned.

"Our dog," rang in union from the backseat.

"Oh," she nodded.

"Does that mean you said no?" Henry inquired in a hopeful voice.

"It means there's a lot of details that would have to be worked out first." I attempted to ease their trepidation.

"I am sorry for the way my dad behaved today." Kennedy changed the subject for which I was grateful.

"He's mourning. It's understandable." Even though I didn't truly understand his rudeness.

"He's not acting like himself." Kennedy said more to herself than to me. "I'm worried about him."

"Me too. He's never treated me this way." I confessed.

"The shocked look on your face told everybody that when you saw the tickets." She informed me.

"Was it that obvious?" She nodded. "Great. I can't imagine how that came across to your family." I mumbled as Kennedy took the O'Hara International Airport exit.

"Believe me, you were not the one my family was judging." She glanced over at me. "Dad simply confirmed what my mom has always said about him."

"What's that?" I had to ask.

"That your son was right in his earlier assessment." She giggled and I couldn't help myself from joining her.

"Please keep an eye on him for me." I turned towards her as she pulled up to the curb on the departure side. "All kidding aside, your father is the love of my life, and I am worried about him."

Kennedy opened her door and I joined her at the back of her SUV. The boys climbed out the back door on the side of the curb while I helped Kennedy pull our overnight bags out. I set them on the curb and turned towards her.

"Thank you again for the ride." I leaned in and hugged her.

"It's been a difficult day. I'm sorry my dad had to be such an ass. I do appreciate everything you've done for him. I know he loves you very much." Kennedy squeezed me. "And I would be thrilled if you married my dad." She whispered.

"Thank you," I let her go feeling better.

Kennedy hugged both of my son's. From the look on Max's face, it was obvious he thought she was attractive. and I tried not to giggle.

"Please text me when you get home, so I know you made it safely." Kennedy placed her hand on my arm. "Try not to worry about my dad. I know he loves you. Just give him some time."

"I will," I gave her the best smile I could muster, trying to hide my broken heart.

A final wave from the boys, we took our bags and headed into the airport.

After a short flight and an even shorter Uber ride, the boys and I walked into the house. It felt eerily quiet without Billie there to greet us. I texted Kennedy while the boys took quick showers, ate a bowl of cereal for dinner, and went to bed without any fuss. It had been an exhausting day for all of us.

I stood under the hot water and felt all the tension in my body wash down the drain. My mind was consumed with worry — my boys, Hayden, our future, and I couldn't help but wonder if we even had one at this point.

I knew grief was a traumatizing thing. I knew it affected everyone differently. And the loss of a child would shatter a parent's soul. Certainly, his behavior was excusable. I knew it was. I knew I would forgive him for practically throwing my sons and I out of the family gathering this afternoon.

I felt positive that once the grief had lessened a bit and he was thinking more clearly, he would understand the absurdity to his logic and realize I was in no way responsible for the death of his son.

But the video.

That damn video haunted me. I felt guilty because deep down I knew I was partially responsible for Mason's death because he defended me and my honor. I hated the thought that Hayden should ever see that video.

But why would he? Surely, he would never ask the detective to see it. What parent would ever want to witness such a thing? And with evidence like that, I couldn't imagine there would ever be a trial.

But still.

I sat down on the bottom of the tub and wrapped my arms around my knees and wept. I missed Mason so much. I missed his easy smile. The sound of his laugh. The way he was when we'd first met and the friendship and love that we shared.

Mason had become such a staple in our lives. Even after our relationship had shifted, his insistence and persistence to remain in our lives and being such a strong mentor for my boys had in many ways grown stronger.

I laid my head upon my knees and wept. Time lost all meaning as I sat there shaking and shivering under the water that had long lost its heat. But the sobbing was uncontrollable. My shoulders shook, my head was throbbing, and I was beyond the point of consolable.

I finally reached up and turned the facet off. I slowly picked myself up off the bottom of the tub and climbed out. My body was covered in goosebumps. My muscles were stiff and achy. I wrapped a towel around my hair and slipped into some fuzzy flannel pajamas. I crawled into bed wishing Billie were there beside me.

Chapter 20

DAYS BLENDED TOGETHER AS THE boys', and I fell back into our familiar routine. None of us mentioned Mason or Hayden in the weeks that followed. Kennedy called every few days just to chat or give me an update on what the detectives were telling her about what was going on with Megan's case.

It seemed Megan's attorney were citing severe emotional distress brought about by the pregnancy and annulment of their marriage. Kennedy told me she had learned that Megan had been diagnosed with borderline personality disorder and as bipolar manic depressive which, according to her attorney, had been exasperated by getting off her medications for the health of her unborn child.

"Do you think they will get a jury to buy it?" Lisa asked a month later as we were curled up on the sofa in her living room.

"I don't know," I shook my head in dismay. "I hope not."

"It's Chicago, so there's a good chance they may." Erik added. "The murder of a wealthy white boy is not likely high on their priority list. I hate to say that, but it's true. Especially one that was murdered by a disgruntled ex."

"Do you believe it will make it to trial?" Lisa cracked open another pistachio. She was determined to lose a minimum of 10 pounds before the wedding.

"I doubt they will do anything until after the baby is born. A pregnant defendant is too sympathetic to a jury. When is the baby due?" Erik looked over at me.

"Well," I speculated. "June, maybe July." I shrugged. "Going off the timeline she tried to entrap Mason with, it would have to be sometime around there."

"She's currently in jail though, isn't she?" Lisa inquired.

"Yes. She was denied bail because of the video. Do you think they would show that video in open court?" A knot grew in my stomach.

"Probably not in open court, but perhaps closed court if it goes to trial." Erik stated.

"I would hate to think of Mason's family ever seeing it. It was horrible." I physically shuddered.

"Most likely due to its graphic nature, the judge would close the courtroom to everyone except the jury. So, it's highly unlikely they would ever see it." Erik tried to reassure me.

"That's a relief. I can't imagine." I couldn't bring myself to finish the sentence.

"Have you heard from Hayden?" Lisa gently asked.

"Nope. He hasn't called or texted. Kennedy said he hasn't been back to work either. She's been running everything and it's taking a toll on her." I explained.

"I think it's great you two have hit it off so well." Lisa lightly touched my arm. "I'm sure it's a great comfort to her."

"To us both," I smiled. "She's been checking on Hayden a couple times a week under the guise of work-related questions, but she said he's mostly sitting in the dark watching Netflix."

"Have you considered going up there to talk to him?" Erik questioned.

"I offered, but Kennedy thought I should give him more time." I understood her reasoning, but it still hurt when she said it. "Besides, I haven't been feeling too hot."

"You're sick?" Lisa sounded alarmed.

"No. I wouldn't have come over if I were sick." I playfully smacked her shoulder. "I'm just nauseated. It's probably my nerves because of Hayden." I quickly dismissed the claim.

"Are you sure?" She raised her eyebrow at me, and Erik laughed.

"Yes. I'm positive. It's lasted more than a week and the boys are fine." I stuck my tongue out at her. "Good grief."

"Okay," she sighed. "You can't blame me for double checking. I don't need a house full of sick kids."

"I'm not sick." I declared.

"Maybe you're pregnant." She laughed causing Erik to snort.

"That's just rude." I flashed her my middle finger. "My tubes are tied, remember?"

"When did you get your tubes tied?" Erik's question caught me off guard.

"When Henry was born." I looked at him inquisitively.

"So, what? About nine years ago?" He smirked.

"Yeah, why?" His smirk made me nervous.

"Are you on the pill or any other form of birth control?" Lisa joined in.

"No. My tubes are tied." I reiterated.

"I thought you guys always used condoms." Lisa stated.

"Mason and I always did without fail. Hayden and I did up until around Christmas, but then we ran out and I don't know," I shrugged. "Didn't buy anymore because we were together and talking about marriage."

"You do realize that some physicians say that the odds of getting pregnant after a tubal ligation are as low as one in two-hundred." Lisa had this shit-eaten grin on her face.

"What? No. That's not possible." I shook my head. "We were careful." I laughed without humor. "And when did you get your medical degree?" I narrowed my eyes at Lisa.

"Erik and I have been doing research. We want to have a baby." She grinned from ear to ear.

"That's wonderful," I leaned over and hugged her. "I'm so happy for you both." I turned and hugged Erik. "I think that's great."

"Am I crazy?" she asked.

"Definitely," I chuckled. "That's what I love about you. But didn't you have your tubes tied too?"

"Yes, that's why we're going to do IVF." Erik joined back into the conversation.

"For the record, I am going to laugh my ass off when you have four or more babies." I could barely get the words out from laughing at them.

"We're not doing more than two fertilized eggs at a time. I was adamant about that." She smacked my shoulder. "I am not a baby factory."

"No one expects you to be, my love." Erik scooted over and put his arm around her and made a goofy face at me.

"Well guys, it's getting late." I glanced at the time on my phone. "It's after six and I need to get the boys some dinner." I got to my feet and slipped my sandals back on. "Boys," I hollered towards the hall. "Let's go."

Lisa and Erik walked me to the door followed by the trampling of a half dozen little feet. I looked around at Lisa three children and Erik's duo and thought about the movie with Henry Fonda and Lucille Ball, *Yours, Mine, and Ours* and smiled to myself. Granted, they didn't have eighteen kids with one on the way, but by today's standards, six perhaps seven children were the equivalent.

It was a little after ten by the time I rounded up my evening and crawled into bed. Billie had happily resumed her position on the vacant side of my bed. She hopped up, did her little circle dance, and curled up in a ball with her head resting comfortably on the pillow. I reached over and scratched her behind the ears and kissed the top of her head.

"Good night, sweet girl." She looked at me with large sorrowful eyes. "I know. I miss him too." I hugged her tight.

I reached over to shut off the light but paused when my eyes landed on my cell. Maybe.

I hated myself, but I looked. No missed calls. No text messages.

I swallowed hard and set my phone face down on my nightstand. I flipped on the TV hoping the noise would drown out my feelings and block the voice in my head that was cursing Hayden. Unfortunately, the voice of my broken heart was even louder, and it was screaming out in pain.

I turned on the second season of *Lucifer*. Lisa had turned me on to it and I had fallen in love with the quirky narcissistic devil and the rest of cast. It had become my refuge and solace during Hayden's continued silence.

Two hours later the sound of my phone buzzing on my nightstand woke me from a dreamless sleep. Disoriented, it took a moment to realize where the intrusion was coming from. I groped around blindly until my hand found the annoyance.

"Hello," I rubbed my eyes trying to focus my thoughts.

"Hey doll, how are you?" Danny's voice rang through my ears.

"Do you know what time it is?" I grumbled.

"Um, it's 10:30 there. You don't normally go to bed until after 11:00. I didn't mean to wake you."

Ever since the funeral, the boys and I had been retiring early. The sad thing was is that each of us were exhausted by the end of the day and were eager to go to bed.

"We've been going to bed early." I mumbled.

"How are the boys?" I was touched by the sound of actual concern in his voice.

"Coping, a bit better than me most days. How was your honeymoon? Where did you go?" I attempted to change the subject.

"Well," he laughed without humor. "That's a long story. The wedding sort of went to shit when I allowed the boys to leave."

"What happened?"

"My parents were at their hotel when I spoke to you and didn't know I'd put the boys on a plane home. When they found out my dad was pissed but my mother went ballistic. The argument escalated, things were said and well, let's just say everything was cancelled, we left Amanda's kids with her parents, and we drove to Vegas." Danny summarized.

"Did you get married by Elvis?" I giggled. The idea of Danny getting married in Vegas was absurd.

"No," he scoffed at the very thought. "At least we got to enjoy our honeymoon in St. Thomas."

"St. Thomas? Damn I'm jealous." I mocked playfully.

"We were two broke kids when we got married."

"Don't remind me." I rolled over and hugged the empty pillow beside me.

"Are the boys still upset with me?"

"No. I explained everything to them."

"How did they handle the funeral?"

"About as you would expect. It was horrible."

"How are his parents? How did you explain your relationship with Mason? I would imagine they had dozens of questions." Danny rambled.

"Neither of them is doing well. They're divorced and his moms remarried. I've spoken with his older sister and she's more concerned with their dad. He's still not returned to work." I tried to be as evasive as possible.

"That's understandable. I can't imagine what he's going through. To lose a son — was Mason his only son?" Danny sounded sympathetic.

"Yes," I choked.

"As a father, as a parent," I heard him swallow the lump in his throat. "I cannot fathom."

"I know," I admitted. "I've been having a hard time even letting Max go over to Aaron's by himself. When Henry wanted to hang out with Logan earlier, I not only drove him, but stayed there with him. Plus, brought Aaron and Max with us. I'm having a hard time letting them outta my sight."

"Don't suffocate them, Alex." Danny attempted to lighten his voice. "They'll eat you alive for it."

"You're right." Tears stung my eyes. "I know you're right. It's just that," I couldn't bring myself to finish the sentence.

"Alex, you study this crap. Your behavior is normal. You just lost someone you care about and as much as I hate to admit it, Mason was someone you and the boys loved very much. How could it not affect you all?

"It's just so hard to believe he's gone. I keep waiting for his car to pull up in the driveway or for him to show up at one of the boy's practices. I know it's ridiculous, but I keep waiting." Just as I keep waiting for Hayden to call — both of which I know in my heart are not going to happen.

"Also, perfectly normal." He tried to assure me.

"No. No, it's not. None of this has been normal, Danny and it's all wrong." The flood gates opened.

"Alex," he tried to break through the sobbing. "Alex?" He gave me a moment. "I understand this has been hard."

"You don't get it," I blubbered. "And I can't tell you. And I hate that I can't tell you." I sobbed.

"You can tell me anything." He tried to sound comforting.

"I used to be able to," I cried. "For years you were my best friend. I could tell you anything. But that was years ago. And I miss my best friend." I had no idea what came over me, but I completely fell apart.

"What is going on, Alex? This isn't like you." He sounded concerned.

"I can't tell you," I reached for a tissue and blew my nose. "I'm just being stupid. I'm sorry."

"Talk to me, doll. You never fall apart like this. You're starting to worry me."

"I'm sorry. I'm just tired," I conveniently blamed. "I'm rambling."

"Alex?" Danny asked being uncharacteristically sincere.

"Danny. Don't. Seriously, just don't." I brushed the tears off my cheeks and sniffled. "I appreciate your concern. I really do. But you know me, I'll be fine. Really, I am."

"Are you done?" He chuckled.

"What?" his question caught me off guard.

"Are you done?" He repeated.

"I don't know what you mean." My head was pounding.

"When you get overwhelmed, you ramble incoherently. You hold everything in, put up your iron façade, and then it sneaks up on you when you least expect it. Something small will happen and the concrete fortress you've build around yourself comes crumbling down." Danny explained.

"Thanks," I grumbled wiping my nose on a tissue.

"I'm not saying it to be mean, Alex. I simply know you. You take on so much that eventually something is bound to give. But as soon as you fall apart, you immediately stand back up and rebuild your fortress. You've always been that way. It's how you cope. You just hate to be vulnerable. You seem to believe it makes you weak. But it honestly doesn't, you know."

"Seriously, Danny?" I mumbled.

"I blame your parents. You were never allowed to be a child."

"Don't psychoanalyze me," I said under my breath. "Right now, I'm sure I'd be diagnosed as crazy."

"Is that a clinical diagnosis?" The pitch of his voice forced me to giggle.

"It should be," I laughed.

"No, doll. You're grieving. I'm not a shrink, but that would be my professional opinion." He speculated. "It's good to hear you laugh."

"It feels good to laugh," I sighed. "Thank you, Danny."

"My pleasure, doll. Despite everything you think about me, I do care. And I always will."

"Ditto"

"Sweet dreams, doll."

"Good night, Danny."

Chapter 21

SPRING FLOURISHED INTO SUMMER along with long humid days. I finished my finals a couple weeks before the boys finished up their school years. Both were finally returning to their old selves and now frequently laughed or joked about something they thought Mason would have found humorous or enjoyed.

It felt wonderful to bring that spirit back into the home. It was almost like a piece of Mason was still with us and it lessened the pain just a smidgen to hear my boys talk about him.

Debbie was hosting her annual Memorial Day barbeque of close family and friends. Her father and Mark were veterans, so this was a sacred holiday for her family. She and her immediate family always spent the morning putting flowers and flags on veteran headstones to honor those who paid the ultimate price for our freedom. I always admired her for doing so and had recently started joining her and her family on these trips and taking my sons along, so they understood the true meaning behind the national holiday.

Max was always intrigued by military and history. It was something we had in common thanks to my father. Although my father had never served, all of my uncles and both my grandfathers had. I held a great deal of respect for service members.

We returned to Debbie's shortly before eleven in the morning. The sun was blazing down upon us and there was not a cloud in the sky. The midwestern weather went from one extreme to the other in a matter of hours. A heat streak this early in the season set the forecast for longer days to come. The humidity started at sixty percent this morning and climbing.

The boys and I ran home to change into our swimsuits. I could hear the boys rustling around in their rooms while I slipped into my red and white bikini. I climbed into an old pair of jean shorts and grabbed my white flip flops out of the closet. With my hair pulled up in a messy bun on top my head, I pulled the potato salad out of the frig I'd made last night and the three of us headed back across the street.

Mark had spent the last week opening their pool and preparing it for the summer season. The water was crystal blue, and the kids were anxious to dive in. Mark agreed to stay outside, get the grill going, and keep a watchful eye on the kids while Debbie and I prepared the food.

Debbie's parents were relaxing on the sunporch with their sweet tea and ceiling fan turned on high. They were a sweet couple who I dearly loved. They had adopted me years ago and I never thought twice about addressing them as mom and dad. I knew it wouldn't be long before they retreated into the comfort of the air conditioner once lunch was served.

"How are you holding up?" Debbie asked as soon as we were alone in the kitchen. "I'm sorry I haven't been over. I figured you needed some time."

"I'm okay," I have her my standard answer.

"I haven't seen Hayden's car lately. How is he doing?"

"He still hasn't returned to work. Kennedy is starting to get really concerned. She said he's barely functioning." I put the potato salad on the counter.

"Perhaps he should see a grief counselor." She suggested peeling the hardboiled eggs for the deviled eggs.

"I suggested that to her a month ago," I shrugged.

"Have you suggested it to him?" She looked over her shoulder at me.

"I haven't spoken to him." I was dreading this conversation. It always picked at that open wound and made me want to break into tears. I was hoping the anger part of grief would happen soon because it seemed everything made me cry these days.

"Seriously? Since when?" Her face held an expression of shocked mixed with pity. I hated that.

"Mason's funeral when he shoved my boys and I on a plane right after the burial." I couldn't hide the distain in my voice.

"What an asshole," she stated through gritted teeth.

"That appears to be the general consensus." I chuckled remembering Max's assessment of Hayden.

"I don't get it," she waved her hands around for emphasis spraying droplets of water about the counters. "Not even three months ago he was begging you to marry him and then he just drops you like yesterday's news?"

"That's putting it nicely," I smirked trying to keep my exterior shell from cracking. "I can't imagine the pain of losing a child and I pray to God I never do," I quickly knocked a couple times on the wooden cutting board — silly and trivial, I know, but I wasn't playing with fate on that one. "But I can't imagine pulling away from everyone and everything that I love at a time when I would need them the most." I tried to reason.

"I would think so too," she sighed. "How are you doing?"

"I'm breathing," I shrugged. "I'm smiling." I flashed her a big fake smile. "You know me."

"Yeah, that's why I'm asking." She threw me a coy look over her shoulder.

"Losing Mason has been devastating. But compounding it with losing Hayden, with him treating me and my boys that way, cutting me out of his life — I don't know if I will ever forgive him for blaming me for Mason's death." I shook my head in dismay. "He has no idea how much he hurt me."

"Have you called him?"

"Nope."

"Not once?" her eyes grew big.

"Not even a single text." I shrugged.

"Wow," Debbie mouthed.

"And from what Kennedy has told me about him, I doubt he's even noticed."

"I can't imagine Hayden falling apart like that. I always thought of him more as a pillar of strength." Debbie raised her eyebrows sympathetically.

"Me too, but Mason was his only son. And the two didn't have the best relationship. Hayden is beating himself up about how much of Mason's life he missed out on. Which according to what Mason told me, was a lot." I explained.

"So, he's consumed with guilt and regret."

"Consumed is an accurate identifier." I pinched my lips together in consideration.

"Tell me the punch is on ice?" Lisa's voice rang through the house as her collective bunch came running through the kitchen peeling off their clothes revealing swimsuits beneath before tearing out the back door to the pool. "I need a drink." Lisa and Erik appeared in the archway.

Her haphazard appearance made Debbie and I laugh and eased the tension that hung over the kitchen for the last half hour for which I was grateful.

"Of course," Debbie crossed over to the frig and pulled out the oversized pitcher she had brewed earlier in the day. "It wouldn't be a cookout without it."

"I love you," Lisa eagerly filled a plastic cup.

"Easy, dear." Erik cautioned her. "You need to eat first."

"Yes, darling." She winked at him before he disappeared out the back door.

"Aw, how cute." I giggled while Lisa rolled her eyes at me.

"The kids have been bouncing off the walls all morning. They were so excited about coming over today." Lisa took another long gulp before setting the cup on the counter. "They were driving me nuts."

"And you want more?" I tried to stifle a laugh.

"Like you have room to talk," she narrowed her eyes in a menacing playful way. "Please tell us, Ms Rose. When was your last period?"

"Oh, shut up and mind your own business." I tossed a dishtowel at her.

"Hold on," Debbie spun back towards us. "Are you pregnant, Alex?"

"No. Of course not" I glared at Lisa. "I had my tubes tied after Henry was born. Besides, everyone's body reacts differently to grief and stress."

"So, when was your last period? Have you taken a test?" Debbie leaned back against the counter. "You do realize it is possible. Weren't you using any protection?"

"I was only sleeping with the man I intended to marry. And yes, we were using condoms up until the holidays. We ran out and just didn't bother to buy anymore. We were in a committed monogamous relationship." I touted.

"Were?" Debbie raised her eyebrows. "Do you really think it's over?"

"I don't know how I couldn't," my eyes dropped to the floor. "He blames me for Mason's death. He hasn't called or texted since he shoved my son's and me on a plane right after the burial. I believe he's made his position clear."

"Are you sure you don't want to take a trip up there and talk to him? You two have been through so much together. Surely, you can survive this." Lisa reached over and touched my arm gently.

"I thought so, but obviously he doesn't share my views." I shrugged trying to hide the dept of my broken heart. "The last thing I want to do is grovel on his doorstep."

"True, that would be humiliating." Debbie empathized. "I believe he just needs more time."

"More time?" Lisa almost shouted. "Bullshit. What he needs is a good kick in the ass. And I'd enjoy being the one to do it."

"Well, you know what they say; easy come, easy go." I couldn't even make my voice sound nonchalant from the tears welling up in my eyes. "Damn it," I looked up at the ceiling willing myself not to break.

"It's going to be all right." Debbie came over and put her arm around my shoulders. "It'll just take time."

"The silly thing is, I'm not mad at him. I'm mad at myself for believing in him." Tears overflowed despite my attempt to stop them. "I'm sorry. I don't know what is wrong with me. I cry at the dop of a hat these days." I hastily brushed them aside. "If you'll excuse me, I forgot something at the house. Can you please keep an eye on my boys for a minute?" Lisa nodded. "Thanks."

I rushed out the front door and ran across the street. The asphalt burned my bare feet as I realized too late that I'd left my sandals by the pool. But I didn't care. I was embarrassed, humiliated, and angry with myself for falling apart in front of my friends. I hated that I had no control over my emotions lately and didn't want to set my boys back after they seemed to finally be accepting Mason's death and starting to enjoy life again.

I collapsed across my bed and sobbed. A mix of emotions ran through me. I was so angry with Hayden. I was certain he would have called or come by weeks ago and apologized for his ghastly behavior. But days turned into weeks and now weeks into months and nothing.

I felt so foolish for believing all the lies he spewed at me. I had believed in him wholeheartedly — in us. And out of our entire relationship, I felt the only thing I had accomplished was hurting Mason and driving a wedge between father and son. I was grateful they had mended their differences before we lost Mason, but still Mason had endured the weight of betrayal from both his father and me.

I laid on my bed for a while and cried until I had no tears left. The pile of tissues scattered across my bed laid testament to my shattered heart. I could only hope that someday sooner rather than later, I could hear his name and remember our time together with a smile instead of tears.

Max took off to Aaron's right after breakfast. I had spoken with his mother the night before and asked her if she would mind keeping an eye on him while I went to the doctors. She was kind enough to accept and offered to watch Henry. But I explained that he was staying over at his best friend's house, and I would retrieve him after my appointment.

I took advantage of their absence and turned on my favorite playlist. The music blasted through the house as I began to dance around like a fool. I had a couple hours until my appointment and for the first time in months I was feeling more like myself.

Three weeks had passed since Memorial Day and the June heat was dripping with humidity. I had stripped down into a tank top and panties while I cleaned up the house. It took me less than two hours to sweep, vacuum, mop, and dust the house. Plus, clean the two bathrooms. I felt rather proud of myself for getting so much accomplished before I had to get ready.

I languished in the shower allowing the hot water it to melt the tension out of my muscles. I tried not to worry about my appointment. But I feared I couldn't get my nerves to settle down and it was wreaking havoc on my stomach and delaying my periods. I mentioned it to Michelle the last time we spoke, and she was certain my nerves were causing my stomach to produce too much acid and therefore, the root cause of my never-ending nausea.

I thew on a light pale-yellow sundress with spaghetti straps and little white daises printed on it and my white sandals. Spinning in front of my full-length mirror, I decided it was perfect for the hot sunny day.

I brushed out my long locks and thought seriously again about cutting it off into a more stylish look. But a part of me loved my long thick ebony shrine and it had been my crowning glory for as long as I could remember. I loved leaving it down, but it wasn't practical given this heat.

So, I pulled it up in a messy bun and topped it off with the necklace Hayden got me for Christmas. I complemented it with small silver hoop earrings and diamond studs. Thanks to my golden tan from lazy hours in Debbie's pool, I really didn't require much makeup. I topped myself off with a bit of mascara and pink lip gloss. I looked very elegant and summery. Satisfied, I took a deep breath knowing I'd feel better at the end of the day.

Dr. James, our family physician came bustling in with his tablet in hand.

"Good afternoon, Alex. How are you doing today?" He sat down on the little stool with wheels and put his tablet on the counter.

"I'm good. How are you?" I smiled trying not to appear as uncomfortable as I felt sitting on the table in the hospital gown.

"It says here you've been nauseated for the last couple months." He read off the tablet screen. "But your temperature and blood pressure look good." He stood up and approached the table.

"Are you hurting anywhere? Sore throat? Any diarrhea? Sharp pains? Shortness of breath?"

"No. No. Nothing of the sort."

He put his stethoscope buds in his ears. "Mind if I listen?" I nodded. "Take a deep breath."

"Oh, that's cold." The icy face touched the middle of my back.

"Sorry. Another deep breath." He moved around to my chest. "Just breath normal." After a couple breaths he removed the ear bud and draped the stethoscope around his neck. "Everything sounds good."

"Well, that's good, isn't it?"

"Will you please lie back?" He pulled out the extension on the end of the table to support my legs.

I laid down feeling extremely exposed despite knowing the ridiculous gown covered more of my upper torso than my sundress. I took a deep breath and closed my eyes while Dr. James poked around on my abdomen.

"Alex, when was your last menstrual cycle?" I sat up as he sat back down on the little stool.

"I don't know." I tried to recall. "I believe it was in February before Mason." I could bring myself to finish the sentence.

"Did you two break up?" I had known Dr. James most of my life. He was a friend of my father's and sometimes it was a mixed blessing and a cruse.

"I am afraid Mason was passed away in March." Those simple words crashed my sunny day into a brick wall and the dam broke.

"Oh, I do apologize." He handed me a box of tissues. "I was unaware."

"I'm sorry," I brushed the tears off my cheeks feeling foolish. "That's why my nerves have been such a mess."

"I can understand." He cleared his throat. "How did he pass? Car accident?"

"No," I shook my head. "If it had been, I could accept that better, I suppose. But Mason was murdered by his ex."

"Oh dear," he scratched his chin. "Was his name Mason Brooks?" I was so shocked I almost fell off the table.

"Yes," I mumbled.

"My wife and I have been following the story on the news. I had no idea he was your boyfriend."

"We lived together for a couple years. My sons and I loved him very much." I sobbed.

"I am so sorry, Alex."

"Thank you," I wiped off my face. "I think the stress of it has just messed up my system. I've been an emotional wreck and cry at the drop of a hat."

"I'm going to have Georgia come in and draw a little blood. I just want to double check your levels and such." He patted me on the shoulder. "You can go ahead and get dress. She'll be in shortly and we'll call you in a couple days if there's any concern."

"Okay," I nodded. "Thank you."

"Let me know if there's anything else you need." He closed the door behind him.

Chapter 22

THE FOLLOWING WEEK I PULLED into the parking lot at the baseball diamonds. Lisa and Erik were corralling their horde of children. Logan and Erik's son, Tanner took off running towards the diamonds with Lisa hollering at them to watch the cars. I giggled to myself getting the rest of Henry's gear out of the trunk.

Bat and glove in hand, Henry ran after them. It felt wonderful to see him so happy and carefree once again.

"Can I have a couple bucks?" Max cornered me by the trunk with Aaron beside him.

"How can you two possibly be hungry? You both just ate dinner." I wrinkled my eyebrows at him.

"Come on, please. We need a snow cone. We're melting out here." Max complained.

"Seriously?" I was interrupted by my phone buzzing in my purse. "Dang it. Give me a second." I told them.

"But mom," Max started.

"Hello," I held up my finger to Max.

"Ugh," he and Aaron walked off towards the field.

"Hello, Alex." I recognized her voice immediately.

"Hello Georgia, how are you?" I leaned against the trunk waiting for her to lecture me on my cholesterol levels.

"I'm doing well. I apologize for interrupting your evening, but I wanted to call you before I left today. I got your bloodwork results back today." She explained.

"I thought you would have had those back long before now." I was confused.

"I did, but I thought the results must be wrong, so I had them run it again." She sighed heavily. "And a third time." She admitted.

"Wow, that good huh?" I chuckled fighting the sudden urge to vomit.

"More shocking, I guess." Georgia fumbled for words. "You're pregnant, Alex."

"What? No." I laughed nervously. "How? That's not possible." I declared.

"Considering you have two sons I'm going to assume you already know the how."

"I had a tubal ligation after Henry was born." I explained. "It's not possible. They must have switched my blood with someone else's at the lab by mistake."

"That's why I had them run it three times." She countered.

"But if my name was on the wrong vial, then it wouldn't matter how many times they ran the text. The results would still be wrong if they're using the wrong blood." I rationalized.

"I am afraid not. It was your vial. I checked it myself. It was your name with my initials on it." She explained.

"But Dr. James never said he was running a pregnancy test." I argued in disbelief.

"After your examination, he suspected, but didn't want to say anything because you were so upset. Especially considering the recent death of the father." Her words hit me like a ton of bricks.

I fell back against the car as if the weight of the world crashed down upon me. How many others were bound to leap to the same conclusion? How could I possibly explain this child was Hayden's and no possibility of being Mason's. My head was suddenly throbbing with an instant migraine.

"I see," I gasped. "But I my tubes were tied after Henry was born." I argued.

"Ideally, a tubal ligation is permanent. But it seems there is always a chance. Some physicians say the odds are one in two hundred after seven years." She informed me.

"Oh, good Lord, that would have been helpful information to know. I would have just had everything removed if I thought this was possible." I stated sarcastically.

"You're not the first lady I've heard say that." She chuckled. "Is Dr. Johnston still your OB/GYN?" Georgia inquired in a calm voice that only made me feel like vomiting.

"Yes, of course."

"Would you like me to call his office and set up an appointment for you as soon as possible? I would be happy to send them the results of your bloodwork as well."

"That would be helpful, Georgia. I would appreciate it." I cleared my throat and tried to speak clearly. "Thank you."

"Great. I will text you once its set. Please let me know if there is anything else you need."

"A cyanide tablet," I mumbled making her laugh.

"Congratulations, Alex." She said cheerfully.

"Yeah, thanks!" I huffed before ending the call and dropping my phone into my purse.

My head was killing me. I closed my eyes as the world began to spin around me. Suddenly, the nausea set in with wretched undertones. I rushed over to the edge of the parking lot and rid myself of everything I had eaten.

I slumped down on the curb and wiped my mouth off with a tissue. I rinsed my mouth out with some water and spit it out in the grass. I looked around hoping no one saw me. I took a couple peppermint Altoids out of my purse hoping they would hide my incident and settle my stomach in the process. I felt horrible.

My mind was whirling. Pregnant. How could I be pregnant? I brought my knees up to my chest, hugged them, and buried my face. Tears poured down my cheeks. This was the worst possible news I could have received.

I cried for the bachelor's degree I'd poured blood, sweat, and tears into possibly washing away. For the reaction of my sons — how could I possibly explain this to them? How would they take it? For the financial strain this was going to put on me.

The muggy evening left a thin layer of sweat on my skin. I finished off the rest of my water but could not bring myself to get up despite hearing the whistle blow indicating the beginning of Henry's game. I felt selfish but did not care.

It seemed my entire adult life I have always taken care of everything and everyone — sometimes at the expense of my own happiness. But I could never begrudge my boys anything. They were my life, the foundation upon everything I build my life upon.

But another child? Starting over? Diapers. Late night feedings. Potty-training. I could not fathom where to begin. I had gotten rid of all the baby things when Henry outgrew them. I was positive he would be my last.

My head ached terribly thinking about how I was going to financially pull this off. The boys and I were doing okay simply because I was careful. I had a low mortgage payment with a low interest rate thanks to the sizable down payment Danny and I had put on it when we bought it and the moneys, I put down on it from my divorce settlement when I refinanced it. Thankfully, I made decent money as a teaching assistant and most of my education was covered by multiple grants. But adding the expense of a baby and all that entailed frightened me to the core of my being.

I am not sure how much time I spent nurturing my own pity party, but I took a deep breath and finally stood up. I wasn't sure what I was going to do but I wasn't going to get anywhere sitting here on the curb feeling sorry for myself. I grabbed another bottle of water out of my car and took a long refreshing drink before I headed towards the diamonds.

I found Lisa and Erik seated about halfway up the bleachers. I climbed the steps slowly to join them. The scoreboard indicated they were in the bottom of the fourth inning. Henry was standing out there on first base. His white pants were already black in the knees, and I could see the sweat-stained dirt streaks across his face. I smiled to myself loving how happy he looked as he watched the batter intensely.

"Where have you been?" Lisa asked when I sat down.

"On the phone," I tried to sound casual. "Have you seen Max and Aaron?"

"Yes, I have been keeping an eye on them." She smirked.

"Thank you," I missed what she was saying.

"Your son seems to have gotten over his aversion to my daughter." She chuckled.

"Huh?" my eyes followed the direction she indicated. "Oh, God," there were Max and Aaron sitting on the bench of a picnic table talking with Brie and her friend who were seated on the table. "So, it begins." I rolled my eyes.

"I think I liked it more when your son insisted Brie had cooties." Lisa joked.

"I know I did."

"Who were you on the phone with?" Lisa leaned over and asked.

"Georgia, my doctor's nurse. She got the results back on my bloodwork." I tried to sound as casual as possible.

"Bad news?" She asked before she jumped up and started cheering Logan who had caught a fly ball to short stop.

"If you call being single, alone, and pregnant bad news, then yes." My voice dripped with sarcasm.

"What?" She froze mid-cheer and stared down at me. "Are you serious?" I nodded. "I knew it!" She broke into hysterical laughter and hugged me tightly. "This is wonderful! I'm so happy for you!"

"What's this?" Erik leaned across Lisa. "What's going on?"

"Alex is pregnant!" Multiple heads spun around and stared at me.

"Hush," I smiled uncomfortably. "The boys don't know."

"Oh," she grimaced. "Sorry. When are you going to tell them?"

"Not until after I see Dr. Johnston. Georgia is making an appointment for me." I explained. "There's no need to upset them before I have all the details."

"Are you going to keep it?" Erik asked in a low voice.

"Yes. Of course." I wasn't surprised by the question.

"Are you going to tell Hayden?" Lisa looked at me with sympathy.

"Why would I?" Truthfully, until that moment I had not thought about it.

"Because it's his child too." Erik stated.

"Hayden has made it clear he doesn't want to be with me. Therefore, I am under no obligation to tell him." I shrugged.

"But don't you talk to Kennedy? I was under the impression that you two had gotten rather close. Are you going to tell her?" Lisa added.

"I adore Kennedy. And yes, we've become close friends, but still, I don't think I should tell her." I reasoned. "It would only cause problems."

"But how are you going to hide it forever from her?" Erik questioned. "It seems dishonest if you consider her a good friend."

"Perhaps, but it's not likely I will ever see her again. She's so busy with running Hayden's business and as far as what I've been told, he's still not back at work. Do you really think he's in the right frame of mind to deal with this?" I looked at them inquisitively.

"I still think you should let that be his decision. He has a right to know. What if you're having a boy?" Erik pointed.

"Boy or girl, does it matter?" I rationalized. "Hayden blames me for the death of his son. He rudely shoved me and my sons on a plane immediately after the burial. He has not phoned or texted me in three months. I believe he has made his feelings crystal clear."

"Anyway, I think it's wonderful." Lisa attempted to ease the sudden tension surrounding us.

"I'm glad you're happy about it." I snorted.

"How could I not be? I'm going to love watching your skinny ass grow fatter each month!" She burst out laughing.

"I hate you," I shoved her away playfully. "Seriously though, please don't say anything to anyone until I get a chance to tell the boys."

"I promise," Lisa pretended to zip her lips closed and Erik nodded.

"Thank you."

Before the week was out, I found myself in the stirrups. Dr. Johnston was my favorite physician. He delivered Max, but unfortunately, his wife went into labor the same day as I did with Henry and a young intern ended up delivering him and tying my tubes afterwards. And while it could not have been helped, I also could not help but wonder if that small detail somehow contributed to my current situation.

"How are you feeling?" Dr. Johnston asked after he finished his examination.

"Honestly?" I chuckled sarcastically.

"Do I dare ask?" He raised an eyebrow.

"Pissed," I snorted. "How could this happen? I had my tubes tied after Henry was born."

"It's rare," Dr. Johnston shrugged one shoulder. "But not impossible nor unheard of, especially when someone with little experience at the helm."

"Are you saying he messed up my tubal ligation?" Now I was really perturbed.

"No. No. I'm not saying that at all. I wasn't there and the only way we would know for sure would be to do an exploratory surgery which isn't covered by insurance. And it wouldn't do you any good now." He laughed lightly.

"You know this never would have happened if your wife was a bit more considerate of others," I said with a snarky tone and laughed. "How is Renee'?"

"She's doing well. Driving me crazy, but hey, that's the joys of marriage, right?" He chuckled.

"It's been so long I can't remember to tell you the truth."

"So, the baby's father?" The same eyebrow went back up.

"Long story short, he proposed. I wanted to wait until after I finished school. He wanted me to transfer to Northwest. I wouldn't budge. We were at a standoff when his son was tragically killed. That was back in March. We haven't spoken since." I pushed back the tears and sighed heavily.

"And what have you decided?"

"I'm winging it. Nothing has been decided."

"Are you thinking of ending the pregnancy?"

"No. I simply want to have time to fully digest everything."

"I understand," he lightly patted my shoulder when he stood up. "I'm going to send in Becky to do a quick ultrasound so we can see where we're at. Since you had your tubes tied previously, you're at a greater risk for an ectopic pregnancy."

"Very well. Thank you."

I laid back on the table as Becky came in with her ultrasound machine. She made pleasant small talk and I tried to respond accordingly, but when she stopped in the middle and excused herself to get Dr. Johnston, my mouth went dry. I knew ectopic pregnancies could be dangerous if they weren't caught in time. Hopefully, this ultrasound meant it had.

Dr. Johnston entered the room with Becky and smiled kindly making me even more anxious. I watched her carefully as she pointed at the screen, but I couldn't make out quite what they were whispering.

"What's going on?" I studied the two of them carefully. "Is everything all right?"

"If I remember correctly, Alex. Twins run in your family, don't they?" Dr. Johnston smiled.

"My mother is an identical twin. I believe she told me there were like sixteen sets of twins on her side of the family." I swallowed hard. The fear I'd felt with my initial ultrasounds with both boys came crashing down upon me. "Why?"

"It looks like you're going to push that to seventeen." He laughed.

"What?" I shot upright. "No!"

"Now lie back," he gently pushed my shoulder down. "And I'll show you."

"Please tell me you're kidding." I closed my eyes.

"See," he tapped my arm with his finger. "Open your eyes, Alex." I complied. "Baby one. Baby two. Both look fine, good size, strong heartbeats." He couldn't stop grinning.

"Boys or girls?" I groaned.

"I'm afraid I can't tell yet. We should be able to tell by your next ultrasound in about six weeks."

"Oh, God." I moaned aloud.

"Everything looks wonderful. You're about 15 weeks and four days along and you're due December 2nd." He flipped the light back on and I sat up. "Thank you, Becky."

"It just keeps getting better and better." I complained as Becky wheeled the machine out and closed the door behind her.

"Alex, I've known you for a long time now. And I hope you know I don't simply view you as a patient. Our boys went to the same daycare and go to the same school. I like to think of us as friends."

"Thank you. I feel the same." I assured him.

"I am concerned," he sat back down on the little stool. "When do you graduate?"

"Next May," I raised my hands hopelessly and laughed. "Figures."

"I know you have a lot to think about, but you also have a lot of people who are here for you and willing to help you in any way possible."

"I appreciate that. Thank you."

"Get yourself dressed and I want you to immediately start taking your prenatal vitamins. Stop and pick some up on your way home."

"I will," I promised.

"Laura will set up your sext appointment. I will see you back in four weeks. Please let me know if you need anything beforehand."

Chapter 23

LISA STOOD ON THE PEDASTAL and twirled around. Her mother and I were sitting on the plush satin bench adding commentary to the dozen gowns she insisted trying on. Lisa had poured through countless magazines in the last couple months and remained clueless as to what she desired.

"I don't know," she twirled once more. "It makes my hips look to wide."

"Darling, you've had three children. You're as thin as a rail." Her mother was growing impatient.

"I think it's beautiful." Boredom had set in three gowns ago.

"Ummmm," she sighed audibly and climbed down. "Can you please unfasten me?" She stopped in front of the bench with her back to us.

"This one is on you. My arthritis cannot take any more of those eyelet buttons." Her mother elbowed me.

"Thanks," I winked and followed Lisa into the dressing room.

"How are you feeling?" She asked as I fumbled with the tiny buttons.

"Good."

"Darling?" Her mother poked her head behind the curtain. "It's later than I thought." She smiled curtly. "I hadn't thought you'd be so indecisive."

"Mother," Lisa growled.

"Never mind," she gestured. "But I must be going. I am meeting some friends for dinner."

"All right. Thank you, mother."

"Love and kisses," She blew her daughter a kiss. "Take care, Alex."

"Have a wonderful time, Mother." I called as she disappeared behind the curtain. "I adore your mom." I told Lisa.

"That's only because she's not your mother." Lisa stepped out of the gown and handed it to me.

"You wouldn't have survived my mother." I snorted putting the gown on the hanger.

"Do you think I should wear white or ivory?" She slipped on her sundress.

"That is up to you."

"If it were you?"

"Well, I'm single, thirty-four and knocked up." I couldn't help but laugh at the irony of it. "The prospect of meeting a man at the alter are slim to none."

"I didn't know how to tell you," she paused. "Erik asked his brother, Chris to be his best man. I'm sorry."

"Don't be. Hayden hasn't had the decency to even say anything to him about the wedding. I expected as much." I shrugged it off.

"Have you talked to Kennedy lately?" She picked up her purse.

"She called last evening." I followed her out of the shop.

"Lunch?"

"Definitely," I climbed into the passenger seat.

"Did you tell her?"

"No," I closed the door and smiled sweetly.

"Texas Roadhouse?"

"Sounds good. I love their rolls."

"Good. And do you plan to tell her?"

"Nope," I continued smiling.

"She should know if she's having a little brother or sister." Lisa pulled onto main street and headed towards the eatery.

"Little brothers or sisters — plural." The look on her face was priceless.

"What?" I was proud she didn't crash the car. "Are you sure?"

"Afraid so," I gazed out the window at life bustling by.

"Hopefully, now you will tell Hayden." She glanced over at me.

"What is that supposed to mean?"

"Look Alex, one baby would be challenging enough, but two?" She looked at me with pity. "The financial burden alone. I mean," She stopped short of saying what I was already aware of.

"Hayden's position has not changed." I continued to stare out the window trying not to cry. "One baby or two, nothing has changed."

"You know Erik and I are always here for you." She gently touched my arm.

"Thank you. I appreciate that." I smiled as she pulled into the parking lot. "I knew what I was doing when I went to bed with him. Granted, I didn't believe this was possible, but I'm an adult and sometimes our decisions have consequences."

"Consequences?" Lisa turned the car off. "Is that how you really view these babies?"

"No. Of course not." I placed my hand on my abdomen.

We took our seats and ordered our drinks. I delayed the inevitable by lingering over the menu I had memorized years before. I picked at the rolls dipping it in the glorious cinnamon honey butter that I adored. After my second one and with our entrees ordered, I realized Lisa was not going to let me off so easily.

"Have you told the boys yet?"

"Tonight," I tore off a corner of my third roll. "I'm not sure how they are going to react."

"What about the rest of your family? Are you going to tell them?" She placed her hand over mine to stop me from stuffing my face.

"I don't know. The only person I speak to is my sister, Sam. And she would be thrilled about the idea of twins." I chuckled.

"What about your parents?"

"Good Lord, no. The last thing I need is the ridicule of my mother. She would have a field day reminding me once again how I was a failure." I snorted. "Believe me, I feel that way enough on my own without needing my mother to reaffirm it."

"You are anything but a failure." She sipped her iced tea. "I cannot imagine going back to school and trying to manage my children and household. Yet, you seem to do it flawlessly. I admire your gumption."

"You are kind. I feel anything but strong. I have managed to completely screw things up for myself. Now, not only am I a divorced mother of two. I am now the single mother of four." I scoffed. "Gee, how appealing is that?" I rolled my eyes sarcastically.

"Well, you have a date this evening." Lisa perked up.

"No. I am not up for one of your dating schemes." I huffed.

"I'm glad you think so little of me," she chuckled. "But as I mentioned earlier, Erik's brother Chris is going to stand up with Erik at our wedding. And since you will be walking down the aisle with him, I thought it may be a good idea for the two of you to meet first. So, don't get your panties in a bunch."

"Sorry, it's just the idea of dating right now seems absurd." I shrugged.

"Well, you and Chris would be in agreement on that account." Lisa giggled. "Seriously, he's a nice guy. And it's not like it's a real date. It's simply a dinner for you two to meet. I'm not setting you two up or anything like that. I promise."

"What does he do?" I knew very little about Erik's family.

"He's a fireman. I believe he works out of the station near Thompson Road near Greenwood, but I am not sure."

"Are you afraid we won't get along?"

"Not at all. He's charming and handsome. You two will get along fine." She waved it off. "So, when are you telling the boys?"

"Actually, I was going to do it tonight, but you just shot that. Tomorrow, I guess." I was dreading it.

"How do you believe they will take it?" She eyed me over her tea whilst sipping it.

"I don't know really. It will be a shock, certainly. I guess I'll have to wait a bit until that wears off to see how they truly feel about it." I reasoned.

"Sometimes I really despise your psych degree," she rolled her eyes at me. "It's given you an unhealthy ability to rationalize everything."

"Wow, I guess that was money well spent." I laughed.

"Will Max be able to keep an eye on Henry for a few hours this evening?"

"I don't see why not. I sat in the boiling sun this morning for their games, they can at least not burn the house down for a few hours this evening."

"Good. We were thinking of La Hacienda. They have the best margaritas."

"Boy, you're enjoying this a bit too much." I sulked.

"Damn, I'm sorry." She wiped her hands on her napkin. "We can pick somewhere else if you'd like."

"Nonsense. I love Mexican food. It sounds great."

"Are you sure?"

"I'm pregnant, Lisa. Not dead. I can survive an evening without having a breakdown over margarita's" I shook my head at the absurdity.

"Very well," she smiled. "How does seven sound?"

"Perfect," I handed the waiter my card. "Lunch is on me, but you're buying dinner."

"Agreed. Thank you," she reached over and touched my hand lightly.

I picked up Henry and my car at Lisa's and headed back home. Henry was all sugared up, filthy, and all smiles. It was wonderful to see him so happy and laughing again. He yammered all the way back to the house about playing in the creek behind Lisa's house catching crawdads.

Henry and Aaron were playing X-Box when we returned. I could hear them hollering jabs back and forth when I climbed out of the car. Henry gathered his things and beat me to the door. He held it open for me.

"Thank you, my dear." I tasseled his hair.

"You're welcome," my little man chimed closing the door behind us. "I'm gonna shower." He announced running off down the hall.

"Make it a quick one. I'm having dinner with Lisa and Erik tonight for the wedding, and I don't want to take a cold shower." I hollered after him.

"Okay."

"Guess that means I'm stuck here with Henry." Max rolled out of his room.

"Would you mind? It would really help me." I smiled.

"More wedding crap?" He rolled his eyes.

"Yes, more wedding crap," I laughed. "Erik's brother, Chris is going to be his best man and they wanted us to meet before things get completely insane."

"I thought Hayden was the best man?" Max leaned against the wall in the hallway.

"Well, I'm not the only person Hayden has stopped talking to." I shrugged.

"So, your boyfriend dumped his friends too?" Aaron poked his head around Max.

"Pretty much," I leaned against the opposite wall. "Ah, they were my friends anyway and he only knew them through me." I shrugged.

"I don't understand him." Aaron shook his head. "If you're sad, you'd want your friends around to cheer you up, right?"

"Everyone grieves in their own way. I can't imagine what I'd do if I lost one of you boys." I grabbed Max and wrapped my arms around him. "You'd have to put me in a padded room cause I'd lose my mind without you guys."

"Keep acting like this and I'll have you committed." Max laughed and squirmed away.

"You're so sweet," I playfully pushed him towards Aaron who in turned pushed me at me.

"I don't want him," Aaron laughed.

"Wow, you're both so sweet." Max rolled his eyes at us. "I'm going to find something to eat."

"Just a snack. I'm gonna order a pizza for later for you guys." I hollered after him.

"Can Aaron crash?" Max yelled from the kitchen.

"Ask his mom, but it's fine with me." I yelled back before closing my bedroom door.

Later that evening I found myself pacing around my closet trying to find something to wear. A half dozen outfits lay thrown across the floor. I had worked so hard on keeping my figure that any fluctuation severely limited my options. I was so frustrated.

I tried on a casual jumper, but it was to tight around my now rounding belly. I could hide it most of the time and was being cautious of what I wore around the boys over the last few weeks. Now, I stood in my bra and panties realizing that my breasts were getting bigger and looked stuffed into a bra two sizes too small. Plus, my panties were so tight I was sure one good cough was going to make the elastic snap.

I was almost in tears. I don't know why but I wanted to look nice. Not to impress Chris, but simply to feel pretty for a change My self-esteem had been obliterated thanks to Hayden and I wasn't exactly feeling very attractive these days. The never-ending nausea and weight gain were making me self-conscious.

I slipped into a loose black sundress that came down almost to my knees, with a little white knitted flowers across the breasts. It's spaghetti straps added a little elegance to the simple dress. Thanks to the polyester fabric it fit but was a little snug. The black helped conceal my rounding abdomen.

I set the boys up with pizza, breadsticks, and the movies, *Remember the Titians* and *Radio* — two of Max and Aaron's favorites they had watched countless times before. The three boys were camped out on the floor with their feast that included Red Vine and Gummy Bears for dessert when I left. I rarely allowed such gluttony but on the rare occasion it was warranted.

Lisa and Erik were already there when I arrived. Lisa was wearing a red flowing summer evening dress and strappy sandals with heels. Her hair was down and complimented her light makeup perfectly. She was the imagine of the gushing bride to be.

"You look lovely." Erik stood and held out my chair for me.

"Thank you," he scooted me up to the table. "You two look like the perfect little couple." I smiled.

"Ah, you're so sweet," Lisa blushed. "You look cute tonight."

"I am starting to have difficulty finding anything that fits." I rolled my eyes with a smirk.

"Congratulations on the twins. I'm surprised you're really not showing yet." Erik remarked and Lisa smacked his arm.

"Why would you say that?" She chastised him.

"I was complimenting her," he defended. "How did the boys take it?"

"I haven't told them yet." I ordered a sweet tea and started on the chips and salsa the waiter left on the table. "I was going to do it tonight, but I got ordered away."

"They will be thrilled." Lisa said optimistically.

"I'm not going to hold my breath," I laughed. "And speaking of disappointments. My track record with men just keeps getting better by the day. Did you tell your brother I'd be here and that's why I'm being stood up on my nondate dinner?"

"You didn't get stood up." Erik laughed at me. "He just got here," he nodded towards the door.

Standing by the door talking to the hostess stood a tall muscular man with wide shoulders, biceps that were larger than my thighs, and golden hair. I accidently snorted when I saw him, and Lisa giggled.

"You're going to make me wobble down the aisle with that?" Lisa nodded. "You must really hate me."

"I love you," she whispered as Chris approached our table.

"Hey, sorry I'm late. Traffic on Rockville Road was a nightmare." His voice was deep and musky. "You must be Alex." He extended his hand, and I shook it. "I'm Chris. Nice to meet you."

"The pleasure is mine." His hand almost crushed mine.

I flexed my fingers and rubbed my hand under the table. I flashed Lisa a questioning smile as if to ask if this man was even housebroken. I had never encountered a man who had crushed my hand saying hello.

"Sorry about that. Sometimes I forget my own strength." He must have noticed my expression.

"No worries," I winced trying to smile. "I'm fine."

"Have you guys ordered yet? I'm starving." Chris started gulping down his water before he dove into the chips and salsa.

The waiter took our order and we made small talk waiting on our entrees'. Chris droned on about the station he worked at and the antics that ensued there. He continually stuffed his face with salsa and chips leaving nothing for the rest of us.

He gulped down his margarita and promptly signaled the waiter for another one. His table manners were worse than a five-year-old. I kept looking at Lisa who did her best to ignore my expressions.

I lost my appetite just watching him.

Chris's behavior didn't improve once our dinners arrived. I picked at my enchiladas fighting the urge to offer Chris a bib. Lisa and Erik did their best to keep the conversation light and pleasant. I tried to keep my eyes on my two friends as the neanderthal seated beside me clearly was raised by wolves.

"So, Alex. Erik tells me you are having twins. Congratulations. That's a lot." Chris remarked between bites.

"Thank you," I narrowed my eyes a bit at Erik. "Do you have children?"

"Four boys," he smiled broadly.

"Never a dull moment at your house, I'd imagine," I smiled. "My two boys keep me busy enough."

"I rarely have all four at the same time, so it's not so bad." He shrugged.

"Huh?" I was confused.

"Chris has been divorced twice," Erik chimed in.

"To be fair, I never married Quintin's mom. That bitch was crazy." He laughed heartily.

"Four boys, three moms, two divorces." Lisa clarified.

"You've been busy," I teased.

"Hey, at least none of them were related, let alone mother and daughter." Chris fired back.

"Excuse me," I was astonished.

"Weren't you sleeping with the dad and the son or at least until the son was killed. Do you know who fathered the twins?" He laughed.

"You bastard!" I stood, picked up his fourth margarita and threw the contents in his face. "Sorry Lisa, Erik." I stormed out of the restaurant as fast as I could without sprinting.

Chapter 24

I CLIMBED INTO MY CAR AND burst into tears. I had never been so humiliated. I noticed Chris standing by the door scanning the parking lot. I started the car and left the parking lot before he could reach me.

I was livid. My phone started buzzing, but I ignored it. I knew it was Lisa and I felt bad for not answering, but I knew she understood. I could only imagine the tongue lashing she was giving Chris. Now I understood why Erik never mentioned his brother and why Hayden had been his first choice for best man.

The boys were watching the end of *Remember the Titians* when I returned. The empty pizza box and soda cans littered the coffee table. I got a chorus of 'hey mom' when I entered. I smiled and waved on my way to my room. I didn't want them to see my smeared makeup.

"Momma?" Max knocked softly on the door. "Are you all right?"

"Yeah, come in," I slipped off my sandals and kicked them into the closet. "I just had dinner with a neanderthal." I sat down on the edge of the bed.

"I thought you were having dinner with Lisa and Erik and his brother." Max leaned against my dresser.

"I did. Erik's brother is a complete neanderthal. He has zero table manners. I wanted to put a bib on him to go along with his funnel as he shoved food into his face." I rolled my eyes in disgust. "It was embarrassing."

"Wow! Was he ugly too?" My eldest giggled.

"Honestly? No. He was good looking. Sort of like a real-life Captain America. His biceps were bigger than my thighs. He's a fireman." I told him. "Still, I'm surprised he used utensils." Max giggled.

"So, you left early?"

"Not before he insulted me, and I threw his margarita in his face. I left after that." I looked at him coyly.

"You threw a drink in his face?" I nodded. "Man, I wish I could have seen that." He laughed.

"You would have been proud of me." I grinned.

"I am. That's badass, momma."

"Thank you," I started to get up.

"What did he say to you?"

"Something about Mason and Hayden." I told him honestly.

"I miss Mason," Max looked down at his feet. "Can I ask you something?"

"Sure," I paused.

"I don't want to make you mad, but I need to know." He started fidgeting with his hands.

"I'm not going to get mad," he glanced at me. "I promise."

"Okay. Well," he continued to fidget.

"Max. I'm not going to get mad." I wasn't sure what to expect.

"Are you pregnant?" I felt like he hit me with a shovel.

"Why do you ask that?" I tried to keep my voice steady.

"Because you've been nauseas. Everything makes you cry, and you've gained weight in your belly and boobs." He kept his eyes on the floor and played with his fingers.

"And that led you to think I'm pregnant?" I was curious who had had been talking to.

"I googled it," a sly grin spread across his lips.

"I love the internet," I laughed. "At least your inquisitive."

"I'm not saying you're fat," he quickly defended himself. "Cause you're not."

"I know, darling. And yes, you are right. I am pregnant." I held my breath.

"Cool," he smiled.

"You're not mad?" I was still apprehensive.

"No. I think it's great." Max leaned over and hugged me. "Are you happy about it?"

"I don't know," I sighed feeling a weight off my shoulders. "I was more worried about how you and Henry were going to take it."

"Why?" he tilted his head eyeing me.

"Because it's been the three of us for so long and changing the dynamics of the house can be difficult."

"If we can survive you going back to school, I think we can survive anything." Max rolled his eyes. "Besides, it would be fun to have a baby sister. Do you know what it is?"

"Not yet, but I'm supposed to have another ultrasound in a couple weeks to find out."

"Can I go with you?" His request caught me off guard.

"I'd love that." I put my arm around him. "But if we're spilling the beans, I guess I should come completely clean."

"Let me guess, we're moving to Chicago?" he groaned.

"Nope, but how would you feel about twins?" I raised my eyebrows.

"Are you serious?" I nodded. "You're kidding?"

"What do you think about that?"

"Double the fun," Max laughed. "Or double the trouble."

"That's what I'm afraid of." I wrapped my hands around his neck. "Don't you think I have enough with you and Henry?" I laughed.

"Apparently not," Max stuck his tongue out.

"Perhaps I'm a glutton for punishment."

"I think so," he squirmed away from me. "Plus, I can't wait to see you get fat with the twins." He ducked before I could grab him.

"You are so mean to me." I laughed.

"And just think, you could have two more boys and I hope they're just like me." He ducked again.

"God must really hate me."

"Nah, I'm a blessing." Max put his hands on his hips and announced proudly.

"You most certainly are," I tapped him on the back of his head and hugged him again.

"I guess you're not going to tell Hayden?" he took a serious tone.

"You think I should?"

"Has he contacted you once since he shoved us on a plane?" he tilted his head eyeing me.

"Not a call nor a text." I said truthfully.

"Then I was right," he held up his hands. "He's an asshole."

"Yes, he is," I smiled in agreement. "And you don't think I owe it to him to tell him about the twins?"

"Why? He walked away. You didn't. So, the twins are ours. Not his." The logic of a youth.

"Exactly," I hugged him again. "And Henry? How do you think he's going to take it?"

"He'll be thrilled," Max smirked. "He won't be the baby anymore. He'll have someone to boss around."

"You're probably right."

"Momma?" Aaron knocked on my door.

"Come in," I replied.

"There's a man at the door with flowers." Aaron poked his head in. "What do you want me to tell him?"

For a split second my heart dropped to my knees, and I had the vivid imagine of Hayden standing on my porch looking remorseful with flowers in hand ready to grovel for forgiveness for his rude and despicable behavior.

"Ask him to wait. I'll be there in a moment." My hand unconsciously and protectively covered my abdomen.

"There's a pick-up truck outside." Max walked over to the window and peeked through the blinds.

It was almost as if my eldest was thinking the same thing I was. My heart held tight that perhaps Hayden had bought a new truck in his grief to uplift his spirits. Max and I exchanged apprehensive yet hopeful looks before we both headed to the living room.

I closed my eyes for a brief second with my hand on the doorknob praying it was Hayden standing on the other side. I took a deep breath and opened the door.

"Yes?" I cautiously opened my front door only to be immediately disappointed.

"I'm sorry," Chris stood on my porch looking nervous.

"Why are you here?" I kept the screen door between us.

"Like I said. I am sorry for my behavior at the restaurant."

"Thank you," I made no effort of hide my sarcasm.

"May I speak with you?" He cocked his head to the side with a sly grin. "I brought you flowers."

"And that's supposed to make me forgive you for humiliating me based on your assumptions that you know nothing about?"

"My brother mentioned you are a psych major." He laughed in an arrogant way that made me want to smack his smug face.

"Let's get one thing straight. You know nothing about me or my life."

"As long as you can agree to the same about mine." Chris pursed his lips and stared at me.

"Agreed," I narrowed my eyes a bit.

"Will you please step outside since you obviously aren't going to invite me in."

"Look, you can tell Erik and Lisa I will be the picture of politeness at their rehearsal dinner and wedding despite my feelings about you. Lisa is my best friend, and I would never do anything to ruin her wedding." I opened the screen and stepped out onto the porch.

"And Erik is my brother. Do you think I want to ruin his wedding?" he huffed.

"I would hope not." I muttered.

"I am trying here. Can you please try not to be a bitch and talk to me like a human being?" Chris shook his head in frustration.

"There are chairs on my deck. Would you like to join me?" I motioned towards the back of the house.

But rather than walking through the house, I chose to walk around through the front yard mainly because I did not want the boys, namely Max to say something off colored to him.

Twilight was underway and the sky was ablaze with colors. The humidity was low, and the air was comfortable. The perennials were in full bloom providing a glorious array of bright colors across the wide flower beds along my house. I smiled proudly to myself walking across the emerald, green lawn to the back of my house.

"Who does your landscaping?" Chris asked as we climbed the steps to the deck.

"You're looking at her." I said with pride.

"Seriously? Wow, I'm impressed." His smug smile was irritating. "You don't strike me as outdoorsy."

"Just goes to show you know very little about me." I voice was cold.

"I suppose it does." He sat down on one of the chairs.

"What did you want to talk to me about?" I took a seat on the swing and crossed my arms across my chest.

"I know you think I'm an asshole." He stated rather than said. "And due to my behavior at the restaurant, I would imagine you would." I kept quiet waiting for him to make a point. "I just got out of a four-year relationship, and it felt like I was being setup on a blind date. I told my brother I wasn't interested in meeting anyone." He crossed his legs and stared me down.

"You honestly think that was a date?"

"You didn't?"

"No," I rolled my eyes in disbelief to his stupidity. "Lisa and Erik simply wanted us to meet so we would be more comfortable around each other going through all the wedding BS."

"You're going to be Lisa's maid of honor?" his eyebrows went up.

"Yes. I told you she was my best friend." I shook my head.

"I guess I really read that wrong, huh?" Chris looked a bit embarrassed.

"Ya think?"

"And well, when you made the comment that I was a 'busy man'" he did the juvenile air quotes. "It felt like you were judging me for having four kids with three women."

"I said busy man because I know my two sons keep me very busy with their sports and schools and I couldn't fathom doubling that."

"But aren't you doubling that?" he smirked.

"Yeah, I guess so." A laugh escaped before I could stop it.

"I understand how it looks to say I have four sons with three women. But it's not like it was something I planned. I got my high school girlfriend pregnant our senior year. Her father forced us to get married. Right after graduation I worked construction trying to support us, but nothing was ever good enough and she was miserable. We argued all the time about money and her being stuck at home all day taking care of the baby. When I was old enough, I joined the department. But then I was never home. The fighting got worse, and we divorced after four years."

I nodded along listening to his explanation wondering why he felt it necessary to share it with me.

"My second wife hated the long hours and time I spent away from home. So, when I surprised her one evening by trading shifts with my buddy to make it home for our son's first birthday, I caught her in bed with another guy. We divorced a month later. And I was engaged to the mother of my fourth son, but she decided after four years together and at 35 years old, she was a lesbian."

"Ouch," I slipped without thinking.

"Now you can understand why I am not exactly excited to be set up on a blind date." He waved his hands for emphasis.

"I get it."

"I do apologize for making assumptions about your character and the father son remark."

"Thank you," I was getting thirsty and didn't want to be rude. "Can I get you something to drink? I have Mountain Dew, coffee, Cream Soda, Kool-Aid, and water."

"Water would be great. Thanks."

I excused myself and went in through the French doors. I grabbed a couple water bottles out of the fridge when Max cornered me.

"Is that the guy you threw a drink in his face?" He grinned.

"Yep. He's apologizing."

"Are you rearming?" he giggled.

"Just in case," I winked and closed the fridge.

"Do I need to fake an injury to pull you away." He offered.

"Code word text Pickles." I laughed.

"Roger," he saluted on his way to the living room.

"Thanks for having my back, buddy." I hollered before I opened the back door.

"Always," I heard him reply from the other room.

"Why are you smiling like the cat that ate the canary?" Chris asked when I handed him the water bottle.

"Honestly?" he nodded. "For the first time since I found out I was pregnant I feel like everything is going to be all right." I returned to my seat.

"Why is that?" He seemed intrigued.

"If these babies are anything like the two I already have, then they are going to be amazing kids." I said proudly.

"Does your ex-husband see them often?"

"No. Danny lives in Phoenix. He moved there several years ago. He used to come see them a couple times a year, but he recently got remarried and she and her children don't get along well with my boys."

"That must be hard."

"It was, but over the last few years they've had Mason as sort of a cross between big brother, mentor, father figure that really enhanced their lives. It was a terrible loss for us when he was murdered." I sighed gazing out over the back yard recalling happier times it had witnessed.

"What happened exactly." I looked at him curiously. "I mean, how did you get mixed up between father and son? I'm not trying to be rude, but isn't that a little cliché'?"

"It's a long story," I sighed.

"I've got time." Chris smiled and settled back into his seat.

Over the next couple hours Chris and I hung out on the back patio sharing the sunset and stories about our lives. I learned he was quite charming once you broke through the hard exterior wall, he kept around him. I discovered we had a great deal in common from our taste in music to movies.

We shared a mutual love for sarcasm and frequent road rage. I found myself laughing at the antics he pulled in his youth and admired the man he had grown into. He was an active father who adored his boys and spent his evenings and weekends coaching their sports and being involved with their upbringing.

I hadn't realized how late it had gotten until Max poked his head out the back door asked if they could make hot fudge sundae's. I glanced at my phone only to learn it was after ten o'clock.

"It's late and I think you boys have had enough junk for one night. Maybe we can make them tomorrow." I reasoned.

"Fine," he muttered.

"Hey Max," I called out to him before he closed the door. "I would like you to meet Erik's brother, Chris. Chris, this is my eldest, Max." Max stepped out on the porch and extended his hand.

"It's nice to meet you." I was proud of Max's display of maturity.

"Nice to meet you too. I've heard a lot of great things about you." Chris shook my son's hand.

"Don't believe a word she says." My young man grinned over at me.

"Your mom tells me you are a talented athlete."

"I enjoy playing." Max kept glancing over at me trying to figure out why I'd been talking so much and for so long with someone I'd thrown a drink at earlier in the evening.

"I coach baseball, football, and basketball for my son's teams down in Greenwood and Franklin." Max must have made a confused expression because Chris clarified. "I've been married twice. Their moms live in different districts."

"Oh," Max nodded. "My dad's been married twice too."

"Your mom mentioned he just got remarried."

"His new wife, Amanda is a witch," Max leaned against the deck railing. "Her brats are even worse."

"Blending families can be hard." Chris told him.

"Amanda made fun of Henry and her kids pick on him all the time. When I do something about it, I'm the one that gets into trouble. My dad doesn't stand up for us and always sides with Amanda." Max scoffed.

"Well, that sucks. Did you tell her off?" A sly grin slid across Chris' shapely lips.

"Don't give him any ideas. He has enough difficult time getting along with his dad let alone his new stepmom." I warned Chris.

"I refuse to acknowledge her as my stepmother. She is just married to my dad." Max stated.

"You could address her as your step-monster." Chris suggested trying to suppress his smile.

"That's better than Amanda." Max giggled.

"Isn't it your bedtime." I asked him.

"Yes, Mommy dearest," he stuck his tongue out at me.

"I knew I'd regret letting you watch that movie." I rolled my eyes. "Get your butt inside."

"Soon, I'll be able to call you Mommy biggest." I reached for him, and he dodged away from me.

"Hey, did you say anything to Henry or Aaron?" Chris had slightly derailed my evening in more ways than one.

"Nah, I was waiting for you. I figured you'd talk to Henry after Aaron went home tomorrow."

"That's the plan." He leaned over and hugged me. "Thanks, buddy.

"Night momma. I love you." He kissed me quickly on the cheek and smiled.

"I love you too. Sweet dreams, baby." He trotted off into the house.

"You've got a really cool kid. I like him." Chris leaned forward in his chair.

"Yeah, I think I'll keep him. He's kinda grown on me."

"Thank you for spending the evening with me. I don't believe Erik or Lisa will believe we didn't kill each other."

"Probably not," I smirked. "I enjoyed it. It's been a long time since I laughed."

"You don't have to act so surprised." He chuckled.

"Given my first impression of you, can you blame me?" I giggled.

"Not really," he leaned a little closer. "Hopefully, you no longer believe I'm an asshole and will not be tossing drinks in my face again anytime soon."

"I'll try," I winked at him.

"I appreciate that," Chris sat back in his chair in a relaxed fashion then stretched with a yawn. "But it is getting late, and I have taken up enough of your time." He stood up.

"I'm glad you stopped by," I got to my feet. "And I'm glad I got to see this side of you." I smiled at him as we stepped off the deck. "It will definitely make a big difference when we walk down the aisle." I nudged him playfully.

"That sounds so odd, doesn't it?" He had a great smile.

"Yeah, but at least we can say it's the one time we can say we'll walk down the aisle and know we'll not go through a divorce." I reasoned.

"True," he bumped into me in a playful manner. "I like the way you think."

We walked around the house to his truck parked on the curb in front of my house. Chris turned around and looked over my yard nodding his head.

"You really did a beautiful job on your yard. It's nice to see someone take such meticulous care of their property." He opened the driver's door, but hesitated getting in. "It was a pleasure to meet you, Alex. Thank you for a wonderful evening."

"The pleasure was all mine. Be careful going home."

"I will," Chris smiled and climbed into his truck.

I stood on the curb and watched him pull away. The turn of events this evening was surprising, but in a good way. I walked up the pathway gazing proudly over my manicured lawn. I was diligent about keeping the flower beds weed-free, the edging elegant, and the beds full of colorful flowers, and shrubbery that complemented each other.

I found the boys scattered about the couch and loveseat crashed out with the television still on and empty boxes, wrappers, and soda cans tossed about the living room. I smiled at the sight. It felt wonderful to see them behaving like their old selves again and enjoying the trivial things like a sleepover party.

After a long hot shower, I slipped into bed. Billy jumped up beside me. I scratched behind her ears as she settled down on the pillow beside me. I smiled to myself thinking of the strange turn of events between Max, and Chris. For an evening that started out in the toilet, it had turned out wonderful. I felt for sure I had made a good friend and I hoped I would have the chance to see him again. While I had no interest in him romantically, he was someone I would enjoy hanging out with.

Chapter 25

I FIXED THE BOYS SOME FRENCH toast, hash browns, and ham for breakfast. They devoured it faster than I could make it. The heckles and jabs they bantered back and forth at each other had all of us in tears. I flipped the last batch on the griddle listening to the never-ending jeering and took a deep sigh of relief.

We had made it through the storm. The boys mentioned Mason frequently and were able to recall the good times they shared and the silly memories they cherished without tears, but with smiles and laughter. I knew they would never forget Mason and it made me feel good that they would be able to someday tell their new siblings about how amazing their big brother was.

Aaron left shortly before noon. His mother was taking him shopping for new sneakers. The kid was growing like a weed just like Max. It amazed me how much the two had changed this last year. My little boy was rapidly disappearing before my eyes and being replaced with a teenager who was going to rival me on being the moodiest person in the house over the next several months.

The boys helped me clean up the dishes and counters. Both were in a good mood and Max kept giving me looks as if to ask me when I was going to tell Henry. Finally, the kitchen was done, and I was out of time. I smiled over at Max and nodded.

"Henry?" he tossed the dish towel on the counter.

"Huh?" he spun around on his heels smiling.

"Can I talk to you for a minute?"

"I didn't do it. Max did." I glanced over at Max who simply shrugged his shoulders.

"Do I even want to know?"

"Probably not," Max pinched his lips together struggling not to grin.

"Then don't tell me," I shook my head with a chuckle. "Living room," I nodded to the boys.

Henry sat down on the couch beside me, and Max parked his rear on the coffee table — something I wasn't crazy about him doing, but let it pass.

"What's going on?" My little man looked nervous.

"I have some good news to tell you." I tried to make my voice as cheerful as possible.

"Are we going on vacation?" Henry chirped up.

"No. Something better," I reached for his hand.

"And bigger," Max muttered still trying to hide his smile.

"We're getting another puppy?" Henry squirmed with glee.

"Nope. I'm pregnant," I said lightly with a smile.

"What?" he stopped and stared at me. "Are you serious?"

"Yep," I squeezed his hand. "What do you think?"

"Are you having a boy or girl?" he asked.

"I don't know yet, but I'm gonna find out in a couple weeks." He slowly grinned. "And we're going to be twice as blessed." I wondered if he would get it.

"Twice? As in two babies, like twins?" His smile grew bigger.

"Twins," I nodded.

"Cool," he reached over and hugged me tightly. "When are you due?"

"December 2nd," Both my sons smiled.

"Maybe they'll be born on Christmas." Henry fidgeted in his seat with excitement.

"Twins are usually born early, not late. And since my due date is more than three weeks before Christmas, the doctors would never allow me to go that far past my expected delivery date." I told him.

"So, maybe closer to Thanksgiving?" Max piped in.

"More likely," I smiled over at him.

"That would put their birthday between ours." Henry grinned.

"I don't know what I ever did to deserve having all your birthdays back-to-back and then get hit with Christmas." I ran my fingers through my hair and exhaled loudly.

"Guess it goes to show what you do when you're bored in the winter." Max giggled turning red.

"Max!" I playfully smacked his leg.

"Just saying," He jumped up and took off down the hall laughing.

Once the moment had passed and the laughter settled, I turned towards Henry. I patted his hand softly before I started.

"How do you feel about two new siblings in the house and not being the baby anymore?" I asked lovingly.

"I think is great. I finally get to be the big brother and have someone to boss around and pick on." He grinned like a Cheshire cat.

"And here I was worried you'd be upset. Guess I mistaken." I nudged him playfully.

"It'll be fun," he jumped up. "Can I play video games for a while?"

"Okay," I felt so much better.

"Thanks," he took off down the hall.

I picked up my cell and stepped out on the back deck. It was a beautiful day. The sky was a robin egg blue scattered with fluffy white clouds. The flower beds were alive with colors and filled the air with a heavenly fragrance. I sat down on my swing and rested back against the plush pillows.

I rocked back and forth pushing off the wooden boards with the tip of my toes. Ever since I was a small child, I had loved swinging. There was something soothing and comforting about the rocking motion. Feeling more relaxed than I had in several weeks, I picked up my phone and called Lisa.

"Hey darling, I'm so sorry about last night. Chris is an asshole." Lisa apologized before I could even say hi.

"Is that why you gave him my address?" I teased.

"Erik did. I didn't." She quickly sold him out and I laughed.

"He showed up on my front porch with flowers." I tried to sound upset.

"You're kidding," she scoffed. "That's probably the first time he's ever bought flowers in his life."

"Imagine that," I giggled.

"Honestly, his behavior shocked me last night. I've never seen him behave that way. He's always been the sweetest guy every time I've been around him. I was so embarrassed and mad at him last night. Erik and I had a bad argument when we got home. He told me Chris and Tara separated about two weeks ago. I never thought he would behave in such a manner." Lisa rambled.

"He came over with hat in hand, apologizing on his knees." I was having fun with her.

"Seriously?"

"No," I laughed. "I'm kidding. Well, partially anyway. He was groveling and he brought flowers, but he never got on his knees."

"Either way, I am happy to hear he apologized. I am so sorry." She sounded remorseful.

"You have nothing to apologize for. He stayed until around ten last night. After you get past the cocky arrogance, he's actually really sweet." I explained.

"I don't know if I'm happy or nervous." She sounded leery.

"Oh, dear Lord. You've got to be kidding me?" I snorted unintentionally. "How could you even think that I'd be interested in anyone. I'm pregnant with twins. I do not believe that's high on the desirability scale. Besides, he's not my type. He looks like a cross between a Ken doll on steroids and Captain America."

"Yeah, that usually keeps women at bay." Lisa scoffed at me. "He's a gorgeous firefighter. Women just hate that."

"Definitely," I scoffed. "But I believe we can agree that I'm not exactly on the market."

"Why not? You're not with Hayden anymore." She paused and there was an awkward silence between us. "I'm sorry. I didn't mean,"

"I know Hayden and I are no longer together. But I am pregnant and that means something." I sighed. "What? I don't know, but something."

"You should ask for a refund." She muttered.

"Refund? What are you talking about?"

"Your higher education. Your university. Cause you got gipped, darling."

"You are such a bitch, sweetheart."

"But you love me anyway." Lisa laughed.

"True," I agreed. "But seriously, once you get past the macho bravado, Chris is a decent guy. Granted, he's not exactly housebroken, but I've certainly met worse."

"I am glad you two found a way to tolerate each other."

"Tolerate?" I scoffed. "I think I may have actually made a friend."

"I'm impressed. I don't believe I have ever heard you make such a declaration." She teased.

"What can I say, I'm maturing."

"Better late than never."

"I told the boys." I switched subjects.

"And?"

"They took it better than I expected. Max even asked to go with me to my next ultrasound, and Henry is thrilled about the prospect of having someone or rather younger siblings to boss around."

"Sounds about right," she giggled. "I'm sure McKenzie will feel the same way. She hates being the baby."

"I get it. I hated being the baby too. Samantha teased me relentlessly." I explained.

"And Colin didn't?" Lisa questioned.

"Colin was too perfect and studious. He rarely spoke to me or Sam. He was born with a stick shoved so far up his ass he coughed up toothpicks."

"That, I believe." She muttered. "Oh, before I forget, you're bringing the snacks for tomorrow's game."

"Dang it. I did forget. Thanks for reminding me. Now I have to run to the store tonight."

"Well, I'll let you go then. I'll see you tomorrow. Have a good one."

"You too."

I disconnected the call and closed my eyes enjoying the warm breeze blowing through the trees. The sound of the leaves rustling brought about feelings of serenity that washed over me. It was such a lovely afternoon, and I was trying my best to embrace the recent twist of events in my life.

I thought about driving to campus this week and speaking to Michelle. There was a daycare on the University campus utilized by faculty and student parents, but I had no idea what it cost. I knew I needed to make sure I had as much taken care of as possible before I was scrambling to complete my final semester of college.

I tried to make a mental list of all the things I needed to buy times two. The list was staggering. I suddenly wished I had held on to Henry's baby things, but I was positive I would never have another child. I mentally rolled my eyes at myself thinking of fates sick sense of humor.

I stretched out on the swing turning my face towards the warmth of the descending sun. I brought my hand up and rested it lovingly on my abdomen thinking about the new lives it cradled. I couldn't help but wonder about them.

Would they be laid-back with an easy-going nature like Mason or a powerful force of nature that is full of gumption like their older sister Kennedy? After having two sons already, a small portion of my heart prayed desperately for that little girl I had always dreamed of since I was a little girl playing with my dolls.

Chapter 26

THE NEXT FEW WEEKS WERE HECTIC. Thanks to Michelle making a few calls and pulling a couple strings, she was able to reserve a couple spots for my twins starting in January. She was so excited she spent several hours telling me the joys and horrors of raising twins. By the time I left her office I was terrified and full of doubts about my capabilities as a mother.

Lisa soothed my fears and talked me off the proverbial ledge after I told her about Michelle's recall of the first year with her twin boys. She assured me that she and Erik would be there to help me out in any way possible. As much as I loved her for it, I reminded her they wouldn't be there at two in the morning trying to breastfeed two crying babies.

I felt like panicking or having a full-blown nervous breakdown. I wasn't sure which, only that one was going to happen soon.

Thursday evening before the Fourth of July celebration, the boys and I stopped by the store to pick up a few things I needed to make potato salad, deviled eggs, and brownies I was taking over to Debbie's. Since the holiday fell on Sunday this year, the community athletic league had decided to hold the annual Fourth of July parade, carnival, and fireworks on Saturday.

The boys helped me cook dinner and clean up afterwards. They had both been trying to do more around the house since learning about the twins. Both were excited about tagging along to my ultrasound next week to hopefully learn if they were going to have little brothers or sisters.

They settled in front of the television playing Mario Kart competing against each other on various tracks. Max was trying to be more patient with Henry and include him in more activities. I curled up on the couch and acted as the peanut gallery when my cell phone rang. I was enthralled in their competition, I reached it without looking at the screen.

"Hello?"

"Alex?"

"Yes," I didn't recognize the voice.

"It's Chris. Erik's brother. Lisa gave me your number. I hope that's okay."

"Sure. How are you?"

"Good. Busy. Last night of a four-day shift?"

"Sounds fun," my attention was still diverted by the final lap of the race.

"I was wondering if you have any plans for tomorrow evening?"

"Tomorrow?" Nothing came to mind. "Not that I can of."

"I got invited to a cookout at a buddy's from work that is shaping up to be more couples than singles and I hate the idea of being a third wheel. Would you be interested in playing the role of my surrogate date?" He explained.

"Surrogate date?" I laughed. "That's a new one."

"Well, after our conversation it was clear that neither of us were interested in dating or relationships for the time being. Still, there are occasions when it is preferable to be part of a couple rather than a single." Chris reasoned.

"True," I went out to the back patio for some privacy. Billy trotted out behind me running out into the yard. "Are you saying we should enact a surrogate date policy?" I plopped down on the swing. "So, those awkward events where everyone is coupled off, we're not standing there as you said, as a third wheel?"

"Exactly," he chuckled. "What do you think?"

"You do remember I'm pregnant, right?"

"Yeah, kinda hard to forget."

"Aren't you concerned what people will say? The natural assumption would be that it's yours. And it would be a bit awkward if you corrected them." I rationalized.

"But that could also be part of the fun you and I could have because I would never say nor deny anything. It's more fun to leave them curious." He teased.

"You have a devious streak in you," I giggled. "I like it."

"Besides, I figured neither of us really want to lock ourselves away and not enjoy life because of our current relationship status, right?"

"I hadn't planned to." I hated to admit it was harder doing everything alone and would be nice to have a friend to hang out with.

"Well, I sometimes find it uncomfortable. I hate going to the movies or restaurants alone. I always feel like people are judging me."

"Don't be silly," I was enjoying myself. "Of course, they are."

"And here I was hoping it was just my imagination." Chris laughed wholeheartedly. "Good to know."

"Ya know, I think it's a great idea. I'd be happy to be your surrogate date tomorrow night. What should I wear?"

"I don't know. It's a cookout. Something comfortable and nice." He stumbled.

"All right," I started mentally running through my wardrobe trying to think of what I could wear.

"Fabulous," Chris' voice lightened. "I'll pick you up at six."

"I'll be ready." I heard Billy creeping around the back yard before she growled. "What is it girl?" I walked over to the railing. "That's odd."

"What's wrong?"

"I don't know. Billy is acting weird. She's growling at something in the bushes."

"Are you outside?" Chris sounded concerned.

"Yes, I'm on the deck."

"Go inside and lock the door."

"It's probably a squirrel or racoon." I squinted in the dark corner of the backyard where Billy was.

Something held her attention, a squirrel most likely. But then she crutched low and let out a deep growl. The hairs stood up on the back of my neck. My feet felt paralyzed with fear. Billy let out a horrible sound, yelped, and I screamed.

"I'm on my way," Chris hollered in the phone. "Stay on the line with me."

I barely heard what he said. My eyes were glued on Billy as she staggered about halfway up the yard before she fell over.

"Billy!" I ran to her dropping my phone in the grass along the way.

"Momma!" Max came running out the back door.

"Go get Mark! Something bit Billy." My son stood there frozen in fear. "Run Max! Go!" I shouted.

I crouched beside Billy. She was whimpering loudly. I stroked her fur softly and she let out a low whine that broke my heart.

"It's all right, girl. I'm here. Tell Momma what happened darling. What bit you?" I whispered in a soothing voice.

Tears poured down my cheeks. Billy was one of my babies, just like the two I was carrying, and the two I'd already brought into this world. I loved them all dearly.

"Alex?" Mark's voice came out of the darkness.

"Over here," I wiped my face with the back of my hand.

"What happened?" Mark knelt beside us. Debbie and Max stood over us with tear filled eyes.

"I don't know. I was talking on the phone while she was running around the yard. She was sniffing the grass and then she started growling this horrible sound. She yelped, staggered up here and just fell over. There's blood around her neck, but I can't tell how bad the bite is, but something bit her." I was barely holding it together looking at the blood on my hands.

"Alex, I'm going to carry Billy over to my truck and lay her in the bed. Max, run and get a couple blankets for her to rest on. We'll run her over to the vet hospital that's open 24/7 in Speedway." Mark glanced up at us.

"I'm going with you." Max hollered running into the house.

Mark lifted Billy and she cried out in pain. The sound ripped my heart.

"Deb, call animal control. This must be a snake bite. If it was a racoon or squirrel, we'd have seen it or heard it by now." Mark reasoned. "Stay in the house with the boys and wait for animal control." He carried Billy's lifeless body across the street.

Max had climbed up in the back of the truck and created a make-shift bed for Billy. Mark laid her down carefully, but she winced in pain. I climbed into the bed of the truck and cradled her head in my lap.

"Let's get going," I said through my tears. "She's fading fast."

"I'm coming too," Max started climbing but Mark put his hand on his shoulder.

"I can't stop your mom from riding in the bed, but it's dangerous Max. Why don't you ride in the cab with me?" Mark noticed the tears and determination in my son's eyes and looked at me. I nodded my okay. "All right, just don't stand up." He helped Max into the bed.

"I'll text you," Mark kissed Debbie quickly on the cheek as he dug in his pocket for his keys.

He hopped into the cab and the engine roared to life. He backed out of the driveway and headed down the road. I stroked Billy's face and rubbed her ears. Max laid down beside her, his head on my knee beside Billy's. He talked softly to her lightly running his fingers over her body. Tears rolled down his cheeks as he promised her a cozy life if she promised to not leave him.

Max begged and pleaded with her throughout the twenty-minute drive. Billy had closed her eyes shortly after we left the neighborhood, and her breathing was growing shallower by the mile. I closed my eyes and said a silent prayer begging God to spare her.

Mark carried Billy into the animal hospital with Max and me on his heels. The veterinary on-call rushed into the waiting room upon hearing the commotion we made at our arrival. He led us into an exam room where Mark gently laid Billy on the stainless-steel table. Billy moaned lowly at being moved again.

"What happened here?" The vet took his stethoscope out to listen to Billy's breathing.

"She was bitten by something in our backyard. I believe it was a snake." I stated. "Billy growled real low, yelped, and staggered about halfway up the yard before she collapsed."

"Do you have woods around the house?" he asked.

"Partially," I nodded.

"Did you call animal control?" he questioned while listening to Billy's breathing.

"My fiancé did," the vet looked confused. "We're neighbors." Mark clarified.

"Did any of you see the snake?" The three of us shook our heads. "Without a witness, it's difficult to know exactly what species," he carefully examined the bite on Billy's neck. "But I do believe you are right about it being a snake bite."

"Poisonous?" I swallowed.

"Looks like. The good news is there is only a select few in this area that are poisonous. And they are rarely found." The vet check Billy's eyes. "I'm giving her an antivenom. It should help her breathing."

"Is she going to be all right?" Max huddled close to my side.

"I'd say if she makes it through tonight, her chances are pretty good. I'll keep her here for a couple days and update you on her progress." Max grabbed my hand and squeezed.

"Is there any way we can monitor her at home?" I asked hopefully.

"She will need to be on an IV for a couple days. I am afraid I cannot send her home until she improves." I heard Max swallow. "I cannot tell you not to worry, because you will. But I promise I will call you if there is any change in her condition." He motioned us towards the door.

"I have some paperwork for you to fill out." The young assistant led us around to the front desk.

I spent the next ten minutes filling out forms. I didn't want to think of what this was going to cost me. But it was Billy and there was nothing I would not do for her. She was a beloved member of our family, and I was not about to give up on her.

"Can we see her before we leave?" I asked the assistant. "She's likely to be scared without one of us with her."

"Let me check with Dr. Davis."

We waited impatiently for her to return. I noticed Mark texting Debbie and I noticed not only did I not have my purse, I also had no clue where I had dropped my phone. It must be somewhere in the backyard. I would have to find it and hope the dew didn't ruin it. I would also need to apologize to Chris. I knew he was still on the line when I ran to Billy.

"Please follow me," the young blond gave us a pitiful look that didn't offer much comfort.

Mark remained in the waiting room while Max and I followed her into the kennel area. Billy was lying on her side with her front paw wrapped in a bandage where the intravenous tube disappeared beneath. Her breathing was shallow but steady.

Max gripped my arm a little harder as we approached her. The vet was crouched beside her stroking her head. Billy's eyes were closed.

"How is she?" Max's bottom lip quivered as he tried to be brave.

"She's sleeping. Her breathing is good. She just needs to rest and let the medicine work," The vet patted Max on the shoulder. "She's strong and she's fighting. You can stay with her for minute. But try not to wake her."

"Thank you," I reached out my hand to the vet.

"I'm Justin Davis." He shook my hand. "I'm going to stay here tonight with Billy.

"I appreciate that," exhaustion finally set in, and I leaned against the wall.

"Are you feeling okay?" Dr. Davis asked.

"Yes, just tired." I rubbed my eyes. "How is she?" I said in a low voice.

"She's strong. This has really taken a lot out of her, but she is fighting. If she makes it through the night, I believe she will make it. The next twelve to twenty-four hours will be telling." He turned his back towards Max and spoke softly.

It was after ten when the three of us headed back home. The atmosphere was sullen on the cloudy night. The moon and stars remained hidden from sight giving me little hope to cling to. I knew it was going to be a long night.

Mark turned down our street to a sight none of us expected. The street cluttered with vehicles and bright spotlights were set up across my backyard lighting up the area like Yankee Stadium. I saw one truck marked Animal Control, another Parks & Services, and one labeled Wildlife Preserve.

"What in the world," Mark growled pulling in his driveway.

"This is ridiculous," I jumped out before he had it in park and ran across the street.

I tore through my front door and almost collided with Chris.

"Whoa," he put his hands on my shoulders to avoid a collision.

"Oh my God, Chris! What's going on here?" I rubbed my growing abdomen. It seemed the twins didn't appreciate my sudden sprint.

"The skittish gal from Animal Control freaked when she discovered it was a Copperhead hiding in the heavily wooded area at the edge of your property. She called Wildlife Preserve who happened to be having dinner with a guy from Parks & Services," I raised my eyebrows. "Don't ask." He rolled his eyes. "Anyway, he tagged along. So, the gangs all here." Chris raised his hands for emphasis with a hearty laugh.

"This is insane," I spotted the troupes on my deck milling about arguing over what to do next.

"What is going on?" Max and Mark caught up.

"That's what I'm gonna find out," I passed Chris, crossed the kitchen, and opened the French door.

"What is going on here?" Five sets of eyes turned towards me.

"And you are?" This stocky woman with a kaki uniform on, demanded.

"The homeowner," I glanced over at a bewildered-looking Debbie and laughed. "Are you sure you don't want to call the National Guard?"

"I only called Animal Control." She smirked patting my youngest son on the shoulder. "Henry can testify to that."

"Where's Billy?" Henry stepped forward and wrapped his arms around my waist. "Is she inside sleeping?" he looked up at me with doe eyes.

"No, baby," I tasseled his hair softly. "She's still at the hospital. The vet gave her the antivenom. And she needs to stay there for a couple days so the doctor can watch her."

"Is she going to die?" his bottom lip quivered.

"I hope not baby," he'd learned a hard life lesson this year. I prayed it wouldn't be reinforced.

"Can I go to bed now?" Henry's voice was shaky.

"I'll come with you," Max slightly nodded his head before he followed his little brother in the house. I noticed Max put his arm across Henry's shoulder in a big brother supportive manner. My heart warmed with pride.

Mark and Debbie joined Chris and me around the table on the deck while the three Stooges crept around my fence-line like Elmer Fudd hunting Bugs Bunny. Debbie rested her head on the table and groaned loudly.

"I am exhausted," she looked up at me briefly. "Why can't you be the dull mysterious neighbor across the street?"

"I keep your life entertaining," I smiled.

"I have 3 children, an incompetent boss, and a worthless ex that are entertaining enough." She playfully slapped the table.

"Should I be scared?" Chris looked at me with a leery expression.

"Oh, I'm rude. Chris, these are my neighbors and good friends, Mark, and Debbie. They live catty-cornered across the street. Mark, Debbie, this is Erik's brother Chris. He's going to be Erik's best man." I rambled.

"Oh, well that makes sense." Debbie laughed. "I wasn't sure what to think when he showed up here asking for you."

"Lisa and Erik introduced us a couple weeks ago. They thought it would be a good idea since we'll be spending time together with wedding preparations." Chris explained.

"Is that what she's calling it? Wedding preparations?" Mark laughed. "She's playing matchup."

"Nah, she knows better. I just broke up with my fiancé and the mother of my youngest son. The last thing I'm looking for is a relationship." Chris laughed.

"Chris had a good idea earlier. Since neither of us are in the frame of mind or position to be in a relationship, we came to the agreement to stand is as each other's surrogate date." I smiled.

"Surrogate date?" Debbie laughed. "Isn't that a mature version of 'friends with benefits'?"

Chris and I both busted out laughing.

"In case you've forgotten, I'm pregnant with twins." I reminded her.

"And are you going to sit there and tell me you never had sex with Danny when you were pregnant with the boys?" Debbie winked at Mark. "Now I understand Danny's affair."

"Ouch!" I playfully smacked her arm. "Yes, of course we had sex when I was pregnant. But we were married." I stated as if that explained it all.

"Okay," Debbie whistled, and they all laughed at me.

"What?" I hated when they did this.

A scream followed by a barrage of colorful language, jerked our heads towards the rear fence. The only view visible to us were three shadow figures scrambling around, jumping back, followed by piercing screams from the two females.

We got to our feet, but none of us left the deck. Considering the nature of their prey the consensus amongst us was to leave it to the professionals. Especially considering how they were fairing, the addition of our laymen contribution, would only be a hindrance.

Another twenty minutes later the trio emerged victorious. The man was carrying a small crate with an angry copperhead squirming about trying to free himself. The women were walking a good five feet off to the side of him looking weary and exhausted.

"We got him," the man announced. "He's not too happy, but we'll take him out to Eagle Creek and set him loose."

"You mean you will," his date added looking none too thrilled with his macho BS.

"But I thought," the look she flashed him shut him up short.

"I'm going home," she wiped her brow.

The two women walked around the side of my house with the man trailing behind arguing with them about who was going to take the lights down.

"It's been a long night. I am exhausted." Debbie leaned over and gave me a hug. "Call me when you hear anything about Billy. I will keep her in my prayers."

"Thank you for everything," I turned to Mark. "You are my hero." I hugged him and kissed his cheek.

"Anytime," he smiled and put his arm around Debbie as they headed home.

"Guess I should be headed home as well." Chris started cleaning up the cups and snacks off the table.

I followed him into the house with the last of remains of the disgruntled evening. I set things down on the counter and peeked in on my boys. Max and Henry were both sleeping in Max's double bed.

I leaned against the doorframe watching them sleep peacefully. It warmed my heart that they had each other to lean on. It reminded me that I still needed to call my sister and tell her about the twins. I wasn't sure what she was going to say. She had gotten engaged to her boyfriend, Oliver last year, yet the two of them had yet to set a date.

"Henry is a lucky young man," Chris walked up beside me and whispered.

"Why is that?" I couldn't take my eyes on them.

"Erik tormented the hell out of me growing up. He never would have let me sleep in his room because I was upset." He shrugged slightly. "Erik was more a practitioner of the tough love school of thought." A smirk formed across his shapely lips as he winked his eye.

"I never would have thought Erik was like that. He always seems so sweet — a little ornery at times perhaps, but a really good guy." I defended the man my best friend loved.

"He is. Erik's the best. I can't think of anyone I trust more or would be so proud to stand up for, but we didn't become friends until my first son was born."

"I'm close to my sister, Samantha now, but not so much when we were growing up. And there's a snowballs chance in hell of us ever getting along with our brother." I motioned towards the living room.

"Why don't you like your brother?" He asked when we reached our destination.

"He and his family are the definition of 'stick up their asses'." I rolled my eyes. "I don't know where he came about his sense of overentitlement, but he married the perfect woman and unfortunately they bred."

"You have a little devil that sits on your shoulder, you know it?" Chris laughed.

"Yeah, but he's been there for years and I'm kinda attached to him. Besides, I must admit, he's got some really good ideas." I gestured for emphasis.

"And on that note, I'm gonna say goodnight." Chris leaned over and kissed me on the cheek. "I will see you tomorrow evening."

"Thank you for rushing over. You really didn't have to, but I appreciate it."

"No problem," he waved back before he climbed in his truck.

I locked the house up and turned off the lights. I was so accustomed to Billy shadowing me through the dark house. I felt so alone without her fur brushing against my leg as I walked or her head lovingly nudging my hand. It had been a long time since I'd had to sleep without her beside me.

I brushed my teeth and took a quick shower. I was becoming so aware of my rapidly changing figure. I ran my hands over my abdomen standing naked in front of the full-length mirror. To my eyes, my body was getting bigger by the day. A matrix of emotions ran through me, and I wasn't sure how I was supposed to feel.

I crawled between the sheets and closed my eyes tightly trying to ignore the empty pillow beside me. In my mind I escaped to that beach in Dublin where things were perfect between Hayden and me. I missed him so much.

I rolled onto my back and stared at the ceiling.

"How could you do this to me?" I whispered in the dark. "How can you do this to our children? I am so mad at you. When I lost Mason in this world, I lost you too. You abandoned me. You treated my sons and me like we're nothing. You couldn't get us on a plane fast enough." I ignored the tears crashing upon my pillow.

"There's so much I want to say to you. I am so angry at you. I wish I could bring myself to hate you. I really do," my voice quivered angrily through my tears. "And I'm trying. I really am, but I just can't. I love you so much. I miss you. I need you. I am so terrified of doing this alone. I can barely manage my two boys most days and they are really good kids. Adding two babies and all they entail," I sobbed. "I don't think I'm strong enough to do this alone."

I rolled over on my side clinging to Billy's pillow.

"I miss you," I whispered in the dark to Billy and Hayden.

Chapter 27

I SPENT A COUPLE HOURS WITH Billy on Friday afternoon. The hospital wouldn't allow the boys to see her, regardless of how many times I asked.

Billy was still connected to the IV and barely opened her eyes for a few minutes and wagged her tail a little bit. I could tell it took a lot out of her to do so. She did not have enough strength in her to lift her head. It broke my heart to see her like this. I was thankful the boys were not with me.

The day-shift vet seemed optimistic. She told me Billy was getting stronger and fighting. But she still had a long way to go. She was hopeful she would pull through. She did mention that the recovery would be long and challenging for her.

Aaron and Max were playing Halo and tormenting each other mercilessly when Chris arrived. I had stopped at Target on my way home and picked up a larger sized dark blue sun dress for the cookout. The material was flowing in an almost sexy way highlighting my figure while being deceptive of my enlarging midsection. It was almost knee-length and looked darling with my white strappy sandals with little heels.

I twisted my hair into French knot and applied my makeup sparingly. I was surprised how cute I looked. And I hated myself for immediately thinking of how I wished I was spending the evening with Hayden at a cookout with him and his friends. I twirled in the mirror and tried to push thoughts of Hayden out of my mind. I was determined to have fun with Chris and enjoy his company.

"Wow, you clean up nice." He was standing in the living room monitoring the battle.

"Thanks," I looked around wondering how long he'd been waiting.

"Oh, Max just let me in about five minutes ago." He explained before I could ask. "I told him not to bother you. He mentioned you saw Billy this afternoon." I nodded. "How is she?"

"The vet is optimistic," I eyed the boys indicating I didn't want to elaborate.

I reminded the boys of the rules and consequences of breaking them. They jeered and pretty much ignored me. I told them there were pizza rolls in the freezer for them and chips and cookies in the pantry. They waved in acknowledgement completely mesmerized by their game.

Chris opened the door for me and held my arm as I climbed into his truck. I fastened my seatbelt while he climbed in and fired the engine. He looked very handsome in his kaki shorts and light blue button-up shirt. The color greatly enhanced his eyes and made him look stunningly handsome.

Yep, he's Captain America.

"Fair warning, my friends are a little nuts." He smiled over at me.

"You're saying this to me knowing who my best friend is? That's frightening." I grimaced.

"Do you know many firefighters?"

"No. Can't say I do." I thought for a moment. "I know a few boys from high school who became cops, but nope, no firemen." Chris made a face. "I'm guessing those are two different breeds?"

"As different as dogs and cats," he laughed.

"But both are necessary for a harmonic existence, wouldn't you agree?" I pointed out.

"Yes, I believe so," he smirked. "I'll let you decide who gets the most props. But I dare say you don't see too many policeman calendars. They are not necessarily known for their outstanding physic, wouldn't you agree?"

"Agreed," I laughed at his overexuberant confidence.

We rolled the windows down and enjoyed the night air. It was a warm and beautiful twilight. The moon appeared off in the distance settling in the sky for the long night ahead. I gazed upon it hardly believing it was the same moon I had shared with Hayden in Europe so long ago.

I tried to push all thoughts of Hayden out of my mind. It would serve me nothing, but surely ruin my evening. I felt as if I were mourning Hayden's death alongside Mason's. My mind accepted the reality of it, but the truth still lay scattered about my broken heart.

Chris turned up the radio and we pulled onto interstate 465. Rush hour traffic was dying down but those determined to take advantage of the warm summer evening littered the highway. He navigated more than a quarter of the way around the city exiting off at Thompson Road.

"Is that your station?" I asked when we turned right.

"Yep, my second home for a decade and a half." He beamed.

"I'm glad you have a profession that you love." I smiled. "I hope to find that too."

"Lisa said you were back in school. What are you going for?"

"I'm getting my BS in psychology."

"A bullshit degree in psychology? That sounds about right." Chris laughed.

"A bachelor's degree in psych isn't worth the paper it's printed on, so I have no choice but to get at least my master's." I told him.

"Are you going after your doctorate as well?" Chris inquired.

"I'm not sure." I was struggling to contemplate how I was going to achieve my master's as a single mother of four. "It all depends." I rubbed my abdomen.

"You must be worried." I nodded. "Lisa said you refuse to tell their father."

"We have not spoken since his son's funeral." I stared out the window.

"Having another child, twins even, may renew his spirit." He gave me a weary smile.

"I don't believe so," I said still looking out the window. "He blames me for his son's death."

"I thought he was murdered in Chicago."

"He was. But he was murdered at his father's penthouse while his father was at my place. He claims if he were home instead of with me, it never would have happened." I explained in a sullen voice.

"That's absurd," Chris raised his voice an octave. "Certainly, he must have realized that by now?"

"If he has, I haven't heard of it. I occasionally speak to his daughter, Kennedy." I told him.

"Does she know about the twins?" I shook my head. "Aren't you afraid they'll find out?"

"No. They live in Chicago." I shrugged. "Without Mason, they have no reason to visit Indy. And even if they do, they have no reason to call upon me."

"Hey, I'm sorry." He reached over and touched my hand lightly. "I didn't mean to."

"I'm fine," I brushed a stray tear off my cheek.

Chris pulled into a neighborhood of cookie cutter homes. The builder rotated between four designs and the sameness was mind numbing. The homes were close together allotting small yards, little space, and zero privacy without isolating the property with a tall fence. It seemed most newer neighborhoods were adhering to this format. This popular new trend made me thankful Danny and I had purchased our home in an upscale older neighborhood with oversized yards, mature trees, and elbow room.

The street was lined with vehicles centered around the house residing at the back of the court. There were people milling about in the circle, front yard, and passing in and out of the house.

Chris parked his truck towards the entrance of the street after completing the circle. Numerous people waved to Chris as we passed them by. He appeared to be well liked amongst his colleagues. He opened my door and held my arm as I stepped down.

"This should be entertaining," I widened my eyes with a smirk.

"It beats sitting at home in front of the television." He remarked.

"Who ever said I would be sitting in front of my TV?" I giggled. "I wish I had time to watch TV. I hear people talking about different shows and I am completely clueless."

"You don't watch TV?" Chris wrinkled his nose at me.

"Do you seriously think I have time between school, teaching, and my children. I barely have time to eat." We stepped up on the sidewalk. "The only time I watch TV is when I go to bed and that usually lasts about five minutes."

"Do you expect that to change anytime soon?"

"I used to be hopeful," I laid my hand on my stomach. "But I guess I shot that to shit, didn't I?"

"You sure did," he shook his head as he opened the front door.

I took a hold of Chris' arm suddenly feeling very self-conscious. There were half a dozen couples milling about with drinks and plates of food. The aroma from the grill flowed in through the windows filling the house with a heavenly mesquite aroma.

"You're late," a robust, burley, man greeted us in the living room.

"I arrived exactly when I meant to." Chris shook the man's hand with a hearty laugh. "Scott, I'd like you to meet Alex Rose. Alex, this piece of work is one of my oldest friends, Scott Harding." I shook his hand.

"What is a beautiful lady like you doing with this fugly monkey?" Scott's bushy eyebrows went up.

"I took pity on him." I smiled up at Chris.

"Obviously," Scott laughed. "It's the only way he can get a lady such as yourself cause you are far out of his league."

"Ah, he's kinda cute." I nudged him playfully.

"Gee thanks. I feel so special." Chris grinned.

"There's food and drinks on the deck. Help yourself. There's plenty." A woman approached from the kitchen.

"Alex, this is Tara. She claims this meathead." Chris explained.

"It's a pleasure to meet you." I smiled.

"You as well," Tara was a cute, short woman with slightly crooked front teeth that added charm and enhanced her features.

We followed them through the kitchen out onto the deck. I was surprised by the size of the gathering. There had to have been at least fifty people eating, drinking, and laughing. Everyone seemed to be having a wonderful time. They were a joyous lively bunch.

Couples had divided into teams on one side of the yard playing cornhole and jeering at each other. Off the side of the deck was a firepit next to the oversized smoker filled with corn on the cob, ribs, chicken, and burgers. The table beside it filled with dozens of side dishes, condiments, and desserts. There was enough food to feed a small country and the men were putting it away at an alarming rate — almost as quickly as their consumption of alcohol.

A group of highly intoxicated men were over by the firepit playing with fireworks, aiming bottle rockets at each other, and tossing blackjacks at each other. They had a captive audience gathered around taking bets on which drunken fool would get injured first.

"And these are trained professionals?" I snickered in a low voice so only Chris could hear.

"Scary thought, huh?" he laughed.

"Very," I tried to bury my face in his arm.

"Would you like something to drink?" A burly intoxicated man stumbled over to us.

"Where's the beer?" Chris asked.

"In the tub," he nodded towards the far end of the deck. "What would you like pretty lady?"

"I'll take a water bottle. Thank you."

"Um, I'll see what I can find ya." He winked at Chris and wandered back into the house.

"I'll be right back," Chris walked over to the tub and grabbed a Rolling Rock bottleneck. He popped the top and took a long swig.

"Feel better," I smiled as he rejoined me.

"You're driving, right?" he gave me a cocky grin.

"So, that's why you invited me?" I laughed.

"Nah, I live just around the corner. I could easily walk home."

"But then I'd have your truck," I teased.

"I know where you live." Chris winked.

"Here ya are," the burly guy returned. "I couldn't find ya a water bottle so, I grabbed ya some tea." He handed me a blue dixie cup with a smile.

"Thank you," I brought it to my lips, took a sip, and promptly spit it back into the cup. "Ugh," I looked up at Chris. "It's a Long Island."

"Seriously, Brett." Chris' voice took a rougher tone. "She's pregnant."

"How was I supposed to know?" Brett stammered.

"Chris, it's no biggie. He didn't know." I was surprised by his tone.

"Because she's with Chris," a tall slender bald man intervened. "He's got children scattered all across the state."

"First off, you're an ass! Secondly, Alex is a friend of mine and these babies," Chris scanned the confused looks. "Yes, I said babies. Alex is having twins and they are not mine. She is my brother's fiancé's best friend and therefore, the maid of honor in the wedding party and I'm the best man," he rambled needlessly.

"Sorry, we see you with a lady and automatically assume she's pregnant because it's well, it's you." A middle-aged chubby guy added garnering laughter from the crowd.

"Fair enough," Chris smiled and shrugged.

"Here," one of the ladies handed me a chilled bottle of water.

"Thank you," I smiled at the pretty blond.

"Don't mind these guys. They are ruthless, but they'd give you the shirt off their back if you needed it," she leaned in closer. "Not that you'd want it, but still."

"Are you a fireman?" I asked.

"EMT attached to their station. They treat me like one of the guys — unfortunately." She laughed. "I'm Robin."

"It's nice to meet you," I smiled. "How long have you been an EMT?"

"Almost five years. I love it," she took a sip of her drink. "What do you do?" I always hated this question. It made me feel inadequate.

"I'm finishing my bachelors and work as a student teacher." I explained.

"I hope to go back and finish mine someday. Life just seems to get in the way." Robin shrugged her shoulder. "Is this your first?" She nodded towards my belly.

"No. Third and fourth." I grinned.

"Wow. I cannot even imagine. I'm a single mom too. I have a six-year-old son. It's hard enough with my ex and parents helping out." She told me.

"My ex-husband lives in Phoenix, and I don't really have family around, but my friends are incredible."

I spent most of the evening talking with Robin. She was really sweet and introduced me around. It wasn't long before Chris was amongst the group playing with fireworks. There were a few close calls when they broke out the Roman candles that required the garden hose spraying the roof and garage door and an incident with a tree. But other than a few minor burns on their fingers, thankfully there was no other carnage.

We headed home a little after midnight. I was completely spent and could barely keep my eyes open. Chris had only had three beers all evening but had also eaten his weight in ribs and potato salad.

"Did you have a good time?" he asked pulling onto the interstate.

"I did. You have some really wonderful colleagues."

"They're family. I went through training with a few of them." He smiled. "You look tired."

"I am."

"I'm sorry. I should have taken you home earlier."

"It's okay. I was having a great time."

"Thank you for coming." Chris reached over and patted my shoulder in a caring manner. "You can lean against me if you'd like. You look like you're about to fall over," he smiled.

"Thanks," I maneuvered the slack on the seatbelt to give me enough room to squirm around so I could rest comfortably against Chris's shoulder.

The next thing I recall was him brushing my hair away from my face.

"Alex?" his fingers traced along my cheek. "You're home, Sleeping Beauty."

I opened my eyes to see his face mere inches from mine. His chiseled features were striking in the glowing hue from the streetlamps and porch light. I caught my breath and sat up straight in the passenger seat.

"Oh, sorry. I guess I dozed off." I tried to stifle a yawn.

"It's okay. I understand," he unbuckled his seatbelt and climbed out of his truck. "You looked so peaceful I didn't have the heart to wake you." Chris opened my door.

"Thanks. I'm just happy I wasn't drooling on you." I smirked.

He closed the door and walked me up to the front door.

"Ya did a little bit," my cheeks burned from embarrassment.

"Oh, God," I covered my face with my hand. "How sexy," I shook my head laughing.

"It's nice to know you're human." He remarked as I unlocked the door.

"Thank you for a great evening. I'm glad we did this. We'll have to do this again."

"I'd like that. It's rare that I ever get a weekend night off without one or more of my boys. I've got three of them this weekend."

"That should be entertaining," I teased.

"I've got the older three for the fourth. My ex wanted to keep Quintin. She's got a family thing to go to." Chris leaned against the railing.

"Any big plans?"

"Not really. I was thinking about taking them downtown to see the fireworks or something. You?" He shrugged.

"We always go over to Mark's and Debbie's. You should come by. Your brother and Lisa will be there."

"Are you sure?"

"Of course, the more the merrier. Just bring a side dish or dessert and whatever you want to drink. We just hang out by the pool, eat too much, and drink too much — well normally," I patted my belly with a giggle.

"I'll think about it. Thanks for the invite." Chris leaned over and hugged me. "I had a great time tonight." He kissed me quickly on the cheek.

"Me too," I opened the door.

"Sweet dreams," he waved on his way to his truck.

I smiled and waved back before I closed the door. I was surprised how much fun I'd had tonight. The house was quiet, and the boys were sound asleep. By the time I closed my bedroom door, I felt guilty for having fun with Chris and his friends.

I undressed and crawled into bed. I knew I had no reason to feel guilty, but I did. I knew things were over with Hayden, but I still loved him. I rubbed my rounding belly and tried not to cry. A part of me was dying to tell him about the twins, but I knew he didn't want to hear from me. He knew how to reach or find me, and he hadn't.

In months.

Our story was over.

Chapter 28

THE ANNUAL FOURTH OF JULY parade was miserable. The humidity was eighty-six percent. By nine in the morning, it was already ninety-two degrees, sunny without a cloud in the sky, and I was in hell. I stood in the blistering sun sweating and drinking water. I felt horrible.

I stood with Lisa, and Debbie on the sidewalk of the parade route. Their men were with the boys finding their team trucks in the high school parking lot. We still had another thirty minutes before the parade was set to begin.

"Erik got a call from Chris last night." Lisa began casually. "He wanted to know if it was all right if he and his boys crashed our cookout today."

"Should I not have invited him?" I asked.

"No. It's fine. I love Chris and his boys are great. I'm just happy you two hit it off so well." She remarked.

"Chris is a nice guy. I went with him Friday night to a cookout with his station. It was fun." I took another long drink.

"And?" she leaned in.

"And what?" I started fanning myself again.

"And you didn't even get a kiss goodnight?"

"No."

"That sucks," she muttered.

"We're just friends." I rolled my eyes.

"There is nothing wrong with friends with benefits. "You're both single, attractive, and enjoy spending time together." Lisa remarked.

"Don't get me started. I already told her the same thing. She blew me off too." Debbie joined in.

"We're friends," I stated again.

"Are you blind?" Debbie shook her head "I may be engaged but I'm not blind. That man is luscious. Don't you agree?"

"Don't look at me. Chris is going to be my brother next month. But yes, you could bounce a quarter off that ass." Lisa winked.

"Oh, I'd love to try that!" Debbie smirked.

"Try what?" Mark asked as he and Erick approached.

"A new recipe for chicken tetrazzini." Debbie quipped without hesitation.

"It sounds delicious," Lisa smiled at Mark.

"I haven't had chicken tetrazzini in years. I love it. You should make it this week." Mark put his arm around Debbie just as the parade started.

"Sure," she grinned up at her him before leaning over to me. "Thanks a lot."

"You asked for it," I giggled.

The sweltering heat did nothing for my disposition. My pudgy abdomen was hardly noticeable to anyone except me. I hid in my closet trying on various bathing suits and all of them felt fight and in my opinion, looked ridiculous.

I wanted to wear my red bikini bottoms with the red and white stripped bikini top, but my belly bulged just a little too much. I stood in front of the full-length mirror looking at myself from every angle wishing I owned a tank-kini or even a one-piece suit, but I didn't.

From the side and the front, it seemed my breasts were growing bigger by the day. I loved having full beautiful breasts, and how the cleavage enhanced my clothes, especially bikinis, but I was now entering into a time when I was struggling to stuff them in. I finally threw on my stars and stripes oversized tank top over my red and white bikini knowing it would hide the twins.

Chris and his sons were already in the pool with the rest of our entourage when my boys and I arrived shortly before noon. I set the boys loose in the backyard and sought refuge from the heat inside the kitchen where Debbie and Lisa were finishing the final preparations for the enormous spread of food.

"Hiding?" Debbie smirked when I entered the kitchen.

"No," I lied setting potato salad on the island and putting my raspberry tea in the fridge.

"Liar," Lisa nudged me playfully. "Chris is out in the pool with his boys, in case you were wondering."

"I wasn't," I stuck my tongue out.

"Brie brought along one of her friends. They were dying to spend the day staring at Max in the pool." Lisa rolled her eyes. "Oh, did you know your son is the hottest guy in school?"

"Um, no." I chuckled. "Are you serious?"

"According to my daughter and her friends." She grinned.

"Oh, Lord. I hope Max doesn't know that." I rolled my eyes. "That's all that I need."

"Hayley has been in love with him for years." Debbie remarked slicing the tomatoes. "But Max has never noticed."

I did not have the heart to tell her that Max had noticed Hayley's crush on him a long time ago. When I playfully teased him about it, he had wrinkled his nose and commented about how chubby Hayley was and stated he was more interested in her friend, Lea who was tiny, petite with a golden mane cascading down her back. She was a beautiful child as a preteen, and I was simply thankful I was not her mother.

I had scolded Max for his comment and told him never to utter something like that aloud. I reminded him to think how he would feel if their roles were reversed, and that Hayley was a sweet girl who liked him. He needed to be careful not to hurt her feelings.

"Max is focused on sports and video games. I'm not sure he's aware of much else." I said vaguely.

"Are the girls outside?" Lisa asked.

"Yeah, their dad is down in the Bahamas with his girlfriend, and they're pissed. They really don't like her." Debbie shrugged.

"I think that par for the course. Look at how my boys feel about Amanda." I put the hamburger patties, Italian sausage, and hot dogs on the platter.

"That's not necessarily true. Your boys loved Mason." Debbie pointed out.

"True, but that took a while and it helped he was closer to their age than mine. Mason was more of a big brother than a father figure." I reasoned.

"And he would have been if Hayden wasn't such a pussy." Lisa scoffed. "I'm sorry, but I am ticked at him for the way he's treated you. I know he's going through hell, but that doesn't give him the right to shit all over the person who he claims to love. That's bullshit."

"I agree," I remarked over my shoulder on my way outside.

I wanted to get out before the conversation got any more intense. I knew how Debbie and Lisa felt about Hayden along with Erik and Mark — none of which was flattering. Adding in the twins only made their disdain for him worse. Plus, none of them understood why I didn't tell him about them or why I wouldn't go after him for child support.

Perhaps it was my broken heart, but I had already felt the humiliating sting of rejection. Hayden had bestowed it on my sons as well. I was not about to subject my innocent twins to being rejected by their father.

"Hello, Ali." Chris climbed out of the pool. "How are you?"

"Ali?" I pinched my lips.

"Yeah, well. It sounds so much more feminine than Alex." The sun glistened off his bare muscular chest. "Don't you think?" His smile was contagious.

"I've always gone by Alex." I shrugged putting the tray next to the grill.

"Fine. Then it'll be my name for you."

"What is it with men," I shook my head in disbelief.

"What?" Chris shook his head making his blond hair stand up in little spikes.

"Why is it men keep trying to change my name. Ali. Lexie. Ahh." I scrunched up my face.

"Okay. Alex it is." He picked up his beer. "I just thought Ali was sexier. But I like Lexie too." He gulped down half his beer.

"Would you like me to call you Chrissy?" I smirked.

"Point taken," he set down his drink.

"Your boys?" I nodded towards the pool.

"Yeah, that's Garrett talking to Olivia. He's fifteen but believes he's twenty-one. Ian is in the red trunks. He's ten," Chris indicated the stocky blond talking to Logan and Henry. "And Zac beside him in the black trunks. He's eight." Chris beamed with pride.

"And your youngest is,"

"Quinton just turned three. He's with his mom."

"You have your hands full." I shook my head how different my life will be next Fourth of July.

"Something to look forward to," he teased.

"I know," I dipped my toes in the water. It was refreshingly cool, and I could not wait to get in.

"Don't worry. You're gonna be great." Chris put a brotherly arm around my shoulder.

"I'm glad one of us is sure," I chuckled and put my head on his shoulder.

The day was idyllic. It had been a long time since I fully relaxed and enjoyed myself. I was still self-conscious about my expanding waistline, but as the day wore on with laugher and easy conversation, I soon forgot about it. We finished the celebration with an obscene number of fireworks picked up by the men. It seemed that they only aged on the outside and deep down they were just as giddy as the children.

Chris and his boys walked us home despite my insistence that we could cross the street alone. It was sweet how considerate he was being, and it was hard to tear our boys apart. They had become fast friends and all of them were hyped up on sugar and excitement rippled through the atmosphere.

Chris and I stopped on my front porch. I unlocked the door and turned towards him.

"Thank you for walking us home." I smiled up at his sparkling blue eyes. "I'll call you this week. Perhaps we can get these monkey's together before they drive us nuts."

"Safety in numbers," he laughed.

"Exactly," I placed my hand on his chest and leaned up on my tiptoes kissing him on the cheek. "Come on boys." I hollered over his shoulder before opening our door.

"I'll be waiting for that call," Chris grinned taking a step back off my porch.

"With baited breath?" I teased.

"You know it," he gathered up his troops and waved a final goodbye as they crossed the street.

I got my sons in the house and waved back before I closed the front door. Henry took off towards the kitchen looking for a snack and Max headed straight to the shower. I took a deep breath and set our things down on the island in the kitchen. I shooed Henry out of the refrigerator and cleaned up the kitchen.

My mind was whirling in confusion. Chris was incredibly kind and attentive. He watched over me consistently throughout the day making sure I had a cold beverage, a dry towel, whatever. He joked around and teased me but never crossed that pervertible line. It was strange.

At times he treated me like a girlfriend yet at others as a sister. And occasionally, I would catch him looking at me and when I would meet his eye, he would immediately look away. I played it off like it was nothing, but I could not help but wonder if he was interested in something more.

I took a long hot shower trying to clear my head and push thoughts of Chris aside. It worked for half a minute until I crawled into bed and guilt washed over me like a scratchy flea infested blanket. Images of Hayden lingered behind my eyelids. His smile, his eyes, his embrace — haunted me.

My hands naturally rested on my lower abdomen. I gently rubbed my fingers over my tiny twins. I tried to refocus my thoughts to the ultrasound only days away. I was curious as to the sex of my babies and I truly did not care which they were if they were healthy.

Chapter 29

THE BOYS AND I PICKED UP Billy on Tuesday afternoon. She was weak, but more alert than when I had last seen her. Dr. Davis carried her out to my car and laid her across the back seat. Max went around to the other side of the car and climbed into the backseat with her.

"She will need a lot of rest." The vet closed the door and turned towards me. "No rigorous activity. No running around. Take her out on a leash at least for another week."

"We can do that," I promised.

"Call me if you have any problems or questions." He reached out his hand to me and I shook it.

"I cannot thank you enough, Dr. Davis for all you have done for my family."

"Please, call me Justin. It was my pleasure. She is obviously very loved. She is lucky to have such a wonderful home. I wish every dog could be so fortunate." He smiled.

"Have a wonderful day." I opened my door. "Thank you again."

"Take care, Alex. Call me."

Henry hopped in the passenger seat and twisted himself around so he could pet Billy. Max was stroking her head and speaking softly to her. It warmed my heart knowing how much compassion and love my sons held for Billy.

Max insisted on carrying Billy into the house once we returned home. He struggled under her weight but refused my help because of the twins. Henry rushed to open and hold the door for him.

Max set her down gently on the oversized plush doggie bed on the living room floor. Henry had moved it out of the corner and over to the center of the room so there was room for everyone to be near her.

The boys and I spent the remainder of the day lying on the floor around Billy watching movies and attending to her every need. It was sweet watching the boy's squabble over who got to take her outside and making them take turns when they couldn't agree.

I met Lisa on the bleachers Wednesday evening for Logan and

Henry's game. She was still wearing her work clothes and heels. Her hair was askew and falling out of the bun she had tied it in that morning.

"Bad day?" I tossed a sweatshirt over the blazing hot metal bleacher before taking a seat beside her.

"My boss is a penis wrinkle." She rolled her eyes. "I've had one of those days when I wish I had the balls to open my own business so I could tell that SOB what he can do with his job."

"You should." I told her. "What's stopping you? You've been talking about it ever since I met you."

"Money." Lisa sighed heavily with despair. "It would take a lot of capital to do what I want."

"But this town needs a café, bakery, coffee, slash bookstore. You could easily make a killing. There's nothing like that around here." I encouraged her. "And you are the perfect person to do it."

"I know," she chewed on her index fingernail lost in her own thoughts.

"Stop that," I wrinkled my forehead and pulled her hand away from her mouth. "That's gross." It was a nervous habit she did when something was bothering her.

"Sorry," she grimaced.

"You'll ruin your nails before the wedding." I informed her.

"Yeah right," she waved her hand at me. "I will be having those professionally done." She grabbed my hand, glanced at my nails, scowled, and tossed my hand back at me. "As will you."

"Thanks. I'm more concerned about Chris having to roll my fat ass down the aisle than my nails." I said sarcastically with a smidgen of truth in it.

"Speaking of which, isn't your ultrasound tomorrow?" She nudged.

"Ten o'clock tomorrow morning." I winked. "Max and Henry want to go. I think they are more excited about it than I am."

"Are you going to find out the sex?"

"I hope so," I cocked my head. "If they decide to cooperate."

"You don't want to be surprised?" She grinned.

"The pregnancy was surprise enough, don't ya think?"

"True," I smacked her for giggling.

"I would like to have some idea of what to get."

"Two of everything," she continued laughing.

"You're such a bitch," I smirked.

"But you love me," Lisa had a cheesy grin on her lips. "Oh, and don't forget you have a final fitting on Friday afternoon."

"Just put me in a Moo Moo and call it a day." I huffed.

"Stop it. You're glowing." She put her arm around me. "Besides, I need you there for a buffer. Lydia is gonna be there too."

"Your sister?" she nodded. "She's in the bridal party?"

"My mother asked me to have her. It's not like she's ever going to have a wedding of her own." Lisa stifled a giggle.

"You're mean," I struggled not to laugh. "She may find someone someday."

"Between her sparkling personality, fashion sense, and highly desirable career choice, I'm sure the men are just lining up."

I'd heard a lot of Lydia over the years, but I had yet to meet her. She rarely came around and hardly spoke to Lisa or their mother. But it never deterred her mom from trying to bring her daughters closer and forge a relationship that in Lisa's mind, was never going to happen.

"What does she do?"

"She's an embalmer?" Lisa wrinkled her nose.

"Like with dead bodies?" It sounded horrific.

"Yep," she grimaced. "Just wait until you meet her."

"Something to look forward too," I put on my happy face.

"So, what is going on with you and Chris? You two seem to be getting along well."

"He's fun to hang out with." I shrugged. "We have lot in common."

"And you don't think he could be anything more than that?" she inquired.

"At this point in my life, no."

"Why not?" she wouldn't let it go.

"Obviously," I ran my hands over my abdomen. "I'm not in any position to start a relationship with anyone. And neither is he. I'm not interested in being someone's transition gal. I have enough problems on my plate without walking into that role."

"Do you really think Chris is like that?"

"Not intentionally, but you and I both know it happens." I cocked my head to the side a bit. "We both just got out of serious relationships. Neither of us is ready or willing to attempt another one — not for a very long time."

"So, you're going to be a hermit? Is that it?"

"No. I still go out." I defended. "Chris and I enjoy hanging out together, but as friends. Nothing more."

"You do know he's not coming back." Lisa said in a low voice. "He's not going to magically appear on your doorstep with candy and flowers begging for your forgiveness." I hated the look of sympathy in her eyes.

"I realize that," I admitted.

"Do you?" She frowned. "I see you pining away; dreaming and wishing, waiting for that call that's never going to come." Lisa put her hand on my arm. "I'm not trying to be a bitch, Alex. I'm just worried about you."

"I'm fine," I lied.

"Right," she sighed. "The man you lived with for two years was murdered and the man you were going to marry practically left you at the alter after knocking you up with twins. Now you're facing raising four children on your own with another year left in school."

"Damn, when you put it that way I might as well slit my wrists right now and be done with it." To hear her put it so bluntly in black and white was like a slap in the face.

"You know we're all here for you." She tried to sound comforting.

"I know," I exhaled loudly. "But I also know you're getting married and trying to have another baby. Debbie is engaged. I haven't spoken to my parents in forever — I'm basically on my own." I hated the sound of my own pity party.

As much as I knew she wanted to deny it, we both knew I was right. Lisa squeezed my arm gently but remained silent for a bit seemingly lost in her own thoughts.

I turned my attention to the game as they entered the second inning. Logan was playing short stop and Henry was following Max's footsteps as first baseman. He looked so cute in his navy-blue jersey, baseball cap, white pants, navy-blue stir-ups, and cleats. He caught an easy pop-up hit between him and second base. I stood up and cheered.

Later that night after the house was silent and the boys long asleep, I could not get the conversation with Lisa out of my head. I had placed Billy in her spot beside me on the bed with her head on the pillow beside mine. I stroked her head and rubbed her ears fighting the urge to call Hayden.

I missed him so much. I wished he was going with me tomorrow to see our twins on the ultrasound. I wondered how he would feel — excited? Terrified? Overjoyed? Would he want to know the sex of the twins?

I wished he would be there, holding my hand, sharing in the anticipation and exhilaration of not just the ultrasound, but the entire pregnancy. I wrapped my arm around Billy and hugged her to me. Tears fell from the corner of my eyes and crashed upon my pillow. I felt so alone.

Somewhere in the far recesses of my mind I heard my cell phone ringing. I must have finally dozed off but was groping around on my nightstand to locate the irritant.

"Hello," I said barely conscious.

"Oh, I'm sorry Alex. Did I wake you?" Kennedy's voice sounded warm and welcoming.

"It's okay. How are you?" I was surprised to hear her voice.

"Much better after today." I heard her sigh heavily into the phone. "We spent the day in court."

I had to stop myself from asking if she was referring to the *royal we* which included both her parents and Tony.

"How did it go?"

"Megan pled guilty to life with the possibility of parole after 25 years with the condition that she be allowed to remain at home with an ankle monitor until she delivers." Kennedy explained.

"When is she due?"

"Next week. Her mother is adopting the baby. She is allowed 48 hours with the baby before she is collected." Kennedy continued.

"But she gets the possibility of parole? After what she did?" The justice system disgusted me.

"That was the condition to her pleading guilty and avoiding putting my family through a trial."

"But the video?"

"It was exhibit A. Thankfully my parents never saw it."

"Did you?" I held my breath.

"No. The Detective and DA showed it to Megan and her attorney. They told her they were seeking the death penalty. So, she accepted life with the possibility of parole after a minimum of 25 years in exchange for taking the death penalty off the table. But she has to serve the minimum of 25 years — no time off for good behavior."

"Still," it felt to me she was getting off easy.

"I know, and I agree. But I wanted you to know that it was finally over."

"Thanks. I appreciate it." I closed my eyes and felt my body give a sigh of relief. "How have you been?"

"Keeping myself busy. I live at the office, but I visit my condo occasionally." Her laugh was dry and without humor.

"I'm sorry. Hopefully now you will get to enjoy the summer now that the sentencing is over."

"Aren't you going to ask me how he is?" Kennedy was never one for beating around the bush.

"I'm trying to move on, Kennedy. That's all I can do."

"Are you dating anyone?"

"No. And that's not what I mean by moving on. I'm simply trying to get over him and it's not been easy. In fact, it's been one of the hardest things I've ever done in my life." I confessed.

"He's not dating anyone either." She hesitated a moment. "He still loves you, but believes he's lost you."

"Did he tell you that?" I hated the smidgen of hope I felt leap in my chest.

"No, of course not. You know my dad. He doesn't talk like that, but I know him, and I see it in him."

"Kennedy, he's never once tried to call me. He wrote me off the moment your brother was killed. He told me Mason's death was my fault." The words ripped at my heart.

"That was the grief talking, Alex. You know that. And he hasn't called because he's afraid of what you'll say to him if he does." She reasoned.

"At this point, he probably should be." I scoffed.

"Probably," her laugh was genuine this time.

"Has he finally made it back to work?" I couldn't help but be curious.

"Sort of," she muttered.

"Sort of?"

"He occasionally appears. What he's actually working on, I don't know. He's driven, but I'm not sure exactly what he's up to. I've asked him about a dozen times, and he just smiles and says I'll find out soon enough. I believe he's closing a deal with a large company, but I'm not positive." I could hear the skepticism in his voice.

"Well, at least he's no longer lying-in bed all day." I pointed out.

"True," she agreed. "Now he's almost like a man possessed."

"You said he was sort of working. Now he's a man possessed?" I laughed. "Which is he?"

"Sort of working, because I assume what he's been doing is working, but who knows. Whatever it is he's doing, he's become obsessed with it." Kennedy clarified.

"I suppose that's good, I guess. At least it's giving him something to occupy his mind with." I rationalized.

"Yeah, it's good for that. I wish I knew what it was though."

"Like he said, you'll find out soon enough." However, I too was intrigued. "You'll have to let me know once you figure it out."

"I will," I could picture the smile on her lips. "I'll call you soon."

"I'd like that. You take care of yourself, Kennedy." I couldn't help the gut feeling I had that this would be the last conversation we'd share.

"I will. You do the same. Good night, Alex."

"Goodbye," I ended the call and set the phone back on the nightstand.

I stared at the phone a moment longer before I closed my eyes. I was thankful for the call. Kennedy gave me what I needed to say goodbye — not just to her, but to Mason and Haydon as well. She gave me the ability to finally close that chapter of my life and turn the page to start anew on a blank one.

Chapter 30

THE BOYS STOOD ON EITHER SIDE of the exam table in the little room Laura put us in. It had been several years since she'd seen the boys and made over them giving them Rice Krispy Treats and suckers. Max was doing his best to act mature, and I giggled when she returned with the Rice Krispy Treats — my son's true weakness. He could not resist and the two of them stood on either side of me munching away when Dr. Johnston walked in.

"Good morning, Alex. How are you feeling today?" He was his usual cheery self.

"Anxious," I swung my legs nervously off the end of the table.

"And this must be Max and Henry." My boys nodded but remained silent. "Well, you two are growing like weeds. Have you started college yet?"

"No," Henry blushed.

"Not yet." Max said proudly. "But soon."

"And where do you plan to go?"

"Not sure yet. I want to go to Notre Dame, but most likely I'll go to Purdue." Max pipped up proudly.

"Both are excellent schools. Do you know what you want to major in?" I sat proudly waiting for him to answer.

"Chemical engineering."

"Interesting. And what about you?" Dr. Johnston looked over at Henry.

"I want to be a cardiologist."

"Another noble career choice." He smiled up at me. "You must be very proud."

"I am," I beamed.

"Well, shall we see how your other two are doing?" Dr. Johnston approached the table. "Lay back for me." He produced a tape measure and lifted my tee-shirt up to the bottom of my bra and lowered my gym shorts to the top of my pelvic bone and measured the distance. "Right on schedule," he smiled.

"Are you ready for me?" Becky knocked on the door and opened it a smidgen.

"Perfect timing. Come on in." Dr. Johnston said over his shoulder.

"Hello Alex," Becky smiled and approached the ultrasound machine. "How are you doing?"

"Good, and you?" I asked.

"Wonderful." She picked up the ultrasound gel and shook the tube. "This will be a little cool."

"I remember," my stomach muscles tightened in anticipation.

Becky coated my stomach with a thin layer of gel and moved her wand over my abdomen. A three-dimensional image appeared on the monitor. My twins were curled together in a little ball holding on to each other.

"There they are," The tech smiled over at the boys. "Are you wanting to know the sex?"

"Yes, if possible." I spoke up.

"Let me see if I can get them to move their legs just a bit," she pressed a little harder with the wand encouraging the twins to squirm about just enough for us to peek.

"There. Can you see?" She glanced over at the three of us.

"Nope," Henry scrunched up his face.

"I do," Max broke out in a smile that lite up his face.

"That's amazing," I couldn't tear my eyes away from the screen.

"Look," Becky grinned at Henry and pointed at the screen. "This is your little brother, and this is your baby sister."

"What? Really? A girl?" Henry frowned a bit.

"Yes. A girl. One of each. That's wonderful, isn't it?" Becky said excitedly.

"No," Henry's bottom lip stuck out. "We don't want any girls in our house."

"Doesn't your mom live in your house?" Becky raised her eyebrow at my pouting little man.

"But she's not a girl. She's a mom." Henry insisted.

"Now there's some logic for ya," Max rolled his eyes and we all laughed.

"What?" Henry looked confused and then got mad at everyone for laughing. "It's not funny."

"We're not laughing at you, honey. We're all just happy about the twins." I reached over and smoothed his hair.

Once everything checked out with the twins, the three of us went out to lunch. I was ecstatic about the thought of having one of each. I thought about Kennedy and how beautiful she was, how strong, how courageous and prayed my little girl would share the traits of her big sister.

And my baby boy.

I couldn't help but wonder what similarities and traits he would share with his lost brother.

Would he have Mason's crystal blue eyes? His dark blond waves? His infectious laugh? His charisma?

We sat down in a booth at Cheddar's and glanced over the menu. After we placed our orders and the waiter dropped off our drinks, Henry was still pouting over the ultrasound results.

"How long are you going to be mad?" Max nudged his little brother. "I think it's cool."

"Me too," I reached over and touched his hand, which he promptly pulled away and dropped in his lap.

"I thought for sure we were going to have two brothers." He stated in a disgruntled tone.

"But this way we have one of each and it will be a new experience for all of us. I've never raised a daughter before." I tilted my head a bit with a smile.

"What should we name them?" Max thankfully tried to change the subject.

"Hmmm, I don't know. What do you two suggest?" I wanted them to feel like a part of this with me.

"What about Sam. Or Dean?" Henry finally smiled.

"You've been watching too much Supernatural," Max teased. "Perhaps we should call him Castiel?"

"Be nice," I pinched my lips together and eyed my eldest.

"Castiel would be cool. We could call him Cas." Henry ignored Max's sarcasm.

"We're not naming your little brother after a character on a television show." I stated. "Be serious."

"Okay. What about Wyatt? That's a great name." Max added. "Like Wyatt Earp. That would be awesome."

"Wyatt Rose? Sounds like he has a lisp." I chuckled. "But I do love the name Wyatt."

"Rose? Wouldn't their last name be Brooks, like Hayden and Mason" Henry looked confused.

"If Hayden was still in the picture, then yes. But he's not. I'm their only parent so they will have our last name." I attempted to explain.

"Won't dad be mad?" Max asked. "I mean, you're giving them his last name and they aren't his kids."

"But Rose is my last name too and has been for fifteen years. This has nothing to do with your dad." I honestly hadn't thought, nor did I care about how Danny would feel about it one way or another.

"Have you told Dad about the twins?" Henry asked.

"No. Have you?" Both boys shook their heads. "I don't mind if you do. The twins are part of our family, so your dad is going to find out about them sooner or later."

"Does Hayden know about them?" Max inquired softly.

"No," I told him honestly. "I haven't heard from him since we left him at the funeral."

"Then he doesn't deserve to know. He shouldn't be a part of their lives or our lives if he's gonna treat you this way." I hated the edge in Max's voice.

"I agree. That's why I haven't called him."

The waiter dropped off our food and the boys started eating. I picked at the lunch in front of me, but I was no longer hungry. I hated this topic and opening up to my boys like this. I felt as if it made me weak in their eyes and incompetent as a parent.

"I only hope I am making the right decision and I pray they don't hate me someday for it." I added without looking at them.

"We won't let them." Max gave me a sympathetic grin.

"Thanks, baby." His words warmed my heart more than I could tell him.

"Do their names have to rhyme or go together? Like Tim and Kim or Stephen and Stephanie?" Henry completely missed what had just transpired.

"No, definitely not." I shook my head.

"I like George," Max stated with a weird look on his face.

"Seriously? You want to name your little brother George? Why do you hate him?" I pinched my lips together.

"George is a strong name."

"But not exactly my style." I eyed him trying not to laugh.

"You named him Henry," Max rolled his eyes. "Like that's a common name."

"I love the name Henry. It's a good, strong, masculine name. Just like Max." I defended.

"Max is a dog's name," my eldest shook his head at me.

"But not our dog," I smirked.

"Yeah, we have a female dog with a boy's name." Max raised his eyebrows at me.

"You have no one to blame for that but yourself. You named her." I stated.

"I was only four years old, and you let me." He giggled.

"So, perhaps I shouldn't ask for your input on naming the twins." I said sarcastically.

"Gee, thanks." Max stuck his tongue out at me.

"What about Tyler?" Henry interrupted.

"Too common," Max replied before I could.

"Agree," I added.

"Okay," Henry scrunched up his face pensively. "Gus?"

"Gus?" my forehead wrinkled up. "Nah."

"Cody?"

"No," Max immediately responded. "There's a Cody in my class and he's not nice."

"Fair enough," I nodded. "So, we need two names not attached to anyone we know." I pinched up the corner of my mouth in thought.

"Can I make a suggestion for his middle name?" Max gave me a thoughtful look.

"Of course," I encouraged him.

"I think his middle name should be Mason after his oldest big brother." Max smiled up at me.

"I agree," Henry added.

"Me too," I smiled at my boys. "I believe Mason would love that." They nodded in agreement.

"So, what goes with Mason?" Henry speculated. "Trevor? Trevor Mason?"

"That's not bad," I had to admit. "But what about his sister?"

"Tonya. Tiffany. Tori. Taylor. Tasha." Max rambled.

"You're just listing names that start with a T." I giggled.

"Well, they would all go with Trevor." Max defended.

"Does it have to?" Henry inquired.

"No," I looked over at Max. "Do you really like any of those names?"

"Not really, but I'm probably not the one to ask." Max shrugged.

"Why's that?" I asked him.

"I've never named a kid," he laughed. "Isn't there a book of baby names that would be more helpful than us?"

"I just thought you'd like some input."

"I do," he looked over at his little brother. "We do. But you haven't suggested anything. What do you like?"

"I've been running names for boys and girls over in my head since I found out I was pregnant." I confessed. "I do believe we should go with Mason for his middle name. For his first name I was thinking Elijah — Eli or Tristen."

"I like Eli. Eli's cool." Max nodded. "I like it better than Tristen, but Tristen is okay."

"Me too. I like Eli." Henry agreed. "And for our sister?"

"Madeline — Maddy or Elicia and we can call her Ellie." I suggested.

"What about Elicia Madelyn? That way they would have the same initials. That'd be cool." Max grinned.

"Elijah Mason and Elicia Madelyn. I love it." I beamed.

"Eli and Ellie. That works." Henry took a big bit of his burger and grinned with his mouth full.

"Gross, Henry. You know better." I chastised him, but he and Max only laughed at me.

We spent the rest of the afternoon over at Debbie's pool. It was hot and miserable out and the humidity made it feel like a steam bath. I lounged on a raft in my two-piece — full belly exposed, sipping on a frozen lemonade and keeping an eye on the boys.

Debbie's girls were playing with the boys. They had a game of Marco Polo going on and it seemed Hayley appeared to be the target of the day. She groaned loudly as she got tagged again by her sister. I watched her close her eyes, count, and the blind hunt continued with her main target being Max as usual.

I swam laps the length of the pool trying to keep myself in shape. I hated jogging and had let my gym membership lapse months ago. Dr. Johnston encouraged me to swim laps to keep my muscles limber and strengthen my core. As I finished my final lap I floated on my back across the pool. Looking down I noticed my stomach protruding out of the water.

I must look like a beached whale, I thought with a smile. It was hard to imagine what I would look like in the upcoming months. I had only gained 17 pounds with Max and 23 with Henry. It was frightening to think where the scale would land by the time I delivered the twins.

I hung out until Debbie got home from work. I was anxious to tell her about the ultrasound. The boys had already spilled the beans to her daughters, and they were overjoyed. They rambled on about all the cute little matching outfits they wanted to dress the twins in and how much fun it was going to be to babysit.

It was humorous to watch Max debate them over babysitting. He was insistent that he would be the primary babysitter, but Olivia said it would be her since she was the oldest. I told them plainly I was staying out of the debate, and I was sure each of them would soon be finding excuses not to babysit two screaming puking babies.

Debbie got home shortly before five. She came around back to find all of us still lounging in the pool.

"Must be nice," she teased as she walked through the gate in her work clothes and heels.

"I'm taking full advantage of having an evening with no baseball practice." I gloated.

"Give me two minutes to change and I'll join ya," she waved on her way into the house.

I rolled off my raft and floated across the pool. It felt so refreshing in the early evening sun. The humidity did not diminish as the day progressed and we were in for a miserable evening.

Debbie returned in her swimsuit with a beer and sat down on the edge of the pool. She put her feet in the water and took a long gulp before setting the beer beside her and stretching out her arms and legs with a deep yawn.

"God, what a long day. My feet were killing me." She complained. "So, how did the ultrasound go? Could they tell?"

"The twins are perfect." I swam over to the edge next to her and held onto the wall. "They had their arms wrapped around each other. The tech had to nudge them to get them to move around. They were a little stubborn,"

"Of course, they were, they're related to you." She laughed wholeheartedly.

"Thanks," I narrowed my eyes at her in a teasing fashion. "Anyway, they finally turned enough for us to have a peek."

"And?" She kicked some water over at me.

I placed my hand on the right size of my abdomen. "I'd like you to meet Elicia Madeline," I place my left hand on the left side of my belly. "And Elijah Mason." I couldn't stop grinning.

"Oh, my gawd!" She jumped into the pool and wrapped her arms around me. "That's wonderful. One of each. And I love the names."

"Eli and Ellie," I added.

"I love it," Debbie was smiling as big as I was. "And everything is going well?"

"Yes, they are right on schedule."

"That's wonderful news." She let me go and ducked beneath the water. "Would you guys like to stay for dinner? I was just going to throw some dogs and burgers on the grill."

"I'm still stuffed from lunch, but I'm sure the boys would like to. They're always hungry."

It was close to eight before the boys and I returned home. Max took Billy out for a short walk to stretch her legs. She was slowly returning to her old self. Henry jumped in the shower while I picked up my phone and a bottle of water retreating onto the back porch.

Lounging across the back swing I called Chris to share the good news with him.

"Alex? Hi, how are you?" His voice was light and cheery.

"I'm good. How are you doing?" I could hear a lot of commotion in the background. "Is this a bad time?"

"Nah. I'm at the firehouse. We're all just sitting around watching movies." He explained.

"Oh, I'm sorry. I didn't realize. Do you need to go?"

"Not at all. I'm here through tomorrow but have the weekend off."

"That's good," I rested back against the pillow and gazed out over the tree line.

The sun was starting its decent lighting the sky up with a collage of gold, pink, and violet. The tress in the forefront appeared black against the canvas leaving a stunning scene across the skyline. Twilight was my favorite time of day when the world took a deep breath at the end of the day and settled down into the cozy evening hours.

"Any plans for the weekend?" Chris inquired.

"Not really. I have the final fitting for my gown for the wedding on Friday afternoon — which is rather comical considering I'm growing by the day, and it will need to be altered again before the wedding." I proclaimed.

"But you're glowing," he objected. "And don't worry, you won't be there alone. I have to get my fitting done for my penguin suit."

"I'm sure you'll look stunning."

"Want to grab a bite afterwards? Perhaps a movie or something?" He offered.

"I'd love to," I barely got the words out before a screeching alarm went off.

"Damn it. I've gotta go. I'll see you Friday. Night darling." And the line went dead.

I set it on the cushion beside me realizing I never got to share with him the good news about the twins. But then I realized he was rushing out to help someone in need. I didn't know whether it was a fire or medical emergency call he was dispersed to. I could only pray for all those involved, and that Chris would make it home safely at the end of his shift.

Chapter 31

I **STOOD ON THE PEDESTAL** surrounded by three full-length mirrors feeling on display. I was uncomfortable being poked and pinned by the boutique's seamstress. She measured and pinned my gown as it would rest with me wearing two and a half inch heels. She pointed out to Lisa the loose flowing design of my gown. The pleats featured under my bodice were created to allow for growth as my body changed between now and the ceremony with the growth of the twins.

The light sage polyester fabric was a stunning shade that complimented my dark hair and golden tan. It was flowing in a gracious fashion but did little to hide my growing abdomen. I made a face at Lisa who was trying to explain to the seamstress exactly how I should look.

Thankfully, Lydia came out of the dressing room wearing a grown created of the same fabric as mine, but in a completely different pattern. The woman had barely uttered hello to me and had only spoken a half dozen words to Lisa since she arrived and those were to complain about the dress.

I soon realized why Lisa did not have much of a relationship with her sibling. I had only seen pictures of Lisa's father, but Lydia was exactly what I would have envisioned of what her father would look like in drag. While Lisa had the feminine grace and features of their mother, Lydia inherited all the masculine traits and characteristics of their father.

Lydia's hair was cut into a short straight bob that did little to deter attention away from her strong jawline. Her nose was large and drew some focus from her extended forehead. It was hard to imagine how these two women were related let alone shared the same parents.

They were very unlike my sister, Samantha, and me. While we looked somewhat different, we shared many features that easily identified us as sisters. We were both feminine and graceful and had numerous attributes that overlapped. However, I envied Samantha's carefree spirit and career driven goals that had established her as an expert in her business field.

"Have you decided on your first song?" Lydia's mother asked from her spot on the chaise lounge.

"*Into the Mystic,*" Lisa held out her hand to help me down.

"Remind me. Who sings that?" Mom pulled out her phone to look up the song.

"Van Morrison, mom. Don't worry. You'll approve." Lisa chuckled. "Unlike the last time," she said under her breath barely loud enough for me to hear her.

"What'd I miss?" I was confused.

"My sister has a knack for inappropriateness." Lydia stated as she climbed upon the pedestal.

"Inappropriateness? What did you do?" Considering Lisa and I held a similar sense of humor, I was sure their idea of what was appropriate and what wasn't surely clashed.

"Fine. You and Danny had a traditional wedding, correct?" Lisa asked.

"Yes, why?"

"What was your song? You know, the first song you danced to as husband and wife."

"*Evergreen* by Barbara Streisand & Kris Kristofferson. It's from that movie in the 70s they did together — the remake, *A Star is Born.* I always loved that song." I clarified for the ladies.

"See. Now that's appropriate." Mom waved towards me. "I'm sure it was beautiful." I smiled.

"It was," I could still recall how stunningly handsome Danny was that day.

"Well, at least you have good sense. My daughter decided to select the tackiest song ever written for her first dance when she married Brian." Mom rolled her eyes at her daughter.

"Fine. But answer me this?" Lisa confronted me. "Did you not select *Evergreen* because it was your song with Danny, and you felt it was a description of your relationship?"

"Of course," I agreed.

"Then my selection — our song was most appropriate for it perfectly described our relationship." Lisa childishly stuck her tongue out at her mother who laughed and waved her daughter off once more.

"Okay, I'm intrigued. What song did you and Brian have your first dance to?" I was wracking my brain and couldn't imagine what she did.

"*Laid*," Lisa grinned widely.

"*Laid*?" It wasn't ringing any bells. "Who sings it?"

"Matt Nathanson," even the name did not sound familiar. Recognizing my confusion, Lisa continued. "Have you seen the *American Pie* trilogy? Specifically, the last one, *American Wedding*?"

"Yes, I bought them on DVD back when they came out. Danny called them the *Porky's* movies for a new generation." I smiled at the memory.

"Do you remember the song on the menu screen for *American Wedding*?" Lisa smirked and it clicked.

"Oh, my gawd," I busted out laughing as I recalled the hilarious song that Danny would never fail to sing aloud whenever we watched the movie. "I love that song!" I declared.

"See, I'm not the only one." Lisa cooed to her mother.

"Dear God, you never told me your relationship with Brian was like that." I snickered.

"Unfortunately, to a T. Why do you think we got divorced? It was toxic." She remarked.

"I'll say," her mom added.

"What did you expect when you have such a vulgar song as your theme? Did you honestly expect the marriage to last?" Lydia spat down from the pedestal at her sister.

"When you find a man to even date you, you can offer an opinion about my relationships. Until then, shut the hell up." Lisa glared at her.

"Forgive me for having standards. I am not like you I refuse to marry a man simply because he asks me." Lydia narrowed her eyes and held her head up proudly.

"You've never been given the opportunity to refuse anyone of anything — not even a date because no one has ever been desperate enough to ask you." Lisa laughed at her.

"Enough," the mother intervened. "We are in public, and people are watching."

Truthfully, no one was within earshot save the seamstress who did look quite uncomfortable.

"I don't know why I'm here," Lydia jerked the hem of her gown out of the seamstress' hands and climbed down.

"Me neither. I certainly didn't want you here, but mom insisted." Lisa said coyly.

"Don't do me any favors," Lydia stopped in front of Lisa. "I didn't want to come to your wedding, let alone be in it."

"Thank God," Lisa turned towards her mother. "I told you. Now can I have my friends stand up for me in my wedding party."

"Really, Lisa?" Her mom shook her head at her before following Lydia into the changing room.

"That was pleasant," I snorted. "Sorry."

"Don't be," Lisa shrugged. "We've always been like this. Lydia isn't happy unless she's making everyone miserable. She's over 40, never been on a date, she's lonely, and hates the world."

"That's sad," I looked back at the dressing room curtain and felt horrible for Lydia even though she had been nothing but vile all afternoon.

"Well, ladies. How do I look?" Chris paraded through the drapery closing off our side of the boutique in a double-breasted tux looking absolutely breathtaking.

"Sir, I told you, you cannot go in there." A small woman rushed in behind him taking him by the arm.

"Hush now, woman. These are my people." Chris teased the frazzled looking woman.

"It's okay," Lisa spoke up. "He's our best man."

"Best Moron, you mean." Erik slid into the tiny area behind him.

"But the best nonetheless." Chris smiled widely. "You look beautiful." I suddenly realized I was still wearing my gown.

"Thank you," I felt myself blush. "I figured I'd better since all the ladies will be drooling over you." I winked at Chris. "You make a handsome best man."

"I try," he mockingly adjusted his tie and cleared his throat straightening his shoulders back.

"Please, don't inflate his ego any more than it already is." Erik groaned.

"You're just upset because I'm going to steal the show, big brother." Chris quipped with a cocky grin.

"Parden me, idgit, but I will be the one stealing the show." Lisa cleared her throat loudly. "Why do you think I have a pregnant maid of honor — so I won't be upstaged by a better-looking friend." She playfully stuck her tongue out at me.

"Gee thanks," I nudged her in the ribs. "The truth comes out."

"Aw, come on. You know I love you." Lisa leaned over and kissed me on the cheek.

"Are you about done?" Chris switched the subject.

"Yes, I only have to change." I replied.

"Do you two have plans?" Lisa glanced between us.

"We're going to dinner." Chris remarked. "We're escaping our children and our responsibilities and tearing up the town."

"I don't know about all that, but dinner is true enough." I smacked him on the arm and headed back behind the drapery of my own little changing room.

I could hear the mumble of voices from the safety of the little cubby. From what I could decipher, Lydia and her mom were leaving. The tone seeping beneath the drapery sounded every bit as hostile as it was before. I was glad I was hidden away.

I really liked Lisa's mother and as a mother I could understand her point of view of wanting to have both her daughters involved in Lisa's wedding in hopes of creating a bond between them. However, at this age the likelihood of that happening was slim. Still, I admired her for trying.

I could not help to think about what may have transpired if Hayden and I had gotten married. I would want Samantha there, but I would have no desire to invite my brother Colin or his snotty wife, Charlotte and I definitely would not want to have their two spoiled entitled brats Hunter and Misti there doing everything they could to belittle my boys.

"Are you heading back to your house for anything?" Lisa asked when I reemerged.

"I wasn't planning on it. Why?" I set my purse down on the chaise lounge.

"I was wondering if Debbie was home. I want to ask her if she'll stand up as a bride's maid.

"My boys are over there now with Olivia and Hayley. Debbie should be home around five." I checked my watch. "So, anytime now really."

"Do you think she will?" Lisa looked skeptical.

"I think she'd love to." I reassured her. "Perhaps it will push her and Mark to set a date. They've been engaged forever and refer to each other as husband and wife."

"Why haven't they?"

"Mark doesn't have kids and Debbie's can be challenging. I don't believe that's the only reason, but I believe it's a contributing factor." I didn't want to go into the details of the numerous arguments the two had over Debbie's inability to effectively control or discipline her daughters and the disrespect they often paid Mark, especially Olivia.

"Understandable, I guess. It must be difficult being with someone who doesn't have children when you do." Lisa waved her hand for emphasis. "But they already live together so why not just make it official?"

"They sort of live together. Mark is usually there, but he does keep his own place. I've never seen it, but Debbie says he had a farmhouse in Putman County with about ten acres. They usually stay there on the weekend's her kids are at their dads." I explained.

"Wow. I never would have guessed. I assumed he lived there." She shrugged.

"It's a bit of a touchy subject." I raised my eyebrows and winked. "Live and let live."

"Are you ready?" Chris poked his head around the curtain once more.

"Yes," I smiled.

"Do you want to drop your car off at your place before we eat?" He asked.

"Sure," I turned towards Lisa. "I guess we are going by my place after all."

"Well, that's good considering we're joining you for dinner." Erik came up from behind his brother. "We'll just leave our car at your place, if you don't care."

"I don't care," I was happy to have them along for the evening.

The four of us walked out into the parking lot debating over where we wanted to have dinner. It was Friday evening, and the restaurants were already standing room only. Even if Chris had made reservations, we were now a party of four, not two.

I pulled into the garage while Chris and Erik parked their trucks in my driveway. No decision had been made on dinner as the four of us converged on the porch.

"Do I have time to run over to Debbie's?" Lisa asked.

"Sure. I'll go with you. I'd like to check on the boys?" I gestured across the street.

"Come on," Erik tugged the corner of his brother's shirt. "Let's go."

The two begrudgingly followed us across the street. We went through the back gate following the sound of laughter that drifted across the street. Debbie and Mark were sitting in the lounge chairs enjoying a cold beer watching the four kids splashing around playing some game only unbeknownst to the rest of the world.

The kids waved when we entered but went right on with their game.

"Hey lady, I thought you were going out with Captain America?" Debbie hollered as soon as she saw me, before Chris rounded the corner and entered her view.

"Captain America?" Chris and Erik said in unison.

"Is that what you call me?" Chris looked directly at me.

"Um," I stammered. "Sort of. Yes. I guess." I didn't want to admit I hadn't meant it as a compliment when I had first said it after our first encounter.

"I've been called worse," he shrugged with a smile.

"Sorry," Debbie mouthed at me. "What ya'll up to?" She asked in her normal voice.

"Trying to figure out what to do about dinner," I said casually.

"And I wanted to ask you something," Lisa plopped down in the chair beside her. "Would you stand up with me on August 7th as my Bride's Maid?"

I left the two of them alone to discuss the details after Erik sat down beside Mark and opened the beer he offered him. I approached Chris with a grimace.

"Sorry about that," I apologized through my embarrassment.

"I think it's a compliment," he put his arm around my shoulders. "As I said, I've been called much worse."

"Haven't we all," I grinned.

"Oh, I wanted to ask you — how did your ultrasound go?" I was surprised he remembered.

"It was great. They were facing each other with their little arms wrapped around each other. It was so sweet." My hand automatically began to rub my extended belly.

"Were they able to tell their genders?" his hand reached out and lightly touched my belly. It was the first time he'd ever done that, and it caught me by surprise. "Sorry," he pulled his hand back.

"No. It's okay. I don't mind." I placed his hand back on the side of my belly and my son kicked him.

"But maybe your twins have a different feeling about it." He laughed.

"That would be Eli." And not to be outdone by her brother, Ellie kicked me on the other side. "Dang," I rubbed the other side of my stomach. "It's not a contest." I spoke directly to her before I looked back up at Chris. "It seems Ellie has an opinion of her own as well."

"Eli and Ellie? One of each?" I nodded. "That's awesome!" Chris leaned down and hugged me tightly. "Do you realize how spoiled Ellie is going to be? The only girl with three brothers? I almost feel bad for her."

"Why's that?" I wondered.

"Can you imagine any guy wanting to ask her out with three overprotective brothers?" he laughed.

"Yeah, but for me that's a good thing." I reasoned.

"True," he hugged me again. "I'm so happy for you."

"Thanks," I hugged him tightly. "I'm excited."

"I can't believe you spent the entire afternoon with me and didn't tell me?" Lisa came up beside me.

"I didn't want to say anything in front of your mom and especially your sister. It didn't seem right with the mood Lydia was in." I explained.

"I get it," she wrapped her arms around me. "One of each. That's wonderful. I'm so happy for you." Lisa let me go and held me at arm's length looking at my belly. "And a bit jealous, I must admit."

"I'll gladly share with you the heartburn and nausea I'm having." I jeered.

"Something to look forward to," she grinned. "So, what do you want to do about dinner?"

"Let's just cookout here," Debbie suggested. "We can make a quick run to the store and grab a few things. What do you think?" she left the forum open to everyone.

"That works for me," Erik opened his second beer.

I noticed Lisa narrow her eyes a bit at Erik. Like me, she was hoping for a night out on the town without children under foot. She and Erik had it arranged with their ex's that every other weekend they had all their children and the next the kids were with their ex's.

I admit I was jealous of her freedom even though I knew it would make me miserable handing the boys over to Danny like that on a regular schedule. It allowed Lisa and Erik the freedom and ability to enjoy time alone with each other and not worry about always finding someone to watch their kids if they wanted to do something.

Despite the evening not exactly going as planned, it turned out wonderful. The kids only came out of the pool long enough to eat — for some reason spending a day in the pool always increased their appetite tenfold and the adults waded in and out of the water drinking heavily.

Debbie had mixed up a batch of her fabulous party punch and it wasn't long before no one was able to drive. That is, except me and the children. I must admit it really sucked being the only sober person with five intoxicated people retailing humorous stories and antics of days gone by.

Of course, Debbie had to regale the group with the story of Isaac's infamous night at the pool after he'd taken his MCAT's. It was several years ago when I was with Mason. Isaac and his girlfriend Heather had shown up at my place almost unannounced. Heather was trying to get him off the road before he hurt them or someone else.

In the first 30 minutes after their arrival, Isaac had broken one of Debbie's chairs and gotten a large piece of wood lodged in his backside. When we tried to remove it, he somehow ended up naked as the day he was born and running down the middle of our street. Thankfully, it was midnight, but he did manage to wake up numerous neighbors who Debbie and I had to pacify.

Debbie and Mark had a wonderful time recalling all the details for the other three that had missed the performance. Erik remarked how he wished they could purchase a house on our street since it seemed there was never a dull moment.

I was almost embarrassed listening to them tell stories as far back as when Danny and I had lived there together. But everyone shared stories from their past, and it was a joyous evening.

By midnight Chris was asleep on my couch, Lisa and Erik were passed out in Max's room and Max was bunking with Henry. I crawled into bed a little after one in the morning after soaking in a long hot shower. The evening had brought back so many memories.

It had been almost two years since I'd spoken to Heather or Isaac, and I wondered how they were doing. They, along with Isaac's son from a previous relationship had moved to Southern Illinois for his med school. I had not heard from them since.

As I closed my eyes, I made up my mind that I was going to give them a call this weekend and catch up. Isaac and Heather were

the most unlikely couple, but always seemed so happy together. Heather was an amazing individual with a gentle soul. I always thought she was a good influence on Isaac and his son. Isaac could not have found a better woman to build a life and a home with for him and his son.

Sunday evening the boys were engrossed in a battle with Mario Kart. I finished cleaning up the kitchen from dinner and slipped out onto the back porch with Billy. The humidity had finally given way and the evening was cooling off in the low 80s. I walked her around the backyard while she took care of business.

Billy was growing stronger each day and it was now often a challenge to keep her on a lease. She hated them and preferred her freedom. She wasn't raised on a leash, and we had never had any difficulty with her following our commands when we took her out. She was well versed on our property lines and only wandered over to Debbie's when one of us were with her.

I led her back up the steps on the patio and closed the gate to the steps — Danny had installed it years earlier when the boys were small to keep them from falling down the steps. I had not used it in five or more years, but realized as I was latching it, that I would be using it again soon and not for Billy.

I looked up Heather's cell number in my contacts list. I hoped she hadn't changed it since they relocated. I hit the call button and waited impatiently. She finally picked it up on the fifth ring as I was getting ready to hang up.

"Alex?" her voice was low and soft.

"Heather? How are you? I haven't spoken to you in forever and thought I'd call and see how you and Isaac are doing?"

"I'm doing well. Isaac isn't." her voice sounded strange.

"What's wrong?"

"I just moved back to Indy last month. Isaac is in prison." Her voice was shaky.

"What?"

"Isaac finished med school and the night he got his acceptance letter for the surgical residency program he wanted at John Hopkins, he went out with some other med student he'd been having an affair with pretty much since we moved here — the two of them got hammered and like he always did, he decided to drive home. His luck finally ran out and this time he hit someone — a 19-year-old boy and his 18-year-old girlfriend, killing them both along with the girl he was banging."

"Oh, my God," I was so stunned I didn't know what to say.

"He was charged with three counts of vehicular manslaughter and driving while intoxicated. He was three times the legal limit.

He was sentenced last month. I moved back home afterwards." I could hear her choking on the words.

"I'm so sorry, Heather. I cannot believe he would do that to you." Isaac was a terrible flirt, but I had always considered him harmless. I guess I was wrong. "Where's his son?"

"I had to give him back to his mom when we returned," the dam broke, and I could hear her crying. "He's been my son for three years and not once during that time did his mom even call him. And I had to hand him back. He held onto me, begging, and crying. She pulled him from my arms, pushed him into the car and told me to never contact him again. I haven't heard a peep from him." Heather sobbed. "I lost the man I was planning on marrying and my son all because of that stupid bastard."

"What an idiot," I was dumbfounded. "He had it all and threw it away ruining multiple lives along with his. What an asshole."

"Yeah, I had to sit in the courtroom with three families who lost their children, brother, sister, grandchild, and listen to them talk about the plans, dreams, and lives that were all destroyed by him. And he just sat there. He never said a word to me, to them — nothing."

"I can't imagine," I felt numb.

"These people looked at me like I was Satan's wife. And in their eyes, I was. They lost everything, but so did I. So, did my son."

Heather and I talked for almost two hours. She admitted she was reluctant to answer the phone and had thought about calling me multiple times, but she was so ashamed of how things had turned out. She said she wasn't sure what to say to me. She had suspected he was cheating on her for some time, but with his insane schedule it was almost impossible to catch him at it, especially since they always fooled around at the hospital or her apartment.

And all the while, Heather was at home being a mom to his son, working full time and handling all the homework and extracurricular activities and sports. The more she told me the worse I felt. Not just for her, but the emotions it brought back to the days when I was in her shoes and Danny was having an affair. The only difference between her situation and mine was I did not lose my boys when he left, and she wasn't dumb enough to marry the SOB like I did.

It was wonderful catching up with her. I discovered she had moved to the same area that Chris lived. We laughed about the irony of how things work out and how neither of our lives had turned out how we thought they would since the last we saw each other.

It was good to hear her laugh. She was excited about the twins but told me how sorry she was for what happened to Mason. She said she had always liked him and thought he was good for my boys and me. However, she did not think very highly of Hayden for his behavior after Mason's death.

Heather and I made plans to get together soon. She said she had to see me simply because she couldn't imagine me fat and pregnant with twins and was going to fully enjoy rubbing in that she was now thinner than me. I loved her for it.

My cell phone had vibrated about an hour into our conversation signaling a text message. I knew it wasn't the boys because they would have just come out when I didn't immediately respond. I figured it was either Debbie, Lisa, or Chris. So, when I finally said goodbye to Heather, I hit the message icon on my phone.

'I remember you'

Three simple words that evoked immediate tears.

Written in the from box at the top of my screen: Hayden Brooks.

I fought the urge to throw my phone out into the yard.

"You bastard," I said aloud to the empty deck. Billy lifted her head at the sharpness of my tone, but then put it back down on her paws. "You just ruined one of my favorite songs."

I hastily brushed the tears off my cheeks. I was angry with myself for allowing him to elicit such a response from me after all this time. I blamed it on the pregnancy hormones and reminded myself I was not in love with him anymore.

Which I didn't even believe.

But never once did I consider calling or texting him back.

Chapter 32

THE SOUND OF RAIN FALLING on the roof and hitting the windows woke me. My room was still dark. A thunderstorm was directly overhead and pounding us. I crawled out of bed unintentionally stirring Billy. She raised her head, looked around, and deciding that nothing was amiss, she rested her head back on the pillow and closed her eyes.

I walked over to the window feeling restless and depressed. That damn text message was haunting me. My heart wanted to call, to hear his voice, to beg him to come back. My head — be it to stubborn, humiliated, or pissed wanted nothing more from the man ever.

The battle between the two was just beginning.

I found Lisa and Erik at the concession stand. Our boys were scheduled to play at six, but it was already ten after and we were waiting around to see if the umpire was going to let the game proceed. It had rained most of the day, but it had finally stopped around three.

The baseball diamonds were a muddy mess. The coaches and the umpire walking around the fields discussing the situation. I was really hoping they would just call it so we could all go home, especially since Max was scheduled for the 7:30 game and if Henry's game were canceled, Max's would be as well. The mood I was in, I felt like crawling under the covers and never coming back out.

"Hey, you two." I approached them while the boys hung out with their friends on the picnic tables.

"Hey," Lisa spun around and looked me over. "Wow. You look like shit. What happened?"

"Um, I'll leave you two alone." Erik patted me on the shoulder. "I'll go see what the coaches are deciding."

"Thanks Erik," I offered him the best smile I could muster before he walked away. "He texted," I looked back at Lisa. "Last night."

"Are you serious?" I nodded. "Show me." I pulled up the text and handed her my phone. "I remember you. What kind of bullshit is that? He'd better fucking remember you, that son of a bitch." Her face twisted in anger and her eyes narrowed. "What's that supposed to mean anyway?"

"The song," I stated the obvious reference.

"The *Skid Row* song? Are you fucking kidding me?"

"When we were in Europe — Germany at the end of our vacation." I stared off into the distance and recalled. "It was raining, and we were walking around this gorgeous little out of the way village. The music — that song came drifting out of a nearby pup. Hayden took my hand and spun me around on the side of the street. He took me in his arms and suddenly we were dancing, and he was signing that song. It was so funny and so romantic." I brushed the tear off my cheek. "That SOB knew I'd remember." I shook my head and waved my arms. "Like I could ever forget."

"Gawd, I hate that man." Lisa looked disgusted. She put her arm around me. "Hold it together," She whispered handing me a tissue from her purse.

"Thanks," I blew my nose and tossed it into the nearest trash can.

"I noticed you didn't text him back. Did you call him?" I couldn't tell from her tone if she was in support of or against the latter.

"No. I was too busy struggling with the urge to throw my phone across the backyard," I shrugged. "I was on the deck when he texted."

"You'd only have to replace it and that's a pain in the ass. You know he's going to text you again and if you do that every time he texts, it could get expensive quickly." She attempted to make me laugh and it worked.

"Good point," I chuckled.

"Besides, you need your money for other things than repeatedly replacing your phone because of that idiot." She smirked.

"I know," I flashed her my phone again. "See."

"Yes. You're the model of restraint. I'm impressed." Lisa rolled her eyes at me. "So, what are you going to do?"

"Nothing," I shrugged. "What can I do? I was so shocked when I received the text. My heart leapt, but then I remembered the humiliation, the months of silence, the complete dismissal of me and my boys after the funeral in front of his entire family. And I just couldn't bring myself to respond. The thought made me feel sick."

"You're still in love with him," she noted.

"I don't want to be."

"I wish you'd fall for someone like Chris," Lisa sighed heavily. "You two would be so good together."

"You're joking, right?" I snorted.

"He's gorgeous. And he's so sweet. I can tell he cares about you."

"Yes, and I him, but only as friends. Can you imagine? Chris has four sons. I have three and a daughter." My hands rested on my baby bump. "In case you really suck at math, Lisa. That's seven boys and one girl." I shook my head laughing. "You would have to have me committed. That's insane."

"Look at Erik and me. We're damn near as bad. I've got three, he's got two, and we're trying for another one. Talk about insane." She laughed. "But I wouldn't have it any other way."

"And I'm happy for you and Erik," I put my hand on her arm. "You know I am. But I'm not interested in Chris like that. Yes, he's gorgeous, but I am still in love with Hayden. Hell, I'm carrying his twins."

"Okay," she put her arms up in a surrendering fashion. "I give. I'll stay out of it"

"No, you won't." I nudged her playfully.

"The games are canceled," Erik walked up and leaned against the beam of the shelter around the concession stand. "The rain is starting back up, so they are rescheduling the games."

"Thank gawd," Lisa said a little too loudly as Erik leaned over and kissed her on the cheek.

"Boys? Let's go." My eyes scanning the tables for my boys.

I am not sure who took the news of Hayden's surprise text message worse — Debbie or Lisa. Both had very strong opinions about it. The main one being that I not respond, which I didn't. Still, seeing it on my phone was like a knife straight through my heart.

A week later, he sent the second one.

'Thinking of you'

I internally argued with myself over whether I should tell either of them since I knew their response would be a replay of the initial one. Therefore, I finally decided to remain quiet about it. I figured my continued silence would deter him from sending a third.

The following weekend Chris and I snuck away for dinner downtown. He was taking advantage of the one night he had off where he didn't have the younger boys. His eldest was spending the night over at Erik and Lisa's with his cousin and he was picking the other three up in the morning.

I was feeling a bit self-conscious as earlier this week I finally gave up and moved into maternity clothes. My sundresses were no longer fitting, and I hated the tent feeling of the red maternity sundress I was wearing. It had thin shoulder straps and came right above my knees. Max said I looked cute before he giggled and rubbed my belly.

"You're lost in thought," Chris noted pulling out my chair. "You've been really quiet this evening."

"Thank you," I sat down as he took his seat. "Hayden texted me — twice in the last two weeks."

"Wow," he rubbed his chin. "What did he say?"

"His first text said I remember you and the second, thinking of you."

"And how did you respond?"

"I didn't — to either of them."

"Why not?"

"I almost threw my phone across the backyard when I got the first one," I laughed. "And the second, I just cried."

"Why are you giving him so much power over you?" Chris shook his head. "You're stronger than that."

"Can I blame it on pregnancy hormones?"

"It's probably a contributing factor," he snorted. "So, why didn't you respond? He opened the door for you to call or text him back. He's obviously realizing what he lost."

The waiter dropped off a couple glasses of water and took our orders. I had barely glanced at the menu, so I just ordered a crispy chicken salad with honey mustard. Chris ordered a double bacon cheeseburger with loaded French fries. I tired not to laugh when he stuck his tongue out at me.

"And that's supposed to make everything better? I'm supposed to forget all the things he did and said? The humiliation? The blame? The anger?" I proposed.

"Alex, his only son was murdered. I cannot begin to fathom what that does to a father. I have four and would kill anyone who harmed them — just as you would for yours. The pain would be unbearable." He reached across the table and took my hand. "You shouldn't judge him for anything that happened during that time. He was out of his mind with grief and there's a part of him that will never be the same."

"I know," I knew he was right.

"And he still doesn't know about the twins?" I shook my head. "I think you should tell him." I raised my eyebrows but didn't comment. "Imagine how he would feel knowing he is having another son and a daughter. This man clearly loves you. I believe he would be thrilled, and it would most likely renew his passion for life after what he's gone through."

"Perhaps," I hated that he was reiterating the internal dialogue I'd been arguing since I first found out I was pregnant.

"You told me yourself how much he regretted missing out on everything with his kids when they were growing up because he was building his business. This would give him a second chance to do it right." Chris rationalized.

"You are forgetting that his business is in Chicago along with his penthouse. I am not moving to Chicago." I waved my hands for emphasis. "You couldn't pay me to live in Chicago with their crime rate going through the roof. Not to mention having Beetlejuice for a Mayor. That woman is insane. There is no way I would ever raise my children in that city or the state of Illinois."

"I can't argue with you on that one." He nodded. "But didn't you tell me he wanted to build a house for you all outside the city?"

"Yes but considering the area around Chicago — it's not the same as here. We've built a life here. I love the schools, the sports, and the community. All our friends are here. I can't ask my boys to give everything up and move out of state or even upstate. It's not just my life. It's theirs too." I tried to explain.

The young waiter dropped off our entrees. I picked at my salad watching Chris tear into his feast. I never understood how men could eat like that and hardly if ever gain weight. I did palates several days a week and was still nervous about eating a cupcake. It was so unfair. I was tempted to reach over and grab a forkful of those fries, but I knew Chris would tease me relentlessly if I did.

"I know what you mean. I'm stuck where I am for the same reasons. My boys are there and since I share custody with their moms, we're all stuck living in the same town."

"You never told me that." He laughed and shrugged. "You live that close with all three of them?"

"Yeppers," his blue eyes sparkled. "And they all know each other. The first two get along well, but neither of them like the third. She likes to use our son as a pawn and doesn't care that it not only affects my relationship with him, but his relationship with his brothers as well. Hopefully, things will get better as he gets older."

"I hope so," I smiled across the table. "I guess I have been fortunate in that aspect. Danny and I get along most of the time. It helps that he lives across the country and the older the boys get, the less I have to deal with him." I chuckled.

"But you get along with your ex and he's remarried?" Chris raised an eyebrow at me.

"Most of the time," I shrugged. "I can't say I like his new wife and the way she and her children treat my boys, but Danny isn't an evil man. He's handicapped by a lack of maturity."

"And what does he think about you having twins?" I knew Chris was intrigued by my relationship with Danny since I rarely spoke of him.

"I haven't mentioned it to him," I shrugged. "We haven't spoken in months."

"I'm surprised the boys haven't spilled the beans." He laughed. "Mine could never keep a secret — not that it's a secret," he quickly corrected himself. "But mine would be so excited they couldn't help themselves. When my first ex-wife got engaged, our son was eight, he was bursting to tell me. And believe me, I heard all about her pregnancy and everything about his little sister. Still do for that matter. But I'm glad he loves her and he's a great big brother to her. She is a pretty little girl."

"My sons haven't spoken to their dad in months." I confessed.

"Is that on your sons or Danny?" Chris leaned forward and put his elbow on the table.

"As Max mentioned, he doesn't care much for his new stepmother or her children. They don't treat either of my boys kindly. They have argued with their dad over her and her children multiple times and Danny sides with Amanda and her children every time. So, when they got married, he forced the boys to come." I closed my eyes for a brief second flashing back on that horrible weekend. "Unfortunately, that was the same weekend Mason was killed. I called Danny and he sent the boys home on the next flight. But he didn't want to tell them about Mason's death so the boys, being put on a plane before the wedding, really took it as a betrayal. Even after I explained to them the truth, they still haven't forgiven Danny for marrying Amanda."

"It seems like Danny got the raw end of the deal having to send his sons home before the wedding and especially, playing the villain in the role when he really wasn't. That seems a bit unfair." He reasoned.

"I agree. I have spoken with my boys about it at length. They understand the how's and why regarding the wedding and getting them home for the funeral. They have both said they are not upset about being deceived to get home and are glad they made it back. Nor do they care about missing the wedding. They simply do not like Amanda or her kids and the fact that their dad never stands up for them."

"I imagine it puts Danny in a no-win situation. He's damned if he does and damned if he doesn't." Chris' eyes widened a bit.

"I'm sorry, but it's a bit difficult for me to feel any sympathy for the man after he's dismissed our son's most of their lives. He only plays father of the year when it benefits him." I rolled my eyes. "Besides, I can't imagine marrying someone my sons didn't like or that treated my children poorly."

"Me neither," Chris agreed. "My boys are everything to me. I don't understand how your ex could do it."

"It's a package deal, in my opinion. When you marry or even date someone who has children from a previous relationship — you can't accept one without the other. It seems if you can't accept their children, you have no business being involved with the parent." I rationalized.

"Yeah, it would seem so, but unfortunately, most people don't share your point of view. It can be challenging, especially if the other biological parent is jealous of their ex's new romance or bitter and poisons the kids against their other parent and new stepparent." Chris sounded like he spoke from experience but didn't elaborate.

"I'm glad I can say I've never spoken ill of Amanda, except to question Danny about her when I know the boys couldn't overhear me. I'm also glad I've never met her." I smirked.

"Your ex must be a special kind of stupid," he shook his head and sat back in his chair. "How he could ever cheat on a woman like you is beyond my understanding. You are gorgeous. And look at you, you're absolutely glowing. Any man would be proud to call you his."

"Thank you. But I'm sure Danny would tell you I'm a royal pain in the ass." I laughed.

"Most intelligent women are," Chris giggled. "Still, they are also the most intriguing. There is nothing sexier than an intelligent woman because you can talk to them about anything, and they can carry on an intellectual conversation with you beyond the material world." Chris picked up his glass and leaned towards me. "A toast to you, Alex. You are a rare lady, and I am so happy we have become friends."

"Me too, Captain America," I couldn't resist, as our glasses clanked, and we drank.

"My witty woman, you have certainly enhanced my life." Chris chuckled.

The evening was splendid. We walked around joking, teasing, and talking while enjoying the beautiful evening. The air was warm but not muggy for a change. It was almost eight o'clock but summer days in Indy were long and we had an hour or so before sunset.

We strolled around the more populated areas of the White River Canal near the baseball stadium and Elteljorg Museum remarking on the various sculptures scattered about the grounds and the array of eccentric individuals wandering about.

Chris wanted to head back before sunset; reminding me that the landscape downtown had changed greatly over the last couple years and was no longer safe after dark. Reluctantly, I agreed even though I was enjoying his company immensely.

Still, our drive home was just as enjoyable. Chris had an infectious smile and a charisma about him that instantly put a person at ease. I glanced over at his profile while he was driving and smiled to myself. His chiseled jaw and strong features set perfectly with his light blue eyes and golden hair. He was a handsome man and his nickname fit him perfectly.

"It looks like they are finally building something on that wooded stretch of land." Chris remarked as we approached my neighborhood.

"I noticed that a couple weeks ago. I was hoping it would never sell." I made a disgusted face. "I love that area. It's so peaceful. The sign said it was 15 acres?" he nodded. "They probably sold it to some damn developer who's probably putting in another neighborhood — dozens of cookie cutter homes with miniscule yards and outrageous HOA fees."

"Probably, but it's prime real estate." He noted.

"I hope they don't cut down all the trees. It's so beautiful, especially in the fall. Plus, the trees are a great buffer between our neighborhood and the high school and sports fields. As it is, we can still hear the marching band practicing in the evening and the football games on Friday nights."

"Well, considering all the sports your boys play in, at least you're able to walk there and not have to worry about parking. That, is a blessing." He smiled turning into the neighborhood.

"True," I glanced over at him and winked. "The location was one of the most appealing aspects of the house when we started looking. I love my home, but I admit I'm a bit worried." I rubbed my belly. "My house is only a three bedroom and the boys have always had their own rooms. The twins will be in my room for a while, but eventually I'll have to figure something out. I hate the thought of putting Max and Henry into one room, but I may have too." The thought had crossed my mind several times and I was worried about it with Max getting older. I hated the thought of robbing him of his privacy.

"You have a huge yard. Why not just add onto the house? You could easily add two more bedrooms and another bath bumping out onto the backyard." He pulled into my driveway scanning over the property. "What size is your lot?"

"About an acre."

"Ah, you have plenty of room." Chris pointed out.

"But that costs money. You forget I'm a student and on a budget." Chris got out and came around opened my door.

"I guess it's a good thing that I used to work construction and one of my best friends owns his own construction company." He took my hand and helped me out of the truck. "I can get all the materials at cost, and I know a group of guys who would be happy to help me build an addition."

"Are you serious?" I couldn't believe what I was hearing. "I couldn't ask that of you. You have so little time as is, off work and that belongs to your boys." I argued.

"I'm not saying they wouldn't be hanging around here at times with me," he smiled. "But you need help, and we take care of our own." I made a face not understanding what he meant. "My unit, the guys in my department, we take care of each other. So, they'd be happy to help me. They enjoy working with their hands just as I do."

"You said you take care of your own. But I'm not," he cut me off.

"Blood does not define family." Chris pulled me into an embrace on my porch. "You are now part of my family. Lisa is your sister just as you are hers. That makes us family." He kissed my cheek. "Do me a favor," he kept his arms around me looked me in the eye.

"What's that?"

"Remember our conversation about Hayden the next time he texts. Find it in your heart to forgive him and help him heal his wounds. Don't judge him for words he said or what he did when he was blinded by unimaginable grief." He kissed my cheek once more and patted my belly. "I'll call you tomorrow."

"Thank you," I smiled lovingly at him.

"Sweet dreams, darling."

Chris' words stayed with me later after I retired for the night. I checked my phone multiple times before I turned out the lights hoping to find a new message from Hayden. But there wasn't.

I considered responding to his previous text, but quickly decided against it — more out of stubborn pride than anything else. Which I reminded myself, was ridiculous, but still, I couldn't do it.

My hands rested on my ever-expanding belly and rubbed it gently. I fought back the tears and rolled over on my side wishing Hayden was there in the empty space beside me. I desperately wanted to rest my head on his chest again and have the sound of his strong heartbeat lull me off into a peaceful sleep like it had in the past.

But that heart was broken now and so was our relationship.

I brushed a teardrop off my cheek and drifted off into a restless sleep.

Chapter 33

L ISA WAS FRANTIC. THE CALM, collected, and excited woman that made it through the rehearsal dinner with ease the night before, had completely disappeared. In her stead was a woman who looked on the verge of tears.

We spent the early afternoon at the salon getting our makeup, hair, and nails done. Debbie and Lisa looked beautiful. Our nails were polished in a pale pink. Our hair hung loosely in a crown of curls accented with sparse baby breath. Lisa had a small comb that would be added at the venue to fix her veil once she dressed for the ceremony.

Erik and Lisa had selected a lakeside venue for their wedding and reception. The ceremony was to take place in a gazebo with a waterfall and lake set in the background. Rows of white wooden chairs had been set up and a white runner adorned the center aisle. The chairs on the end of each row held bouquets of wine, dusty rose and rose quartz tied with sage silk ribbon cascading down and matching all the bouquets in the wedding party.

The tables for the reception under the shelter were a short walking distance from the ceremony. They were decorated with white linen tablecloths, matching bouquets as centerpieces and long stem candles in the middle. Her mom had closely monitored the setup and delivery of the three-tiered cake. Everything was elegantly formatted and designed around the dance floor including the rows of twinkling lights running through the boughs overhead.

Lisa and her mom had done an astounding job. Every detail from the location to the flowers, to the cake was stylish and elegant without being overdone and gaudy. But with all the I's dotted and T's crossed, the three of us couldn't get Lisa to calm down.

Brie was a junior bridesmaid set to walk down the aisle with Erik's oldest son, Finn. McKenzie was serving as the flower girl. Somehow during all the commotion, the hairclips specially designed to match the girls' dresses, were nowhere to be found. Lisa swore she told Brie to grab them off the island before they left the house. Brie was in tears because she was positive, she had them in her hand when they left. But none of us could locate them.

"I promise, I had them," Brie sobbed.

"If you had them, they'd be here." Lisa angrily stated the obvious.

"Lisa. Stop," her mom put her hands on her daughter's shoulders forcing Lisa to look at her. "Brie didn't lose them on purpose. You're only making things worse by lashing out."

"Let's retrace your steps," I put my arm around Brie and led her out of the dressing room and her mother's line of fire.

Brie and I walked down the halls covering every inch of the building she had been in that day. We didn't find anything. She was baffled and kept assuring me that she had them.

"Did you look in the car? Maybe they're still there." I smiled down at her squeezing her shoulder.

"I hope so," she said in a low voice. "I don't want to ruin my mom's wedding. She was so happy and I'm ruining everything."

"No, honey. You're not. Even if we don't find them, the ceremony and reception will be beautiful. It's not the end of the world. You and McKenzie look lovely with or without the hairclips."

I pushed open the side door to the parking lot. The late afternoon sun was almost blinding. Brie and I walked down the cobblestone walkway towards the gravel parking lot. A ray of light reflected off something shiny in the lot as I carefully navigated the gravel in my heels.

"Brie," I hollered. "Over here." Brie came running up behind me and over to where I was pointing.

"Got em'," she squealed picking them up.

They were a bit dusty but no worse for the wear. She rushed up beside me placing them both in my hands.

"Here," a smile blossomed through her tears.

"Fabulous," I blew the gravel dust off them and carefully clipped the piece in her hair. "You look beautiful." I put my arm around her shoulders and walked back into the building with her.

Crisis averted; Lisa calmed down once I had McKenzie's hairclip perfectly placed. Her daughters looked darling. Lisa primped their hair and fluffed their dresses. She handed Brie her bouquet and McKenzie her white wicker basket with a sage ribbon braided through the handle and filled with dusty and wine rose petals.

The ceremony went flawlessly. Lisa's daughters joined her mother in the front row after reaching the alter. Chris and I walked joined Debbie and Erik's best friend, Jason on the gazebo steps. Chris kept glancing over at me throughout the ceremony making goofy faces angled so that only I could see. It was hard not to laugh, and I had to keep pinching my lips together to stop from giggling.

Thankfully, the gathering was just under a hundred guests. I knew most of the people there except for those who were coworkers of the bride or groom. It was a festive celebration, and everyone was in great spirits.

Erik and Lisa could not have selected a more perfect evening for their outdoor wedding. The weather was divine — warm with a slight breeze to keep everyone from getting too hot while dancing. The live band was talented and experienced. I was so happy they had decided to use a band and not a DJ. It added a little something extra to the ambiance.

After the happy couple finished their first dance to a song her mother approved of, Chris came over and asked me to dance. I checked on the boys and reminded them to behave before letting him lead me out onto the dance floor.

"You look very handsome," I placed my hand around his waist and my arm around his neck.

"You took the words right out of my mouth," his grin widened up to his eyes making them sparkle in the twinkling lights.

"I look handsome, huh?" I laughed.

"I was going to say gorgeous." He flashed me a coy look.

"Well, thank you."

"Any news from Hayden?"

"Not a peep," I shrugged. "Perhaps, he decided better of it."

"I doubt that," Chris rolled his eyes like I was being ridiculous.

"What's make you so certain?" I raised a questioning eyebrow at him.

"May I cut in?" I felt my stomach drop to the floor while my heart jumped into my throat. My grip on Chris tightened and my eyes widened.

I exhaled softly and swallowed the knot in my throat. I lowered my arm from Chris' neck and turned around slowly. Hayden was standing before me in a suit and tie. His sandy blonde hair combed back in soft waves. His emerald, green eyes glistened in the slow glowing lights. I had never seen a more handsome man in my life.

"My God, Alex. You look so beautiful." It was then that I realized it was the tears in his eyes making them glisten. "I am so sorry I hurt you." Hayden took a step forward with one hand reaching out towards me.

"Hayden, what are you doing here?" it was then that I realized I still had my arm around Chris' waist and that I was holding onto him tightly as if he were my life preserver.

"Can you forgive me?" He paused mid step and dropped his hand back to his side.

"Hayden," I didn't know what to say.

"Why don't you two go for a walk around the lake so you have a bit a privacy?" Chris suggested squeezing my shoulder. He leaned in closely and whispered, "Remember our talk and put yourself in his shoes." He kissed me on the cheek and surprisingly shook Hayden's hand as if the two had some kind of understanding I was not privy too.

I glanced over my shoulder and saw Lisa leaning down between my two boys seated at the table eating their second piece of cake. I was baffled as to what she could possibly be telling Max and Henry as I walked out of the pavilion with Hayden beside me.

"I imagine you are surprised to see me here?" Hayden remarked when we reached the gazebo where the ceremony had taken place a short time ago.

"Yes," I managed to squeak out before sitting on the bench.

"I behaved badly," he sat down beside me. "When you didn't respond to my text messages, I wasn't sure where your head and heart were at. So, I visited Lisa on Thursday evening and had a long conversation with her and Erik."

"And?"

"And we talked for several hours. They read me the riot act about the funeral and rightfully so. They also said you've had a lot to deal with, but they refused to elaborate." I nodded and fidgeted with my hands in my lap wondering if he had already noticed the obvious. "Lisa said you've spent the summer with the boys and become good friends with Erik's brother, Chris." Again, I nodded. "Was that who you were dancing with?" I nodded once more feeling like a bobble-head doll.

"Alex?" he reached over and put his hand over mine to stop my fidgeting. "Please say something."

"I don't know what to say," I stared down at my hands.

"Do you hate me?" I looked up and saw the pain on his face.

"I love you," our eyes locked. "I love you still." I couldn't help myself. It was the truth.

"I love you, too. Alex, I never stopped. I never will." Hayden placed his hands on the sides of my face and pulled me towards him kissing me passionately.

My lips and body responded eagerly to him. I had waited so long to feel his touch, to hold him, to be in his arms again. Every barrier I'd built around my heart over the last several months came crashing down into a million pieces with that one single kiss. I had completely forgotten all the tears, the pain, the anger. It all fell away into nothingness.

"God, how I've missed you." He continued to cradle my face in his hands and looked at me like he hadn't seen me in decades.

"I missed you, too."

"So, what have you been up to? How are the boys?" Hayden's smile brightened up my heart.

"They are good. Baseball season is finally over. Football starts in two weeks, same as school." I rattled on. "How is Kennedy?"

"She's a blessing. She kept everything going through the spring, landed several key accounts I'd been working on, and she was the one who brought me back to life."

"How did she manage that?" I eyed him with curiosity.

"By literally smacking me back into reality," he laughed. "It's sad, but true. She got in my face, screamed at me, and finally smacked me for being a selfish brute." I giggled at the imagine.

"I can see her doing that."

"She was right. I'd been a selfish asshole since Mason was taken from us and this is not what my son would have wanted." Hayden admitted.

"Mason would never want you to give up on life," I agreed.

"Would you like to go on a walk around the lake?" He glanced at the waterfall and lake behind us. "It's a perfect evening." He stood and held out his hands to me.

"Sounds lovely," I slipped off my heels, picked them up the ankle straps, and got to my feet taking his hand.

"You look so beautiful," Hayden leaned down and kissed me once more.

"And you look very handsome as well," I was almost afraid to stand in front of him.

Sitting, the shape and flow of my dress hid my growing belly. Standing, and moving about, it was much more difficult to hide. Thankfully, the sun had almost set leaving the world basking briefly in warm evening hues.

I placed my hand in his. My heart leapt at the warm familiarity of his skin. It felt like coming home after being torn apart by forces beyond our control. I followed him down the gazebo steps, off the pathway, and onto the grass.

The grass felt cool under my bare feet. My heels swayed slightly with each step over to the water's edge. We followed the waterline a quarter way around the lake, neither of us saying a word. My mind and body felt at peace — something I haven't felt in months.

"There is so much I want to tell you," Hayden leaned against the railing on the dock. "Where to begin?" He reached out and placed his hands on my waist — instantly, my body froze.

Hayden's face looked at if I smacked him. His muscles locked for a moment then, much to my horror, he ran his hand over my abdomen.

"What the hell? You're pregnant, Alex." His face was bewildered.

I slowly nodded but could find no words.

"How far long are you?"

"About 28 weeks," I met his eyes. "They're yours."

"They?" I nodded again. "Twins?"

"Yes," I searched his face, but it was too dark to read his eyes and I got nervous. "I'm due December 2nd."

"Are you sure it's twins?" Hayden reached back and gripped the railing.

"Yes. I've had two ultrasounds to confirm." I admitted.

"And when were you going to tell me?"

"I don't know," I confessed. "I've been struggling with it, especially since I received your texts."

"Are they okay? Healthy?" Hayden stammered.

"They're perfect," I smiled nervously.

"That's good," He sighed heavily. "Do you know their sex?"

"Yes, a boy and a girl. One of each." I said proudly.

"We are doubly blessed," Hayden straightened up and wrapped his arms around me. "I guess I cannot be angry with you considering the way I behaved. But I must ask, how did this happen? I thought your tubes were tied."

"Apparently, it's not as uncommon as you might think. I cannot say I was so happy to learn that myself." I stated honestly.

"And now?"

"Now?" I took his hand and placed it back on my expanded belly. "Now I cannot wait to meet our children."

"And us?" Hayden looked up at me with imploring eyes.

"I love you. That will never change, Hayden. I want us to be a family and raise our children together. I know we have some geographical issues to figure out, but I believe we can." Or at least I wanted to believe that.

"Well, I guess I'll be calling my contractor on Monday morning."

"Huh?" He wasn't making any sense.

"Kennedy told me she mentioned to you that I've been working on a new project," he shrugged. "So, to speak." He had a mischievous grin on his face.

"She mentioned you were working on something, but she wasn't sure what."

"I went into grief counseling at the end of April." Hayden leaned back against the railing. "I knew I wasn't handling things well."

"And it helped?" I was curious.

"Yes, a great deal. I even joined a support group with other parents who lost their children. I listened to their stories and noticed a trend — nine out of ten allowed their grief to destroy their relationships. They pulled away from their biggest support and wallowed in self-pity. I knew I was on the same track, and I decided I didn't want to be another statistic." He offered a slight smile.

"Is that when you started texting me?" I was trying to piece the timeline together.

"Not quite. I wasn't ready. I was afraid of being rejected after I hurt you so badly, especially after what I said." He shook his head slowly.

I couldn't tell him how badly he'd hurt me. I didn't want him to know those words sliced my heart to pieces and continued to haunt me making me feel responsible for what happened to Mason.

"I knew you didn't mean it," I lied. "So, what was your project?" I tried to lighten my voice.

"After spending many hours talking with my counselor and group, they made me consider our geographical situation from your perspective." Hayden rubbed the bottom of his chin as if he was carefully considering his words. "So, I started looking into the business market around Indianapolis, mainly around town. Then I remembered the wooded acreage across from your neighborhood."

"You bought that land? For what?" It didn't make sense.

"Well, we're gonna need a place to live, aren't we?" a smirk crossed his shapely lips.

"I don't understand," Certainly he couldn't be saying what it sounded like.

"But now, given what I just learned, I'm going to have to tweak the blueprints."

"For?"

"I wanted to surprise you. I'm building us a house on the land across from your neighborhood. That way, you and the boys won't have to switch schools, leave their friends, and Billy will have plenty of room to stretch her legs lease-free." Hayden reached out taking my hands and pulling me close to him.

"But your business?"

"Given the landscape of Chicago and city officials doing nothing to improve it, we've decided to relocate here. Plus, given the incentives the city tossed in, I'd be a poor businessman not to do it."

"But what about your employees?"

"All but ten are relocating. The ones that couldn't are staying due to their spouse's careers. I was honestly surprised how many jumped at the chance and can't wait to leave Chicago. Everyone is simply sick of the dangerous city. Businesses are leaving by the droves. Mine is one of hundreds vacating that hellhole." He explained.

"I can understand why? But what about your penthouse?"

"I sold it in May. I've been living down here for the last few months getting everything completed with both the house and the new office building."

"You've been here for months, and you didn't tell me?" He could tell by the abrupt change in my ton I was pissed. I dropped his hands and took a step back. "How could you do that?"

"I was afraid," he looked down at his feet. "It got worse after I texted you and you never responded — twice." I took a deep breath and exhaled loudly. "I began to wonder if I was doing the right thing with building us a house and relocating my business. I was starting to panic. That's how I ended up on Lisa's doorsteps."

"And they invited you here?" I softly smiled at him.

"They thought it would be romantic." He held his arms in a surrendering gesture. "Did it work?"

"I haven't run away yet?" I rolled my eyes playfully at him.

"Can you run?" Hayden's eyes dropped to my belly so, I smacked his arm.

"It's good to know some things never change." I shook my head and smirked. "And for the record, yes I can run — just not very fast at the moment."

"Please don't," he smiled coyly at me. "So, was it?"

"Was what?"

"Was it romantic? Me showing up here, remorseful and apologetic, on my hands and knees begging for your forgiveness."

"On your hands and knees, huh?" I glanced down at the wooden planks beneath our feet and back up at Hayden.

"I meant metaphorically, but if you are more interested in literally," he dropped his eyes as well and started to kneel, but I grabbed his arm.

"Stop," I smiled and drew him to me. "Please, don't do that." I pressed my lips against his.

"Does that mean you forgive me?" A smile grew across his face.

"Only one thing is going to make me forgive you?" I gave him a quizzical look.

"Does that mean you've changed your mind?" A hopeful look glistened in his eyes.

"Our situation has changed," I leaned my head against his chest.

Hayden kissed the top of my head and wrapped his arms around me holding us tightly. I melted into his arms. For the first time in a long time, I felt like I was home. I felt safe, secure, and most of all loved.

Hayden released me and knelt in front of me. I inhaled sharply as he reached into the inside pocket of his suit and pulled out a little box. He opened in and held it out before him. Inside, displayed a vulgar diamond on a white gold band.

"Oh, my God!" My hands went up to my mouth.

"Alex, our relationship — Christ, I don't even know where to begin." He laughed softly, "has been intense, interesting, and entertaining. I have never known anyone like you. I know I've been a fool, but would you consider being this fool's wife?"

"Yes," I squealed with elation. "Yes, I will." I pulled him to his feet and pressed my lips over his. "I love you," I held him close never wanting to let him go.

"I love you," Hayden's smile reached is emerald, green eyes that glistened with tears. "You have made me the happiest man on earth." He kissed me again, before slipping the ring on my left hand.

❧

We took our time walking back to the reception. As eager as I was to share the glorious news with our family and friends, I didn't want to give up our time alone. We strolled around the lake, hand in hand basking in each other. I could not seem to stop touching him. It was almost as if something inside of me feared if I did, he would disappear again.

I knew my fear was irrational, but if I had learned anything in the last several months, was that time is precious and your life can change forever in the blink of an eye. I said a silent prayer that we had been through enough and could finally have our happily ever after.

The reception was in full swing when we returned. The lights sparkled against the black sky and the outline of the trees around the pavilion were barely visible. A cool breeze swept around us lifting the loose strands of curls off my neck and shoulders. The dance floor was packed with couples and singles enjoying themselves. Even Max was dancing with Brie.

Hayden slipped his arm around my waist as we crossed over the threshold. I spotted Lisa and Erik seated at a table near the dance floor. I started to make our way over to them when a face I didn't expect to see stepped in front of us.

"Surprise," Kennedy appeared out of nowhere.

"Indeed," I gasped. "When did you get here?"

"About 30 minutes ago, but I drove down this morning after Dad told me that he was coming to the reception to talk to you after his conversation with the bride and groom." She was all smiles. "I couldn't sit around and wait for dad to call."

"I'm guessing you knew all along what he was up to?" I chastised her.

"Not at first," she defended herself. "But I did the last time we spoke. I'm sorry. Do you hate me?"

"No. Of course not." Kennedy made it impossible for me to be upset with her.

"Good," she beamed. "Let me see." She grabbed my hand. "Congratulations!" She hugged me tightly, but stopped abruptly, dropped her arms, and took a step back. "You've been keeping your own secrets." My hands ran down my abdomen showing what the flowing pleats of my gown were hiding. "Seriously?" Hayden and I nodded. "When are you due?"

"December 2nd," I grinned rubbing my belly.

"It gets better," Hayden stated proudly, placing his hand over mine resting on my stomach. "We're doubly blessed."

"Twins?" Kennedy's voice kicked up an octave with glee. "I can't believe it. This is wonderful." She wrapped her arms around both of us. "Okay, mom. Can we go tell my little brothers the great news?" She smiled with a twinkle in her eyes that warmed my heart.

It was after midnight before I got the boys asleep. It felt strange even though we were engaged, to have Hayden in my bed with my sons in the house. The boys were so excited after their initial shock and being reassured that we were not moving to Chicago, about the prospect of Hayden and I getting married. They hugged Kennedy and Hayden and welcomed them to our family.

We waited to make the announcement to everyone else since we didn't want to take the spotlight from Lisa and Erik. It was their day, and I would never do anything to steal their thunder. Watching her twirl around the dance floor in Erik's arms, I'd never seen her so happy.

Hayden crawled into bed with his hair still damp from the shower. He was wearing dark gray pajama bottoms with no shirt. His bare muscular chest was even more rippled than I recalled. He had mentioned that he had spent time in the gym working out his frustration and the results were evident as he hovered over me with a devious smile on his lips.

"I missed you," he whispered lying down beside me.

"I missed you too." His hand cupped the side of my face lovingly.

Hayden's lips brushed over mine. The distinctive yet subtle stubble on his face rub against my chin. His lips parted slightly as the tip of his tongue touched mine. He became more forceful as his tongue hungerly lapped at mine. He pressed his body against mine, his arms wrapping tightly around me.

I nudged him onto his back. Our lips devouring each other fervently. I climbed on top of him taking the weight off the twins. Hayden's hands ran over my thighs, caressing my ass, before cascading over up my back. He pulled my white lacy nightgown over my head and tossed it onto the floor.

The low glow from the television enhanced the mystique of him below me. My hands explored his chest as I teased my way along with happy trail. I could feel his cock throbbing between my legs. I pulled on the drawstring on his pajama bottoms with a devilish grin as they came undone between my legs.

I slid down his legs taking his pajama bottoms with me. My feet touched the floor as I maneuvered them down his legs and discarding them carelessly. I traced my fingers lightly up the inside of his thighs. Hayden squirmed delightfully in anticipation.

"Climb on me," his words were breathless.

"Not yet," I teased him tracing my finger around his throbbing cock without touching it.

"Please," he begged arching his hips.

I shook my head with a rascally grin and run my tongue over his thick shaft. Hayden groaned and inhaled sharply. I took the head into my mouth and sucked on it gingerly. I slid it down my throat and slowly maneuvered my way back up. I twirled my tongue around the head loving the way it made him wriggle around the bed.

Hayden tugged on my arms pulling me up to him. I straddled over him without allowing him to penetrate me. He arched his hips into me, but I lifted my hips up to heighten his arousal and prolong his torment.

"You're killing me," he complained.

"I know," I giggled maleficently.

I kissed his neck lightly enjoying the look of desire on his face as he closed his eyes. My lips found his and pressed against them hungrily. I had missed him so much I wanted to savor every moment with him.

I lifted my hips and maneuvered myself over him. His fingers gripped my thighs and guided me down onto his quivering cock. I arched my back straddling him, leaning my head back with my eyes closed. I loved the glorious way he filled me.

Hayden's hands guided my hips riding his hobby horse. The friction of his pelvic bone rubbed against my clit beautifully driving me to eutopia. I moaned loudly intertwining my fingers with his, gripping them tightly. My body exploded with his as our rhythm increased into intoxicating spasms.

I collapsed beside Hayden trying to catch my breath. My arm and leg were draped over his artistically sculpted body. My head finally found its way back to where it belonged — on his chest listening to the sweet sound of his powerful heartbeat.

"I missed you so much," I whispered in the dark tracing my fingers lightly over his chest.

"I'm sorry it took so long for me to get my head out of my ass." Hayden stroked my hair lovingly.

"It's understandable," I swallowed the lump in my throat. "You're living through my worse nightmare. I cannot imagine what you have been dealing with and I wish I could do something to ease your pain."

"I know I was horrible to you, and I wish I could change that. I just fell into a hole of grief and anger I couldn't see my way out." He explained. "I knew you weren't to blame, but you were a safe and convenient target."

"I understand," I reached up and cupped his face. "I love you. I will always love you."

"I love you too."

Chapter 34

LISA AND ERIK RETURNED FROM their honeymoon in the Bahamas eight days after the wedding. Her ex-husband, Brian and mom traded off watching her kids while they were away. She called me the Monday evening after she'd gotten the kids to bed.

"How was the honeymoon?" I snuck out onto the back desk for privacy with Billy lapping at my heels.

Billy was doing much better. She trotted down the steps but kept her roaming no further than midway down the yard. The snake bite incident had cured her curiosity and desire for adventure. I sat down on the swing and watched her sniffing the grass.

"Beautiful. Romantic. Heavenly. I didn't want to come back." Lisa's voice was light and cheery.

"I can imagine. I saw your pictures on Instagram. I'm so jealous."

"If you ever get the chance, you definitely need to go. So, spill it," she paused to giggle. "We're dying to know what happened."

"Yeah, thanks for the heads up by the way. Was Chris in on it too?" I recalled his not so surprised look when Hayden asked to cut in on our dance.

"Erik and I talked to him about it after the rehearsal dinner. He said he'd been trying to get you to talk to Hayden, so he was all for it." She defended her actions.

"Nothing like being ambushed. Thanks for that." I snorted as Billy jumped up on the swing and put her head on my lap.

"And where is Hayden now?" She asked coyly.

"In my living room with the boys." I admitted.

"You're welcome." Lisa said sarcastically.

"Bitch," I laughed. "How did you know I wouldn't blow up at him and make a scene at your reception. That was quite a gamble, don't you think?"

"Not at all. I know you. And you love him. You simply needed a little push is all."

"No. What Chris did was a little push. You shoved me off a cliff." I stated.

"Well, Hayden was there to catch you." Lisa said matter-of-factly. "Did you see the house?"

"He told you about that?" Unbelievable.

"Yep, and about relocating his business to Indy — which I think is really smart considering." She didn't need to elaborate.

"Yeah, I agree."

"I'm so happy for your both." I could practically hear the smile in her voice.

"Thanks. Hayden's even coming with me to my OB appointment this week." I told her.

"Have you two decided on a date yet?"

"We're still discussing it. We're thinking October since we both love Fall and Halloween."

"Just remember, your Baby Shower is on the ninth." She reminded me.

"I have it marked on my calendar, and I will have the guest list for you by the weekend."

"Sounds good," I heard Erik whisper something, but I couldn't make out what. "Hey, I've got to go. I'll call you later this week."

And the phone went dead.

I rubbed Billy's ears for a moment enjoying the peace and quiet. Hayden had mowed and trimmed my yard earlier in the day and the smell of fresh cut grass still hung in the air. It was still in the mid-80s, warm and comfortable. I dangled my feet over the swing with my toes touching the deck. I slowly swayed back and forth thinking how bizarre this last week, last year had been.

Saturday afternoon Lisa and Erik and their children joined

Hayden and me along with my boys at Debbie's. The ladies had decided it was the easiest way to get anything done — keep all nine children occupied playing in the pool while the guys grilled and drank beer. And it worked, mostly.

The three of us were gathered around Debbie's kitchen table with baby shower invitations and a party planner Lisa had picked up. Her organizational skills rivaled my own when it came to event planning. She was meticulous in seeing to every detail and I loved and hated her for it.

"Okay, so we have the menu, Debbie's ordering the cake, and we'll take care of the decorations. Will the new house be done by October 9th?" Lisa chewed on the end of her pen.

"We hope so, but I'm not sure. The changes Hayden made for the twins will likely delay them a month, perhaps longer." I hoped it would be completed by then, but I seriously doubted it. "We won't know until we get closer to the date. I'm sorry."

"I'm just wondering what address we should put on the invitations?" Lisa continued chewing lost in thought. "Would it be done enough?"

"Lisa?" I rolled my eyes at her.

"Sorry," she started tapping the pen on the table. "The guest list?" I handed her the spreadsheet I'd printed out for her.

"Is this everyone?" I nodded. "Twenty people?" I placed my hand over hers to stop the tapping.

"Yes, why?" I asked.

"I was expecting more."

"I didn't want it to be overwhelming." I shrugged.

"And your mom and sister-in-law are not on the list," she observed scanning over the it before setting it down. "Are you sure you don't want to at least invite your mom?"

"Do your parents even know you're pregnant and getting married?" Debbie inquired.

"I don't know. It's a small town. It wouldn't surprise me if someone's told them, but they haven't tried to contact me." I confessed.

"Perhaps you should offer them an olive branch." Debbie suggested.

"Look, I'm not trying to be a bitch, but you both remember how fond my parents were of Mason, especially my mother. Can you imagine how they'd take it if they knew I was pregnant by his father and marrying him?" I shook my head in disbelief. "I really don't think I have it in me to deal with them right now."

"Okay. It was just a suggestion." Debbie's voice dropped.

"I'm sorry, but my life is just simpler without my mother's drama and hateful attitude." I rolled my eyes in a disgusted manner. "And don't even get me started on my lovely sister-in-law. She is a ray of sunshine full of condemnation and self-righteousness."

"So, just Samantha." Lisa pipped in with a smirk.

"Just Samantha," I agreed. "She's going to flip." I laughed. "This could be entertaining."

"Didn't she get engaged last Christmas?" Lisa started chewing on the end of the pen again.

"Yep," I opened a bottle of water and took a long drink. "Oliver finally proposed."

"Have they set a date?" Debbie inquired.

"Not yet," I shrugged.

"What about your wedding? Are you two any closer to setting a date?" Lisa fidgeted with the pen.

"We've talked about it," I looked at them mischievously. "We thought it would be wonderful to do something fun and out of the ordinary." I confessed.

"Such as?" Debbie glanced over at Lisa to see if she had any clue.

"What do you have in mind?" Lisa shrugged slightly at Debbie.

"Taking full advantage of our favorite holiday." I smiled.

"Please tell me you're talking about Christmas?" Debbie looked hopeful, but I shook my head.

"Halloween?" Lisa giggled as I nodded.

"But Christmas would be so beautiful." Debbie defended.

"And Halloween would be so much fun. Think of all the creepy foods, entrees, desserts, and decorations we could come up with." I got all giddy.

"Are you talking like costumes, full Halloween horror, the works?"

"Absolutely," I leaned forward. "Think of how much fun we can have with this. Hayden and I were thinking of a gothic old world Victorian wedding. Halloween is on a Sunday this year so kids will be Trick or Treating on Saturday night, right?" They both nodded. "So, we have the wedding start at 12:05 a.m. on Halloween."

"Why not get married late afternoon or early evening on Halloween? Wouldn't that be easier?" Debbie looked conflicted.

"Because people have to work on Monday." I reasoned.

"But people also have children," Lisa cocked her head. "And dealing with a five-year-old at midnight is not pleasant. Or have you forgotten?"

"No, I haven't forgotten," I sighed. "And I want McKenzie to be my flower ghoul. I guess we can do it late in the afternoon on Halloween."

"And what size are we thinking for the wedding? Have you thought of a venue?" Lisa started chewing again.

"Um, we should probably take this outside. I'm sure Hayden has a better guesstimate than me."

We gathered up our notebooks and joined the men at the water's edge. I kicked off my sandals, sat down beside Hayden and put my feet in the water. It felt so refreshing on my achy, swollen feet. They were beginning to look like sausages to me despite Hayden rubbing them every night.

"Our party planners are grilling me about the wedding. They want to know how many guests? What venue? Etcetera. Any ideas?" I playfully bumped into him.

"Why did I know this was coming?" Hayden chuckled. "Let's see, workers, close clients, family, friends?" he splashed his feet in the water and took another swig of his beer. "500ish."

"What?" Debbie, Lisa, and I all said in unison.

"You have got to be kidding me? I don't even know 500 people." I hoped he was kidding.

"It's not like I have a whole lot of choice on this one." Hayden tilted his head a bit. "There's certain things necessary in the business world and this is one of them."

"Where are we going to host a wedding that size? And don't you think it's inappropriate to have a wedding that size considering the bride will be a month-ish from her due date?" I pleaded. "I mean, it's one thing to get married that far along amongst family and close friends. I'm not sure I would want to do that in front of a bunch of business associates who are virtually strangers."

"I understand, but you have to consider the entire picture. My company is transitioning and relocating. Things like that makes some companies, clients, a bit nervous. And that could cost us business — a lot of business. Weddings are reassuring, comforting, stability to many people."

"I hate to say it, but he is right Alex. There's a bigger picture. Business is all about networking and stability." Erik joined in. "However, finding a venue large enough to host such an event with such short notice could be difficult."

"You just bought fifteen acres. Is there any way to make sure the construction is completed, and landscaping done by then?" Mark asked.

"It'll be close with the additions. They just broke ground on the pool last week. I know the foundation on the twin's room and the atrium is done." Hayden said casually.

"How big is this place? And when do we get to see it?" Lisa leaned forward.

"You will, just not yet. I want it to be a surprise." A devilish grin slid across his lips.

"That's just cruel." Debbie childishly stuck her tongue out at him. "I don't think I like you anymore."

"Yes, you do." Hayden grinned mischievously while Mark and Erik laugh.

"You are onery," Lisa giggled.

"Did you tell them about our theme?" Hayden looked over at me.

"I thought you were joking." Debbie rolled her eyes. "Only you would come up with something like this."

"What?" Mark looked confused.

"This has got to be good," Erik mused.

"A Gothic Victorian wedding on Halloween." I announced.

"Awesome. This is gonna be fun." Erik smirked. "Do we all get to dress up or is it just the wedding party?"

"Well, considering you are part of the wedding party, I'm counting on it. But yes, the wedding party as well as guests are required to dress up for the ceremony and reception." Hayden leaned across the group. "I mean, what's the point of having a wedding on All Hallows Eve if you can't Goth out in classic style?"

"I agree. We could have a lot of fun with this. But it really would help if we could get an idea of the venue." Lisa glared at Hayden in a playful manner.

"In time," Hayden laughed. "Don't worry about the venue. I'll take care of it."

"Now I'm worried." I rolled my eyes.

"Trust me," Hayden winked. "I know exactly what you have in mind."

"Well, it should be anything but dull." Debbie's eyes widened and we all laughed.

Chapter 35

FALL SETTLED INTO THE MIDWEST with all its brilliant majesty. The warm days faded into cool evenings where bonfires were a prominent feature in our backyard. The trees were full of fire in a vast array of red, orange, and gold. The air held the aroma of pumpkins, apples, and hay.

Hayden spent the last couple months getting to know my sons and building a relationship with them. It took a little bit of time and patience for Max to warm up to him, but Henry took to him immediately. Hayden went to every football practice and game. He spent hours helping with homework and running plays with the boys.

I never said anything to him about his enthusiasm. I was afraid it would only upset him, but I couldn't help but wonder if he was, in some ways, making up for all that he missed with Mason. Either way, I was happy that our family was melting together.

Our new home was coming along beautifully, and Hayden was monitoring its progress closely, especially since he had made numerous adjustments adding more space and additional bedrooms for the twins.

The home was a two-story red brick house with five ensuite bedrooms, seven bathrooms, four fireplaces, a theatre room, playroom, mancave, an office for me, a professional kitchen, and a four-car garage. He also added a pool house with a guest house above it and full outdoor kitchen. The inground pool and surrounding walkways were flagstone. In addition, he put a hot tub, grotto, and flagstone waterfall and slide. It was just under seven thousand square feet and exquisitely designed.

The curved wooden staircase was breathtaking, and I was at a loss when they delivered the eight-burner gas stove. The kitchen had a farmhouse copper sink, red brick backsplash, and red brick covering the wall that housed the double ovens, microwave, and warmer along with more cabinets than I could ever fill. It was overwhelming and a bit intimidating. I was in love with it. I have never imagined in my wildest dreams living in such a place.

The boys were so excited about the new house. Most days Max and Aaron would ride their bikes over to the house to check on the progress. They had earmarked where they wanted the basketball goal, and the treehouse. I told Hayden I thought it was too much — all of it, but he said he was enjoying himself.

When I brought Lisa and Debbie out to the new house, they were in awe of it as much as I was. When Lisa pressed me further on the price tag of it, I was embarrassed to admit I was completely clueless.

"How can you not know?" she pressed. "You're getting married in a couple weeks. Haven't you two discussed finances?"

"Not really. Every time I bring it up, he just says, 'I got it covered. Don't worry about it'. It's frustrating, but what can I do? Demand to see his checkbook and latest bank statement?" I shrugged.

'Um, yes." Debbie joined it. "I know all of Mark's finances." She waved her hand for emphasis. "If we're going to be married, I have every right to know."

"And when will that be," I smirked.

"Probably after Hayley's graduation." She giggled. "Either way, you should have a serious talk about it."

"Hayden told me in Europe that some or rather most women he's dated in the past were more interested in abusing his generosity and his bank account." I leaned against the half-installed kitchen cabinet with no countertop. "I know he's successful. I mean, he just sold his penthouse and God only knows what that that went for."

"Erik said it's over seven figures." Lisa shared her husband's speculation.

"Can you imagine what the payment on this place is?" Debbie asked Lisa walking through the oversized pantry off my new kitchen.

"Want to trade husbands?" Lisa smiled over at me. "I could definitely learn to live like this." She nodded.

"Very funny, ladies. It's just a house." But we all knew it was so much more than a house.

The fall semester was well underway. The boys were doing well, and I was enjoying my final year of student teaching and classes. I was required to take American History for my degree and Max, being in the eighth grade, was also taking American History.

Even though the material for my class was more in depth than his, it allowed us to study together, work on homework together at the island, and it sparked some lively discussions. Max and I were discussing the end of the American Revolution and which of the founding fathers where responsible for what when my cell phone rang.

Engrossed in my conversation with Max, I picked it up without looking.

"Hello."

"Hi, Alex. How are you?" Danny's voice came ringing through my phone.

"Hi," I climbed off the barstool, grabbed my jacket, and walked out on the back porch.

Danny hadn't called in months, not even to check on the boys. We had only spoken twice since Mason's funeral. I was so upset and disappointed with him for walking out of their life the way he did, not once but twice.

"How are you?" I shivered as I sat down on the swing.

"I'm good. How are you?"

"Fine," my legs were shaking up and down trying to generate heat to the rest of my body.

"That's good. Aren't you in your last year of school?" I couldn't figure out why he was making small talk.

"Yes. I graduate in May."

"I'm happy for you." Danny stammered.

"Um, thanks."

"How are the boys? Are they playing football this season? Are they enjoying school?"

"The boys are doing well. Max is playing for the school team and Henry is enjoying junior football. They're both doing well in school." I was scared to elaborate.

"I would like to see them." Danny lowered his voice.

"Their Fall break isn't for a few weeks." I was tempted to remind him of what he'd said before about forcing the boys to come to Phoenix.

"I will be in town next week for a conference. Would it be possible to see them?"

I glanced down on my enormous belly. I was seven weeks from my due date and waddled instead of walked these days. There was no possibility Danny would not notice and I hadn't told him I was engaged or pregnant. I wasn't sure why except I was afraid of what he would say if and when he found out Hayden was Mason's father.

"Alex?" He interrupted my thoughts.

"I'm here."

"You got quiet. Is everything all right?" He almost sounded concerned.

"Yes, everything is fine." I lied. "When are you coming into town?"

"I'm flying in late Sunday night. I will be in meetings all day Monday, but I'd like to see them afterwards. I should be done no later than five."

"Max has practice right after school until five and Henry has practice at six." I explained. "Tuesday may be better."

"I could meet you at practice. I'd love to watch." Danny sounded hopeful.

"Can I call you tomorrow? I would like to talk to the boys. I know they're still upset about you marrying Amanda." I proceeded cautiously.

"I'll be traveling alone, Alex." He pleaded.

"Okay. I'll talk with them and call you tomorrow evening."

"All right. Please tell them I love them and miss them." his voice sounded so sad, I almost felt sorry for him.

"I will. I promise."

"Thanks, Alex."

"Good night, Danny." I hung up the phone before he could say anything else.

Four days. I had four days before my ex-husband would be back in Indiana. I dreaded telling the boys. Henry might be a little more receptive than Max, but probably not much. Plus, I wasn't even sure how to begin the conversation with the boys. I didn't know how to explain to them the challenges with Hayden, Mason, and now the twins. Their misinterpretation could possibly cause many problems.

I knew Danny wasn't completely unreasonable. And even if he blew my love triangle out of proportion, I seriously doubted if he would fight me for custody considering the intense distain between Amanda and our sons. Still, I was skeptical and a little apprehensive about putting any faith in Danny.

I walked back in the house and found Hayden getting his butt kicked by Henry at Mario Kart in the living room. I watched the two finish their tournament and then waved Max to come in a join us. He plopped down on the couch beside me and gave me a questioning look.

"Sorry, guys. But I need to talk to you for a second. That was your dad that called." Both boys looked disheartened.

"What did he want?" Henry asked.

"I'm not spending my Fall break in Phoenix. He promised." Max declared.

"No. This has nothing to, do your Fall break. And I believe he's trying to keep that promise. The reason he called is that he's flying in Sunday evening for business. He'll be here all next week and he'd like to see you guys." I explained.

"Is he coming alone?" Max inquired.

"Yes," I put my arm around him. "He's trying guys. I really believe you should give him a chance."

"Are you going to make us see him?" Henry asked.

"Technically, he has visitation rights. So, I cannot stop him from seeing you." I shrugged.

"Fine. But I have practice after school every day that I can't miss." Max stated. "He will have to wait until afterwards. But I also have homework. I can't let my grades slip or coach will kill me."

"I have practice on Monday and Wednesday too." Henry chimed in. "At six, remember?"

"Yes, I remember." I assured him. "Don't worry, you're not going to miss it. What would you say if he wanted to come watch you practice?"

"I guess it's okay," Henry didn't look overly thrilled.

"Have you mentioned to your ex about the wedding or the twins?" Hayden raised his eyebrow at me.

"I think I'll ask Danny to meet me on Monday evening. I get out of class at 4:30 so I can just meet him downtown. It's probably a good idea to explain everything before he sees you and the boys."

"Do you think that's wise?" Hayden looked concerned.

"Well, the baby shower is tomorrow, and the wedding is three weeks away. When do you think a more appropriate time may be?" I reasoned.

"Okay. If this is what you want to do." Hayden stood up and stretched. "Does that mean we'll see him on Tuesday?"

"Yes, I believe so." I looked over at the boys. "What do you think?"

"All right," Max shrugged.

"Fine," Henry bit his lower lip looking upset.

"Yeah," he looked over at Hayden. "Dad's not going to make us go back to Phoenix for Christmas, is he?"

"No," I knew Danny had given up that fight when he married Amanda.

"Good, cause I want to have Christmas in the new house with the twins." Henry smiled.

"You will," I tousled his hair with a reassuring grin.

"Good," he jumped up. "I'm gonna take a shower."

He trotted off to his room looking relieved. Max got up and disappeared into the kitchen to finish the rest of his homework. I reached out and took a hold of Hayden's hand.

"Are you all right?" I asked him.

"I knew I was going to meet him sooner or later." He half smiled down at me. "It's not like you didn't meet my ex."

"Everything is going to be fine," I stood and put my arms around him. "I promise."

"I love you," he held me tightly rubbing the side of my belly.

"I love you too."

Debbie and I arrived at Lisa's Saturday afternoon for the baby shower. She insisted on playing hostess since the new house was not quite ready and she agreed with Hayden to keep it a surprise for the wedding. She had decorated her house in blue and pink pastel decorations with storks and teddy bears in abundance.

My sister, Samantha came charging out of the house before we got the car door closed. She was wearing a beautiful auburn maxi-dress with knee-high boots looking stylish and elegant as always. She ran up and wrapped her arms around me almost knocking me over in her excitement.

"Oh, my gawd, look at your belly — you're huge!"

"Thanks, Sam," I laughed hugging her back. "You look wonderful, as always."

"I try," she smiled and flipped her thick locks over her shoulder. "I can't believe you're having twins and marrying that gorgeous hottie."

"Speaking of hottie's, how is Oliver?" I asked closing the car door.

"He's wonderful. He'll be with me at the wedding. He's in Boston this week. He'll be home on Thursday." She put her arm around me. "You are simply glowing," she gave me another squeeze.

"Hello, Samantha," Debbie came around the car. "How are you?"

"Fabulous," my sister beamed.

"Does mom and dad know anything?" I bit my lower lip.

"Not from me," Samantha cocked her head slightly. "I finally gave in and answered my phone." She rolled her eyes. "That woman would not give it a rest. She actually tried defending herself, giving me all this bullshit about how I couldn't understand how dad was back then, blah, blah, blah."

"Figures she'd blame her actions on dad." I huffed. "I'm not surprised."

"Me neither. Like there is any justification for what she did and lying about it all these years." My sister's tone displayed how disgusted she was. "Hell, dad only drinks because he lives with her," she scoffed. "We all did, except for her perfect Colin."

"I'm sorry. I didn't mean to cause you any problems."

"Yeah, like fighting with our parents is something new for me," she mocked. "I pride myself on being their biggest disappointment." Samantha's laugh was jovial. "But I admit, you're giving me a run for my money these last couple years." She put her arm around my shoulder and walked up to the house rubbing my belly.

"You're such a bitch." I tilted my head and rolled my eyes at her which only made her laugh harder.

Lisa had invited several of the mom's we knew from the boys' teams, Aaron's mom, Rhonda, Heather, Kim, Michelle and several professors and students I'd become friends with over the years. It was clear that Michelle had helped Lisa with the guestlist on the campus end rounding out the party with twice as many people as I expected.

Lisa took our jackets and ushered the three of us into the great room. I was met by a chorus of greetings that felt overwhelming. Everyone was excited about the idea of twins and my upcoming nuptials. I plastered on a smile as I was forced to endure two hours of baby shower games, finger foods, and constantly being petted like a Buddha.

When the party dwindled down to Michelle, Samantha, Debbie, and me, Lisa broke out the wine and poured a glass for my companions. The five of us made ourselves comfy in the great room amongst the piles of baby gifts, scattered wrapping paper, and little confetti pastel cutouts in pink and blue baby feet that Lisa would be finding around her house for the next six months.

"Are you getting nervous?" Lisa settled onto the loveseat beside me.

"About the twins or the wedding?" I sipped my green tea.

"Take your pick," Samantha sat down on an oversized cushion by the fireplace.

"Yes, and yes."

"I would think you'd be excited, overjoyed even. You're getting everything you've always dreamed of. Hell, what we've all dreamed of since childhood." Michelle smirked.

"Let's see — sexy as hell, check. Wealthy, check. Knight in shining armor, check. You got the dream, woman." Debbie leaned forward on the couch waving her glass in a mocking toast to me.

"Hayden is not perfect," I protested.

"No, but he makes one hell of an effort and that's more than most." Lisa raised an expressive eyebrow at me.

"That he does," I agreed with a sly grin upon my lips.

"All right, enough of the sentimentality. It's time to discover what we've all wanted to know." My sister had a devious smile on her face as four sets of eyes turned towards me.

"Huh?" I forged innocence.

"Pray tell little sister — which one is better in bed? The father or the son?" Samantha's eyebrows raised in inquisitively.

"Oh, my God!" I busted out laughing. "Seriously?"

"Oh, hell yeah!" Lisa nodded her head enthusiastically. "Inquiring minds demand to know."

"That's so unfair. Mason was barely 21 when I met him. He was a child." I explained. "And more importantly, an eager student." I giggled mischievously.

"But he was a man when you got done with him," Michelle leaned forward laughing and helping herself to some more wine. "I am absolutely envious of you. He was simply edible."

"I'm guessing you haven't met Hayden yet?" Debbie cocked her head to the side. "Talk about the whole 'like father, like son'!"

"Really?" Michelle cooed. "Do tell," I shook my head in dismay at her cheesy grin.

"Hayden has these exquisite green eyes — Mumm," she closed her eyes and exhaled dreamily. "Sculpted chest and abs, cutest bubble butt God ever put on a man. I swear it's so firm you could bounce a quarter off it." She exclaimed.

"Can you?" Samantha asked all giddy.

"You guys are terrible," I rolled my eyes at them.

"Oh, don't forget the hair," Lisa leaned back with her hands behind her head with a tawdry grin showing off her dimples. "You must run your fingers through those waves every chance you get." I simply shook my head and smiled.

"Oh yes, the hair," Debbie continued. "Hayden has the same wavy dirty blond hair as Mason, except his is highlighted with traces of silvery gray giving him that distinguished sexy physique that's just irresistible." She was waving her hands about for emphasis.

"I've got to see this guy!" Michelle declared.

"So, spill it all ready." Samantha leaned up and tapped my knee encouragingly.

"You guys are terrible," I set my drink on the coffee table and slipped off my dress shoes getting comfortable. "I trained Mason well — very well." I raised my eyebrows smirking. "But Hayden — Ah, Hayden, there are no words to describe how talented that man is." I flashed them a shit-eating grin with no further explanation.

"I hate you," Michelle informed me. "My husband has so many damn intimacy issues," she shook her head in disgust. "I'm just sick of his excuses. I remember when sex was fun. Not some routine where it's simply a race to reach the finish line so you can get some sleep."

"Brian was like that too," Lisa emphasized. "I hated it. He never kissed me. When I said something to him, he got upset because to him, a simple peck on the lips was kissing." She took a sip of her wine before continuing. "I missed those long deep kisses that curl your toes and leave you breathless. You know what I mean, ladies." Four heads nodded in agreement.

"Danny was always big on the kissing. That was one of the things I loved about him." I admitted. "Still, there wasn't an affectionate or romantic bone in his body."

"Danny's an asshole," Samantha stated. "I'm so glad he's in Arizona now. You and the boys are so much better off without his sorry ass."

"Did I mention he'll be here tomorrow?" I asked the group.

"No," Lisa playfully slapped my shoulder.

"Oh, shit," Debbie's eyes widened.

"I'm guessing from the look on everyone's faces you haven't told him about Hayden and the twins?" Samantha's face crumbled up in confusion.

"I may have failed to mention them to him." I confessed.

"Are you serious?" Michelle looked stunned. "He doesn't know you're pregnant?" I shook my head. "Or getting married?" Again, I shook my head. "Or the father of your twins is also the father of the — ," she turned towards Lisa, "what did he call Mason? The paper boy?" Lisa nodded as I hung my head in shame. "I'm glad I'm not in your shoes. How are you going to explain this one?"

"I don't know," I conceded. "We're having dinner on Monday night before he sees the boys on Tuesday."

"Are you going to introduce him to Hayden?" Debbie asked with a weary expression.

"I don't see how I can avoid it," I reluctantly stated. "It's not like I can hide Hayden or who Hayden is from him forever?"

"Do you think he'll try to use it against you?" Concern burned on Michelle's face.

"No. He doesn't want the responsibility. Plus, his wife hates the boys, and they would fight him all the way. Danny isn't up for that kind of battle." I shrugged. "Don't get me wrong, I expect him to threaten and chastise me like a child, but I don't believe he'll follow through on anything."

"Are your parent's coming to the wedding?" Michelle poured herself some more wine before settling back on the couch making herself comfortable.

"No," I said immediately.

"I still can't believe you haven't told them. You know they're going to blow a gasket when they find out." Samantha pointed out.

"I don't have it in me to deal with their drama." I readjusted myself suddenly feeling like I was being judged. "But Uncle Rick and Aunt Misha are coming." I looked over at my sister.

"You're kidding?" I shook my head. "God, I haven't seen Uncle Rick in years."

"Who's Uncle Rick?" Debbie inquired.

"Our Dad's younger brother. They had a falling out years ago. He stopped coming to all family functions." Samantha explained. "It will be so nice to see them. I'm glad they're coming. How did you convince them?"

"I just invited them," I shrugged. "And I may have mentioned that our parents wouldn't be there." I smirked.

"Well, I'm glad they're coming."

"Me too," I locked eyes with my sister knowing we were both thinking the same thing — the family we create for ourselves is sometimes stronger than the one we are born into.

"Did you tell your uncle that your dad's not your dad and I guess that makes him not your real Uncle then?" Debbie said innocently, but Michelle's eyes widened in surprise.

"Wait. What?" Michelle boggled.

"Yes, I told him. Shockingly, he wasn't surprised at all." I flashed Debbie a look telling her to drop it before I turned my attention to Michelle and explained to her what I had uncovered earlier this year. Still, I left out the part about the blood test results before my parents were married. It was humiliating enough having a mother who was a promiscuous whore but adding syphilis and her claim of a rare blood type on top of it all was mortifying.

"I can't believe you haven't demanded the truth out of your mother." Michelle stared at me with disbelief. "I would be going ballistic."

"It's pointless," I wagered. "She's never going to be honest with me when she can't even be honest with herself."

"You know her behavior is typical for her diagnosis," Michelle looked at me sympathetically.

"I understand that, but it's one thing to read about it, and study it, but when it directly impacts your life in this way, you feel a lot less charitable and forgiving about it." I reasoned.

"Maybe you should sit down with both of them and confront them." Debbie suggested.

"It wouldn't do any good. Neither of them is going to be honest with me." I knew my parents to well to believe in them.

"I feel bad for your dad," Lisa pursed her lips in a frown.

"He knew, and he stayed." I pointed out.

"I believe he may have suspected, but never knew emphatically until you confronted mom. Even if he always thought it or whatever, he never wanted to believe it and I think in a way, convinced himself it wasn't true." Samantha stated. "At least until he confronted the guy before he showed up on your doorstep."

"I wish I knew who he met with," I wracked my brain as I'd done a thousand times since February trying to figure out who was in their life during that time, but no longer was and I was still drawing a blank.

"That's so weird — to think you have another family out there, brothers and sisters, grandparents, aunts, uncles, cousins, that you'll never know." Debbie said without thinking.

"Yes," I felt even worse considering all that I had lost. "I know."

"I didn't mean it that way," Debbie back peddled. "I just think it would be frustrating not knowing."

"It is," I grimaced.

"Have you considered doing one of those genetic websites to see if one of them are on there too?" Michelle inquired. "You never know. Maybe they know you exist, but not who you are, and they could be looking for you too." There was a hopefulness in her voice that was endearing.

"I don't think I'm ready for that," I confessed. "I don't know which is worse — realizing the only biological parent you know is a bipolar whore with borderline personality disorder or learning that the one you were closest to isn't even your *real* parent?" I admitted. "Besides, obviously this man knows about me, and he's made zero effort to find me so, that means he doesn't want his family to know about me and he doesn't want to know me either." It was a heartbreaking rationalization.

"You can't know that." Lisa reached over and touched me arm. "He may be scared about facing the truth too. His children or wife, may hate him for leaving you."

"That's true," Michelle joined in. "He may have been married at the time too. This could open a whole can of worms that would destroy his life also."

"Well, it certainly imploded mine." My voice took on an unintentional edginess. "It ruined my relationship with my parents — not that we had much of one to begin with, but still."

"I confronted our mom about it and she's never going to be honest about who Alex's father is." Samantha admitted to the girls.

The five of us chatted into the evening enjoying the comradery and closeness of the trials that binds us together — husbands, children, motherhood, and wine. It felt so freeing to laugh, tease, and joke around about all the craziness that life continually throws at us. Teetering on the edge of major life changes, it was exactly what I needed.

Chapter 36

I DROPPED MY BACKPACK IN THE trunk and slammed it shut. It had been an exhausting day. My feet were swollen. My lower back was on fire with an aching pain that no amount of massage could cure. I felt miserable. The idea of another two months of this was unfathomable.

The last thing I wanted to do was spend an evening with Danny being interrogated.

The dreary evening did nothing to improve my mood. Light raindrops splattered across my windshield just enough to be annoying. I gripped the steering wheel and sighed loudly in the empty car. I skillfully maneuvered my way through downtown traffic to the restaurant off the circle.

Per Hayden's request, I used valet parking. He wasn't crazy about my being downtown after dark and it was the only way I could appease him. Thankfully, the hotel Danny was staying at hosted a four-star restaurant and offered valet parking. It was a blessing since I knew Danny would be drinking heavily this evening. And considering the shock I was about to give him, he was gonna need it.

I was wearing a maroon jumper dress with a cream, long-sleeved tee-shirt. My jewelry was subtle and tastily — small diamond hoops and an elongated necklace. The knee-high, lace-up brown leather boots accented my Fall attire perfectly. My hair was pulled up in a French roll, and I had touched-up my makeup before I left campus. I don't know why I was so nervous. I looked cute and elegant — the perfect vision of an expectant mother-to-be.

A kid in his early 20s opened my driver's door and held an umbrella over me while helping me out of the car and over to the canopy. His colleague jumped him as we stepped upon the curb and sped away towards the garage. He politely handed me a tag and went out to greet the next couple.

My legs felt like lead as the butterflies fought furiously in my stomach. I swallowed roughly, my throat feeling parched. One of the twins kicked me swiftly in the diaphragm causing me to exhale and wince in pain. My hand automatically rubbed the side of my belly encouraging my unborn child to reposition themselves. It was as if they too could sense my apprehension and wanted to make their feelings known.

I passed through the automatic doors and scanned the exquisitely decorated lobby looking for a sign. I could hear the low sounds of classical music coming from the far right. The gold emblazoned sign on the wall indicted the restaurant was a short way down the corridor.

My boots reverberated off the marble floor as I made my way down the hall. The constant clambering sounded like my pulse ringing in my ears to the rapid beat of my heart. I paused in the entryway scanning the vast rows of tables for Danny. My eyes found him seated at the bar nursing a martini.

He was engrossed in a lively conversation with the bartender and had not noticed my arrival. I walked up behind him, winked at the bartender with a finger to my lips and tapped Danny on the shoulder.

"Good Lord," he jumped turning his head and smiled. "Alex."

Danny, reached behind himself to put an arm around me, noticed the obvious condition I was in. His eyes widened, bulging in disbelief. His lower jaw dropped open as he lost his balance on the barstool and fell off. He caught himself on the corner of the bar regaining composure and what was left of his dignity. People turned around, eyes glistening with amusement at Danny's shocked reaction to my pregnancy.

"That's not mine," Danny looked over at the bartender laughing. "I swear."

"How can you say that?" My voice squeaked; an expression of hurt and betrayal covered my face.

"That's not funny, Alex," Danny pinched his lips, his brows furrowed. "You're gonna make me look like a louse."

"Of course, it's not yours," I playfully smacked his shoulder and leaned over to the bartender. "He's only a deadbeat dad to his other children." I said mockingly.

"You can be such a bitch," Danny laughed while the bartender looked confused. He shrugged his shoulder and headed to the other end of the bar to wait on another customer.

"Always," I leaned up kissing him on the cheek. "You look good, Danny."

"You're glowing, Doll." He shook his head with a sweet grin. "You always looked so radiant when you're pregnant." He dropped his arm around my back, picked up his drink with his other hand, and led me over to the host. "Our table should be ready."

The host ushered us to our white linen table with a small boutique with a lit candle in center. Danny held out my chair for me with a twinkle in his eye. I smiled and placed my napkin in my lap before taking a sip of the ice water.

"I must say I am speechless, Doll. This was the last thing I expected." He sat down and unrolled his napkin placing it across his lap. "Do his parents know?"

My stomach tightened. I knew he was going to assume Mason was responsible for my current condition.

"Yeah," I cleared my throat. "About that." My mind scrambled for where to start.

"Don't get me wrong, I'm happy if you're happy." The waiter dropped by, and Danny ordered another martini and an iced tea for me before turning his attention back at me. "How are the boys taking it?"

"Excited. Henry is thrilled about not being the youngest anymore and Max has been wonderful. They went with me for my ultrasound." I could feel the heat rushing to my face waiting for his next question.

"And? What are you having? Do you know?" For a moment, his expression took me back to when I was carrying our boys and how excited he was for their arrival.

"A boy," I placed my hand on the left side of my abdomen, "And a girl." I put my other on the right.

"Dear Lord," Danny finished off the last of his martini and eagerly took a drink of the new one the waiter handed him. "Twins?"

"Yes," I laughed at the expression the waiter gave Danny.

"Wow," he stammered running his fingers through his hair. "How are you going to finish school. Aren't you supposed to graduate in May? I mean, when are you due?"

"December 2nd. I'm planning on going back in January as scheduled. Ideally, I can get all my classes clumped together in the mornings or hopefully, two or three days a week. The twins will be in the daycare on campus so that will help." I explained.

"But how can you manage this? I mean, Alex, this isn't going to be easy, even with the boys helping you. Financially, it's going to be a struggle." I was touched by the genuine concern I heard in his voice.

The waiter came by and took our entre orders giving me a momentary reprieve. I wracked my brain trying to think of how to begin my explanation of Hayden and my relationship. I knew Danny could be judgmental, but I quickly reminded myself of his tract record which ultimately led to our divorce. Still, I truly didn't want to go there knowing it could escalate rapidly into a heated argument.

Once the waiter disappeared, I fidgeted with the bread he'd left in a basket on the table. Danny was eyeing me conspicuously waiting for me to say something.

"Are you taking me back to court?" He raised his eyebrows suspiciously.

Of course, he would immediately jump to that conclusion.

"No," I let out a deep breath. "Nothing like that." Relief passed over his face.

"Then why do you look so anxious? Like you're nervous sitting here with me. That's not like you, Doll." Danny leaned forward looking apprehensive.

"Do you remember my European vacation when you had the boys the summer before last?" he nodded. "Well, Mason and I ended things when he left at the end of the term before then and I started seeing someone else."

"Someone more age appropriate, I hope" Danny chuckled under his breath as I narrowed my eyes at him. He cleared his throat and sat back in his seat.

"Anyway, when school resumed in the Fall, Mason was still around coming to the boys' football games and such. We weren't together, but the boys had grown so close with him, I didn't want to take him away from them. Mason knew I was involved with someone else, and he was dating some girl from Northwestern." My hands felt clammy as I continued to play with my napkin.

"The girl who murdered him, right?" I nodded. "I watched the news coverage on CNN. I didn't realize Mason's Dad owned Brooks Enterprises. He handles all our marketing and advertising. He's a big deal." Danny rambled on aimlessly. "I had no clue Mason was his kid until our VP told me after I got back from our honeymoon." He picked up the olive out of his martini and shook it off before popping it in his mouth. "That's why I'm here. Brooks Enterprises is moving to Indy. The VP and I came down here to meet with Mason's Dad."

"Huh?" my body went numb as I stared at him stupidly. "You met Mason's Dad?"

"Sure," he finished off his martini and waved to the waiter for another one. "Spent four hours with him today. We're teeing off at 9 a.m. tomorrow morning. Nice guy. Have you met him?"

"Did you mention that you met his son?"

Surely, Hayden would have called me if Danny had said something to him about Mason or his relationship with me.

"No," Danny lowered his eyes. "I figured it would be in bad taste considering what happened. Plus, I didn't know if he knew anything about you and Mason." He shrugged nonchalantly.

"Only in my world," I propped my head in my hands, covering my face trying to come to grips with the fact my ex-husband and soon-to-be husband spent the day together and were playing golf in the morning.

"Alex?" Danny leaned forward taking my hands away from my face. "Talk to me."

The waiter dropped off our plates. The food looked and smelled fabulous, but the thought of eating anything suddenly made me nauseated. I stared down at my glazed scallops that had sounded so delicious and edged my plate forward just enough to keep the aroma out from beneath my nose.

"Long story short," I took a deep breath after the waiter disappeared. "Mason went to Cancun on Spring Break after we started dating. He charged the entire trip on his dad's credit card that he'd given Mason for emergency use only. Well, Hayden wasn't too happy when he got a couple thousand dollars' worth of charges on it and drove down to confront Mason. Mason, in turn, lied to his father about who I was alluding that I was Alex's mother. Not Alex." Danny's eye's widened in surprise.

"Ouch!" he pinched his lips. "I'm sure that made you feel really good about your relationship."

"To say the least," I grimaced at the memory. "I ended up telling Hayden the truth, but Mason didn't know it and carried on with this whole charade. It was humiliating." I confessed. "Then Hayden made Mason work for him that summer to pay back the money he charged."

"Good for him. I would too." He took a sip of his martini before he continued. "But I would also beat his ass for it. Our boys better never pull a stunt like that."

"Mason called Hayden a sperm donor with a checkbook. His parent's divorced before his second birthday and his stepfather raised him. They really didn't know each other."

"Still," Danny shook his head. "That's ridiculous."

"I agree."

"So, you've met Hayden Brooks." He looked at me carefully. "What was your impression of him?"

"Confident," I stated honestly.

"Yeah, with a little bit of arrogance. But he has the goods to back it up. I'll say that much for him." Danny chuckled leaning forward. "I never see Michael, our VP, kiss anyone's ass, but boy he puckered up to Mason's Dad."

"Seriously?" I was curious. "I thought you guys were his clients. Shouldn't it be the other way around?"

"Normally, yes. I would say so." He cocked his head to the side. "When I questioned Michael in a roundabout way, he told me that Brooks Enterprises is in great demand, and they are extremely selective with their clientele. It's some elite, prestigious thing to be represented by them so," he waved his hands for emphasis. "Mason's dad has managed the impossible. Instead of searching for clients and beating down doors, he's turned the tables and has everyone begging to be represented by them. It's quite ingenious and apparently the man's made a fortune at it. It's a good thing you're carrying Mason's twins, you're gonna clean up, Doll." Danny sat back laughing and finished off his martini waving to the waiter for another.

"Danny," I smirked. "These are Hayden's twins." The look of astonishment he'd had on his face earlier after realizing I was pregnant was nothing compared to the look on his face at this moment.

He was speechless. He stared at me with bulging eyes and his mouth agape. I struggled not to laugh as I could see him slowing coming to grips with the information, I just told him.

"Your European vacation? Hayden?" I nodded. "Did Mason know you were sleeping with his father?"

"He found out we were together over Christmas break." I left out the how since it really didn't make a difference and I still felt horrible about it. "But he was also already married to someone else when he found out."

"What kind of daytime soap opera have you been living? That's fucked up." Danny crossed his hands on the table leaning forward.

"I know," my heart was racing waiting for him to tear into me.

"And the boys? How much of this were they exposed to?" His eyes watched me intently.

"They knew I went to Europe, but not who with. They knew I was seeing someone, but they didn't know who. I was extremely careful. But eventually, yes. They found out and I explained to them how Hayden and I are closer in age, more compatible, and they didn't know anything about him until after Mason had told them he was married to someone else. They knew Mason and I had separated long before." The explanation sounded absurd even to my own ears.

"How does Hayden feel about you having twins? His children are grown. Is he at least going to pay support for them?" Danny's eyes narrowed.

"We're getting married in two weeks." I held my breath to scared to breathe.

"Wait. What?"

"We're getting married on Halloween."

"Halloween?"

"Yes," I nodded.

"So, I'm guessing you and the boys will be selling the house? I'm sure it's a bit below Hayden's standards." He mocked taking a long drink. "Unbelievable," he muttered under his breath.

"What?" I raised my eyebrows at him.

"You're marrying Hayden Brooks?"

"Yes," I repeated cocking my head to the side eyeing him trying to decipher what was going on in his head.

"Do you realize who he is? What he's worth?" Danny questioned. "Jesus Christ, Doll. I'm supposed to play golf with him in the morning." He ran his fingers through his hair. "How am I supposed to look at this man who is screwing my ex-wife?"

"He's not simply screwing your ex-wife. We are getting married." I said hotly. "And I had no idea you were coming here to see him."

"I had no idea you were knocked up by him." Danny countered.

"What difference does it make? You act like this is a bad thing for you?" I questioned.

"What if you got pissy with me? You could screw my career in a heartbeat."

"You really think I'd do that?"

Unbelievable.

"You've been pissy with me in the past? And it's not like you'll need my child support after this month. This would be your opportunity to fuck me over since I did you."

I couldn't believe he really thought I was so vindictive.

"Danny," I reached over and took his hand. "Regardless of what happened in the past, you are the father of my sons, and my first love. You will always have a special place in my heart. Hurting you would be the same as deliberately hurting them and that's something I would never do."

"I feel the same," his face softened. "I just can't believe you're pregnant and getting married." He squeezed my hand. "Are you happy?"

"Yes, very."

"Good," a small grin spread across his shapely lips. He let go of my hand and sat back in his chair. "So, where is this new house? I hope the boys don't have to transfer schools."

"Nope. They don't." I fiddled with my now cold dinner suddenly starving. "You remember the woods across the street from our neighborhood?" He nodded. "Hayden bought it."

"All of it?" Danny finished off the last of his steak.

"Yes," I tasted the scallops. They were as delicious as they smelled. "I'll take you on a tour before you leave."

"Tour? How big is this place?" I raised my eyebrows and he laughed. "Like I even need to ask."

All in all, I couldn't have asked for things to go better. Danny took it all in stride, the surprises, twists, and turns — he was a trooper. Never once did he threaten my custody of the boys. I didn't believe he would, but still — there was a part of me that feared it.

Thankfully, we spent the remaining time we shared for the evening laughing, joking, and teasing each other. I saw traces of the man he used to be once he let down his guard and relaxed. I couldn't help but wonder if Amanda ever saw this side of him or if she only wanted to business suit she'd seduced? Either way, I knew she would never have the same type of relationship we had once shared because Danny and I grew up together, became parents together, and shared a bond she would never break.

Even though I had never met the woman, her treatment of my son's made me loathe her with a passion. Danny refrained from mentioning her the entire evening which only made me wonder if there was trouble in paradise. But I didn't ask, nor did he offer.

I couldn't help but wonder.

Chapter 37

HAYDEN WAS SITTING UP IN BED watching a movie when I returned. I leaned over and kissed him feeling his stubble rub against my chin. I pulled back, but he grabbed my arm pulling me down on the bed. He laughed leaning his face towards me trying to rub his whiskers on my cheek.

"Stop," I struggled to free myself from his grip.

"But I love you," he wrestled me down to the bed and leaned over me.

"I love you too, but," I squirmed and smacked him playfully. "Get off me."

Hayden rolled to the side and put his hands behind his head. I sat up and unzipped my boots. I kicked them onto the floor and laid by on the pillow beside Hayden.

"My feet hurt," I moaned.

"Fine," he sat up. "I know what that means."

"You're an ass," I pushed him away.

"Rub my feet," he said in a whiney mock feminine voice. "I'm pregnant and my feet are swollen. And my back hurts. Can you get me some Häagen-Dazs?"

"I hate you," I pushed him away again, but he only laughed and leaned down to kiss me again.

"How was your dinner? I'm happy to see you weren't calling me for bail, so I guess that means you didn't kill him." Hayden loved to tease me.

"You're not going to believe me if I told you." I propped myself up on the pillow as Hayden started massaging my aching feet. I moaned out in pleasure it felt so incredible. "First, tell me about your day." I couldn't help but be curious of his take on it.

"Nothing too exciting. Meetings with clients. Luncheons. Paperwork. Boring." He ran his hands under the ball of my foot caressing it roughly working out the pain.

"Tell me about your clients." I adjusted the pillow making myself comfortable.

"Just a couple guys from Arizona," Hayden's hands froze for a second and turned towards me. "No," I giggled. "Tell me that's not your ex." I nodded. "Dan?" I laughed aloud. "Jesus Christ," he looked like I'd smacked him across the face.

"Hey," I nudged him with my feet to get him to start rubbing them again.

"Sorry," he started massaging again but looked dazed. "You know I'm supposed to play golf with him in the morning." He looked down at me and rolled his eyes. "Like this isn't going to be uncomfortable."

"Look at it this way, at least you no longer have to worry about meeting him." I chuckled.

Hayden's eyes narrowed with a dark glint. "I'm glad you think this is funny."

"I do," I failed to keep a straight face causing him to tickle my foot. I kicked out at him in defiance. "That's not fair."

"Life isn't fair," he stuck his tongue out childishly at me.

"Boy, I wish I could be a fly on the golf course tomorrow."

"Just for that, I'm not putting out tonight." Hayden announced pushing my legs off his lap.

"Wow, you went there." I giggled and climbed off the bed with Hayden's assistance. "I swear, I get much bigger you're going to need a forklift for me." I groaned.

"Doc Johnston said your weight is fine. Twenty-three pounds is not that much, especially for twins." Hayden wrapped his arms around me and kissed me on the forehead.

"Yeah, but I've got two months to go, and I feel like a duplex." I stuck out my bottom lip and pouted.

"You're gorgeous," he dropped his hand to my abdomen and gently rubbed it. One of the twins decided to kick back. "Did you feel that?" he laughed. "Hello, little one." He leaned down and rested his face beside my stomach. "Be nice to your mother you two. You may have the upper hand for the next couple months, but she has eighteen years to get even with you for any pain you cause her now."

"Don't tell them that," I smacked his shoulder lightly. "You're awful."

"What? You know I'm right." Hayden chuckled. "Do you really want me to lie to them right from the get go?"

"I expect you too," I glared down at him. "Things like Santa Clause, the Easter Bunny, and Fairy Tales are the staples of childhood, and they are going to believe in them for the short time this cruel world allows."

"I'll even dress up as Santa on Christmas Eve if that's what you desire, my love." He kissed my belly sweetly then rested his head against it. "I want to experience every aspect of their childhood. I missed so much with Kennedy and Mason. I don't want to make the same mistake again. I've been given a second chance and I intend to make the most of it." He kissed my belly again before standing upright and kissing me on the cheek. "I love you," he whispered stroking my hair.

"I love you too."

Hayden unzipped my jumper and helped me undress. I was so self-conscious now that my belly was growing bigger by the day. He claimed he loved the shape of my expanding figure and rubbed my belly every chance he got. It made me feel both loved and like a Buddha doll.

The bathroom filled with steam from the shower as we both crowded around the sink brushing our teeth. As we continually bumped into one another it made me more anxious to move into the new house. Since Hayden had moved in our little ranch house had shrunk to a matchbox. His business documents cluttered my desk forcing me to join my sons at the island to complete my homework.

Hayden's wardrobe rivaled my own for space in the closet. I spent a weekend last month packing away all my non-maternity clothes and moving them over to the new house simply to make room for the enormous amount of elaborate suits he owned. His collection of shoes amounted slightly shy of my own and those my swollen feet could no longer tolerate were already awaiting me at our new house.

The movers were due Friday morning. Hayden chastised me every time I attempted to pack a box or organize anything for the movers, and it was making me crazy. I was not accustomed to releasing authority and responsibility to anyone. It wasn't that I was a control freak, I simply relied upon myself to complete tasks. I never had the fortune to hire someone to take care of things I had always done myself nor did I intend to now.

Hayden followed me into the shower. The space was limited before, but now with my expanding figure, it felt miniscule. I found myself looking forward to our new walk-in double headed shower closet with a third rain facet hanging from the ceiling. It would quadruple our bathing space. Plus, Hayden had added a corner bench that could be utilized for various sexual exploits that weren't currently possible.

"You realize if you weren't expecting, I would force you to play in the morning." Hayden lathered my hair with shampoo.

"I don't golf well," I looked into his eyes with a sarcastic smirk upon my lips.

"Regardless, I wish you were coming." A doomed look passed over his face.

"You spent most of the day with him today. Don't tell me your nervous about a simple round of golf with him now?" I teased.

"That was before I knew I was about to marry his ex-wife and help raise his sons. How does he feel about that?" A look of concern clouded his face. "Did he ever meet Mason?"

"Yes, he did. He referred to him as the paper boy." I smiled at the memory. "He enjoyed tormenting me greatly about our age difference."

"And what did he have to say about us?" Hayden raised his eyebrows in curiosity. "Is he going to give us grief or fight us for the boys?"

"None whatsoever," I rinsed my hair and added conditioner. "As I said before, his new wife is more than happy to be rid of them and Danny doesn't have the balls to stand up for them."

"I wish I could tell him how big of an idiot he is. I missed everything with my first two children and I'm fortunate Kennedy has forgiven me. But Mason never did." His eyes looked sorrowful and glistened with tears. "Things were better before the end, and I have you to thank for that because of this weird, twisted mess we got ourselves into, but I would give anything to go back twenty years with them." I wrapped my arms around his neck, leaned up on my tippy toes and kissed his cheek.

"Your son loved you very much," I whispered lying my head on his chest.

"I know," he swallowed hard. "Sometimes I look at Max or Henry and how you are with them, and I realize how much I missed throughout their childhood. You realize Danny is me only a decade behind."

"At least you were committed to building your own empire, and not sleeping and brown-nosing your way up the corporate ladder in someone else's empire." The distain was evident in my voice.

"Do you believe that mattered to them?" Hayden tilted his head and eyed me carefully.

"Perhaps not when they were younger, but I believe it does now. Look at the legacy you've built for them. Kennedy is an amazing businesswoman who takes a great deal of pride in her position. You have much to be proud of with her." I placed my hand on his warm chest.

"I'm sure Mason didn't feel the same," I hated the mournful look in his eyes.

"Perhaps when I met him, but after his internship he had a new respect for you and what you've built. He learned a great deal that summer and admired your staff. He rambled on endlessly about your office and its politics and antics after his return." I smiled to myself recalling the vacation destination board put up in the conference room.

"I would have loved to someday pass the business onto him and Kennedy." Hayden placed his hand on my belly. "And to them and Max and Henry if they are interested." His shoulders relaxed as a warm and loving peacefulness formed upon his face.

"You are a wonderful man, Mr. Brooks." His sentiment touched my heart. "I don't know what I ever did to deserve you."

"I could say the same thing." Hayden kissed my forehead tenderly under the hot water. "I feel like the luckiest man alive. I feel so blessed."

"We both are."

"The sad thing is, even if I explained to Danny — told him my story and all the regret I have with Mason and how my heart is shattered that I will never get the opportunity to make it up to him — it wouldn't make a difference to him one way or another. He is too power hungry to learn from my mistakes." Hayden rested his head upon mine while the hot water rained over us.

"I know you're right. He destroyed our marriage and gave me sole custody of our sons for his career. Sadly, I know the knowledge of your experience won't make any difference to him. And from what I can gather, Amanda is no better — worse in some ways." I closed my eyes and listened to the strong steady rhythm of his heart.

"All we can do is what you have been doing." Hayden gently rubbed my hair. "Love the boys and teach them to be good, honest, hardworking men." His lips touched the top of my hairline. "And you have done a remarkable job thus far."

"Thank you," my heart swelled with pride.

"Alex," Hayden placed his hand under my chin and lifted my eyes up to meet him. "I give you my word. Your sons will be loved and cared for just same as the twins. I promise I will never treat them any different." His eyes glistened with devotion.

"I never had any doubt," a small smile turned up the corners of my mouth. "Still, I believe I would serve Kennedy better as a friend than a stepmother."

"Perhaps you are right on that account," a smile hovered in his eyes. "She is so excited about the twins, the wedding, and her new little brothers. Not to mention she adores you."

"And I her. I love her spirit. I like to think I would have been somewhat like her if I had made different choices." I confessed.

"You have a lot of spunk." Hayden kissed my nose. "It's one of my favorite things about you."

We crawled into bed, exhausted from the day's exploits. Each lost in our own thoughts. I curled up on my side with my head resting upon his chest. My belly was snuggled into his side. I closed my eyes nestled into him. The soft glow of the television illuminated the room just enough for me to make out the sculpted curves of his chest and abdomen.

"Hey," a deep chuckle escaped his chest. "That not fair." His hand rested one the side of my belly. "It's not nice to kick your old man."

"Old man?" I snorted. "You are in the prime of your life." I declared.

"I am afraid that passed some time ago, my love." The low rumble of his chuckle vibrated through me.

"Stop being silly," I playfully smacked him lightly on his chest.

"Silly? I'm starting to take it personally. Our son kicks me every time you snuggle up to me." Hayden's fingers traced lightly over my belly. "I'm afraid he doesn't like me."

"Now you are being silly. Your son loves you. He's simply practicing for soccer or football." I smiled up at him.

"Or how he's going to manage his older brothers," his voice was lighthearted.

"The most likely explanation," I laughed aloud. "He's certainly going to need it, especially with Henry."

"Ah, Henry will be fine. He'll be so overprotective of the twins it will drive us all batty." Hayden reassured me.

"I'm sure your right, my love." I closed my eyes and felt completely at peace and happy with the world.

Chapter 38

THE FOLLOWING WEEK PASSED IN A whirlwind of panic, tears, and tension. The boys were on fall break which was both a blessing and a curse. I had them organizing their rooms, going through clothes, and getting rid of things they couldn't fit into or didn't want any longer.

Max was enthusiastic, sorting through his closet, and giving Henry some of the things he'd outgrown that his little brother wanted. But Henry was being obstinate and fighting me every step of the way.

The golfing outing was as successful as possible. I cannot say I was surprised when Danny showed up with Hayden on Tuesday evening for dinner. There was no evidence of cuts or bruises on either of their faces, no broken bones. For that, I was thankful.

They were in good spirits and seemed to be getting along well for which I was grateful. Hayden took Danny on a tour of the new house. The boys, Aaron, and I joined them since we were spending our time going back and forth between the two houses.

The art of balancing school and family was growing more difficult daily. Plus, the anxiety of having Danny and Hayden spending so much time together. I knew Danny was curious about the man who spends so much of his time with his children and rightfully so. I was happy to see how much Danny liked the house and Hayden. But it was odd having the two of them so chummy with each other.

Still, once Max and Henry got accustomed to seeing the two men getting along so well, both were in much better spirits. They even attended the boys football practices together and shot hoops with them in the driveway. As hectic as my week was, I was thankful for the extra set of hands.

Danny extended his trip to help us get things moved in. The movers handled all the packing and moving things to the new home, but the unpacking was overwhelming. Thankfully, our friends offered a hand and worked for pizza and beer.

The last box was in the new house by three o'clock Saturday afternoon. Hayden and I had offered the house to Kennedy, and she was thrilled. She was already talking with her dad about remodeling the master bath and extending the master closet. She was so excited to move out of the apartment she was renting closer to the city and be closer to us before the twins arrived.

The boys said goodbye to Danny on Monday morning before they left for school. The cloud covered sky was dark gray and threatening rain. The autumn air was warm, but the cool breeze was enough to raise the goosebumps on my arms. Hayden had an early meeting, so I was taking Danny to the airport. He put his bags in the trunk and climbed into the front passenger seat.

"Ready?" I fired up the engine and turned the car around. It still felt strange being at the new house full time.

"I believe so," he smiled over at me.

"I truly appreciate you extending your stay to help us get moved and settled." I pulled out onto the street.

"It was no bother. Afterall, they are still my sons, and I am invested in their wellbeing." He reached over and patted my belly. "And given your condition, I felt obligated to pitch in. Plus, my VP would have extended my stay a month if I'd asked since I was helping Hayden move. He was practically dancing a jig when I told him who you were marrying."

"What a tool," I laughed. "Either way, I do appreciate it. And I'm glad you and Hayden got the chance to get to know each other outside a business setting." I glanced over at him, but he was staring out the side window.

"It's good to see you happy." Danny's voice was low. "Regardless of how you two came about, it is obvious you two belong together."

"Thank you," I reached for his hand. "That means a lot to me."

"I know I wasn't the best husband and I've made a lot of mistakes with you and the boys," I nodded, but remained silent. "I am sorry for that. I truly am." He squeezed my hand tenderly. "I know it sounds selfish, but I must say I really hate the thought of you getting married."

"Need I remind you that you are remarried?" I crinkled my eyebrows at him.

"I know, I know," his eyes glistened in the hazy morning light. "It doesn't make sense and I have no right to feel this way."

"No, you haven't and I'm sure Amanda wouldn't approve of you saying such things to me." I tried to stifle a giggle but failed miserably.

"I say them because we grew up together, became adults and parents together," he pinched his nose between his eyes, a gesture he always did when he teared up. "You were my first love and are the mother of my children. It's just hard seeing you marry someone else."

"Danny," I traced my thumb lightly over his hand that still held mine. "Don't you think I felt the same way when you married Amanda. There's a part of my heart that will always belong to you because you were all those things to me."

Large raindrops splatter across my windshield as I pulled onto the ramp that led to the backway into airport. It felt fitting considering the solum mood in my car. Danny continued staring out the window and remained silent until I pulled up to the terminal.

"I wish you all the happiness this world has to offer." Danny squeezed my hand one last time before he opened the car door.

"And I, you," I pushed the button to open the trunk and climbed out of the car, leaving it running.

"Please text me when you get home, so I know you've made it safely." He lifted his garment bag and suitcase out of the trunk and set them down.

"I will," he patted my belly. "Take care of yourself and these two. Our boys are going to spoil them rotten." I reached up and wrapped my arms around his neck and hugged him tightly.

"Take care of you," I whispered as I kissed him on the cheek.

Danny picked up his bags and disappeared behind the sliding glass doors. I watched him until he was no longer in sight. A small part of my heart ached for the man I used to know and love, but as I watched my past vanish before me, I climbed into my car eager to get home to embrace my future.

Classes became a nuisance and an inconvenience. I was aggravated with having to take the time out of my day to attend them or teach. There were so many last-minute details I needed to attend to before the wedding. The bridesmaid, maid of honor, and flower girl gowns were all finalized as were the flowers and tuxes. Even my gorgeous Victorian gothic luxury gown was beyond my expectations.

But Hayden's idea of hosting a Gothic Victorian wedding on Halloween at our home proved to be more than my nerves could take. The landscape architect was constantly present with a gaggle of workers from dawn to dusk milling about the yard, building the trussell, installing lights and the fountain in the pond, and dozens of plants, shrubbery, flowers, and trees scattered about the yard and driveway.

The wedding planner, Kari, hired by Hayden, was grating on Lisa's last nerve since she assumed authority over the wedding. Lisa spent most of her time rolling her eyes behind Kari's back and being egged on by Kennedy who had arrived Wednesday morning. She found Kari annoyingly cheerful and perky. Every time she was around Lisa and Kennedy finished off a bottle of wine between them.

Kennedy was still running the daily operations in the Chicago office until it closed the second week of December so Hayden wouldn't have to travel up there nearly as often. Still, he was going up there at least a couple days every other week. She was floating back and forth between the two locations while Hayden handled the finalization of the new Indy office. Her strong business sense and work ethic was a true blessing, and I knew Hayden was relying heavily upon her.

The tents were erected on Thursday before the wedding. The day was filled with a constant flow of trucks delivering tables, chairs, cutlery, linens, and dozens of other things I was unaware of. Kari was floating about the house and grounds barking orders and attending to all the details. I spent the morning on campus and found my car headed along a country road afterwards simply to avoid the chaos at the house.

I turned the radio up and let the warm autumn breeze flow through the rolled down window. Golden amber leaves tried desperately to cling to the branches but failed repeatedly as the warm breezed rustled through them. The sky was filled with fluffy clouds against the robin blue sky. It was a lovely afternoon, and I wanted a bit a time alone with my music and thoughts before jumping back into the circus ring.

I propped my elbow on the widow and ran my fingers through my hair. I was exhausted. My feet were killing me, and my back was aching with all the extra weight I was carrying in the front. I loved Hayden for all that he was doing, but I was unaccustomed to such lavishes or vulgar displays of wealth.

Debbie and Lisa were enjoying it much more than I. They had no problem adding their two cents for added things or improvements on various aspects of the house and wedding. Neither could understand how difficult it was for me to have Hayden take care of everything. They felt I should be sparing no expense on the house and the wedding.

It was embarrassing, even humiliating in many ways. I had never given much thought to Hayden's wealth either way. I knew he was very successful, but to hear others including Danny speak of him, you'd have thought he was the next King of England. It was all rather foolish.

The florist was waiting for me in the library when I arrived. Hayden met me in the driveway with a broad smile. He was pleased with all the hustle and bustle both inside and outside the house. Personally, it was giving me a headache.

"There you are," Hayden opened my car door. "I expected you more than an hour ago."

"I'm sorry," I took his hand as he helped me out of the car.

"What kept you?" he kissed me on the cheek.

"Trying to dot all the I's and cross all the T's," I handed him my backpack.

"You had an appointment with the florist a half hour ago. Kari has been handling it. They are in the library." I followed him through the garage entryway.

"Then why am I needed? Kari has made all the decisions anyway. My opinion doesn't matter." I muttered under my breath.

"Don't be silly," Hayden dropped back putting his arm around my waist. "You're the bride. You can have anything you want."

"Except control over the wedding preparations." I pointed out through gritted teeth.

"I hired Kari to assist you and attend to all the little details that you don't need to bother with it. I know the move has been difficult on you, especially with teaching and keeping up with your schoolwork." He pulled me closer to him. "I didn't want you to exert yourself, my love." He kissed me softly, his eyes full of genuine concern.

"I appreciate it, darling. I do." I offered him the best smile I could muster. "I am just used to doing things on my own. I find it unsettling to let a stranger make intimate details about our wedding."

"Just remember, Kari works for you. Not the other way around." Hayden raised an eyebrow.

"Yes, sir." I teasingly rolled my eyes as I made my way into the library.

Kari and the florist were wrapping things up when I opened the pocket doors to the library. Photographs of floral designs and sketches were laid out across the oversized table in the center of the room. The florist looked relieved when I entered the room. I could only fathom how demanding Kari was being.

"Ms. Rose, it is so good to see you." She breathed a heavy sigh of relief.

"Thank you for your patience. I was held up at school." I slid the door closed. "How are things shaping up?" I sifted through the designs on the table. "These are beautiful."

"I told her I think the black candle holders would be more appropriate as well as the black tablecloths." Kari reached for the picture.

"I still believe using the cooper taper candle holders with the ivory tapers in various sizes on top a rose gold tablecloth draped over a smoky gray tablecloth with a black lace runner would be more elegant." The florist picked up another photograph on the table and handed it to me. "We could highlight the center with black and silver pumpkins with the deep purple flowers accented with baby breath, a few black plumes, and sage in large blush vases."

"These would look perfect with the black metal lanterns and brass birdcages. They complement each other well with the Victorian gothic theme." The florist looked triumphant.

"Exactly. Plus, the octagon black dinner plates on top the gold dinner plates accented with the black patterned wine glasses with the Victorian place cards — you'll create a full Hallows Eve table-scape." The florist enthusiastically beamed.

"But I feel," Kari intervened.

"I appreciate your feedback, but this is my decision and I want this one." I looked at Kari and tried not to sound condescending.

"Perhaps we should ask Mr. Brooks which he would prefer?" Kari said in a perky tone.

"I do not need to ask Mr. Brooks." I smiled sweetly at her. "He trusts my judgement."

"Of course," Kari nodded with a solum expression.

"Fabulous," I looked over at the florist. "Is there anything else?"

"No. I believe that is everything." She made notes and gathered up her things. "We will be here to set up by noon on Halloween."

"Perfect," I extended my hand and shook hers. "Thank you. I look forward to seeing you then."

"You too. Have a wonderful afternoon." She put everything into her satchel and followed me out the door.

"You do the same."

I left Kari in the library and found Hayden in the kitchen. He was putting together a plate of cheese and crackers to snack on before dinner. He grabbed a cream soda Dr. Pepper out of the refrigerator and set it on the counter beside his plate.

"How did it go?" He raised an eyebrow as he took a bite out of a cracker and cheese.

"I don't think Kari is nearly as happy as I am." I walked up behind him and wrapped my arms around his waist leaning my head against his back.

"Why am I not surprised by that?" he chuckled.

"She wanted me to check with you regarding the flowers, tabors, and tablecloths."

"What on earth for?" he asked between bites.

"Probably because you are the one paying her." I smirked.

"We're paying her. Not me." Hayden insisted spinning around and facing me. "We are a team, remember? What's mine is yours, and vice versa." He cupped the side of my face in his hand and kissed me gently.

"I'm exhausted. If you don't mind, I'm going to rest a bit before the boys get home."

"Sure," I kissed him again and hugged him tightly. "I love you." I whispered before leaving him in the kitchen.

Chapter 39

THE MORNING WAS OVERCAST WITH thick clouds hovering over our small town. Hordes of people I had yet to meet poured onto the property. Hayden had hired a half dozen valets and gotten permission from the high school to park cars in their student lot.

I stood in the nursery window looking down at the parade of people arriving for the wedding. A part of me felt sad that my parents were not here. Despite all the hurt feelings, years of childhood emotional and physical abuse, the scars that remained raw, I still loved them — although I did not like them.

I stood peering down at the circle driveway in front of our home in a long ivory silk robe and satin ivory slippers that Hayden had bought me. I ran my hand over my expanding abdomen leaning my head against the side of the plantation shutters. I felt huge and awkward, nothing like the graceful lady I always strived to be.

The Jack and Jill nursery wing designed by Hayden was a fairy tale. Elicia Madelyn or Ellie's room was decorated in soft ivory, sage, and pale pink, with little bouquets of blooming flowers held together with satin ribbons. Little plush bears, elephants, rabbits, and birds in a variety of pale pastels accented the room. From the ceiling hung pale pink sheer canopy covering the circular crib that stood in the center of the room. The dressing table and rocker were a rustic white accented with pale pink cushions.

Elijah Mason — Eli's room had pale gray shiplap across the back wall. The other three were painted a blueish gray. His crib was shaped like a pirate ship with the mizzen, main mast, foremast, and shrouds mounted above it. It was so unique and could be converted into a full-size bed with a loft that served as a deck and plank as he grew. Max and Henry loved his pirate themed nursery and couldn't wait until the crib was transformed.

Both nurseries had complementary shelves, changing tables, and walk-in closets filled with everything they would need for at least six months. Hayden had gone overboard in his excitement purchasing more clothes than they could possibly wear before they outgrew them.

It was such a contrast to the nursery's Max and Henry had. Both were cute and they had plenty of clothes and everything they needed, but neither had designer everything. And from what Hayden had told me, Kennedy and Mason had even less when they entered this world. Now that Hayden had the financial capability to give his new children the best, he wanted to.

Given the theme of our Hallows Eve wedding, when we sent out our Victorian wedding invitations complete with the wax seal stamped with a fancy B, we encouraged guests to participate in the costume gala. From the look of those arriving they were happy to oblige. Many of the ladies carried lace parasols and the men looked dapper in their top hats and tails. Their expressions and demeanor expressed delightfulness and ease as they exited their vehicles and made their way to their seats for the ceremony.

I sat down in the soft cushioned glider and closed my eyes, rocking gently. My back ached and my feet were slightly puffy, but nothing too bad. Debbie, Lisa, Samantha, and I had spent the morning getting mani-pedi's and our hair done. They were downstairs in my dressing room getting into their Victorian bridesmaid gowns complete with a corset, petticoats, elliptical crinoline slips, and bustles with the supporting flounce. The dark purple taffeta silhouetted with black lack gowns were full in the back, gathered into a train of soft folds and draperies. The ladies loved their heeled, black ankle-length laced boots, black lacy slouch socks, and their black-lace fingerless gloves.

I nervously glanced at the clock above the door. I was sixty minutes from becoming Mrs. Hayden Brooks.

The men were getting ready in the pool house leaving the women and girls to roam about the main house freely. Chris, Ian, and Aaron were serving as ushers taking guests from their cars over to their seats for the ceremony. Even those who were not direct participants in the wedding were excited about getting dressed up for the special event.

Hayden, Erik, Mark, Oliver, and the boys were dressed in their black tailcoats and trousers, dark purple satin vests, bowties, and white shirts. Their tall black top hats gave them a distinguished air. McKenzie and Henry were to walk down the aisle together as ring bearer and flower girl. McKenzie's attire matched the bridesmaid's gowns perfectly right down to the black lace gloves. She was going to carry a black wicker basket with a dark purple satin ribbon woven through the handle filled with purple and black rose petals.

"Are you all right?" Lisa cracked open the door and leaned in.

"Yeah," I smiled. "I was just taking a moment to gather my thoughts."

"I love this room," she stepped in gazing slowly around the magical bliss radiating through the room. "It is so beautiful." She ran her fingers over the edge of the crib railing.

"Thanks," I continued rocking. "You look very elegant." Lisa spun around to give me the full effect of the dress.

"I feel like such a lady," she curtsied before me laughing wholeheartedly. "But now it's time for the bride to get ready." She held out her hand to me.

"Fine," I took her hand and followed her down the stairs.

After much squeezing, huffing, and a few tears, the layers were finally on. I felt like a creampuff about to explode. I spun around in front of my full-length mirror in my dressing room wishing I looked half as elegant as the three ladies surrounding me.

"The only blessing is that my dress isn't purple. Otherwise, I'd look like a big fat grape." I frowned at my reflection.

"Don't be ridiculous. You look gorgeous." Samantha kissed me on the cheek and squeezed my shoulders in a side hug.

My wedding gown was a black silver sparkle gothic Sakura with lace appliques and a six-foot train. It had an extended black sheer cape. The corset was fitted right above my extended abdomen. The skirt was specially pleated to obscure my pregnancy as much as possible. My lace-up ankle boots and stockings matched my court ladies. They were soft and comfortable providing the support I needed for my swollen feet.

The black lace veil surpassed my train and cape billowing out behind me in a mystical fashion. My hair was styled in Victorian curls with a white gold crowned hairpiece accented with black opals holding my veil in place. It was elegant and stylish without being gawdy.

"I don't believe I felt this anxious on the day I married Danny." I nervously turned towards my sister, my hands shaking.

"Trust me, you were worse." Samantha fluffed my skirt and adjusted my veil. "I know you're waiting for the other shoe to drop, but Alex — it's not going to." My sister placed her hands on my shoulders. "The boys are happy. The twins are healthy. Danny is supportive. It's past time you enjoyed all the happiness you deserve." She leaned down and kissed me on the cheek. "I love you, little sister."

"I love you, too." I hugged her tightly.

"Now, let's go get your happily ever after." Samantha beamed.

"Momma?" followed a small knock on the door.

"Yes?" Max cracked open the door a smidgen.

"May I come in?" his voice sounder older than his years.

"Please," my eldest son looked dashing in his coat and tails.

The broad smile upon his face erased all doubt I clang to. My son was happy. For a single mother about to remarry, that meant more to me than anything.

"You look beautiful, Momma." Max entered the room with the new air of confidence of a teenager.

"Thank you," I said proudly.

"Can I talk to you a moment?" He leaned against the shoe shelves in the dressing room.

"We'll meet you on the veranda." Lisa checked her watch. "You have about ten minutes," she warned Max who nodded in acknowledgment.

Samantha handed me my flowers and distributed the rest to all the ladies around her. McKenzie was twirling in front of the full-length mirror admiring her dress. She looked darling so caught up in her reflection that it took Lisa two times calling her name to get her attention.

"Is something wrong?" I asked as the door closed behind them.

"No," he sat down on the chaise lounge appearing much younger than he had a moment ago.

"Something is bothering you," I sat down beside him placing my hand over his.

"Nothing's bothering me. I just wanted to tell you something before we go out there." Max looked down at our hands. "You know I'm proud to walk you down the aisle today, but I don't like the line the minister said at the rehearsal — who gives this woman." He brought his eyes back up to mine. "You are not mine to give away and I cannot give you away. You're my momma and always will be."

"Of course, I will." I was so touched. "So, what would you like the minister to say instead?"

"How about, who blesses this lady to join this man?" His eyes glistened with tears.

"I love that," I glanced at my phone. "Let me text Hayden and have him tell the minister." I quickly typed it into my phone. "Hopefully, he's got it with him."

"Can I run out there and tell him? I don't want to chance him not having his phone." He looked a bit anxious.

"All right, but you must hurry. Go around the outside of the chairs. Don't cut through the aisle." I told him as he jumped up and headed for the door.

"I will," he scurried off.

"I'll meet you on the patio." I called out and heard an 'okay' drift back from a distance.

I straightened my gown and double checked my reflection in the mirror. I hardly recognized the image staring back at me. So much had occurred in the last three and a half years. The naïve girl who drove the wrong way down a one-way street on her first day of college and befriended the sleeping boy with blond curls sticking out from beneath his beanie no longer existed.

In her place stood a lady who had learned much and not just academically, but personally. She excelled in her studies, and student teaching. She had traveled across Europe with the man she loved. But she'd lost someone dear to her. She'd had her heart broken, leaned on her friends for strength and comfort. And then had all of her dreams and wishes granted and it was more blissful than she ever imagined.

So why was I so nervous?

Hayden was my Knight in Shining Armor.

He was every dream I had ever had of whom I wanted to marry since I was a little girl. He was flawed, imperfect, and a little arrogant at times, but he oozed confidence, loyalty, and was fiercely protective of those he loved. Granted, there were little things I would love to tweak about his behavior, but nothing I wanted to change.

I touched my reflection and glanced around the huge closet dressing room Hayden designed for me. I was still in aww that this was now our home and I lived here — this was my life. In the span of one summer, I went from being a struggling single mom on a strict budget, stressed and fearful of what the future held to living in a multi-million-dollar estate with the man I love, two happy and healthy sons, and anxiously awaiting the arrival of my twins.

Life was so wonderfully weird.

My hands felt sweaty and shook nervously. I picked up my black lace handkerchief, twisting it around the stem of my bouquet. I exhaled loudly and took one final look at myself in the mirror.

"You can do this," I said to the vacant room.

The girls and my boys were waiting for me on the veranda. We were a short distance to the ceremony area, but it now looked a mile away.

Lisa took ahold of McKenzie's hand with Henry walking alongside them to the aisle. After they flounced and fluffed my gown, straightened my train, and adjusted my veil one last time, Debbie, Kennedy, and Samantha followed behind. Max straightened his shoulders as if to appear older than his years and held out with arm for me to take. The proud expression in his eyes overwhelmed my heart.

"My lady," his full lips formed a shapely smile displaying his deep dimples.

"It would be my honor, sir," I wrapped my hand around my son's bicep.

In harmony with each other, our steps matched as we crossed the emerald lawn. We strolled slowly with the pressure of my grip on his arm getting tighter the closer we got to the aisle. As we reached the beginning and our guests rose to their feet. Max placed his right hand over mine and squeezed it momentarily. He smiled into my eyes giving me the strength to me forward.

"I got you," he whispered as if reading my thoughts.

"I love you," I said softly with tears glistening in my eyes.

My son was growing into an amazing young man. I was so proud of him.

Right foot first, we stepped forward into our future.

Hayden was a breathtaking sight. His sleek black tails and top hat with his gleaming emerald eyes was a devastatingly handsome combination. I felt as if I were walking through a Victorian dream fog. His broad shoulders and structured features only enhanced the attire and gave him a gentleman aura of a time long forgotten. He swayed nervously under the trestle. Erik placed a hand on his shoulder to steady him. Our eyes locked. I concentrated on him, blocking out the hundreds of guests on either side of me most of whom I did not recognize.

Step by step Max and I made our decent. We stopped beside Hayden in front of the minister.

"Thank you all for joining us this afternoon. You may all be seated," the minister addressed our guests. "Who blesses this lady to join this man?"

"My brother and I do," Max turned towards me and lifted my veil. He leaned up and kissed me softly on the cheek. "I love you, Momma." He whispered placing my hands in Hayden's and then taking a seat in the front beside my Uncle Rick and Aunt Misha.

I handed Lisa my bouquet and joined hands with Hayden. He smiled nervously at me, his hands were damp with perspiration, and I was thankful for the black lace gloves I was wearing.

Hayden and I had written our own vows. The words I spent hours composing were nowhere to be found in my brain. I prayed for something to jog my memory when the minister put the spotlight on Hayden.

"Alexandra Lee Rose, I never thought I would get remarried or find someone I wanted to share my life with. But through a crazy twist of fate, we found each other," he grinned knowingly. "And you have shown me how to laugh again, to live each day to its fullest and never take the precious time we have together for granted." His voice cracked and tears glistened in his eyes. "I love you for bringing me back to life and giving me a second chance to be a husband and father. I promise you, that you and our family will always come first." He slipped the elegant white gold band on my ring finger.

"Hayden Gabrielle Brooks, you are my best friend, my lover, and the foundation of our home. I love your sense of humor, your playfulness, and how you never fail to make me see the silver lining in every situation. You are so loved and cherished." I reached up and touched the side of his face. "I promise to love you, treasure you, and to continue to steal the covers from you until my last breath." I placed his white gold band with three small diamonds symbolizing me and my two sons, on his ring finger.

"By the power invested in me by the state of Indiana, I now pronounce you husband and wife." Our minister beamed down at us. "You may kiss your bride."

Hayden pulled me closer to him and eagerly pressed his lips upon mine. I wrapped my arms around him passionately kissing him back. Behind us, we heard our friends, family, and colleagues erupt into a loud round of applause and cheers.

Hayden and I separated, each with plastered silly grins upon our faces giggling like fools. We did it.

"It is my pleasure to introduce to you for the first time. Mr. and Mrs. Hayden Brooks." Our Minister concluded.

I took ahold of Hayden's arm and followed him back down the aisle.

I could not stop smiling.

The reception was a blur. I met dozens of Hayden's business colleagues, clients, and associates — all of whom wished us well, but became an endless stream of names and faces I knew I'd never remember. Everyone had loved our wedding theme and dressed up in the most glorious costumes making it almost impossible for me to connect people. I felt exhausted by the time we made it through the procession line, and everyone made their way over to the reception tent for dinner and dancing.

Kari had done a phenomenal job putting everything together. The scale of it was beyond my comprehension. I was suddenly very appreciative for all her hard work and meticulous attention to detail. There was no way I could have handled this on my own on top of school and moving — all the while being seven and a half months pregnant with twins.

Victorian lamp posts lined the driveway, which I was thrilled to learn were permanent. Several more carefully placed about the grounds, also permanent. In other places where light was needed for this evening, antique brass, bronze, and oblique lanterns hung from figurines, spikes, and trees. It gave our vast backyard still heavily wooded a paranormal mystic appeal.

The caterers had done an amazing job. Each dish was exquisite and pleasing to all the senses. I felt as if I were walking around in a dream that I never wanted to awaken from. I squeezed Hayden's hand adoringly.

"Thank you," I leaned in and whispered.

"Is it what you wanted?" He beamed proudly.

"It's better," I admitted.

Hayden led me out onto the dance floor. He had never asked me what I wanted our first dance to be of and with everything going on, I hadn't remembered to suggest anything. I was happily surprised when I recognized the intro to Justin Timberlake's song, *Mirrors* ring through the sound system.

"It seemed aptly appropriate for us," Hayden held me close as we waltz across the dance floor.

"It's perfect," I stared lovingly into his emerald eyes. "You have made me so happy."

"Then I'm doing my job right." He kissed me tenderly before twirling me around.

I held onto his hand spinning around feeling the full measure of my Victorian gown cascading around me. I couldn't imagine Cinderella feeling this happy and loved at her ball. I leaned my head back and laughed aloud finishing my final spin and landing up against my husband's chest with his arm holding me securely to him.

"I love you," a smile reached his bright emerald eyes making them gleam in the twinkling lights.

"I love you too."

I danced with Max, Henry, Chris, Erik, and Mark before I was allowed to finally sit back down. I was thankful for our little ankle boots and how comfortable they were. I hated to think how my swollen feet would be feeling in heels.

I had barely caught my breath when Kari leaned over my shoulder.

"Excuse me, Alex. The father daughter dance is up next. Where is your father?" She innocently inquired, but it felt like a slap in the face.

"Right here." Thankfully, my Uncle Rick who was seated across the table from us, rose to his feet.

He set his napkin on the side of his plate and smiled over at me with all the love of a proud father. He came around the table and held out his hand just as the song finished and the band leader broke in.

"Please clear the floor for our father daughter dance," he announced, and our guests slowly returned to their seats.

Uncle Rick led me out to the middle of the raised hardwood dance floor. He placed his one hand in mine and his other around my waist. I rested my hand on his shoulder and smiled up at him.

"Thank you," I whispered.

"My pleasure," he kissed me gently on the cheek. "I may not be your dad, but I have watched you grow up and am so proud to be your uncle."

You'll Always be my Baby by Alan Jackson rolled softly across the floor. Beautiful lyrics written by a father who adored his daughter. I rested my head down on my uncle's shoulders. The song brought tears to my eyes as I couldn't stop myself from thinking about the father I never knew and the alcoholic one who had raised me.

"You know, if you keep this up, you're going to smear your mascara," my uncle always knew how to make me smile.

"I know," I looked up at him and grinned. "I'm being silly — wishing for something I will never have." He didn't say anything but offered me a weary grin. "The sad thing is, I believe he could have been an amazing dad if he'd have just left that crazy bitch." I whispered.

"I know it hurts because you just learned the truth," he looked at me with such gentleness. "But you must concentrate on what's important now. You have two sons that love you, a good man over there that would move heaven and earth for you, and a sister who is standing beside you in all of this. Plus, you seem to have a strong group of friends that seem pretty amazing to me." He lifted my chin with his finger to look him in the eye. "That is what is important now. You may have been born into a shitty family, but you have built a pretty amazing one all by yourself. So, don't miss what you never had and treasure what you do. Besides you're gonna need them when you're up to your elbows in spit-up and dirty diapers by Christmas." He chuckled softly before kissing me lightly on the forehead.

"I know," I felt the tension ease out of my shoulders. "You're right." I looked over at Hayden standing next to Samantha, Oliver, Lisa, and Erik and winked at him. "I am blessed."

"Yes, you are." He smiled at me lovingly.

Chapter 40

I FOUND HAYDEN STANDING beside Kennedy and several of his employees. He was holding a glass of champagne and laughing. I was standing beside Lisa and Erik rubbing the side of my aching belly. All these hours standing on my feet were taking a toll on me.

"Why don't you sit down?" Lisa suggested touching my arm lightly.

"I will," I set my cream soda in the champagne glass down on the table beside me. "Let me check on my husband first." It felt so wonderfully weird calling Hayden my husband.

I could not take my eyes off him as I approached. He was strikingly handsome, and I could not help but notice how so many of our female guests let their eyes linger on him. I had been told too many times since the reception began how I had landed one of the most eligible bachelors in the Midwest, if not the country.

"There's my beautiful bride," Hayden greeted me as I approached.

"And there's my Knight in dented armor." I smirked.

"If I were slaying the dragon for you, you'd most certainly be standing on the sidelines telling me I'm doing it wrong." Hayden laughed. "Don't do it like that," he attempted to mimic my voice. "Step to the side and stab it like this." Everyone laughed as he put his arm around my waist. "Then it would be followed with, 'damn it, just let me do it'." The small crowd around us roared.

"Well, if you did it right, I wouldn't have to correct you." I teased along with him.

"And that is why I love her, she's not afraid to put me in my place." A broad smile gleamed on his shapely lips as he leaned over and kissed me playfully on the cheek.

"Someone has to keep you in line," I simpered.

"I cannot believe he managed to keep you a secret for so long," His employee remarked. "We were all betting where he took off to last summer and with whom." She shook her head knowingly at her boss. "I could not be happier for you two. And twins as well." She patted me gently on the arm.

"They were a bit of a surprise," I rubbed the side of my abdomen again.

"Are you feeling all right?" Concern clouded over Hayden's face.

"I'm afraid my back and feet have reached their limit." I rubbed the small of my back arching it a bit.

"Would you please sit down," Hayden held me tighter to him.

"I need to lie down," I spoke softly, but my eyes were pleading with understanding.

"I'll walk you up to the house," my husband offered.

"No, please," I placed a hand on his chest. "The reception is going so well, and everyone is having such a good time. I don't want to spoil it," I patted his chest with a slight tired smile. "Kennedy, would you mind escorting me up to the house?"

"Of course," Kennedy addressed our guests. "Please excuse me."

"And me," I kissed Hayden again and took ahold of Kennedy's arm.

We walked up the pathway towards the house. The lanterns offered a soft glowing hue of comfort guiding us towards my new home looming in the distance. The stars glittered the cloudless sky peering down at us.

Kennedy looked radiant in her elegant Victorian gown. Her dark hair looked ebony with the lanterns giving it a mystic purple tone that served only to enhance her ivory skin and doe eyes.

"Are you having contractions?" Her face was pinched in concern.

"No," I squeezed her arm. "Just exhausted."

"Isn't your OB here?" she raised her eyebrow in question.

"Yes, but I believe he's hit the champagne and spiked punch a little too hard." I chuckled rolling my eyes.

"Most of the guests have." She grinned. "You know there's not a vacant hotel room in this town thanks to your wedding."

"That doesn't surprise me," I opened the back French door into the great room. "I think I know about twenty people here out of what — 500?"

"Dad has done well with his business connections." She crossed over the threshold behind me and closed the door.

"He certainly has," I agreed collapsing on the oversized sectional. I put my legs up on the edge of the cushion, with my shoes dangling off the side. I leaned back against the plush pillows and rubbed my extended abdomen with both hands.

"Do you want to take your shoes off?" She sat down near my feet.

"If I could reach them, I would." I snorted. "But Hayden's been helping me with that for about a month now."

"You look beautiful. You're glowing," Kennedy placed my legs over her lap and began untying my ankle boots.

"I believe that's fat lady perspiration." I shook my head with a slight grin. I let out an unintentional moan of pleasure as she slipped off my boots and began rubbing my feet. "That feels amazing."

"You must be exhausted." She looked at me sympathy. "It's been a long day."

"Yes. A long and wonderful day." I smiled sleepily up at her. "I cannot believe we got married. If someone would have told me a year or even six months ago that we would be sitting in a beautiful new home, married, and excited about the future, I would never have believed them." I confessed.

"I know," she firmly yet tenderly continued to rub my feet. "I am so glad you never gave up on my dad for his behavior after losing my brother." Her voice was genuine.

"Do you think Mason would have approved?"

"I know my brother is looking down at us tonight and he is very happy for you and dad. He loved you both very much." Her expression and tone were warm and comforting.

"I truly hope so," I brushed a worn-out tear off my check. "I hope you know how much Mason meant to me and my sons."

"I do." A sadness clouded over her eyes briefly. "You know, it's funny to think — I lost one brother this year but gained two more today and soon to add a third and a baby sister." Kennedy playfully shrugged her shoulders with a cute tilt of her head which I'd seen Mason do countless times before.

"And you're okay with all the changes?"

"Alex, I've spent my entire life watching my dad slave away at his business. But as he grew this empire, he withdrew from having a personal life." She sighed heavily. "Of course, he always had dates for business functions and such, but then he'd dismiss them." She shook her head slightly with dismay. "I'm not saying that's a bad thing since most of them were simply gold diggers." She chuckled sarcastically.

"I guess your dad was a bit of a playboy?" I smirked recalling some of the comments Mason and Hayden had made about the previous women in his life.

"I knew you had to be something incredible for my dad to pursue you so fiercely." Kennedy cocked her head to the side. "Although I still find it a bit twisted how you guys met." Her eyebrows raised pointedly.

"Believe me, no one thinks it's more twisted than me." I admitted. "I wish I could change a lot of things about the last couple years."

"I know what you mean. I still can't believe I worked with that woman for twelve weeks. She spent her time glued to Mason, flirting with him, giggling, and acting like an air-headed tart. I wanted to fire her before dad left for Europe, but he said to give her a little time to get her bearings." She shook her head. "I wish I'd followed my gut and fired her as soon as dad left. If I had, maybe Mason would still be alive." Her eyes dropped to the floor.

"His death was not your fault." I reached over and touched her arm swallowing hard. I wondered if I should mention the haunting words from the video but pushed it aside. But my thoughts were interrupted when Hayden walked through the door.

"There're my lovely ladies," His broad smile was highlighted by his deep dimples. "Are you feeling all right?" He took a seat beside me.

"I'm fine. My feet are tired and my back hurts —the joys of pregnancy." I cupped the side of his face staring into his emerald eyes.

"What can I do?" He lovingly offered with concern written across his face.

"Nothing. Kennedy is taking care of me," I grinned at my new stepdaughter.

"Well, I hate to say this, but guests are wondering where you are. Are you up to coming back out and sitting at the table?" Hayden rose and held out his hand.

"Do I have to wear my shoes," I looked at him pathetically.

"It's your wedding. You can do anything you want." He cocked his head knowingly.

"Thank you," He helped me off the couch. "I feel like a beached whale."

"You are the most beautiful women in the world to me," Hayden cupped the side of my face and kissed me tenderly. "Thank you for marrying me."

"Thank you for asking me." I poked him playfully on the nose.

"It took you long enough to say yes," he flashed me a devilish grin.

"So, your solution was to knock me up?" I teased laughing at the surprise look on his face.

"Damn. If only I would have thought about that," he rolled his eyes at his daughter as Kennedy held open the back door for us.

"Come on, you love birds." Kennedy shook her head at the two of us closing the door behind us.

The next three hours crawled by. I sat at the head table with my feet up on the chair beside me. Hayden paraded so many faces before me, I felt like the plastered smile on my face would need to be surgically removed.

Everyone was kind, festive, and tipsy. It was almost midnight before the final guests departed. Lisa was taking Henry back to her place for the night and Max had left with Aaron and his mom a short while ago. I was so drained as I leaned on Hayden as we made our way up to the house.

"I'm sorry we can't have our honeymoon yet," Hayden led me up the luminous pathway of lanterns. "I would love to take you back to Europe for a few weeks." His emerald eyes sparkled under the bright moonlight.

"That would be heavenly," I said dreamily. "Unfortunately, we don't have Danny to watch the boys this time. They'd never go out there with Amanda and I can't do that to them."

"I guess we'll have to take them with us." He squeezed my waist a little tighter, but I wrinkled my nose making him chuckle. "What?"

"It's not exactly a romantic honeymoon if we take the boys with us."

"We'll have separate rooms," he chirped happily.

"And the twins?" I raised my eyebrows at him. "A 14-hour flight with two babies doesn't entice me much."

"Looks like we're screwed for the next few years, darling." Hayden raised his hands in defeat.

"I guess so," I shrugged nonchalantly.

"Gee, if only we had the resources to hire a nanny." The devilish glint in his eye told me this was merely intermission on this topic. "My dear," he opened the French doors, stepped back, and swooped me up in his arms. "I have to carry my bride over the threshold." He leaned over and kissed me deeply as he carried me into our new home.

Hayden kicked the door closed with his foot without missing a beat. I wrapped my arms around his neck giggling and feeling like a queen. He carried me effortlessly to our room and laid me down on the bed.

"Don't move," he winked opening the little cabinet beneath the drawer in his antique night table. He scurried about setting long elegant black and ivory tapers in luxurious silver candle stick holders on the shelves above our wet bar, our night tables, and along the bay window.

"You've been planning this," I leaned on my elbow and watched him intensely.

"Guilty," Hayden strolled around the room lighting the candles. He paused by the shelves above the wet bar, lit the tapers, and then flipped the switch on our sound system. The room was flooded with soft classical music. It was barely audible in the background not to deter any conversation.

It was perfect.

I stifled a yawn and dropped my feet over the edge of our bed. The double-sided pillowtop mattress on the 19th century canopy frame made our bed almost twice the height of a normal bed. Once Hayden realized it was difficult for me to climb into bed, he bought a little wooden step stool with black iron legs and an ornate design that blended seamless with the antique décor in our home.

"Can you please help me with my dress?" I stepped down onto the floor.

My new husband approached me slowly. His eyes glistened mischievously in the candlelight. His full lips tilted upwards in eager anticipation. The fingers on one hand traced feather-like over my torso as he looked longingly into my eyes, stepping around to stand behind me. His lips lingered on the lap of my neck.

The magnetic heat of his breath sent shivers down my spine and goosebumps along my arms as he slowly undid each of the tiny eyelet pearl buttons down the back of my Victorian wedding gown. It fell billowed out at my feet in a pool of silver lace taffeta.

"I cannot imagine how the men felt 150 years ago," I felt the chuckle in his chest graze against my back with his hands resting softly on my shoulders. Hayden's voice was a husky whisper. "They must have had great restraint, not to mention stamina and control or they would have cum in their britches in anticipation before they got through all these damn layers." I stood there giggling foolishly in my corset, crinoline slip, and pantaloons.

"Perhaps the men knew they were worth the wait," I whispered over my shoulder as he untied my crinoline slip allowing it to fall to the floor on top my gown.

"Indeed, you are," Hayden pulled the laces on my back of my corset undoing the bow. His fingers lingered unlacing the string down my spine heightening my desire and drawing out my anticipation for him. "But I admit, I am loving this corset pantaloon look." He brushed his lips longingly over my shoulder.

"Really now?" I giggled. "I wondered why you were so excited about having a Victorian wedding."

"You look so sexy, Mrs. Brooks," his lips traced along my shoulder and up my neck.

I closed my eyes loving the sound of my new title rolling off his shapely full lips. I leaned back into him, melting under his hot breath on my skin.

I turned towards him, pressing my mouth gently over his, and pulling back just as his lips began to part. Our eyes locked as I ran my fingers down his chest. I slowly worked my way back up his torso undoing each button. Our eyes never wavered, but the grin on his face widened with the release of each one. The devilish mischievous look in his eyes gleamed

Standing there in his dress shirt unbuttoned, bare sculpted muscles visible in the illuminating candles. I ran my fingers over his chest and up his broad shoulders lightly pushing his dress shirt off them.

Hayden shook his arms slightly until his shirt dropped onto the floor. I reached out and took a hold of his belt buckle tugging it a bit with a giggle before unfastening it. I pulled the buckle allowing the belt to travel around him through the loops. His hips jolted towards me causing him to chuckle as my attempt to seduce him.

I unfastened his pants and slid his zipper down. I ran my hands around him, allowing his pants to drop to his ankles pulling him closer to me as I gripped his buttocks. His black boxer briefs bulged with anticipation.

Hayden lifted me effortlessly onto the bed. I propped myself up on my elbows as he pulled me to the edge of the bed. He removed my pantaloons and corset stood over me looking admiringly at me.

"You're so beautiful," his emerald eyes glistened.

Hayden nudged my legs apart and ran his hands over my thighs lifting my knees. He knelt between my legs and lapped at my clitoris enthusiastically. I rested my feet on his shoulders and allowed my knees to drop to the side. His fingers pushed up inside me, locating my G-spot immediately. I closed my eyes moaning loudly.

I loved how he played my body like an instrument, strumming me perfectly making me hum with pleasure. He knew exactly what I loved and how to send me off to eutopia. The rhythmic strokes with his fingers working in harmony with his tongue curled my toes and set my body on fire.

"Come here," I gasped, but Hayden vehemently shook his head. "I want you."

Hayden rose and removed his boxer briefs. I looked up at him standing in all his naked glory before me and smiled.

This is my husband!

Damn!

Hayden held onto my thighs and entered me slowly, teasing me, hovering before me, watching my face intently. I reached for me, grabbing ahold of his buttocks attempting to increase is thrust, but he wouldn't let me. He was enthralled in his torment. He was angled skillfully to where the head of his cock rubbed my G-spot sending me right along the edge of the cliff, but then he stopped, withdrew, and climbed up on the bed.

"Why?" the frustration inside me was so intense I wanted a release before I screamed.

"Not yet, my love." The devious twinkle in his eye told me he was not done tormenting me. "Roll over," he playfully smacked my thigh.

I giggled and turned over, getting up on my hands and knees before him. Hayden positioned himself behind me with a coy look and smacked me a bit harder on the side of my ass before thrusting inside me.

I laid my head upon the bed with his hands on my hips, controlling the depth of each thrust. He reached around and began rubbing my clit with his finger. I pushed harder against him, loving the feel of him deep inside me. The friction against my clitoris spread throughout my body sending me into a frenzy of euphoria.

I tore at the sheets screaming out in pure ecstasy as wave after wave rippled through my body uncontrollably. I was breathless, sweaty, and spent. Hayden's hold on my hips tightened as he moaned loudly pressing firmly against me cumming deep inside of me.

Our breathing was labored, and our bodies locked together — our muscles frozen in elation. With a final thrust, Hayden collapsed beside me. I rolled onto my side trying to catch my breath. He reached over and touched my breast with a sly grin.

"I love you, darling." He gazed lovingly upon me.

"I love you too."

"Thank you for marrying me." He smiled.

"Thanks for asking," I grinned leaning over to kiss his full shapely lips.

Chapter 41

THANKSGIVING DAWNED UNDER A thick cover of dark clouds threatening to dampen our holiday. I reminded myself that I needed to get up and put that 30-pound bird in the oven. My mind ran over the list of all the preparations I needed to get done before everyone started showing up around noon today.

I was glad I made the cream cheese pumpkin roll, peanut butter pies, and pumpkin pies last night, so I didn't have to worry about them today. But I still needed to get the dough made for the yeast rolls so they would have time to rise and take care of the dressing.

Uncle Rick, Aunt Misha, Lisa and Debbie and their families would be joining us along with Chris and his three older boys. Lisa and Debbie were helping with the sides and Chris was picking up the apple pies. Our table was going to be overflowing today and I was looking forward to it.

I rolled over on my back and stretched, moaned, and rubbed my hands over my huge abdomen. The twins squirmed and stretched their own legs kicking their tiny feet straight into my diaphragm. I coughed as the air escaped unexpectedly out of my lungs.

"Move your feet," I scolded them rubbing hard on the top of my belly attempting to make them adjust.

"You okay?" Hayden's eyes were still closed on the pillow beside me.

"Yeah, just arguing with your children." I mumbled trying to roll over to my other side to get my feet to the stool.

"Why is it you call them *my children* only when they are irritating you?" He peeked through one eye still half asleep.

"Because you did this to me," I struggled to get myself into a seated position once my legs were over the side of the bed dangling above the stool.

"Hang on," Hayden crawled out of the foot of the bed. "Let me help you." He took my hands and I slid off the bed bypassing the stool.

"Thanks," I smiled as my feet hit the plush rug.

I waddled into the restroom and undressed to take a shower. Hayden started both shower heads to warm up the water while we brushed our teeth. I spit in the sink, turned off the water and set my toothbrush on the counter when a sharp pain ripped through my side. I grabbed the counter with one and my abdomen with the other.

"Hayden!" No sooner had the word passed through my lips, my water broke all over the rug.

"Um," he sputtered standing there naked with one foot in the shower. "We need to go." He reached in to turn the water off.

"What are you doing?" I tightened my grip on the counter as another pain ran over me. "I need to shower."

"Your water broke," Hayden came over and took my arm. "We don't have time."

"I'm not going to the hospital until I shower." He looked flabbergasted. "I am not giving my babies razor burn on their way into this world. I am showering and shaving my legs first." I declared slowly making my way towards the shower.

"I thought you told me your labor with the boys took less than two hours." Hayden held my arm as I stepped into the shower.

"I did. Therefore, we have plenty of time." My smirk turned into a grimace as the first true contraction tore through me. I dug my nails unintentionally into Hayden's arm as we both screamed.

"Alex, please," his eyes looked frightened. "The twins and Dr. Johnson could care less about the damn stubble on your legs."

"Just hold onto my arm and help me balance." I tried to put on a brave face in my determination. "I promise I will make this fast."

Hayden washed my hair and body with rapid speed. He helped me balance as I quickly shaved my legs as best I could. It was a spotty job at best, but at least I felt better.

Wrapped in an oversized plush towel and leaning against the bed, my dripping wet hair getting water down my back and over the bed, Hayden climbed into his boxer briefs. I tried not to laugh at him as they stuck to his body because he had forgotten to dry himself. He took off at a mad dash through the great room to the front stairs hollering for the boys. Both came scrambling down in their pajama bottoms with hair askew and bare feet.

"Max, call Lisa and tell her what's going on. Thanksgiving dinner will," Hayden stood in the middle of the great room rambling and stammering trying to think straight. "I don't know. Call Debbie too. I've gotta get your mom to the hospital." He ran back into our room. "You ready?"

"No," I held onto the wet towel and the edge of the bed waiting for the contraction to pass. "I need my nightgown at least." I was enjoying seeing him so flustered when it was far out of his normal character.

"Oh," he turned around twice as if he were lost. "Right. Um, which one?"

"Any of them. I don't care," I winced trying to control my breathing.

"Where?" Hayden was rooted in his spot by the foot of the bed with both of my sons standing in the doorway.

"Third drawer on the right in my dresser in the dressing room." Hayden looked at me like he hadn't registered anything I said.

Max shook his head and took off throughout room to the dressing room. I heard the drawer open and close and then another. He returned tossing a pair of jeans, a sweatshirt, and socks onto the end of the bed.

"Get dressed," Max's voice snapped Hayden out of whatever trance he was in and prompted him to move. "Here, momma," He set my nightgown on the bed beside me.

"Thank you," I offered him the best smile I could muster. "Could you please close the door so I can slip this on?"

"Do you need anything else?" My eldest looked so calm and collected I couldn't help but feel proud of him.

"My slippers and my purse. But let me get this on first." I glanced over at Hayden pulling his sweatshirt over his head.

"Okay," Max left the room closing the door behind him.

"Are you okay?" Hayden sat down on the end of the bed to put his socks on.

"Huh?" He glanced over at me. "Yeah, I'm fine. How are you?" He struggled to get his jeans on.

"Better than you," I laughed at him. "Can you please help me with my gown?" I dropped the bath towel to the floor.

"Arms up," I raised my arms over my head as he slipped the gown over me. "Just a sec," Hayden disappeared back to the dressing room and returned with my slippers and his sneakers.

Max and Henry followed us out into the garage. Max handed me my purse as Henry held open the car door.

"Can we go, Momma?" Fear shown in his dark brown eyes.

"Baby, you don't want to sit around the hospital all day waiting for the twins. You'd be bored silly." I took his hand in mine. "I promise, Lisa will bring you up there just as soon as the twins are born."

"But momma," his bottom lip quivered, and Max put his arm around Henry's shoulder.

"I'll be fine. I promise." I squeezed his hand before Hayden closed the door.

"Keep me updated," Max told Hayden as he went around the car.

"Will do," Hayden smiled nervously at my sons before closing the car door.

The rain cut loose by the time we hit main street. Hayden turned on the wipers and cussed at everyone out on the road slowing our progress. I grabbed the door and clenched my teeth as another contraction ripped through my body. I doubled over and moaned loudly.

"Keep your legs crossed. Don't get anything on my car." Hayden smirked, as I glared at him. "Of course, we wouldn't be here if you'd kept your legs crossed." He chuckled.

"Seriously?" If I wasn't in so much pain, I would have smacked him.

"It's true," he shrugged with a smile still on his lips. "Besides, you know how much I love my car."

"You're such an asshole," I let out a breath I hadn't realized I was holding.

"Aw, come on babe." Hayden took my hand in his. "You know, I'm only teasing. I wanted to make you laugh."

"Ha ha," I stuck my tongue out at him.

Hayden made it through several yellow lights. I closed my eyes and held on through each intersection, but never complained. A few sharp turns and bellowing horns later, we pulled up in front of the hospital emergency room awning.

An orderly came out with a wheelchair and my nervous husband helped me into it. He left the car running with the driver's side door open. He held my hand and scurried alongside the wheelchair.

"Sir," the young man stopped Hayden before we passed through the sliding doors. "You need to move your car." Hayden's head whipped around as if he was just realizing it was there.

"Oh, yeah," he stammered but still didn't move.

"I'll take her up to labor and delivery on the third floor. You can meet us there." The orderly's voice was smooth and comforting as if he'd given this speech dozens of times before.

"Right. Okay," but Hayden still didn't move.

"Honey, I'm okay." I reached out and took his hand. "I'll meet you up there." Hayden's eyes softened as he looked down at me.

"All right," he leaned over and kissed me. "I'll be right behind you."

Our fingers lingered for a couple of steps as we passed through the entryway. The florescent overhead lighting was blinding along the sterile hallway lined with tacky pictures painted by unknown artists.

Dr. Johnston greeted me as I was rolled out of the elevator. He looked to bright eyed and cheerful for this early in the morning.

"Happy Thanksgiving, Alex. I thought you were going to come see me on Tuesday?" He beamed holding a to-go cup of coffee.

"And you told me two days ago I had plenty of time." I raised my eyebrows and exhaled loudly gripping the arms of the wheelchair. "I guess we were both wrong. I hope you brought the good drugs cause this hurts!" My voice went up a couple octaves as another contraction took a hold of me.

"Let get you settled first." He led the orderly around the corner to a birthing suite. "How far apart are the contractions?"

"Two minutes, maybe less." I grunted. "I need to push." I leaned forward raising myself up on the arm of the wheelchair. "Agh! Where's Hayden?" I bellowed.

"He'll be here in a moment." A nurse grabbed hold of my arm and the orderly took the other.

"Don't push, Alex." Dr. Johnson stood in front of me touching the side of my face. "You'll tear, darling."

"Damn it," I cried and reached for his hand.

"Let's get you into bed and see where we're at." His eyes were soft and caring.

The three of them helped me into the bed. They were scurrying around talking to each other, but I couldn't hear anything they were saying. The pain was too intense. The nurse did her best to shield me with a sheet as she pulled up my gown to attach the fetal monitors. At that moment I'd have cared less who saw what as long at they got these babies out of me.

Dr. Johnston lifted my legs and carefully placed them in the stirrups. He draped the sheet over my legs, but who was he kidding — all modesty I had went right out the window when my water broke with Max.

"Alex," Dr. Johnson leaned around my leg so he could see my face. "I'm going to massage the birth canal, so you don't tear, and I don't have to do an episiotomy and stitches."

"Okay," I squeaked.

"You're going to feel some pressure. I'm going to see how many centimeters your dilated also." His voice sounded like butter, but a second later I screamed. I wanted to push from the intense pressure. It felt like I was being split in two.

"What the fuck are you doing to my wife?" Hayden's face was bright red in the doorway.

"Happy Thanksgiving, Hayden." Dr. Johnson seemed immune to Hayden's hostility.

"Huh?" his distraction worked as Hayden looked confused.

"I'm massaging the birth canal, so your wife doesn't tear or rip requiring stitches after the birth." Dr. Johnson explained without missing a beat.

"Hayden," I reached out for him.

My nervous, puffed-up husband edged his way over to my bedside without taking his eyes off Dr. Johnson. If I were an outsider, it would have been comical. But considering it was my feet in the stirrups with my bare ass on display, I wasn't laughing.

"Okay, Alex. You're fully dilated. I want you to push with your next contraction." Dr. Johnston said in an upbeat tone.

Hayden picked up the washcloth from the tray and wiped my brow. He lifted me into a more seated position and scooted his body behind mine. I leaned back into him taking ahold of his hands in mine.

The next contraction hit me like a wave of pain ceasing hold of my entire body. I screamed, squeezed Hayden's hands with every ounce of strength I had in me, and pushed.

"Your baby's crowning," Dr. Johnson cried out triumphantly.

"Girl or boy?" Hayden called over my shoulder.

"I don't know. It's just a head." Dr. Johnson laughed. "Now really push, Alex. You've got to get the shoulders out." His voice took on a stringent tone. "Push," his voice got louder.

"Push, baby. Come on, push!" Hayden hollered over my shoulder like a cheerleader on steroids.

"Would you shut up!" I screeched back at him baring down until my muscles screamed in protest.

I felt a sudden gush like my insides fell onto the floor. I let out a breath I hadn't realized I was holding when I heard the sweetest sounds — the first cry of my baby.

"Here's your son," Dr. Johnston announced holding him above the sheet.

"He's so tiny," The little gooey infant with balled-up fists, a head full of dark hair, looked like he was covered in Jell-o was demonstrating his healthy lungs.

"I have a son," Hayden's voice was soft, almost a whisper behind me.

"Dad, would you like to cut the cord?" Dr. Johnston stood and set Elijah just under my breast.

"What about Elicia?" Hayden stammered.

"She'll be along momentarily." Dr. Johnston reassured him.

Hayden scooted to the edge of the bed and stepped down. He approached Dr. Johnston with trepidation and apprehension.

"What do I do?" My husband chewed on his bottom lip.

"Cut it right here," Dr. Johnston handed him a pair of small scissors.

"Wow, that's spongy." Hayden chuckled nervously.

"Agh," I gripped the side of the bed as another contraction wave swept over me.

"Looks like his little sister is ready." The nurse carried Eli over to the little bed near the wall. "I'm just gonna clean this little guy up so he looks presentable to meet his baby sister." She smiled out of the corner of my eye.

"Okay, Alex." I heard Dr. Johnston exhale loudly. "Big push."

"I can't," Hayden moved me around like a rag doll sliding back in his place. I flopped back against my husband. "Leave me alone." Every part of my body hurt, especially my nether regions.

"Come on, Alex. You can do this." Dr. Johnston encouraged me.

"Agh," I screamed, tears rolling down my cheeks mixing with beads of sweat. "I can't," I cried pushing through my exhaustion and pain.

I could feel the fire of her head crowning and the pressure of Dr. Johnston maneuvering her around to get her shoulders out. The pain was blinding. My addled brain couldn't remember being in so much pain with Max or Henry. There's a reason your brain forgets the intense pain of childbirth because no woman would ever do this twice.

It is the strangest sensation, the explosion of fire followed by immediate cessation of pain that occurs as quickly as flipping a switch. I heard the glorious cries of my baby girl. She was determined to prove her lungs were as healthy as her brother's.

"Here she is," Dr. Johnston announced with joy holding her up before us. "Ten fingers, ten toes." He laid her down on my abdomen.

Elicia's little face was scrunched up and beat red as she screamed with all her might. Her tiny little fists shook, and her legs kicked about with all the fire and spirit of her siblings. She was going to need spunk and gumption to survive three protective brothers.

"My little princess," I held her in my arms and stroked her tiny cheek.

"Daddy's little angel," Hayden leaned over and touched her mass of dark curly hair.

"Let's see how long that lasts," I snorted with a smirk.

"That's something that she'll always be," Hayden kissed my forehead before sliding off the bed to cut her umbilical cord.

The nurse whisked her away also while Dr. Johnston took care of me. After passing the placenta, I was thrilled when he announced there was no tearing and no stitches required. Max and Henry had been born so quickly and were such big babies that I had required not only stitches, but reconstructive surgery. In comparison, the twins had been a breeze.

"I swear, you are one of those women who are made to have babies." Dr. Johnston removed his gloves and peeked over the pediatrician's shoulder at the twins. "They are perfect."

Hayden was hovering behind the medical staff eagerly awaiting his chance to hold his children. The twins did not appreciate being manhandled, poked, and prodded for measurements and scores. They reminded me already of their father's temperament.

I closed my eyes for a moment relishing in the absence of pain and peace of not having someone touching me. I listened to Hayden talking to the doctors gushing like a proud father. He was snapping pictures and making gooey faces at the twins. I smiled to myself feeling truly happy.

The nurse and Dr. Johnston brought the twins over to me, setting one in each arm. The overwhelming feeling of joy and fear consumed me. Eli had his fist in his mouth. He was bright-eyed and intently watching everything around him. Ellie, on the other hand was sucking her thumb and sleeping peacefully. Both had a head full of dark hair and whisps of Hayden's wavy curls.

My heart was full. Hayden stood beside the bed gazing down lovingly at the three of us. He reached over and brushed my hair away from my face before kissing me softly on the forehead.

"You are the most beautiful and amazing woman I have ever met." He lightly touched the heads of our angels. "We are blessed." His voice was barely more than a whisper.

"Yes, we are." Our eyes locked with unspoken words of a bond that would last a lifetime cemented with the birth of two children we created.

"You have two very healthy babies," Dr. Johnston stood at the foot of the bed. "It's probably a good thing you went early."

"Why is that?" Hayden asked taking Ellie out of my arms and snuggling her.

"Because Eli weighed in at 5 pounds, 8 ounces and little Miss Ellie here is 5 pounds, 2 ounces. If you'd have carried them a couple more weeks, they would have easily been another pound each. Their weight looks very good for two preemie twins."

"That's wonderful to hear." Hayden kissed Ellie's forehead. "We should probably call the children. I know they must be pacing around." Hayden glanced down at his watch. "You're efficient. I'll give you that." He chuckled. "It's not even ten o'clock."

"As I said, Alex was made for having babies." Dr. Johnston smiled. "I swear, she could fart and have a baby."

"Dr. Johnston," I was appalled. "I can't believe you just said that."

"I meant it as a compliment." Dr. Johnston defended with a sly grin.

'That didn't exactly sound very flattering," I raised an eyebrow at him.

"My apologies," he patted my leg. "We need to take the twins down to the nursery for a bit. You should get some rest."

"I'm gonna take a shower. I feel disgusting." I allowed the nurses to take the twins from me.

"We'll bring them back shortly." The older of the two assured me. "But you really need to rest. We don't allow new mothers to shower less than an hour after giving birth." She laid Eli down in the plexiglass crib.

"I'm showering," I swept the covers aside and swung my legs over the side of the bed.

"No, you're not," the nurse said more firmly and reaching for my arm. "You could pass out, fall down, or any number of things."

"Don't ever grab me," I shot her a nasty look. "And don't tell me what to do." I shook my arm away from her. "Dr. Johnston," I turned his direction where he was talking quietly with Hayden.

"Would you explain to this woman that I am going to take a shower, just as I did after giving birth to my sons." Anger was prevalent in my tone.

"Rita, it's okay. There were no complications, and her husband will be standing right beside her if she needs anything." Dr. Johnston reassured her.

"That goes against protocol." The older nurse pinched her lips together in defiance.

"Yes, I know. But she breaks protocol every time she's here." Dr. Johnston smiled slightly and shook his head at me. "It's okay."

"Fine. But I will not be responsible," she turned and wheeled Eli out of the room.

"Duly noted," Dr. Johnston hollered after her.

"Please keep that woman away from me and my babies. I do not want to see her again." I asked as my feet hit the cold floor.

"I will do that," he eyed me carefully to make sure I was steady on my feet.

"Thank you, I appreciate that." I stood a little hunched over from the cramps. "When are you going to let me outta here?"

"Tomorrow morning," He calculated.

"But it's Thanksgiving," I protested. "I was thinking late afternoon or early evening." I suggested with a coy smile.

"Tomorrow morning is the best I can do." He tilted his head and eyed me. "And you shouldn't be on your feet cooking Thanksgiving dinner anyway. You just gave birth to twins." He turned towards Hayden. "She needs to take it easy, and she should sleep when the twins sleep. Hopefully, you can get them on the same schedule." He chuckled slightly.

"We have friends and family coming over to cook." Hayden added. "She's not going to be doing much of anything."

"Wow, I've never met anyone who could control Alex." Dr. Johnston smirked. "Good luck with that."

"Her bark is much worse than her bite." Hayden looked over at me with a smirk.

"As much as I'm enjoying this banter, I would like to take a shower if you two don't mind." I was still leaning on the bed.

"I'll be back to check on you in a little while." Dr. Johnston closed the door on his way out.

I took a long hot shower with the curtain partially open so Hayden could stand on the other side making sure I didn't fall and crack my head open on the ceramic tile. He was busy sending pictures to the boys and all our friends and family.

"Hey darling, Lisa and Debbie think we should just celebrate Thanksgiving on Saturday. Is that all right?" Hayden's voice was muddled through the curtain.

"That's fine," I poked my head out of the curtain.

Hayden was leaning against the wall texting almost as quickly as Max could. I leaned against the wall and pushed on my abdomen. It was the strangest sensation, my fingers sunk all to my spine. All my abdominal muscles were gone.

"You okay?" Hayden poked his head in.

"Yeah," I grinned with tired eyes. "I'm almost done."

I stood beneath the hot water for another minute loving the feeling of the hot water rolling off my skin. The heat absorbed into my skin making me melt. Hayden handed me a towel as soon as I turned the water off.

"Thank you," I felt the blood rushing into my cheeks at him seeing how my body naked body looked after giving birth. My abdomen looked like a deflated beachball, and I hated it. I wrapped the towel around my body quickly hoping he hadn't gotten a good look.

"You're beautiful," He gazed at me with love and adoration, and I felt myself suddenly forget about feeling self-conscious.

"You're blind," my heart soared.

Hayden helped me dress and dry my hair. I suddenly felt very tired and weaker than I expected. I climbed into bed and sank into the plush pillows. But I was still freezing.

"Would you mind getting me another blanket?" I asked.

"Are you hungry?" I shivered as Hayden placed a warmed blanket over me pulling it up to my chin.

"No. Just tired." I closed my eyes and snuggled back into the pillows.

"Get some rest," Hayden kissed me lightly. "I'm going to make a few more calls."

Chapter 42

THE TWINS SLEPT PEACEFULLY IN THE arms of their eager adoptive aunts. Our friends and family had all come over to celebrate Christmas. The house was alive with laughter and Christmas decorations hung from everything that would stand still. Lisa, Debbie, and I had spent the last three weeks putting it together. Our table was filled with those most precious to us.

Midway through our holiday feast, the doorbell chimed. Everyone looked at one another stupidly since it was a rarity anyone embarked our long-wooded driveway to our hidden chalet amongst the trees.

"Got it," Max rose from his chair placing his napkin on the side of his plate. "Excuse me."

Erik, Chris, Mark, and Hayden continued making plans for their hunting trip after New Year's. I was half listening to them when a commotion in the foyer caught my attention.

"I don't care if she's eating or has company, get your mother." The familiar voice sent ripples of fury through me.

"Excuse me," I shot Hayden a look of pure disdain as I rose from my seat.

My parents were standing in the foyer clearly being blocked from the rest of the house by Max. My dad looked more uncomfortable than annoyed, but my mother's face was so pinched up she looked as if she'd been constipated for more than a week.

"What's going on?" I asked Max.

"I explained we are in the middle of dinner," The gleam in my son's eyes told me it was no mistake he omitted any further details.

"We came by to offer our congratulations. I understand you not only got married but you also had twins that you failed to mention to us." My mother crossed her arms as her voice became salty and venomous.

"Why didn't you call?" I stood rooted clearly indicating they were not welcomed.

"Do we need to call to visit our daughter and grandchildren on Christmas?" My dad raised an eyebrow.

"Well, I figured you had Colin and his family at your place today." I shrugged casually.

"We took a drive after dinner. Your brother and his family are in the car." My dad looked around uncomfortably.

"He doesn't believe he'd be welcome in your house." My mother spat.

"Then why is he here?" I snorted with disbelief. "It's not like we ever talk."

"He is still your brother and a part of this family." Mom glared at me, and I knew she knew exactly where Samantha was.

I glanced over my shoulder wondering if my sister was going to poke her head in.

Nope.

Coward.

"Well," my mother shifted her weight impatiently.

"Hello," Hayden entered the foyer looking skeptical. "Is there a problem?"

"My parents stopped by," I raised an eyebrow at him. "Mom. Dad. This is my husband Hayden Brooks." Hayden shook hands with my father, but my mother remained facing us with her arms folded.

"Nice to meet you," Hayden smiled warmly.

"Tell me Hayden, I realize because of your social standing you believe common courtesy doesn't apply to you, but do you believe it's proper to marry a single mom without meeting her family first?" My mother stared hard at my husband who graciously side stepped her snide remark.

"Well, Mrs. Carlton. I met your daughter, Samantha and her fiancé, Oliver. I've spent a great deal of time with Max and Henry, as Alex did with my daughter, Kennedy. Plus, I have met Danny,"

I glanced over at Hayden who was clearly enjoying himself. "In fact, I even played a round of golf with him. I also met Rick and Misha a while back." I was thankful he didn't say 'at the wedding'.

"And yet you didn't find it odd you never met her parents?" Mother pinched her lips into a thin line.

"Not when my wife tells me she isn't on the best of terms with them, why would I?" Hayden slipped his arm around my waist and continued being his truly gifted charismatic self.

"Are you going to invite us in and show us your new house or are you going to leave us standing in the foyer?" Mom turned her glare in my direction once more.

"I thought Colin and his family were waiting in the car?" I asked coyly.

"Should I invite them in?" My dad asked hesitantly.

"Of course," Hayden flashed his fake smile. "The more the merrier."

"I'll get your brother," Dad opened the front door and exited quickly.

I followed Hayden and my mother into the dinning room where our guests and family were still gathered finishing up their dinner. Samantha looked astonished, but quickly composed herself. She got up and walked over to greet our mother.

"Merry Christmas," My sister hugged her lightly.

"I figured this is where you'd be when you said you had plans for today." Mom patted her on the back with no emotion.

"I did have plans," Samantha's voice was icy.

"Hello Oliver," Mom nodded in his direction.

"Merry Christmas, Connie" His face looked plastic.

"I can't believe you had time to cook such an elaborate feast with two infants and a house full of guests." Mom surveyed our dinner.

"Everyone helped," I leaned against the back of the chair wishing she'd leave.

"With a kitchen that size," mom stepped through the doorway into my kitchen. "Fixing something this elaborate would be simple." She turned towards me. "Eight burners, a grill, double oven, and a warmer? That's a bit excessive, isn't it?"

I didn't bother to respond but noticed all the women in the room narrow their eyes at her.

Lisa was holding Eli and Ellie was sleeping peacefully in Kennedy's arms. After so much fuss, my mother was concerning herself with my kitchen appliances and had yet to make a remark about or even attempt to hold either of her new grandchildren. It truly shouldn't have surprised me since she also had not yet acknowledged Max or Henry either.

"I know Lisa and Debbie, but who is this?" My mother turned her focus on Chris, Kennedy, Hayden's sister, and her family.

"This is Erik's brother, Chris, Hayden's daughter, Kennedy, his sister, Lauren, her husband, Dennis. The younger children are at the kitchen table with the other children." I explained.

"It's nice to meet you," mother almost smiled. "What do you think of your brother's outlandish new house?" She turned her eyes on Lauren while Samantha, Lisa, Debbie, and I all shot her a look of disdain.

"Really, mother?" I snapped. "You just can't be civil for one day."

"I love it. He's worked hard and deserves it. I'm happy my brother has found a wonderful woman to share his life with and two amazing stepsons and his beautiful new twins." Lauren poured on the fake charm. "The only thing I hate is that he moved to Indy, and it'll take me twice as long to get here."

"Do you live near Chicago?" mother inquired.

"We are about an hour outside the city." Lauren explained.

"Oh, are you staying close by?" I could tell my mother was fishing.

"We're staying in the guest house." Lauren looked over at me clearly becoming uncomfortable as I knew she could sense my mother was going someone with this.

"You have a guest house?" Mother turned towards me. "How appropriate." She scoffed. "Are you staying in the guest house also?" Her eyes landed on my sister.

"Nope. We're upstairs." Samantha rolled her eyes blatantly.

"Guest house?" My dad paused in the entryway with Colin and Charlotte lurking over his shoulders and their brats behind them.

"It's nothing," I shrugged nonchalantly. "We have a lot of family and business associates from out of town and it was just more convenient." I don't know why I felt it necessary to clarify that to my dad.

"I see," dad smiled over at me.

My anal brother and his prudish wife pushed their way into the dining room forcing me to go through another round of introductions. Tension clung to the air like mid-July humidity.

"Can I get anyone something to drink? Perhaps some dessert? We have several different kinds of pies, cookies, and a mocha cream cheese roll." I offered just to break the silence.

Samantha and Lisa broke away from the table and followed me to the kitchen. I began slicing up the pies and roll placing them about the island while Samantha started a fresh pot of coffee.

Ellie stirred in Lisa's arms indicating she was ready for her early dinner as well.

"Just a minute, darling." I pulled out a bottle from the refrigerator. "Momma's gotta warm this up." I put the bottle in the warmer and kissed my baby girl on the forehead.

"I thought you were still nursing them." Lisa remarked trying to rock my fussy little girl.

"I am," I lightly rubbed the top of Ellie's head. "I'm going back to school the second week in January so I'm trying to introduce them to a bottle to make the transition a bit easier on the nanny."

"Are you ready to go back?" Samantha leaned against the counter nibbling on a cookie.

"I've already been back." I shrugged. "I had to go back for finals. Besides, I've only got one semester — 14 weeks until I graduate. I can't quit now."

"Can I feed her?" Max joined us in the kitchen.

"You want to feed her?" Lisa looked surprised.

"Yes," Max leaned down and kissed the top of Ellie's forehead. "Little Miss Ellie and I have our own thing going, don't we baby girl." He smiled down at his little sister.

"I think it's sweet," Samantha grinned and patted Max on the arm. "You're such a good big brother."

"Yes, you can feed her," I handed Max her bottle. "Over on the couch." Lisa followed him into the great room and handed him Ellie.

"I think you're amazing," Lisa beamed returning to the kitchen. "I know I couldn't balance it all."

"You're going back to school this spring?" my mother asked as she and Charlotte walked into the kitchen.

"Yes," I looked at her inquisitively.

"Why?" Charlotte wrinkled her nose.

"Because I'm one semester from graduating." It felt stupid to state the obvious.

"But why bother?" Her face was all scrunched up making her look constipated.

"I don't understand what you mean. I've spent the last three and a half years busting my butt to get my degree. It's a big accomplishment." I couldn't believe she didn't get it.

"It seems a bit unnecessary, especially with two new babies, a middle schooler and a grade schooler." My mother added her two cents. "I would think you're inviting a lot of undue stress into your life for no reason."

"How can you say that when you know how hard I've worked." I took a deep breath trying to not let her bait me.

"Because you have a family now and a husband who has made it possible for you to never have to work again." My jaw hit the floor at my mother's words. "Let's be realistic. It's not like you can actually do anything with a degree in psychology anyway." She picked up a thumbprint cookie and popped it into her mouth like she was discussing nothing more important than the weather.

"Thanks," I muttered through gritted teeth.

"How about a tour?" Charlotte finished off a piece of peanut butter pie and set her plate in the sink. "I'd love to see your new house."

"Sure," I poked my head in the dining room and told everyone that desserts and drinks were on the island, and they were welcome to help themselves. Hayden looked up at me with a look that said he was miserable. My brother had barely shut up long enough for me to make the brief announcement, then immediately resumed his pitch about the company he worked for and what they were doing.

Lisa and Samantha joined me as I took my mother, Charlotte, and her daughter, Misti around the house. I showed them the library, laundry room, and master suite biting my tongue as my mother continually made snide remarks about extravagance and gluttony. My sister and Lisa kept rolling their eyes and muttering under their breaths keeping my spirits up.

They followed me up the grand staircase located in the two-story foyer. I gripped the banister and bit my bottom lip listening to Charlotte compare our curved wooden eighteen-step staircase and banister with the average twelve-step one and estimate the price difference. I had to remind myself that I wasn't allowed to drink while breastfeeding the twins.

Everyone gushes about how cute and beautiful the twins' rooms are and loves the tunnel connecting balcony and hideaway in the boys' rooms. But taking my mother and sister-in-law through them, I had to endure their petty remarks about how my husband was flaunting his wealth to buy the love of my sons.

I gazed out the window of my daughter's bedroom. Fat fluffy flakes had started to fall. The grass was still visible beneath the snow, but it wouldn't be long before it was completely covered. The serene image, an hour ago, would have had all of us pressed against the windows admiring the beauty and mystical atmosphere that brought Christmas to life. Now, the tension and irritation could be felt by everyone in the house.

The mention of Hayden's name piqued my interest. Charlotte was whispering to my mom, but she wasn't nearly as discreet as she thought. She mentioned something about an article in the New York Times regarding the new marriage of one of the country's most eligible bachelors, followed by the pressure Colin's boss was putting on him to connect with Hayden to ensure their marketing. I took a deep breath and closed my eyes trying to calm myself.

It was apparent this impromptu visit had nothing to do with holiday spirit or meeting the twins and my new husband, but everything to do with my snotty-ass brother wanting to suck-up to Hayden.

I was not amused.

"I'm sorry, but I don't believe Hayden's firm is accepting new clients at this time." I turned away from the window and caught Charlotte and my mother by surprise.

"Certainly, your husband would make an exception for your brother to help his career." My mother put her hand on her hip and eyed me closely.

"I have nothing to do with my husband's business, including who he represents." I explained.

"But you can ask him for a favor," Charlotte's fake smile was nauseating.

"You all are unbelievable. You almost had me fooled," I scoffed. "I wanted to believe you actually cared about me and my family. But no, you only care about who I married and what he can do for your husband's career."

"That's not true, Alex. You're being overly sensitive as usual." Mom was quick to defend her angel's wife.

"Get out," I stood there shaking with furry.

"What?" My mother gasped. Neither of them moved.

"Get out of my house," I repeated and pointed to the door for emphasis.

"Alex, you need to calm down. You always overreact to everything." Charlotte stated. "Family helps family. That's just the way it is in the business world."

"Yes. I am aware. Hayden represents Danny's employer. But he will never represent Colin's." I said flatly. "And it is time for you all to leave."

"I am your mother. You do not talk to me that way." Mother's face was red and distorted.

"I am trying to be polite, but if you do not leave, I will have you removed." My patience was wearing thin, and I was struggling to maintain my composure.

"I imagine you would too. And by your own private security, no doubt." Charlotte scoffed.

"Nah, not necessary. We have an excellent police department here in town." I said sarcastically. "Would you like to find out?"

"Your brother was right about you. You are nothing but a slutty bitch. I wonder if those twins are even your husband's or that little twinkie you've been screwing for the last several years. I'll bet your husband doesn't even know about him." Charlotte spat.

Lisa and Samantha both busted out laughing. I looked over at them with a coy smile shaking my head.

"Then you'd be wrong on both counts. My husband does know about him, and Hayden is the only possibility to have fathered the twins. We've been together for a couple years — not that you'd know that because you know nothing about my life. And as for my sex life — that's also none of your damn business, but I will say I'm glad I'm not a frigid prude like you who's probably never accomplished anything more risqué than missionary style." I laughed fully enjoying myself for the first time since they arrived.

"Well, I never," Charlotte looked like I'd physically slapped her.

"Yeah, we know," I roared with laughter as she stormed out of the nursery with my mother and her daughter right behind her.

"You're terrible," Lisa brushed the tears of laughter off his cheeks. "But that was priceless."

"It had to be said," I couldn't stop smiling as the three of us headed back downstairs.

Mother and Charlotte were yanking their coats out of my front closet and tossing them at their travel companions.

"Put them on. We're leaving," Charlotte glared at me as I stood on the bottom step watching them.

"But we were discussing," my brother whined.

"Now," my sister-in-law raised her voice.

"What happened?" Dad stood there holding his coat, but not putting it on.

"We've been asked to leave," my mother was visibly rattled.

"Why?" Dad looked confused.

"I'll tell you in the car. Let's go," Mom gritted her teeth.

"Don't you mean you'll greatly distort the truth or out-right lie to him in the car." I leaned against the banister and asked her.

"What's that supposed to mean?" She looked accosted.

"I asked you, Charlotte and her family to leave, not dad." I raised my eyebrows at her. "Because Charlotte let it slip upstairs that the only reason you all are here was so my slimy brown-nosing brother could suck up to my husband and try to convince him to represent his employer." I turned towards my mother and brother. "They could care less about me or my family. Only what my husband can do for his career."

"Is this true?" Dad spun around and looked at the three guilty parties whose culpability was written plainly across their faces. "Unbelievable." He shook his head in disgust before turning back towards me. "I am so sorry. I did not know." He faced Hayden with his hand extended. "My apologies. I would never disrespect you or your business in such a manner."

"I appreciate that, Mr. Carlton." My husband shook his hand.

"Jack," my dad placed his other hand on top my husbands.

"Thanks, Jack." Hayden seemed to exhale for the first time since they arrived.

"Daddy, you can stay. I can run you home later." I offered.

"Jack, if you even think," my mother jumped in before my father could respond.

My dad looked over at me and smiled, reached into his pocket, and handed my mother his car keys. "Head on back to the house. I'll be home later."

"I will never forgive you if you do this," Mother's voice dropped an octave or two.

"Then add it to my list," Dad snorted with a shrug.

I bit my bottom lip trying to stifle a laugh and looked at my sister who was not trying to hide anything. She leaned against the railing laughing and never paid attention to the look Oliver shot her trying to calm her behavior. If she noticed the evil look my mother and Charlotte threw at her, she gave no indication.

Once the door closed behind them, my house was finally at peace, and we could resume our Christmas. My dad settled onto the sectional with a twin in each arm. The children decided they wanted to watch *National Lampoon's Christmas Vacation*. Hayden had the workers install a gas starter on our wood-burning fireplace. He fired it up and joined me on the couch beside my dad.

I snuggled into Hayden and looked around at my nontraditional family scattered about our great room. My boys were happy and chatting softly with their friends and new cousins. Our family was far from perfect, but it was mine.

I woke after midnight to the sound of Ellie crying. I groaned and rolled over turning down the volume on the baby monitor.

"I'll get her," Hayden sat up and kissed me on the cheek. "There's still a couple bottles in the frig."

"Are you sure?" I was exhausted but I knew he was also.

"Sure," he rubbed the sleep from his eyes. "Call it father daughter bonding." He slipped on his fleece robe and cozy slippers before heading to the kitchen.

I rolled over and cozied up to Hayden's empty pillow. The world drifted away as I thought about how I was suddenly so grateful for bottles.

An hour later I stirred to the faint sound of a baby crying. I checked the monitor, and it wasn't registering anything. Listening closely, I could still hear a muffled cry. I tossed the covers aside and climbed out of bed. I grabbed my robe and stepped into my slippers and set off in search of my crying child.

Normally, I could tell the different between Eli and Ellie's cries. They were very distinctive to my ear, but this sound was so muffled I was not sure which one it was.

I followed the sound up the stairs past the bedrooms and down the corridor to Hayden's man cave. The light was shining under the door. I opened it and immediately knew it was Ellie having a tantrum.

Hayden was sitting on the couch with his feet propped up on the oversized five-foot squared ottoman watching a *John Wayne* black and white western. His hair was disheveled, and his eyes were bloodshot. I could tell he was at his wits end.

"Where's Ellie?" I could hear her wailing but did not immediately see her.

"Over there," Hayden pointed to the far corner of the room. "In the corner."

"You put her in the corner?" I walked over and found her sitting in her infant seat facing the corner.

"It was her or me," Hayden looked over at me with leaden eyes. "So, I put her in a time out because I needed one." I couldn't help but laugh as I picked her up.

"She's six weeks old," I chuckled.

"She's got stamina and a stubbornness that is only rivaled by her mother." He smirked.

"You're horrible," I swaddled her close to me and began swaying back and forth.

"I tried that, and she threw up on me," He opened his robe to expose his bare chest and nodded towards the wadded tee-shirt on the end table.

"Wonderful," I remarked but continued anyway. It was the only thing I knew that would calm her when she got like this.

Within a few minutes, Ellie was sucking her thumb and sleeping soundly in my arms. I rocked her for another few minutes before joining Hayden on the couch.

"Are you okay?" I rested my head against his shoulder.

"Yeah, just tired."

"Are you ready to go back to work?" I glanced up at his face and saw a calm wash over it.

"Who ever thought that going back to work would be a vacation?" He raised an eyebrow. "Don't get me wrong, I'm happy I took time off to spend with you and the kids over the holidays, but I had no idea how much work was involved. I don't remember Kennedy or Mason being so much work."

"That's because you were 25 years younger and Marcie did all the work," I smirked.

"True," he agreed with a quick peck on top my head. "I love you."

"I love you too. Merry Christmas, darling."

"It was an interesting one, that's for sure. Your family," he sighed heavily. "I can see why you avoid them. Your mother is a bitch, and I don't even have words to describe your brother and that cunt he's married too. And what's with his kids? They're a bit strange."

"That's an understatement. Now you see why I avoid them?"

"Your dad seems like an all-right guy. He loves you and your sister, but I'm not sure if he loves your mother." Hayden stated the obvious. "I can't imagine why they stay married."

"It's cheaper to keep her," I muttered making him laugh. "I believe it's more out of habit than anything else. They've been married almost 40 years. Besides, no one else would have them."

"I believe that about your mom," his lips formed into a thin smile.

I tilted my head and listened closely for a moment. "Eli's up."

"I got him," With a grunt and a couple groans, Hayden rose from the couch. "I'll bring him back and we'll swap."

"Are you grabbing a bottle?" I rested my head back against the cushion and closed my eyes.

"Why? Isn't that why I have you?" A devious smile slid across his lips.

"You're lucky I'm holding your sleeping daughter."

"That's why I dared to say it," He playfully stuck his tongue out before trudging off to retrieve our son.

Chapter 43

THE TWINS FLOURISHED AS WINTER melted into spring. Ellie had all the men in the house wrapped tightly around her little finger. I had to constantly get on the boys to quit carrying her around. She was so spoiled she got fussy whenever I put her in her swing or laid her in the port-a-crib beside her brother.

Eli was a happy laid-back little man who always had a smile on his face and never let anything bother him. I could vacuum under his crib while he slept, and he never flinched. Unlike his sister, he preferred nuzzling with his momma over his brothers or daddy. But no one could make him laugh like Henry. It was clear early on; Eli was Henry's pet, and he would be his fierce protector and ally.

Mid-terms quickly turned into finals, and it wasn't long before I was in the Dean's office picking up my graduation cap and gown. I was so overwhelmed with emotions; I could hardly scribble my name down fast enough on the clipboard and get out of the office before the tears broke.

Two weeks later I stood in the hallway of the Indiana Convention Center in downtown Indianapolis. I was wearing a cream-colored strapless dress that hung to my knees that was accented with black paisley across the bodice and the bottom third of my skirt. It was elegant and stylish and matched well with my black strappy heels. I had bought the ensemble last weekend when Lisa and I had snuck away for a couple hours.

I paced nervously with my peers all wearing our caps and gowns. We had all worked four or more years to obtain this accomplishment. It had not been an easy journey for any of us.

"There you are?" I spun around to the sound of Michelle's voice. "You look so beautiful." She hugged me tightly.

"Thanks," I immediately felt a rush of relief.

"I'm so proud of you," She gushed. "Are you sure there's no way I can change your mind about graduate school?" Her eyes pleaded. "I hate the thought of not having you as my assistant next year. And I know you would excel in the master's program."

"I'm sorry, but no. I want to focus on my family. I need some time off. And I don't know when I'm going to go after my master's." I shrugged. "I've got enough on my plate right now. Max heading into high school. Henry starting intermediate and the twins are starting to crawl." I shook my head. "That's enough for now."

"I understand. But I'm still going to miss you." Michelle touched my arm lightly.

"You're not going to get rid of me so easily. I'll still be around." I assured her.

"I'm so proud of you." She hugged me again with tears glistening in her eyes. "And I'm so happy for you and Hayden."

"Thank you for always being there for me." I was going to miss her too.

"Ladies and gentlemen, your attention please." a large boisterous woman touted down the center of the wide hallway. "It's time to line in alphabetical order. We are heading into the auditorium."

"I'll see you afterwards," Michelle rolled her eyes annoyingly at woman as she passed by.

"You're coming to the party?" Michelle nodded as she took off walking as fast as she could in her heels.

"I'll be there," she hollered over her shoulder.

Hayden and my sons were sitting in the auditorium waiting anxiously for the ceremony to begin. Students were limited to the number of guest seats they could fill so; Lisa and Debbie were at our house taking care of the twins and most likely annoying Kari — who was taking care of the last-minute details for my graduation party.

I followed the young man in front of me through the double doors at the back of the auditorium. My eyes nervously scanned through the audience searching for my family amongst the sea of faces. I numbly followed the young man to the second row of seats.

The students took their seat while some prominent man I had never heard of approached the podium and adjusted the microphone. He covered the obligatory greeting and droned on about our prospects, goals, and success.

A few minutes into listening to his monotone voice drone on my mind began to drift over my years in the Purdue School of Science at Indiana University Purdue University Indianapolis. I remembered how frightened I was driving to campus for orientation, vomiting before every exam in finite math and calculus, and countess sleepless nights studying for exams and drinking so much coffee my head was spinning.

I remembered being so upset after my first psychology exam I was ready to quit. I was so distraught I called Lisa on my way home from campus sobbing and telling her I was done. She told her boss she had a family emergency, rushed over to my house, and spent the rest of the day convincing me to stick it out. In a way, this graduation was just as much her victory as my own.

I felt so proud to have my name on a Bachelor of Science degree in psychology from Purdue University. I felt a little tug of sadness for not completing my bachelor's in nursing because it was too overwhelming with trying to balance school, teaching, and all the men in my life. Plus, I loved psychology so much more than nursing. And the only thing I missed about the medical field were my patients, not the arrogant doctors.

I felt proud that despite not completing my nursing degree, I finished my psychology degree with a double concentration in the psychobiology of addictions and neuroscience with a 3.8 grade point average. The scared single mom returning to school in her early thirties had grown into a confident woman ready to tackle the next chapter in her life.

I rose with the rest of my row and followed them to the side of the stage. The academic honors and Psy Chi cords dangled off my shoulder and I was very aware of them. I nervously fidgeted with my wedding band trying to watch each step I took. I feared falling on my way to the stage, on the steps, or accepting my degree.

I watched the students before me shaking the hands of faculty members when their name was called and ending with Michelle, who was now the Dean of the School of Science and handed us our degree. I took a deep breath stepping closer to the stage and tried to swallow the lump in the back of my throat that felt as dry as sandpaper. I would kill for a glass of water.

"Tyler William Brannon," the tall sandy-haired athlete stepped up on the stage and went through the congratulatory procession.

"Alexandra Lee Brooks," I climbed the six steps and became very aware of the sound of my heels crossing the wooden stage.

I numbly smiled and shook the hands of half of dozen professors I had been a student of at some time or another over the last four years. Michelle, standing at the end of the line, smiled broadly and squeezed my hand. I could see the immense pride in her eyes as she looked at me and it filled me with an overwhelming joy in acknowledging how integral a part she played in my career.

I followed the procession back to my chair and took my seat. That was one of the downfalls of having a last name at the beginning of the alphabet — although I was through the line, I was stuck there through the other twenty-four letters. Then my mind turned to Mason and how he never got the opportunity to make his walk. He was so close to graduating when his life was abruptly stolen from him.

It seemed so unfair that in one night so many lives were changed forever. I knew being here for my graduation was bringing up the painful reminder that a year ago Mason should have been making this same walk. I knew Hayden loved our family and he was an amazing dad and stepdad, but that hole in his heart that belonged to Mason would never heal.

The sun was blinding after we stepped out of the auditorium despite being late afternoon. My graduation party was supposed to kick off at six o'clock and it was already five. Hayden and I had agreed to meet on the westside of the convention center over by the statue of *Peyton Manning* in front of Lucas Oil Stadium. However, it seemed many others had the same idea, and it was a struggle to make my way over there and another ten minutes to find them.

The boys were giddy and climbing around the base of the statue when I located them. Henry spotted me first and ran up practically jumping in my arms.

"Congratulations, momma!" he hugged me tightly.

"That was long and boring," Max complained with a smile as he hugged me. "I'm so proud of you." He beamed warming my heart to bursting.

"Thank you," I couldn't stop smiling. "You're next."

"I know," he rolled his eyes playfully. "But I doubt it'll be from here."

"Oh really," I wrinkled my forehead. "And where are you thinking of going?"

"Notre Dame," Max's eyes sparkled.

"Notre Dame," I repeated shaking my head slightly. "You'd better get those grades up."

"Football scholarship," he replied smugly.

"It takes more than just football to get you into that school. You need brains along with it." I put my arm around his shoulder. "You should try using yours if that's your goal."

"I know," he offered me a pinched-up smile. "I'm working on it."

"You can do it," I squeezed his shoulder. "I know you can."

"Congratulations, beautiful!" Hayden pushed through the storms of people to reach me.

"Thanks, darling," his arms engulfed me tightly.

"I am so proud of you," he kissed me passionately.

We fought our way through the crowd over to the parking garage. Hayden had elected to park several blocks from the mess surrounding the convention center. My feet weren't as accustomed to wearing heels as they used to be and were killing me by the time we reached the car.

I climbed into the passenger seat and immediately removed them. I rubbed my feet fiercely dreading putting them back on for the impending party. The boys were hyper after being cooped up in the auditorium for the last several hours and rambled on the entire way home.

Lisa met us in the driveway when we pulled up in front of the house. She was holding Eli who was squirming in her arms as soon as I opened the car door. She passed him over to me before giving me a hug.

"Congratulations. I'm so proud of you," she gushed with such enthusiasm. "I don't know how you did it, but you pulled it off flawlessly."

"I wouldn't say that." I chuckled planting a kiss on Eli's chubby cheek. "Where's Ellie?" I followed her into the house.

"Your dad took off with her," she looked back at me. "You know how Ellie is — every man in her life is at her beck and call." Lisa laughed.

"We should all be so lucky," I chuckled going into the kitchen with her.

"No shit," she picked up an envelope off the bar and handed it to me with a smaller card. "This was delivered with a gorgeous floral basket and balloons. I put them out by the cake but that's the card from the florist who said this was to be delivered with it." She shrugged.

I opened the smaller envelope first which had balloons and streamers across the background. Handwritten on the card was 'Congratulations from St. Lucia. We'll see you soon. Love, Uncle Rick and Aunt Misha'. I handed Lisa the card as I adjusted my chubby little man on my hip.

"I was wondering where they were," she remarked after reading it.

"They had this trip planned since last November. I couldn't begrudge them lounging on the beach in the Caribbean." I shrugged. "Hold him a sec," I passed Eli back to her so I could open the envelope.

Dear Alex,

I was so pleased, after the paramedics had restarted my heart, to behold that a Carlton advanced beyond high school! I would say that it is in the genes, but our gene pool is murky, at best, and I suspect a few relatives with flippers hidden away somewhere – mostly on the Wyatt side, of course. So, it must have been hard work that got you where you are now. Congratulations!

I am puzzled and a bit alarmed that your being in the field of psycho-babble-ology is a classic example of the inmates running the asylum. Though I am now on in years and my brain is riddled with syphilis (oops! That's a secret, OK), I do recall that at one time (a very long time) you could have made a budding psychologist's whole career. Humm. I guess you are a testament to the value of electro-shock-therapy.

My regrets for not being able to come but you know the deal. Jeez! You try to bugger one little boy, and everybody goes nuts! I wasn't smoking and I had a helmet on, fer Chrissakes.

Because of the theme of your note, I have waited til this is appropriately dilatory (a.k.a. late, college girl!).

Hope we'll catch up someday soon, but for now I am proud of you and your accomplishment. For now. Just remember: Psychology enables us to correct our faults by confessing our parents' shortcomings.

Love,

Uncle Rick

"Oh, my Gawd!" I busted out laughing. "I love my Uncle Rick." I handed Lisa his letter and took Eli back from her.

"Your great uncle is a silly man," I told Eli while Lisa read it. Eli squealed happily in my arms and pulled my hair for good measure. "Ouch," I blew raspberries into his chubby little neck making him squeal with laughter. "Don't pull momma's hair you, naughty little man," I playfully chastised.

"That's fabulous!" Lisa leaned against the counter laughing. "Your uncle is a riot. If I were you, I'd frame this and hang it in your office."

"I will," I glanced out of the window and wondered who all these people were milling about the party tent and grounds. "Can you believe the size of this?" I asked without really expecting a response.

"You've moved into a different league now, sweetheart." Lisa stepped up beside me at the window and raised her eyebrow. "I can't imagine what it would feel like to be in your shoes."

"Overwhelming," I took a deep breath.

"But you're happy," Lisa put her hand on my shoulder. "And so are your boys. Hayden is a great husband, and he loves your sons."

"I am blessed," I kissed the top of Eli's head. "It's just hard to believe this is where we live," I looked over at my best friend. "That this is our lives now."

"Trade ya," she cocked her head to the side with raised eyebrows.

"As cute as I think Erik is, I've gotten a little attached to Hayden," I smirked. "I think I'll keep him."

"Figures," she muttered with a laugh. "You'd better get out there or Hayden's going to send in the troops for you."

"Tell him I'll be there in a minute."

"Here," she reached out and lifted Eli from me. "Let me pacify the insurgents with chubby cuteness."

"Thanks," I cupped his little face before she disappeared out the back door with my baby boy.

I watched Lisa bouncing down the walkway with Eli laughing in her arms. She barely made it to the tent before Kennedy swooped in and stole him from her arms. She was in love with her baby siblings and adjusting to living in Indy. I was shocked to see her mother Marcy, and stepfather, Tony, stroll up to make goofy faces at Eli as he laughed. I had no idea they were invited to the party. I had not seen them since Mason's funeral.

Scanning over the grounds, I recognized Lauren, Dennis, and their children along with several faces I remembered from the wedding. Still, most I could not recall.

I closed my eyes and thought about the view from the deck of my old home — one I lived in most of my adult life. I loved the tree-lined yard, our little beige shed with green trim and the pine trees that stood on either side of the double doors. I smiled to myself thinking about the day I planted them. I had been drinking frozen Sangria's on a hot July day. I dug two holes for the two-foot pine trees Danny, and I picked out.

No sooner had I planted the second one Danny came around back and stopped mid-way to the shed. He cocked his head to one side and then the other eyeing my work with meticulous scrutiny.

"What?" I brushed my hair away from my face smearing dirt across my forehead.

"The right one's crooked."

"No, it's not." I turned and looked at it again. "It's perfectly straight."

"How much have you drunk?" his lips curled up around the edges.

"Second pitcher," I felt insulted. "Why?"

"I think you've done enough gardening for the day." Danny had laughed at me.

It had taken him another hour to fix the lopsided pine tree and it never was truly straight. I thought about how silly it was to remember something so trivial, but it was those little things that had made that house our home.

This huge, gorgeous house with its elaborate pool, pool house, guest house, putting green, tennis and basketball courts had been professionally designed and landscaped. Each week a maintenance crew showed up with their truckload of equipment and spent the day cutting, pruning, and trimming the vast lawns surrounding our home.

Professional designers, painters, and party planners had taken over all the little things I had once enjoyed handling myself. Twice a week a house cleaner showed up and cleaned our home from top to bottom and took care of all the laundry.

Not that I can say I enjoyed doing housework, but I missed those days when I would blast the stereo with some 80s metal hair band and the boys, and I would dance around the house singing as we cleaned. It was goofy and absurd, and I am sure we looked comical to anyone from the outside, but it too, was one of those little things that made us a family and that our home.

After seven months of living in this oversized home, it still felt sterile. I knew in time I would adjust, and this place would be home.

I looked up and saw Billy chasing Henry across the yard. I smiled to myself realizing that it wasn't the size of the house that made our old place a home, it was the people who lived in it. And I knew, I was home.

Author Bio

ADDISON WINTERS HAS A MASTER'S in military psychology and is currently completing her doctorate. She is the author of the bestselling *With Honors* series and the new *Heat of Arrest* series. When she is not buried in research, reading, or lost is a world of her own creation, she enjoys gardening, hiking, volunteering with The Lone Survivor Foundation, and spending time with her family and friends. Addison lives in east Texas with her husband Eric, their daughter, and spoiled puppies.

Don't Miss Out on Addison Winters' New

~Heat of Arrest Series~

Mounting Deuce, Book 1

Arya Lucas finally had her life back. After a nasty and drawn-out divorce and moving fifteen hundred miles from everything she had ever known; freedom was finally hers and she was enjoying it to the fullest. Her small consulting firm was growing rapidly and affording her the life she'd worked so hard to achieve. She had everything — or so she thought.

With the urging of her best friend Arya joins a dating site with no desire to start a relationship with anyone, until she met Detective Deuce. He was unlike anyone she had ever dated and definitely not her type. His enticing blue eyes and smirky boyish grin drew her to him. His witty sarcasm was undeniably charming. He held a sense of mystery and adventure that she had never experienced before.

But what she hadn't counted on was his impact on her entire world. How one day she would wake up and find herself in a life she no longer recognized; and realizing she could not have been happier about it. Still, was he worth risking her heart for? Could he be more than just a tryst?

Addison's Closet

Welcome to Addison's Closet where you will find the perfect attire to workout in or snuggle-up in with your favorite sexy read. And for those more intimate nights, you will love what you will discover in Addison's ToyBox.
But remember, Shhh . . . It's a Secret

https://addisonwinters.com/addisons-closet/

For Eric . . .

The End